1 · 0

D0329076

WHERE THE *Sweet* BIRD SINGS

Center Point
Large Print

**This Large Print Book carries the
Seal of Approval of N.A.V.H.**

WHERE THE *Sweet* BIRD SINGS

ELLA JOY OLSEN

CENTER POINT LARGE PRINT
THORNDIKE, MAINE

This Center Point Large Print edition
is published in the year 2018 by arrangement with
Kensington Publishing Corp.

The text of this Large Print edition is unabridged.
In other aspects, this book may vary
from the original edition.
Printed in the United States of America
on permanent paper.
Set in 16-point Times New Roman type.

ISBN: 978-1-68324-651-0

Library of Congress Cataloging-in-Publication Data

Names: Olsen, Ella Joy, author.
Title: Where the sweet bird sings / Ella Joy Olsen.
Description: Center Point large print edition. | Thorndike, Maine :
    Center Point Large Print, 2018.
Identifiers: LCCN 2017046870 | ISBN 9781683246510
    (hardcover : alk. paper)
Subjects: LCSH: Large type books. | Domestic fiction.
Classification: LCC PS3615.L7236 W48 2018 | DDC 813/.6—dc23
LC record available at https://lccn.loc.gov/2017046870

Dedicated to:

All the people who ache to have a child,
to those who have lost one, and to
every person who loves a child and worries
about things that are beyond their control.

I WOULD LIKE TO THANK

The first, and most important, acknowledgments must always go to family. Life (and writing a story) wouldn't be as worthwhile (or as much fun) without all of you.

My friends and my book club. You are my best cheerleaders and my street-team.

The Badass Writers who hear the good, the bad, and the ugly. And don't judge.

The Tall Poppy Writers who have all the answers and make me laugh.

Women's Fiction Writers Association for giving me a home.

My early readers: Aimie, Bobi, Courtney, and Lauren for honest and pointed feedback.

My agent, Rachel Ekstrom, who can always talk me from crazy to calm.

My editor, Tara Gavin, who sees the bigger picture.

My publicist, Lulu Martinez, who answers all my questions, even the silly ones, and who puts the plan into action.

Kensington Books for pushing *Sweet Bird* out of the nest. And helping it fly.

All of the bloggers, reviewers, and fellow writers who have been amazingly generous with their advice, promotion, and love.

Every single person who read and loved *Root, Petal, Thorn*. Without readers, I'd be out of a job.

The Family History Library, operated by the genealogical arm of The Church of Jesus Christ of Latter-day Saints (LDS Church), which helped me to explore.

23andMe for breaking the code.

PROLOGUE

His hand was clenched in a loose fist, but today he wasn't fighting. It lay motionless against the mattress like an object in a still-life. I traced its shape against the sheet, not touching his fragile skin, but celebrating the heat it radiated and what it meant. Alive.

After several moments I circled his wrist with my fingers, feeling the flutter of his pulse against the base of my thumb, waiting for his response, aching for even the smallest indication he was aware of my presence. There was nothing.

How many times had I brought the tips of his fingers to my mouth, or pressed his knuckles to my lips? But the nurse told me this was to be expected. She explained it was impossible, at this point, for him to respond. Slipping my hand under his, I tucked his fingers so our palms touched. "I'm here." As my words met his ear, the strands of his hair caressed my cheek like the fluttering wings of a butterfly. "Stay with me."

In response to my plea, his chest rose and fell, filled with manufactured life. How long could he balance a breath's edge away from death? But if I lost him? It was unimaginable. And if he was gone, *when* he was gone, who would I become?

CHAPTER 1

Grass clung like a dearly beloved to the color of winter. On this day, enormous swaths of olive-drab blades stretched forever, still flattened from the pressing snow of an especially bitter season in the Wasatch Mountains. I squinted, hoping to see pinpricks of brave green on hills that faced the southern sun, but in the exaggerated distance of the cemetery, the dun lawn seemed to roll eternally, ending only at the horizon.

The bright springtime branches of the forsythia were the one exception. A twiggy bush glowing with explosions of gold, it burst through the dreariness of March, heralding the end of winter. I focused on those cheerful branches because I didn't want to look at the casket, the family assembled, or my mom. And I didn't want to see if they were looking at me.

The forsythia in question was the size of a small car hovering like a lesser sun near one of the narrow roadways threading through the Salt Lake City Cemetery. These paths meandered around thousands of headstones and the occasional twenty-foot obelisk marking the burial site of one important founder of the city or another, rising from the ground like a skyscraper in a small town.

11

The largest of these monuments were reserved for prophets from the Mormon Church, as this was the oldest cemetery in Salt Lake City, but here and there a local tycoon, one who'd made a mint in mining or some other gentile pursuit, purchased a stone memorial large enough to stand toe-to-toe with the powerful men of the priesthood.

My grandpa Joe would be buried in the shadow of one of these monoliths. His last name, Barlow, was common here in the older part of the cemetery. Today I noted close to a dozen headstones surrounding his, all bearing the same surname. However, these distant family members were no one I knew. Most had passed a century earlier, meaning this historic plat was sparsely adorned. A few graves sported bouquets of faded silk standing sentinel a season or two, but this section of the cemetery didn't see a parade of regular visitors. For the most part, loved ones of the deceased were deceased themselves.

My grandparents' side-by-side graves would be the exception.

I let my focus slip from the safety of the golden branches and followed the concrete walkway with my eyes, past the low sandstone wall built at the base of the hill, and continued up the stairs. It was one hundred yards. Maybe two. I'd visited this cemetery almost daily and hadn't realized the proximity of my grandma Ginny's grave (and now my grandpa's) in relation to my son's.

A light breeze lifted my hair, the edges frosted with the remnants of winter, and I shivered. Noah pulled me against his side, his large palm warm against my waist. It was all so similar—the brown lawn, the thin sunlight, my dress, his hand, the forsythia. I shook again, and this time my teeth chattered. Noah touched the back of my neck, running his hand the length of my hair. I leaned into his shoulder and closed my eyes.

A familiar voice drifted through the crowd as we watched the casket being lowered into the ground. "It seems like we were just here, doesn't it? Same type of day. Same place. Where is she anyway?"

"Shhh. Over there by the tree. In the sunglasses."

I knew at once who was speaking: my cousin Becca. She and her brother Doug had flown in for the service. Becca's voice was one of those that carried. Easter egg hunts and birthday parties when we were children, family party murmur switched to circus tent megaphone whenever she entered the room.

"Was it this time last year? Or was it two years ago?" Doug asked.

"Last year. Hold on. What's today?"

"Second to last day in March."

"I think—" This time Becca lowered to a stage

13

whisper. "I think it's possible they were buried on the same day. Oh my God, do you think she realizes?"

I felt Doug's eyes find me as he processed this information, and I was happy for the reflective lenses of my sunglasses.

"Mom told me she's not doing so great. Hasn't gone back to work, stays in the house most of the time. . . ."

I backed away from their words, pulling myself from Noah, hoping to hide behind a nearby tree. Though barren of leaves, the width of the trunk would be my shield. Several mourning doves that were perched in the highest branches startled as I ducked out of sight, their swooping descent draped like low-hung party streamers over the gathering. The tips of their feathers vibrated at their retreat, whistling, and my cousins glanced skyward. This welcome distraction allowed me to tuck myself deeper into shadow.

Of course, I would have spoken with my childhood playmates after the service in other circumstances, in the manner of grieving family members at a somber occasion. Smiles without teeth, a quivering chin. But it was nothing I was capable of today. If I uttered a sound, if I made eye contact, it would be the end of the masquerade.

Pressed against the gnarled willow, I watched the crowd disperse and planned my solitary escape. It wouldn't be easy, because my brother, Ethan, was also in town for the funeral. On most visits the two of us couldn't be separated, and though it made me ache to ignore him, today I avoided him like I had all the others. Once or twice during the service he attempted to approach me, and I grasped at Noah's arm with frozen fingers. Noah must have glared him away, because Ethan's girlfriend, Anusha, kept a tight grip on my brother's arm, giving me the space I needed.

No one else sought my company for the remainder of the gathering—or maybe no one dared—until only a handful of close relatives remained. My mom and my aunt Marsha stood together by their father's grave, arm in arm, their scarves and sweaters billowing flags of windblown fabric. Then, as if they'd coordinated the movement in advance, they turned away. My mom's scarf fell, and as she draped it over her elbow it was clear the strands that tied them to childhood had been severed.

Not long afterward, my mom found me. "Emma?" She took off her sunglasses in an attempt to get me to follow suit, to judge my emotional state without a disguise. I shook my head, denying her unspoken request. Noah had resumed his place at my side, his arm over my shoulders feeling more like a weight than a comfort. It was too much. I needed to get away.

With a pivot I extricated myself, lurching away from both of them. Noah followed me for several paces.

"Please, can I have a few minutes?" I begged him without turning around. I wouldn't cry.

"If you're going to see him, I'd like to come with you."

"Would it be okay if I went alone?" I touched his outstretched arm, trailing my fingers from his elbow to wrist as I stepped away, out of his grasp. "I need to say good-bye to Grandpa."

"Noah, you can ride to the luncheon with me." My mom stopped him from following me with her hand. "Leave her the keys. Maybe a little chat with Grandpa Joe is just what she needs. Really, I think she'll be fine."

"Will she?" Doubt filled his voice as, resigned, they made their slow retreat.

"His death would have been hard at any time, but . . ." My mom's words faded as they departed, choked with her own emotion.

I stood with my shoulders squared and rigid until the car doors slammed in the distance. My husband and mother idled near me for several seconds, giving me a moment to reconsider, and I waved them on without looking away from the patchy lawn. I would be fine. Wouldn't I?

A man from the mortuary lingered at a respectable distance, but I knew he wouldn't approach my grandpa's resting place until I

16

walked away. I'd done this type of thing before. On a different day I'd stayed near a tiny grave for hours because storm clouds were approaching and I couldn't bear to leave my son alone in the rain.

I inched my way to the side of the open grave. "Grandpa?"

If I concentrated on the memory, I could almost hear him reply. *Emma. My girl.*

"Will you keep watch over him?" The casket blurred as I spoke. "He's just so tiny." My grandpa had never visited Joey's grave. By the time we buried my son, Grandpa Joe was no longer mobile. A series of strokes had left him bedridden, though still alert, for two years.

"You're neighbors now." I assumed a childlike tone as I spoke to the most important man of my childhood.

Count your steps, Emma. You'll see it's not too far. He said these words when I complained about the distance from his house to my elementary school. I made the seemingly endless trudge every day when my mom went back to work full time, leaving me on school mornings at my grandparents' house.

Not too far. I would find Joey's grave from where I stood and I would count. I'd never approached it from this direction. Most days, I would drive as near his grave as possible. For practical reasons, I wouldn't have quite so far to carry flowers, carved pumpkins, or my library bag bulging with a collection of thick-paged children's books. But in reality I couldn't bear to meander, to consider that each stone in this cemetery was a monument dedicated to pain. I could barely hold my own.

I kept a whisper-count each time my foot touched the ground (my intent to report back to my grandpa), but as I had anticipated, my attention drifted to the names and dates on the burial plots I passed. Unlike Joey, whose early death was an unusual circumstance, a rare thing defying statistical odds, a mother at the turn of the century would likely bury many of her children. After wandering for several minutes, I stopped in front of one headstone reading *The Snow Children*. One marker for how many? I circled the stone. Five:

ALICE SNOW 1914   TWO YEARS

ROLAND SNOW 1916   ONE YEAR

INFANT SON 1917   ONE MONTH

INFANT SON 1917   ONE MONTH

MARY SNOW 1920   SIX YEARS

A woman named Marguerite Snow was buried next to her children. *Beloved Mother.* Her title was etched in granite, her role lasting forever. I leaned close to the grave, darkening her name with my shadow. This woman lived to be over fifty. Even without her children she went on. The enormity of this mother's loss dwarfed my own, five children to my solitary child. At the same time, witnessing the carved-stone evidence of grief, I knew sadness wasn't a shield against more of the same.

"I'm so sorry," I whispered. Swallowing several times to clear the lump threatening to stop my breath, I spoke again, louder this time. "What a stupid response. *I'm so sorry?* Sorry is what people say when they don't understand. I understand. And this—" I touched the stone bearing the names of her dead children with the tip of my satin flat. With only a moment of hesitation, I kicked it so hard that the knuckle on my big toe popped and flamed red-hot in the flimsy shoe. "This is so damn unfair."

A couple of long yards past the Snow gravesite, up a short stairway onto a plat terraced by modern machinery, lay my son. In this newer section, the headstones were placed horizontal to the earth (easier to mow over), traffic was steady, burials often, and the graves continually refreshed with seasonal decorations. People mourned those buried here. Emotions were still raw.

From a distance I saw that someone had arranged flowers on Joey's grave, recently too. A handful of sticks covered in bright yellow blossoms were a cheerful bonfire on his headstone. Forsythia. A note wrinkled with spring rain lay on his grave, kept in place by a rock.

One year, Jo-Jo. Momma and
I miss you. So much.

Noah. I knelt next to the headstone and touched the paper. The damp ground soaked the knees of my nylons, and blades of dead grass pressed like a bed of nails into my legs. One year.

My grandpa and my son were bound in name: *Joseph*. The name was intended to honor the most significant man in my childhood, my grandpa Joe. And now my grandpa and my son shared something else. They were bound in death. They were buried on the same day. One year apart.

Like an old woman easing her frail body into bed, I lowered myself to the ground and imagined Joey sleeping cocooned next to me. Near the end I couldn't bear to be separated from my son. What if he took his last breath and I was doing something as mundane as the dishes? So I never left his side. We slept like this every night. We napped like this every day. But it didn't matter. Despite my vigilance, my hands holding his, he still managed to slip away.

The engraved letters on his headstone pressed

solidly against my cheek. Though I loved my grandfather with the adoration of a child, if I'd known what story lay behind this particular name, and if it would have made any difference in what happened to Joey, would I have chosen another for my son? Absolutely.

CHAPTER 2

"Emma? Where are you?"

I'd been home from the cemetery for over an hour when Noah arrived. Before I could respond, he pushed open the partially closed door leading to Joey's room and found me sitting in the gliding rocker. Instantly his face relaxed. I raised my hand in greeting, unable to smile. Like mine, his eyes were worn, the whites shot with red, the corner creases deeper than usual.

"Long day, huh?"

"It was." Inside the room the sheer curtain blocked the sharpest rays of the evening sun illuminating the space with washed light. Everything lay outside this room—the whole world beyond the door—but inside lay nothing. Together Noah and I had assembled the perfect nursery: purchasing a crib that could be converted into a toddler bed, painting the walls a soft gray so they wouldn't be too baby-like when Joey got a little older. But Joey never graduated to the toddler bed. And now he was gone.

"How was the luncheon?"

"Everyone asked about you. They're worried. They want to know how you're doing."

"And what did you tell them?"

"I said it was a hard day but that you're doing

better. Overall." Noah pressed his forehead to the doorjamb. "Are you? Doing better?"

We were both quiet for several minutes, the gliding movement of the chair the only activity in the room. "I don't know."

I shoved my toe into the thick carpeting and the rocker responded by hitting the wall with a thud. Noah stepped toward me and placed a hand on each wooden armrest, stopping the erratic motion. Once the chair was still, he sat at my knees and laid his head on my legs. The weight on my lap felt like I was cradling Joey, and I closed my eyes to imagine rocking my son to sleep while the night-light combined our shadows into an indecipherable and inseparable form.

Loosening my grip on the chair, I placed my hands on Noah's head, smoothing the coppery brown strands of his hair. Slowly I traced his cheekbone to the bridge of his nose and back again, until he opened his eyes, beloved, deep brown, surrounded by a thick fringe of lashes. Joey's eyes. I couldn't bear to look at them and yet I couldn't look away.

"I'm sorry you had to make up excuses for your crazy wife today. I can't believe I couldn't hold it together long enough to make it through Grandpa Joe's funeral."

"Everyone understands. I understand. There were other things on your mind."

Other things.

"Will I ever be the same?" I asked myself, but Noah raised his head at my question, searching my face to see if I had the answer. "Will *we?*" I whispered, but I already knew.

It had been months since the two of us were on the same team. Every single day we forced kindness on one another. We tried to create a normal routine, but there was always an undercurrent of anger, or expectation, or something. I expected him to fix everything and he wanted the same from me, and instead of coming together we ricocheted like errant pinballs until we were more broken than before.

Noah answered for me. "We won't be the same, Emma. How could we? But we could be happy again." He hesitated, wary of his next statement. "You know, we could still have a family. We don't have to stay like this forever."

"A family?" And there was the crux of it, the one truth. Noah and I could never have children together because of the disease that had claimed our son. We would never have a family.

"Emma?" I must have recoiled because Noah's voice reverberated against the walls of the abandoned nursery, panicked. He caressed my chin, pulling me toward him. "What are you thinking about? Your face . . ." He touched the corner of my mouth. "Talk to me, please."

I gently pushed his hand from my cheek and stood. "Should we go to bed?"

Noah followed me into the bathroom. He smeared toothpaste onto his brush as I took out my contacts. Together, going through the regular routine of our evenings, tucked into the tiny room, we could dwell in close proximity without actually facing each other. Our connection flickered in the mirror, both of us concentrating on an unfocused point in our future, wondering if we could come together somewhere in the distance.

Even this was too much. I rubbed a washcloth over my face, taking extra time with my mascara, hiding my expression.

"I was just thinking . . ." I said after a couple of minutes. My jaw was rigid as I spoke, my words compressed by the pressure of my teeth. I covered the quivering in my chin with the cloth, but I found him with my eyes. The bond between us was forced, but it loosened the lines of worry between his brows. "I was just thinking how much I love you. You're the best man I know, and I'm so lucky you've been mine."

"And you're mine," he whispered, his declaration in the present tense. Mine, I realized, in the past. He rinsed the brush, flicking the water into the sink, where the drops slid into the drain like tears. He pulled me to him, leading me to the bedroom. And because I was susceptible to his touch, I let him.

After unzipping my black funeral dress, he

dropped it to the floor and like a layer of dark sorrow, it puddled at my feet. As we joined and loved, I clung to him, touching him everywhere, memorizing him: the stubble on his chin, the mole below his collarbone, the fleshy lobe of his ear. We sunk into each other, and I willed myself to absorb this perfect moment. Forever.

Noah's breathing deepened after we parted. He always descended into slumber first, midsentence sometimes. I would wait for the familiar cadence, audible proof of safety and calm, before I could allow my own consciousness to blur at the edges.

Minutes passed, and as I drifted, his voice found me in a fog. "Do you remember the night we conceived Joey?"

I rolled from him, believing his voice part of a dream, but the familiar inhale and exhale were gone.

"It was a new moon, remember?" he continued, his voice filling the still room. "Dark enough to throw a blanket in the yard without the neighbors seeing what we were up to. We'd been trying for three months and you'd heard some wives' tale at the studio that women are most fertile during the new moon. And, of course, I was willing." He chuckled at his joke, and I recoiled.

"Four months," I whispered into my pillow. He didn't hear me. We'd been trying for four months.

"And so there you are—" His voice fell into the well-worn rhythm of a story told often.

"Lying on that denim quilt in the yard, in what was it? Goddess Pose? Flat on your back, naked as a jaybird, legs splayed open to increase pelvic flexibility. And the sprinklers came on."

He snorted, now fully involved in this beloved memory we hadn't repeated since Joey's diagnosis. It was the story recounted to Noah's buddies as they clapped him on the back the evening we publically announced the pregnancy. It was the tale that brought my brother to mirthful tears in the retelling.

"And you just lay there, icy water soaking you." He touched my shoulder in the dark, and I reflexively pulled from him. "What did you say next?"

I was silent.

"Come on, Emma. What did you say as the sprinklers rained down on you, after I'd bolted to the porch?"

"I think this one is going to stick." My throat closed at the words.

"And he did."

"Joey," I whispered.

"I've never been happier than those months, when you grew roly-poly, like you carried a watermelon in your shirt. And then we held our boy. We knew right away he had a dimple in his chin, just like you."

And he had your eyes, I thought, but I couldn't speak.

Noah rested his hand between my pelvic bones, lightly, barely enough pressure through the sheet to sense his touch, but the imprint of his hand burned like a branding iron.

"Are you forgetting how this story ends?" My voice was as soft as his fingers on my skin, but he heard.

"It seems like we've been in this awful place for so long, Emma. I'm just—" Noah's voice caught on the word. "I'm just trying to remind you of the good times."

Movement came from his side, a leaning pressure, and I could sense he'd rolled toward me, searching for my silhouette in the dark. The pressure from his hand increased, and he inhaled deeply. He had more to say. "Don't you think we should try again?"

I sat up like I'd been catapulted from the mattress and picked up his hand with two fingers, as if it were a dead sparrow delivered to our mat by the neighbor cat, bloody and mauled. I flung it back toward him and his palm smacked against his chest, but he was undaunted.

"I know it's a risk."

"But you're a risk taker. I've heard that before. Noah, this isn't a game. Don't you remember what came next?"

"I know it's not a game."

"You're right. It's a gamble."

"But it could be okay."

"It's a bet no gambler would make."

Silence filled the room after I spoke. I listened desperately for his sleep-breathing to tell me this conversation was over. I lay flat on my back, as rigid as a knife, my knees locked. Waiting.

"I would," he whispered. "I'd roll the dice, because the odds are—"

My fingers curled around the edge of the mattress. "I wouldn't." I cut through his declaration with the serrated edge of my voice. Then in a weaker tone, on the verge of tears, I added, "I couldn't."

Silence. Longer this time. So long that I thought he may have left our darkened room. Then he shifted, sheets crinkling under his weight, and I purposefully lengthened my breath, feigning sleep.

"So what do we do now?" His voice was hollow. His question was to himself.

I didn't respond, timing my inhale, faking it, until his exhale matched mine. Deep and rhythmic. Cocooned in the warmth of our night bedroom, I finally relaxed, but instead of sleeping I sobbed.

CHAPTER 3

The phone rang at seven the next morning, and I jolted at the shrill sound. For months I'd waited for an ill-timed call like this as my grandpa's condition worsened, but now that he was gone, who would call at this hour?

It was my mom. She'd suffered through Grandpa Joe's funeral the day before, like I had, perhaps not spending so much time in the cemetery, but I expected I wouldn't hear from her for days. "Emma." She was chipper, and I held the phone from my ear. I felt hungover, forehead and eye sockets pounding with the residual ache of spent tears. "I need your assistance today. I'd love it if you'd help me move some things out of Grandpa's house."

"Today?" I lay back on the pillows. Noah had left for work before I woke, which was not uncommon. A construction manager at a large local firm, he often began near dawn. I touched his pillow, the indentation where he'd slept a lingering shadow of his presence.

"We need to get the place cleared out. I'd like to put it on the market before the end of the summer. Aunt Marsha said she'd like her portion of the sale money sooner rather than later. Apparently Becca's planning quite a wedding."

"Today?" I sat up in bed, absorbing her request. "Today . . ." Perhaps this was my next step. Perhaps my mom, with her call, was leading me where I needed to go. My grandpa's house would be my distraction, a reason to leave the house, the solid thing to fill my hours while I figured out the rest of my life.

"You know Grandpa would have wanted you, more than anyone, to sort through the rest of his things. So I want you to take a shower, get dressed, and meet me at ten-thirty. We'll grab a coffee and go." Her insistent tone was laced with awareness of the months she tried unsuccessfully to entice me out of my living room. Home sentry had been my routine for nearly a year, an uncalled-for duty filling my days while I waited for a child who would never come home.

"Emma." The cheerleader deflated when I didn't reply. "These past couple months when Grandpa was worse and you sat with him, keeping him company, well, it pulled you out of a dark place. I can't let you retreat. Your life has purpose," she said softly. "Even without him."

I crossed my arms, grasping my elbows, holding myself together. Forcing strength into my limbs, I dropped my legs over the side of the bed. "You don't need to convince me, Mom. I want to come."

"You do?"

"It's time to make some changes." I pressed

my lips against the receiver so fragility would be disguised by volume.

"It's time?" She coughed, caught off guard.

"But I need an hour or so to pull some things together." I swallowed to keep steady. "I'll be there soon."

"You will?"

I smiled at her surprise.

After showering, I towel dried my hair and wrapped myself in Noah's robe, letting the soft fleece sleeves enclose me in an embrace. Fresh coffee waited for me in the kitchen. Like usual, my husband had brewed the perfect amount to fill my favorite mug and left it in the carafe to keep warm. This was his love letter, his morning greeting, even after he'd left for work. The cream swirled through the dark liquid, and I leaned close to study the spiral of brown, considering the hours in my day, and all the days beyond it, until I'd sipped the full mug to empty.

While rinsing the dish, I absently let a spray of water from the faucet soak me to the forearm. After using paper towels to mop up, I wrapped the ceramic cup in half a dozen more, like a sales clerk would package a fragile item, and wandered into the bedroom pressing my hands into the padded surface.

My clothing for the day lay on the bed. I slipped it on, then hastily pulled several more shirts from hangers. Before I could stop myself, I had the mug, my laptop, makeup, and toothbrush shoved into a couple of discarded shopping bags, using my shirts to bubble wrap several of the smaller framed photos of Joey.

As I moved about the room cataloguing my items, my actions indicated I planned an absence much longer than one innocent afternoon. All at once, I realized I had no idea what I was doing with these haphazardly packed bags. My true intent wasn't clear, even to me.

Bile filled my mouth, nerves twisting my stomach. I ran to the bathroom and leaned over the toilet. Nothing came. After digging through my clothing to find my toothbrush and brushing my teeth again, I stared at myself in the mirror, forcing steel into my spine. "I am *not* leaving him," I told my reflection. "That is not what I'm doing. I just need some space to get my head straight without any pressure."

I found a pencil, and after several false starts I finished a note telling my husband I needed some time away. I didn't say I was leaving forever, but without some distance I knew I'd fall back into his arms in a second. And I knew I couldn't follow where he wanted to go. I couldn't imagine my life without Noah, and yet I had no idea how to bridge the chasm between us, the void that once held our son.

Standing at the bar in the kitchen, I imagined him studying my plea, his body bent at an angle like when he'd skim the Sunday paper while I made breakfast, reading aloud the best tidbits from the front page. My words would likely surprise him, perhaps anger him. Or would he be relieved?

Spring rain fell as I made my way to my mom's, fat drops reverberating into an ear-shattering drum solo on the metal roof of the car.

"This weather—it's something, isn't it?" I spoke into the upholstered emptiness without thinking. The lull of the familiar twenty-minute drive south to my childhood home, the sedation hum of the engine, the patter of the droplets, and I was talking to my baby boy again.

Here was the thing about having a child who could not speak but who let me know he was listening by finding me with his soulful eyes. I talked. Constantly. For three years I'd been the commentator calling a baseball game, except I called the action in every mundane moment, during each waking hour of the day. At first I spoke to fill the silence, memorizing and repeating names of trees and flowers, zoo animals and their traits, the steps in a recipe. I used my words to soothe my son. It didn't matter to me that he'd never retain the information I gave him. It was my role as his mother to fill his days. So I spoke.

A few minutes later I stopped the car in my

mom's driveway. "We're here, buddy." How long would I narrate into the emptiness of each drive, each meal I prepared, or each shirt I folded? Aware of my mistake, I still couldn't stop myself from pretending, from wishing things were as they'd been before.

As I closed the door, my mom walked from the porch and pulled me into her arms. I'd leave the clothing, and my shaky plans, hidden for the moment. "You really came."

"I'm not a complete basket case," I said, hoping she didn't notice I was speaking in the empty car as I arrived.

"I didn't say you were. But I'm happy to have your help. So, bagels first? Then Grandpa's. I'm driving." And I let her whisk me into her world because I needed her. And I let her because she was my mom.

CHAPTER 4

An hour later we were at my grandparents' house. The place stood on a road that became busy and double-lined through the decades, the sound of constant traffic replacing the quiet of a neighborhood. My grandpa had arranged to sell the lot and house as commercial property after his death, since it was the last residential dwelling on the street. I anticipated it, but now that it loomed large, the end of this place ached in my bones.

I stood behind my mom as she twisted the key in the lock.

"You're like a church mouse this morning, Emma. I know going through Grandpa's things won't be easy, not for either of us, but is there more going on?"

She asked the question without facing me, giving me a minute to compose myself. I didn't want to tell her about Noah, not yet. I needed a distraction from the rest of my life, and although it would be a different kind of sadness to sort through my grandpa's things, I wanted to throw myself into it, to be embraced by the past rather than examine my future. "I'm okay. Let's just go in."

She nodded, allowing my half answer.

This house. The empty silence of the place

hung heavy, a weighted blanket pressing on me from all sides. My grandpa was gone. Taking a deep breath to steady myself, I filled my lungs with the smell of my youth. It was more penetrating now, as if the house, when void of human activity, intensified the essence of all of the years that filled these rooms. This house—these rooms—they had been the one sure thing of my childhood because I'd spent more waking hours in them than I had in my own home.

Decorated in cozy midcentury modern (called *modern* at purchase), my grandparents were excessively practical when it came to home décor. While their furnishings survived decades of being old and reliable, of being dated and scorned by my mom and her sister, all of the cousins clambered for the kitschy (now popular) items when my grandpa became confined to a hospital bed. And he was happy to let them take everything. Over the last few months, the living room had been stripped, piece by piece, but indentations in the worn shag were ghostly footprints of what had been.

I touched my toe to an imprint against the far wall of the living room. In this spot once sat a long, sleek-backed royal blue couch made of faux leather so sticky that if I sat on it in shorts, I'd have to break the vacuum seal to stand. On the opposite side of the room was an enormous box television, which smelled like ozone when switched on. Even as an adult, an impending thunderstorm reminded me of morning cartoons. There had been a kidney bean chrome and laminate coffee table holding an unused rotary phone (once they got a cordless for the kitchen). And behind the couch, a brass sunburst clock had counted down the seconds of my grandparents' lives.

Not intending to tiptoe—after all, there was no one left to disturb—my mom and I made our way through the abandoned front rooms, the empty whisper of worn carpet bristling beneath our feet. The door to the hall closet was ajar. I could picture my grandfather's green down jacket hanging inside, the one he wore when he shoveled the walks, and his long trench he wore over his scrubs on the way to the hospital, intending to keep them clean. I could always tell the minute my grandpa opened this door because I could smell the sweetness of the Butter Rum Life Savers he carried in all of his outerwear.

"This closet always smelled like sugar," I said to my mom as she followed me into the tiny enclosure. "Grandpa would give me a candy to suck on as I walked to school in the mornings. 'A little sweetness to start the day,' he'd say. He kept them in every pocket." I inhaled. "Even though the coats are gone, the smell is still in here."

"He carried them when I was a girl too." She paused. "He had his reasons."

"There's a reason for Life Savers?"

"Well . . ."

"What were his reasons?" Her reaction was strange.

"Sorry, Dad," my mom spoke to the popcorn ceiling. "You're gone now, and I'm revealing your little secret."

"What are you talking about?"

"Sweetie," she said. "Grandpa was a smoker. He used the candy to hide the tobacco smell on his breath."

"What? That's impossible. I was here all the time and I never saw him smoke. Besides, he was a doctor."

"Smell again," my mom said.

I inhaled until my nose burned, determined to tease out the fragrance. Butterscotch. But there was something else too. I always thought it was part of the complex flavor of the candy itself, but she was right. Smoke. "How could he hide this for so many years?"

"He'd walk outside for his cigarette and pop a candy into his mouth on his way inside," she said. "When I was young he smoked in the house. But for you, he was trying to be the best role model possible. He tried to quit several times after you started spending mornings here, but he couldn't make it stick. In the end, he hid it."

I leaned into my mom, weakened with the realization I could never ask my grandpa about this secret he'd kept for so many years. "I don't know why this *aha* moment about Grandpa is making me feel so out of sorts. Maybe it doesn't matter now, but I thought I knew him."

"Oh, baby, it's not a big deal. Besides, everyone has a secret or two."

Maybe, but I wanted my grandpa to remain exactly as I remembered him. No surprises. As my mom led me by the hand out of the closet toward one of the back bedrooms, I hesitated, willing the rooms to reappear furnished and tidy, the way they presented when I was young. But the sunburst clock was gone, a shadow of dust indicating where it had hung, and the kitchen cupboard doors were ajar, as if a hungry thief had visited in the night.

"The spare bedroom in the back is stuffed with things no one's claimed, so that's where we're headed. There are a few pieces of broken furniture, old paperwork, a bunch of photograph albums. Who knows what else? I want to keep the photos, of course," my mom continued. "But most things we'll have to throw away."

I shook my head as she spoke. After we were done sorting the remnants, my grandparents' lifetime would be erased by a wrecking ball. My heart begged me to refuse the task, to leave things alone, so I could always come home. I needed this sanctuary I could always count on, especially when I had recently left another.

Standing in the doorway, I observed the

hodgepodge of items stripped from other rooms, now stacked haphazardly in all corners. Soon after my grandma died, about the time I was ten, this spare bedroom had become a resting spot for everything my grandpa didn't want to deal with. He refused to discard the annual photos of each grandchild, the holiday and birthday cards, the elementary school artwork generously given for display on the fridge, Grandma Ginny's magazine subscriptions (which he continued to renew), any appliance that wasn't reliable, and the suitcases stuffed with worn, but not worn-out, clothing. Eventually he shut the door, saying it was full of things already broken or things he didn't want to become broken, and asked everyone to stay out.

My mom and aunt added to the original compilation as they cleaned. Organizing these items could take weeks, maybe months. As my mom studied my reaction, I realized this was part of her plan to get me back on my feet, to keep me from fruitlessly waiting for my son, physically breaking my cycle of grief.

Relief saturated my thoughts, understanding her gift, realizing I had a task before me that could be all consuming, if I wished. Even as I recognized my mom's ulterior motive, to provide a distraction from my daily life, part of me—the ten-year-old part of me who yearned to enter the forbidden room—begged me to dig in, to explore.

"Come in," my mom urged. "Here's a collection

of storage containers to save the best stuff."
She touched a tower of stackable Rubbermaid
with her toe. Grabbing my hand, she pulled
me through the door. "I really need your help,
Emma. I've taken so much time off work I'll lose
my clients if I'm not careful."

She dropped my hand and dragged over one
of the folding chairs employed during family
Thanksgiving and Christmas dinners. Flipping it
open, she touched the back of my knees with the
metal. I crumpled onto the cold surface.

"You don't need to knock me down so I'll stay,
Mom." I spoke from my seated position. "I want
to be here."

My mom sunk onto her own metal chair, secure
for a moment that we were in this together.
"What's different about today? You usually want
to race home."

"I'm making some changes." My voice broke
as I edged closer to revealing my indecision
about my marriage, and I pressed a finger into
the corner of each eye, forbidding the tears.

"Baby girl." She pulled me against her shoulder,
and I pressed into her like I would when I was a
child. "What's going on?"

"I think I'm taking some time away from
Noah," I said without uncovering my face,
moisture now finding its way to my palms. "Can
I stay with you for a while, until I figure out
where I'm going next?"

"You can always stay with me, baby. I know things haven't been easy, but why now? Are you fighting?"

"He wants a family and he deserves one. I can't give him that."

"Did he tell you he wants to separate?"

"Not exactly, but he said he can't be happy without children. He wants to try again." I could hear his voice shimmering with hope as he asked the question.

"You could adopt, Emma. There are other options. You should continue with marriage counseling. There are things you could—"

"It's not fair for me to hold him. I know he wants a biological child, and I can't go there. It's too much pressure."

My mom shifted in her chair, and I could feel her slip into her professional role, like a superhero revealing a concealed cape. Although she was worried about me as my mother, her second role, her profession, was of marriage counselor and social worker. If she couldn't reach me as a daughter, she would attempt to reach me as a client.

"Tell me about your conversation."

"No, Mom. I'm not ready. Can I have a few days to come to terms with it myself? Noah doesn't even know I'm not at home."

"This is another stage in your grief, Emma. Your sadness is renewed because Grandpa died, and that he died on the same day as Joey. Tragedy tore a hole in your relationship with Noah, but it will mend. You need to be patient."

I removed my hands from my face and grasped both of hers. "Please, just be my mom today. No counseling. Distract me. Let's talk about Grandpa. I don't want to think about myself today, or about Noah, or about Joey. Can we do that? Together?"

Her face softened, and she braided her fingers through mine. Clasped together, entwined in this task, she said, "Okay. Let's surround ourselves with memories of Grandpa, together."

"Thank you."

"But first a snack. Stay here." She stood and placed a hand on my head, holding me in place. Seconds later she set an unopened package of Velveeta cheese on my lap. A sticky note that said *For Emma* was pressed to the plastic. The writing was faint, the letters jostled. I held the chilly plastic to my cheek.

"Grandpa knew you'd been visiting, though he didn't say much when you were here." She pulled a tissue from her pocket and touched it to her red eyes. "He had me buy this for you last week. It took him over an hour to write the note."

I slid my fingers over Grandpa Joe's last note to me. *For Emma.*

When Grandma Ginny died, leaving me and Grandpa Joe to fend for ourselves in the dark mornings, a reminder of her absence—very noticeable to a ten-year-old—was the empty cookie tin she'd always keep full. Several days after her funeral, my grandpa caught me pawing the bottom of the metal container, whimpering, less about the cookies and more about my grandma. The next day he took charge, presenting me with my own package of presliced, individually wrapped Velveeta (a waste of money and nutritionally insignificant according to my mom, but heaven to me).

From then on, I couldn't remember a day I didn't indulge in my favorite snack. Even after I was married and would bring Joey for an afternoon visit, I'd eat a piece. And like the days when I was a child, I'd remove the slick cellophane and fold the cheese repeatedly until I had a stack of postage-stamp-sized mustard yellow squares, which I'd place on the tip of my tongue, one after another, allowing them to melt. During my youth, my grandpa would sit with me through this ritual, never in a rush, keeping me company while I ate. These last few years, I was the one who pulled up a chair and sat next to him.

I smoothed my hand over the package my mom had placed in my lap and sniffed, pushing away another round of tears. "Oh, Grandpa."

"Yep, that's your grandpa Joe," my mom agreed. "Should we begin?"

CHAPTER 5

I nodded, then pulled myself from the uncomfortable metal chair. A stack of precariously placed textbooks, phone books, and encyclopedias blocked access to the first item I wanted to delve into. I made myself as narrow as possible, slid past them, and reached with outstretched fingers for the inset handle of an enormous rolltop desk, feeling very much like I was getting into something I wasn't supposed to.

"Can we start here? Grandpa wouldn't let me touch this desk when I was little because he claimed I'd pinch myself. He made me put my hands in my pockets every time I came into this room."

"Same thing when I was a girl." My mom laughed, realizing we had the same butterfly nervous feeling reaching for the out-of-bounds object. "Well, guess what we get to do today? But for Grandpa, I'll remind you to watch your fingers."

"Ha," I said, as I maneuvered the accordion cover. The ribs reticulated into a hidden pocket at the top, sounding like the staccato click of an old-fashioned typewriter.

The surface of the desk was littered with piles of papers and boxes of several sizes—some wrapped with ribbon, some bound with rubber bands. As I pulled a Buster Brown shoe box, circa 1950, from the desk, I couldn't suppress my smile. The distraction was working.

"Hey, I had Buster Browns," my mom said, standing next to me, waiting for me to open the lid. "I wonder if they're mine."

Inside, instead of a pair of worn leather shoes, lay two Madame Alexander dolls, each partially dressed and topped with matted hair. They rested on a green-glass dish my grandparents always displayed on their coffee table. I'd played for hours with the two dolls, parading them around the yard, bathing them in the sink, and attempting to curl their hair with the barrel of a pencil. Wrapping a snarled tress around my little finger, I smoothed the knotted strands. My mom took the candy dish from the box into her hands.

"Remember Grandma would always fill that dish with that awful ribbon candy at Christmastime?" I said. "And black licorice the rest of the year. She was the only person in the world who liked black licorice." I wrinkled my nose at the memory. After placing one of the dolls on the cluttered surface of the desk, I touched the scalloped edges of the platter. "I never realized how much this thing looks like an—"

"Ashtray." My mom and I said it at the same time.

"And it was full of ashes when I was a girl."

"I'm not sure which would be worse, the candy or the spent cigarettes."

"I know." My mom laughed. "Grandma always bought the worst candy so she wouldn't be tempted to eat it."

"But she made awesome cookies." I thought about the empty cookie tin.

"For you grandkids. For Marsha and me it was black licorice, and nothing but." As she spoke her phone buzzed. She silenced it, grumbling, "I have the day off." Immediately it chirped again.

"Just get it, Mom. It's making me nervous."

She huffed and studied the screen. "No. Oh no."

"What?"

"It's the hospital. One of our in-and-out schizophrenics is back in, but James is on call. I'll text him." As she quickly pressed the keys on her phone, I shifted through several stacks of ancient mail, the envelopes addressed with the careful type from a manual typewriter rather than the mass-printed checks and bills sent these days.

"Oh, Emma," she groaned after several minutes.

"You have to go?"

"For a bit. Can you stay here without me?"

I expected a tightness to roll in from my shoulders, up the tendons in my neck, to surround my brow like a band of fire at the mention of her leaving me here, alone and away from my home.

It would have been the instantaneous response for the whole of the past year, but it didn't come.

After a pause I said, "I guess that would be fine." The calm feeling, in its unfamiliarity, made me feel superficially fragile, like a wineglass made of plastic.

"I'll hurry."

"Don't worry, I'll be fine."

As I heard the front door click shut behind her, I reached deeper into the recesses of the desk. Under a ceramic mug stuffed with pencils lay a full-size manila envelope. Across the front my grandpa had written *Do Not Bend*.

Carefully I pinched the brass clasp and reached inside. The package held an eight-by-ten black-and-white photo in remarkable condition, as if it had been kept flat in a book or tucked into the bottom of a seldom-used drawer . . . or hidden away from my sticky childhood fingers in this carefully guarded desk.

The image was clearly an antique based on the attire of the people in the photo. I smiled and pulled it closer. Historic photos echoed things unsaid, moments captured but not contained. Maybe because there were so few images to analyze, the importance in every facial expression or every subtle nudge of body language meant more than in our hundreds of selfies or digital snaps. I loved to speculate about what was happening right outside the frame to draw the subjects' attention, to make them smile (or not), to pull them close to one another or push away. Whose hand was draped across a knee? Why the subtly clenched jaw?

"Who are these people?" I asked the empty room as I flipped to the back of the photo, checking for inscriptions. I wasn't disappointed. The fading cursive said: *Barlow Wedding 1916.* Barlow? So these must be Grandpa Joe's parents, my great-grandma Emmeline and great-grandpa Nathaniel Barlow.

I'd heard so much about them, especially my great-grandma Emmeline, who was my revered namesake and a source of much familial pride. Uncommon for a woman in the early 1900s, Emmeline Barlow graduated from nursing school during World War I, was a full-time working mother, all the while raising six boys. Later in her career, she practiced as a nurse-midwife with my grandpa at his medical practice until her death a couple of decades before I was born.

Now that I'd placed her, I vaguely recognized her from other photos taken when she was an old woman, her elbow supported by my sturdy grandfather, her son. In this photo, she had the same aquiline nose I remembered, the same narrow chin, though her face glowed in vigorous youth, her happiness evident even a century later.

Her groom, and my great-grandpa, had been a decent-looking guy. He was tall and thin and sported no facial hair, no beard typical for the times. He wore a dark hat and a three-button jacket with lapels, dressed in formal fashion. Emmeline stood to his left, her arm linked through his. She was also quite tall and trim. Her dark, wavy hair was cut in a short bob and pushed behind her ears.

Wearing a light-colored dress with a long peplum and lace sleeves, she held a large brimmed hat in one hand and a bouquet of flowers in the other. She leaned into her husband with a slight smile on her face, almost as if she'd whispered something naughty in his ear. His eyes were crinkled in response to whatever she'd said.

I'd seen the exact expression on Noah's face when I'd tell him at a fancy restaurant I wasn't wearing any panties. My God, photos were supposed to be serious events a hundred years ago. She wasn't coming on to him when this picture was taken, was she? But it was a wedding, so of course they were planning to get busy that night. I giggled at the thought.

Witnessing my great-grandparents as frisky newlyweds was interesting, but there was more. Even as Nathaniel leaned against his bride, a second woman stood on the opposite side of my great-grandfather. He had his arm wrapped protectively over the second woman's shoulders, pulling her to his side. Her arm was bent at the elbow, and it appeared she was resting her hand on his. Were their fingers entwined, or was she pushing him away? It was hard to tell because of the angle of the camera. But regardless, who was *she* to get such a favored spot in a wedding day photo?

The second woman was fair, her light hair pulled back in a bun, her dress more conservative than my namesake's. She looked anxious, her hips and legs angled away from Nathaniel's youthful body, like she might leave the photo if only she could get away. But he wasn't letting her go. And yet it was clear from the tilt of her head against his shoulder that she didn't want to leave. They were bound together, somehow.

A tiny child dressed in short pants and suspenders was holding the opposite hand of the blond woman. "Who are *you*, little guy?" Since I had plenty of time, maybe I'd trace this unidentified woman and child back through the years, using the photo albums scattered among the detritus.

As if in response to my question, my phone rang, shattering the silence of the empty room. I jolted, lurching toward my purse draped over the folding chair. *Joey! He needs me!* Just as quickly I remembered the truth, and as the adrenaline leaked away I sat with a heavy thump, the chair catching my weight. A photo of Noah hovered on the screen and disappeared. He was home.

"Hello?" I whispered the word, uncertain how he would have received my note.

"Emma? Are you still at your grandpa's?"

"I am."

"And you're going to stay the night at your mom's?"

"Yes."

"Just for tonight, right? To work through your grandpa's things? Because I'm reading your note and it has a weird finality to it."

"I need some time to sort things out."

"Sort things out? At your grandpa's? I don't get it. Do you need all night long? I'm confused, because for months you barely left the house, and it's a little surprising to have you gone, is all. . . ."

I pressed my finger against the speaker to mask a sharp sob that came out sounding like a hiccup. I wanted to crawl through the phone and curl up in his lap. But I wouldn't.

"What was the best thing that happened to you today?" I uncovered the speaker and changed the subject.

Since Joey was diagnosed, to put a little perspective on our experience—to minimize the gravity of the future—every day Noah and I would play the Today Game. Best and worst from *today* only. No projection, no forecasting. How truly bad or good was *this* day? Living without anticipation was easier, and as it turned out, each day, taken one at a time, was not so bad.

Noah chuckled, the vibration warming the earpiece. "Okay, I'll play. I had great Mexican food at this little dive joint near the airport. We were on our way to the airport bid opening, which meant we were all in good spirits. I had a margarita." I could hear Noah moving around in the bedroom, closing the closet, opening a drawer. I imagined him changing from his work clothing into his running attire. "What was your best thing?"

"Let's see . . ." I searched the ceiling, trying to pull one purely good thing from the day. "There are some amazing things at Grandpa's. I found this photo of my great-grandparents' wedding. I'll have to show you." As I imagined tucking close to him on the couch and together speculating about the photo, I had to stop myself from grabbing my keys and driving to him on the spot.

"What was your worst thing?" I forced myself to continue.

"That you're gone. I'll miss you tonight, but I understand. I guess. Like I said, it's strange only a couple of months ago you never wanted to leave the house, and now you're not here."

"I did go to the cemetery, back then," I said softly.

"It's true. You went to the cemetery." He exhaled. "What was your worst?"

"Same. I miss you." And because I knew more

54

about the intention and duration of my absence, I worked to control my breathing so he wouldn't be suspicious.

"Will you come home for breakfast tomorrow? It's Saturday and I have some things I want to show you."

"My mom and I will be busy at Grandpa's and I need more time. . . ."

"Emma. Please?"

I was crumbling. "Okay, but could we meet somewhere? I can't come home."

CHAPTER 6

Noah was reading the paper, his back to me as I approached the new breakfast place on the corner of Ninth and Ninth. His shirt stretched at the shoulders, silhouetting the muscles in his back. I could imagine tracing the terrain with my fingertips as we lay together in bed.

"This place is lively," I said as I approached him, determined to keep things light. I kissed him on the forehead.

"It appears to be quite popular." He folded the paper, turning his attention to me.

Although the springtime sun was obscured by trailing vaporous clouds, it was warm enough to eat outside and the breakfast place was hopping. Jog strollers with large rubber wheels were parked along the perimeter of the semicircular patio, like spokes on a hub.

"Circle the wagons, son, we're under attack." I ached even as I made light of our dining companions, wishing one of those carriages were ours.

"Hi." A small boy who was feeding himself from a carton of strawberry yogurt greeted me from the adjacent table. I raised my hand to acknowledge him. He responded by banging his spoon against the wrought-iron surface with a splatter of pink. His mother grinned indulgently, scolding him with laughter in her voice as she swiped at the mess.

My eyes darted about the restaurant, searching for somewhere to land. I wanted that little boy, and the girl in the striped sun hat, and the baby asleep in a portable car seat, and the four-year-old who was eating pancakes with her fingers, to vanish.

Noah winced, understanding. "You know what *we* can do that these other folks can't?"

"Have a mimosa?"

"Yes." Noah grinned. "And we can leisurely read the paper." He winked as he handed me a folded piece of newsprint. "But I see you came prepared."

I'd taken the envelope containing the sepia photograph of my great-grandparents from the room of memories, figuring the things in the room were castoffs, meaning nobody claimed them, which meant the photo was essentially mine. I brought it with me, determined to keep the conversation squarely on my duties at Grandpa Joe's rather than falling into a discussion about my absence in our home. I didn't want to provide an explanation to questions I couldn't answer, even to myself.

"Yes, I guess I did." I held the envelope in front of me like a shield. "This is the photo I told you about, the one of Grandpa Joe's parents, my great-grandma and great-grandpa Barlow." I pulled my chair close so we could look together, and I allowed the warmth of his arm to soothe my skin.

"This man is my great-grandpa: Nathaniel Barlow." I touched his face in the photo. "And this woman is my great-grandma Emmeline, who I was loosely named after. Look at her face. I think she just talked nasty to him."

Noah laughed. "So who's this woman?" He pointed to the woman with light hair.

"Ah, and that's the question. I don't know. I was going to search for her in the family photo albums, but I haven't had a chance. I'll get back to it."

He held the photo at arm's distance and glanced several times at my face. "Pull your hair back."

Grabbing the hair hanging long in front of my shoulders, I pulled it into one hand and held it against my neck, aware of my steady pulse.

"No, pull it high, in a bun."

"Why?" I asked, using two hands to lift the sides. I sucked in my cheeks and turned my face from side to side. "How's this?"

Noah put the photograph next to my face. "You look just like her," he said. "It's kind of creepy."

"Who? Emmeline? I don't think we look alike at all. She's tall and has dark hair, after all. I'm short and a blonde, remember?"

"Not Emmeline, the other one. Whoever she is, there's some obvious family resemblance. You should figure out who your doppelgänger is. . . ." He set the photo on the table. "And maybe wear your hair in a bun more often. It's hot, in a pioneer girl sort of way."

I finally smiled. Oh, how I loved him. This banter was familiar and easy, as it had been before we had Joey. But there was no erasing our child. He bound us together in heartbreak more deeply than any companionable conversation.

The waitress reached across the table to turn our mugs upright. "Coffee for both of you?"

I put my hand over the top of the cup. "I'm already a little shaky this morning."

The server reached for Noah's. He shook his head. "None for me either, but you know? I could use a mimosa."

"Such a great idea." I could feel myself leaning into the numbness of the alcohol even before I had a sip. "I'll have one too."

We stared at each other while we waited for our drinks, each daring the other to speak. Something hovered between us—a caged energy—a sorrow as heavy as an approaching thunderstorm. I glanced down first, focusing my careful attention on straightening the artificial sugar packs in their ceramic container.

Noah coughed, and I sensed he was ready to

talk. He lifted a stack of papers he'd been hiding on his lap. He tapped them twice on the table surface, taking his time to organize the crooked edges, and placed them in front of me.

"What's this?"

He took a deep breath. "What if instead of looking back and concentrating on all we've lost, we thought about moving forward?" His words were quick, as if he were pulling out a thorn—if you didn't linger over the action, it wouldn't hurt as much. His face was full of anticipation. Or fear.

I leaned in so I could see the pamphlet at the top of the pile and read it aloud. "Reproductive Options for Families with Increased Risk?" My question resonated between us. "Was this where you were headed the other night?"

Noah's face was a study in contrast. His timid grin was wide and unassuming because it was the shape of his generous mouth, but his cheeks were tight.

"I want to have a family with you, Emma. If we try again, there are lots of options. We can take control of this thing. We can stack the deck in our favor." Stack the deck? So he really did think this was a game.

Noah opened the trifold, the ridged creases already flexible from rehearsal of this conversation. He touched the bullet point on the top. "If we wanted to have a biological child, there's in vitro where they test the embryo before implantation. It's expensive, but we'd know for sure. Or number two . . ." He touched the second bullet point. "We could have the fetus tested with an amniocentesis. And if it had the condition, well—"

"Stop." I put my hands over my ears. "You'd consider conceiving, knowing there would be a one-in-four chance we'd have to abort the child?"

"It wouldn't be my first choice, but—"

"Like I said the other night, I'm not ready to talk about this." He winced as my words stabbed him, and his face crumbled. I softened my tone. "Not yet." *And maybe not ever.*

Noah opened his mouth to speak, then stopped short as the server handed him a mimosa. He took a long swallow, emotions and responses moving across his face like shadows.

I grasped mine directly from the waitress's hand like a lifeline and didn't set it down until it was empty. "I think I need to go," I said, placing the fluted glass on the metal surface with a jagged clank.

"Wait." Noah stood as I backed away from the table. "When are you coming home?"

I shook my head.

"At least take these." He handed me the photo, once again enclosed in the envelope. I tried to pluck it from the stack of information he was forcing into my hands, but he wouldn't release it until I accepted the remaining paperwork.

"Can we talk about this soon?" I heard him call across the crowded patio. I retreated, clutching the unwanted items, and I didn't turn back.

CHAPTER 7

Job Hunting for Dummies. That was the name of the book I picked up at Barnes and Noble after fleeing breakfast. It took an hour of wandering the aisles of the nearest bookstore for the mimosa buzz to wear off. At the end of sixty minutes, to justify my stay, I picked up the title closest at hand. As it turned out, the subject matter was perfectly apropos. Maybe it was time to get a job.

Back at my mom's house I realized the title also fit my mental state. I felt directionless, like a "dummy" with it next to my laptop. What was I doing with my life? After turning to the chapter on crafting a résumé, I opened a blank document on my computer. The book was a sign. It was time to do something productive, but I couldn't very well send out a résumé if I didn't have one to send.

I slid the sunshine yellow volume over the top of the pamphlets given to me by Noah, obscuring them completely, and stared at the laptop screen. In all honesty, I didn't have a deep pocket of consistent employment, or much of a post–high school education, so finding a decent job wouldn't be a simple proposition. A "creative," my mom always called me, reassuring herself I wasn't a complete failure when I couldn't settle.

In my revolving carousel of paychecks and schooling, I'd gone for several semesters to the community college, my intent to get a degree in early childhood education. After finishing my general courses, I gave up and decided to train as a birth companion, or doula. I wanted to help women through the birth process like Grandpa Joe did as an OB/GYN, but in a more holistic way (and without the years of medical training). I almost made it through my residency, but a month before I was certified, I branched into Ayurvedic massage.

From there, I designed a line of scarves made of sustainable bamboo and hemp, which I tried to pitch to Whole Foods, and was eventually forced to sell for several summers at the farmers market. At the market I also painted henna tattoos. The real cash came from the henna.

With any money I earned at the farmers market, I'd buy baskets of fresh herbs and crusty baguettes to create cookbook-worthy meals and considered becoming a professional chef. One winter, after I failed to sell through the stockpile of scarves, but before I applied to cooking school, I got certified to teach yoga, and I was a year into that profession when I met Noah.

I was aware I'd been productively drifting, and lucky that Noah thought my scattered interest and variety of careers was endearing. But the birth of my child was solid and certain. The flitting about, the training in other fields, it was something to pass the time. The moment my son was conceived I knew becoming a mother was my true purpose. I craved a physical connection with Noah stronger than a marriage certificate, and I yearned for a child I could call my own. But now my purpose was gone. I was starting over, and I didn't know where to begin.

I figured my current work experience of caring full-time for a disabled child could be applied to home health assistance for an elderly person. I certainly knew how to unfold a bulky wheelchair, administer antiseizure medicine, clear a feeding tube, decipher obscure medical directions, and get in and out of the hospital encumbered with pounds of equipment. But I'd already raised a child with no future, and the idea of watching another person wither under my care deflated my balloon of good intentions like a hot pin.

Discouraged, I closed the book and picked up the pamphlet on reproductive options. For Noah's sake I would review it, but I needed to do so without him studying my face. Upon skimming, I realized I'd seen a compilation of information very similar to this on one of Joey's numerous doctors' visits. I'd studied the odds back then and promptly attempted to forget them.

Yes, we could perform in vitro, fertilizing each egg with Noah's sperm in a petri dish, abandoning the diseased specimens before they could become *actual* babies, wreaking havoc on my soul in their dangerous imperfection. But I had a soft spot for these damaged would-be children. They were Joey (in cell form), the whisper of him, the tiniest essence of a baby I ached to hold. Plus, I didn't think Noah had considered the full cost of the procedure.

And testing a child by amniocentesis after I cradled it, growing it inside my body? If it tested positive and we decided to abort, I would mourn a child I created but would never have a chance to know. Next, our options were adoption, sperm or egg donor, or a life void of children. And I couldn't ponder any of those options. Not yet.

Hoping for something new and more hopeful than the information Noah had given me, I opened the laptop and typed the website address listed on the topmost pamphlet into the search bar. In two clicks, my online search led to a genetic counseling site intended for Jewish couples. One additional option, one not included in the stack of papers he'd presented, read, *Many couples who test positive for one of the Ashkenazi genetic disorders choose not to marry at all.*

So, if we'd sought genetic counseling, the counseling I wished we had received before we conceived Joey, Noah and I would have been encouraged *not* to marry. At all. Oh, God.

But I'd chosen him and he'd chosen me. From

the moment Noah and I met, our connection was more than attraction. It was fated, electric. If we were a genetic mismatch, shouldn't we have been physically repelled from one another? If we couldn't achieve our biological destiny to conceive a healthy child, shouldn't there have been some sort of pheromone revulsion? But it was quite the opposite. Noah and I were like magnets.

In our early days of dating, we compared childhood activities we both attended, separately but together: Pioneer Day parades, fireworks at Sugar House Park, half-price day at the water park, football games at rival high schools. As college students we studied at the same student library and frequented the same bars. We were two planets orbiting ever closer to each other, destined to collide. Once we got close enough, nothing could pull us apart. But if we'd received this logic-based, genetically critical counseling, we'd have been warned against one another, entirely.

The grief counselor we went to after Joey was diagnosed told us some studies indicated that 80 percent of parents who lose a child will divorce. After this ominous prediction he gave us tips on grieving together. I followed his suggestions without fail until I was certain we were strong. And we were. Noah and I held together while Joey was sick. But things changed once he died.

Noah tried to move on, and I tried not to move. At all.

Unable to help myself, I typed into the search bar *Chance of divorce due to infertility*. If we had an 80 percent chance of divorce due to the death of a child, what about this next little detail? Because that's essentially what Noah and I were: infertile. The first study stated infertile partners divorced three times more often than typical married couples. If I added the death-of-a-child statistic and the infertility statistic together, we were more than 100 percent certain of divorce.

But I wasn't *actually* infertile. And neither was Noah. Both of us could have children. We just couldn't have a biological family together. Would I be fulfilled without a child? I stared at my empty hands as I considered this option.

Or I could have a different life. A different husband. Were Noah and I wasting time trying to create something together, the two of us continually wondering what could have been?

"Stop," I said out loud. I clicked back to my fledgling résumé and tucked the family planning pamphlets out of sight at the back of the book.

I was exhausted from the morning of mimosa and emotion. Sleep had evaded me the night before, missing Noah's steady breathing next to me in the dark. I rested my cheek against the cool surface of the book, and I must have slept. Because I started to dream.

• • •

Noah and I were at the hospital. Over the years, the frequently trafficked corridors became as intimate and familiar as my own home. I held Joey. He was an infant, young and fragile. An early visit. We were led into a tiny room with no windows. It contained a round conference table, three chairs, and a box of tissues that sat like a bull's-eye in the center of the faux wood surface. There was no paper-topped examination table, no rubber gloves, and no sink.

"What is this place? We've never been here before," I asked Noah, fearing the answer.

"If all we need are tissues, I've got a bad feeling." His hands were shaking, and he tried to mask it by tapping on the table surface, feigning nonchalance. "You know, like the horror film where the girl decides to go into the barn filled with chain saws and pickaxes." He continued with his rambling story, lacking other less terrifying words.

It was the day of diagnosis. The worst day. Until, of course, later.

I blinked and turned away. I didn't want to consider why the table contained a single item, an item used to absorb grief. Seconds later the doctor arrived, sat across from us, and slid the box of tissues our direction as if to say, *You might need these now.*

He spoke. "Most children with Canavan disease

will die within their first decade." His inflection was robotic, without emotion. I'm sure the doctor's explanation was intended to be soothing, but the content was so unbelievable, in my dream it was rigid, brittle with cold.

I touched my son's cheek as he slept in my arms: *He won't attend prom.*

"Some children smile, at least initially, but most do not communicate." The sterile voice continued. I tried to wake myself. I didn't want to hear what he had to say, not even in my dream, but I couldn't pull myself to the surface.

"He will not be able to sit, feed himself, or walk. Any developmental milestones he reaches will regress as the brain atrophies."

He won't go to kindergarten. He won't read a book. He won't eat a cookie, he won't, he won't, he won't . . .

I jerked awake, hearing an echo in my mom's empty kitchen. *He won't . . . he won't.*

"Oh, my God." I rubbed the sleep away with rough hands, determined not to drift.

For two months after learning Joey had Canavan disease, Noah and I sought gene therapy, called specialists, searched for cures. All waking hours were spent researching the disease online, Joey draped across my lap. Every so often his tiny body would stiffen with a seizure, but they were mild. I could press him against my chest, convincing myself the

70

movement was nothing more than a quick bout of the hiccups.

After learning gene therapy was in the trial stages and no further studies were being conducted, I created a letter campaign targeting the hospital that funded the initial genetic research. I urged them to undertake another trial. I begged my doctor to petition my local children's hospital to purchase the fledgling technology. After two months of fruitless activity and sleepless nights as I fought to cure my son, I gazed into Joey's soulful eyes and I understood we were being wasteful of the time we had. We were allowing these fleeting moments with him to wither like fragile blossoms on thin stems while we searched for the perfect vase.

That day, I rested Joey over my shoulder, and while his breath tickled my neck I closed every tab on my computer pertaining to Canavan disease and turned off the machine. After stacking the books on development in the first year into a paper grocery bag—the ones I'd checked out from the library, trying to figure out what was going on with my son—I dressed Joey for a day at the park. I dropped the books into the library's metal return bin with a resounding clang and spent the next two years savoring.

Joey's brain, initially so full of promise, gradually destroyed itself. Noah and I were forced to watch him go, moment by tortuous moment, until he was gone.

But there was more to the story. Something I'd never discussed with Noah. I knew it wasn't fair, but it still existed. The day of Joey's diagnosis, I believed in the power of my husband. That day, he told me we would fight. He promised we would win. If Noah believed we could save our child, then I did too. So when Joey began to fade and Noah was as helpless to fix him as I was, something broke inside me, a blind confidence. An innocence.

I wanted Noah to have all the answers, to wield the mightiest sword and slay the foe. But he wasn't a hero who could save the day. He was just a man. As hard as we raged against the disease, we both lost the war. How could we pull together now? Because it was not so easy to wave a white flag when both hands were gripping weapons. And, in all honesty, sometimes being angry was so much easier than being sad.

With shaking fingers I refreshed the screen on my laptop and opened a new tab. I pinched my eyes closed several times to clear the sleep, to remove the bittersweet memories of the years with my husband and child, and sat mesmerized by the blinking cursor for several minutes before typing *How to file for a divorce.*

Knuckle joints stinging from the pressure I placed on the keys, without meaning to I ended my prompt with a string of random characters. Before I had a chance to press Enter or Delete, I slammed the lid of the laptop, shielding myself from the words, and rested my cheek against the warm surface until the fan stopped whirring and the machine switched itself off.

CHAPTER 8

"You're still here? I thought a breakfast date with Noah might have changed your plans."

I startled as my mom entered the room. She had been gone most of the day to a weekend couples-counseling session, and in my brooding I hadn't heard her come in. "What are you working on?"

"Job hunt," I answered without lifting my head.

"Looks like it's coming right along," she teased. "So, how was breakfast?"

"Not awesome."

"Do you want to tell me about it?" She leaned across the table so she could see my face.

Forcing a smile, I said, "Not really."

She pulled a chair next to me, sat down, and slipped off her heels. "These things fit better when I was younger." She flexed her toes. "Do you want me to make you something to eat and we can get back to Grandpa's this evening?"

I ran my fingertips along the edge of my laptop. "I could use a little distraction. So yes, let's go to Grandpa's. But I'm not hungry. Let me fix something for you while you change."

She reached into her briefcase, which was sitting near her abandoned shoes, and pulled out a page of the *Salt Lake Tribune* that was folded in quarters, then handed it to me. "I'll just make

74

myself a frozen burrito, so don't get up. But first, I brought something home you'll probably want to see. I haven't had a chance to read it, but the receptionist at the clinic saved the paper for me."

"The obituaries?" I swallowed. I hadn't read them since Joey died. The thing was, I used to love the obituaries, and Noah loved to tease me about my obsession. My favorites were the ones with before-and-after photos, the ones where the reader could witness a dashing young chap morphing into a sagging old man. It happened to even the most handsome, and I was never sure if the deceased included a youthful picture so friends from years gone by could recognize them or so they could show the young people that no one was immune. Or maybe it was so they could recognize themselves.

Years earlier, it was the first section of the paper I reached for while Noah skimmed the front page. That is, until our son was listed in the fine lines of black and white. As I tried to etch my pain into a two-by-eight column, I imagined other mothers reading the words and feeling immune, almost as if learning about something as tragic as Joey's death was a vaccination against it.

"It's Grandpa's," my mom said as she shuffled barefoot to the freezer to find her meal. I pulled the paper closer to study my grandpa's write-up. Though the newsprint photo measured only one inch by one inch, there he was.

"Hi, Gramps." I returned his bright smile, the one I hadn't seen in two years. The first stroke made his grin lopsided and the second removed it from his face entirely. It was nice to see it again. His steel-gray hair was cut in a 1940s style, which went in and out of fashion several times during the many decades of his life: short on the sides, with a longish top combed back from his forehead, waves kept in place by Dippity-do.

The narrative was something most readers would skim over, meaning no tragic death, no puzzle, an expected passing due to advanced age. It was short, lacking the gushing of a grieving spouse, and Grandpa Joe had refrained from postmortem chest pounding.

BARLOW—Joseph Lewis (Dutch).
Born September 15, 1913, in Manchester, England. Became an American citizen in 1916. Son of Nathaniel and Emmeline Barlow—he was one of six boys. Joe loved to read, garden, and play cards. Received his doctorate from the School of Medicine at the University of Utah in 1940. Joseph worked side by side as an OB/GYN physician with his mother, an OB/GYN nurse, until her death in 1955. He continued to practice until age seventy. He loved his job. Joe married Virginia Bertrand in 1944. Together they

raised two of the prettiest daughters: Diane Barlow Gontrum and Marsha Barlow Spears. Proud grandpa to seven grandchildren: Emma, Ethan (Diane), Kristen, Kyle, Doug, Angie, Becca (Marsha). Preceded in death by parents and four of five brothers: Blake, Deacon, Hyrum, and James. And by two sons: Robert and Ronald. Also preceded in death by beloved wife, Ginny. Graveside service only. *Interment at the Salt Lake City Cemetery.*

I put the paper down and ran my hands over the surface several times, pressing the stubborn folds from the newsprint, turning my fingertips ashy. My grandpa was born in England? Why had this not been mentioned when I was doing the required immigrant report in fifth grade? I spent a week envious of the kids who could interview their Grandma Martinez or Uncle Yang. After several days of fruitless brainstorming and questioning (as far as I could tell, my family had lived in Utah forever), I was forced to interview our grumpiest neighbor, Mr. Kuklachyov, who'd emigrated from Russia.

His house smelled like sauerkraut, and I couldn't understand anything he said. Neither could my mom, who joined me for the interview because I was too frightened to go alone. When

I wrote the mandatory five pages, I fabricated at least half of the answers, adding stories about persecution from the KGB, time spent in a Russian orphanage, and his role as a sniper during World War II.

"Fiction will serve as fact," my mom told me after reading my last round of edits. "Mr. K should be happy you think he's led such an eventful life. And I dare your teacher to question him in person."

Did my mom *not* know her own father was born outside of the United States? Or did she want me to dig a little deeper for information on my report? I remembered her complaining about the length of the assignment. She would have taken the path of least resistance, surely, especially since she was so busy being a single working mom.

"Anything interesting?" My mom rejoined me at the table and poured bottled salsa onto the steaming plate.

"It says Grandpa was born in England."

"What? He was?"

"It says so in his obituary."

"Hmm. Maybe they got it wrong? I wasn't part of the process. Grandpa wrote it years before he got sick and had one of the hospice workers help him update it a couple of months before he died." Her tone was unconcerned. She put a piece of burrito into her mouth and finished chewing before she spoke again. "Or, you know he always said Grandma Emmeline trained as a nurse during World War One, so maybe she was in Europe for her studies. He never spoke of it. Who knows?"

"Well, no one knows *now.* I can't believe you're acting like this is no big deal. Grandpa's dead, he was born in England, *and* he was a smoker. And no one even told me."

"You know why he hid the smoking. He did it for you. And maybe the fact that Grandpa Joe was born in England wasn't a secret either. Maybe it didn't matter in the scheme of things. I mean, Grandma and Grandpa Barlow were both from Utah, right? Maybe they were vacationing when he was born."

"Maybe," I conceded. "But it's so unsettling to discover huge details about my grandparents after they've died. Remember when I learned Grandma Ginny was married before she met Grandpa?"

"It took you months to recover." She smiled and put a hand on my leg.

"It seems like they hid things on purpose."

"Well, honey, *I* knew about Grandma. Her first husband was no secret, just not relevant to *your* life."

My grandma Ginny's funeral was the first I'd attended and one of the most powerful memories of my childhood, for one reason: I learned she'd lived a lifetime before I came along. Until that point she was one thing: my grandma. Her world revolved around me. After the funeral, I wasn't sure who she was.

That day, ancient people filled every church pew, and all the women were bedecked in enormous hats. Woven and wide-brimmed, they were adorned with flowers, plumes, and netting. It was as if I were surrounded by a flock of tropical birds.

My grandma, in dramatic fashion, had insisted that all the ladies come well topped to her funeral. "In celebration of my fashionable life." And the crowd didn't disappoint. My mom even insisted I wear one, and I begrudgingly agreed to an Easter bonnet from several years earlier. It mashed my ears.

As we sat, a woman tapped the microphone up front. She was old, her gray bangs curling across her forehead, the remainder of her hair covered with an orange hat plumed with sunshine-gold feathers. To me, she resembled Big Bird, but it turned out she was my grandma's older sister, Betty, who lived in Idaho. I shrugged at my mom. Grandma had a sister?

Her speech was entitled "Life Sketch for Virginia Leigh Bertrand Cartwright Barlow." What a name! She was Grandma Ginny to me. Betty's voice crackled with age as she spoke. I figured I already knew everything about my grandma, but there was nothing else to do, so I attempted to concentrate on the life sketch of my grandma Ginny.

Born in 1920, my grandma was the youngest of four girls who lived in a house with no running water. *No running water?* They made all of their own clothing, and she developed a style she carried to the last day of her life. Though she didn't go to college, she taught elementary school in a one-room schoolhouse until she married her husband. I waited for his name, glancing at Grandpa Joe, who sat on one of the wooden benches right at the front: Robert Cartwright.

What? Who was Robert Cartwright, and why wasn't my grandpa pounding his fist and insisting to this silly old lady she had the name wrong? I glanced at my mom, who smiled without concern and squeezed my knee.

But Robert Cartwright died in 1942, in France, during World War II. *Whew,* I thought, and continued to gape at my grandpa's face. He must have known, because he wasn't protesting, but why hadn't anyone told *me?*

She met my grandpa, Joseph Lewis Barlow, at a wartime dance, where she was swept off her feet. She quickly agreed to marry the dashing doctor several years her senior, and they were married for the remainder of her life.

But again anguish. She had a stillborn son,

Robert, and lost another child, Ronald, to a high fever when he was only two years old. Even still, she went about her days with a smile and high style. Before long she had her two darling girls: Diane and Marsha. I glanced again at my mom. Did she know all this? Did she know about her dead brothers? My mom held a tissue and was dabbing at her cheeks.

Betty continued to speak, and when she got to the part of my grandma's life I recognized, she spoke two sentences about her seven beloved grandchildren and sat down. We weren't even mentioned by name!

According to the printed schedule, the next performance was a piano rendition of "Crazy Bone Rag," and as the music pinged in my skull, I pondered all I learned in fifteen minutes about Grandma Ginny. How could she have lived so much of her life before I came along? Had she kept these things secret on purpose? I thought I knew her. But it turned out I barely knew anything at all.

"Emma, you look tired." My mom was finished with her meal and was staring at me. "Are you sure you don't want to talk about your day?"

"No. Sorry for drifting. I was just thinking about Grandma Ginny's funeral."

"It was a long time ago."

"I know, but going through all of their things . . .

I feel like I should second-guess everything I look at now."

After retrieving the kitchen scissors from the junk drawer, I trimmed Grandpa Joe's obituary and stuck it to the refrigerator with a magnet. "You know, Mom, I *am* tired. Maybe I'll go to bed now and take a day or two off from Grandpa's. Is that okay? I'll get back to it, I promise, but I might continue with my job hunt, with serious intent."

My mom stood next to me and leaned her shoulder into mine. We wore the same size clothing, bought the same perfume, and had the same aversion to cilantro. She was my comforting shadow. Together we read the obituary, my grandfather's last message to us. She touched his face on the newsprint. "Don't fret about Grandpa, okay? It's impossible to know everything about everyone."

Her fingers shook slightly as she spoke, and she crossed her arms, tucking her hands into the creases of her elbows. Before I could question her, she'd turned her back to me. She was walking down the hall as she finished her thought. "But it doesn't change who they are."

CHAPTER 9

I woke in the spare bedroom next to my mom's, disoriented for a moment where I lay. Though I slept all the years of my childhood in this house, I'd never slept in this particular room, because this room was reserved for my little brother, Ethan.

Though it sat empty for fifty weeks of each year, our mom had decorated annually for him, updating his barely used bedspread from dump trucks to dinosaurs, hanging striped wallpaper through his baseball obsession. Eventually she graduated his room to the teen phase and filled the walls with posters of grunge bands like Pearl Jam.

During the long days of elementary school summer, when the house was especially quiet, when I ached for my baby brother to live in the hopeful room where I now lay, I'd leave Ethan notes hidden in his chest of drawers, taped behind posters, or tucked like secret whispers into his empty shoes. But I was the visitor now, sleeping in this vacant guest room, having run from my own home. I needed a plan, because I couldn't stay here forever.

An hour later I was tucked at the kitchen table, cold coffee next to my keyboard, scrolling through job listings. I told my mom this was my plan, but boy did I long for the old-fashioned want ads, impressive pages of newsprint I could fill with jolly red circles indicating two things: I was employable and I was trying.

Though the desire to visit Grandpa Joe's house tugged at me, insistent like a hungry child, I also knew I needed some distance before I could lose myself, again, in his past. Revealing my grandparents' history would be intriguing only if I started thinking of their memories as a puzzle rather than a betrayal.

Time away from Noah . . . sifting through my grandparents' memories . . . finding a job. Part of me wanted a five-year rewind, back to a time before I was married, before Joey, when Grandpa Joe was still alive, before my world had been shattered. If I could avoid the undetermined parts of my life, each of them trailing like an unfinished tune, reverberating in my head, begging me to finish the lyrics, I would, because I didn't know how this song would end.

The text notification on my phone vibrated the table next to my laptop. I grabbed it, aching for a word from Noah, even as I hoped it would not be from him. It wasn't Noah. It was Ethan.

Are you home and do you have a minute to talk?

I'm free, I responded. A minute? I'd talk to him the whole damn day if it meant avoiding the rest of my life.

Where are you? came his quick reply.

After much maneuvering via text, my brother explained he and Anusha wanted to see me before they went back to California. He told me he wanted to give me some time after the funeral, and he was sad we didn't have a chance to talk that day. Which, of course, was my fault.

I texted that I'd been cleaning Grandpa Joe's house for the past couple days and was taking a short break back at our mom's place. I kept the explanation on the surface because, like train cars tightly coupled, if I revealed to Ethan that I'd spent the past two nights in her spare bedroom, it would be a clear indicator I'd replaced sitting on the couch with abandoning my life in a different manner. I wasn't ready for that conversation.

So, is Mom with you?

I knew he'd ask, because a ballad of discord resonated behind Ethan's seemingly innocent question. Throughout the years of childhood, Ethan and I were the weapons our parents used to keep the wounds of their broken marriage fresh. The fact that Ethan lived full-time with my father was the reason he didn't have a relationship with our mom. It's hard to continually drink poisoned water and not feel a little sick. And though my mom didn't say negative things about my dad on a daily basis, it didn't mean I liked him much either. In a child, familiarity is what makes the heart grow fonder.

Despite the physical distance between Ethan and me, and the drama between our parents, my brother and I were entwined at the roots. If he texted to say he was still in town, no matter what I was doing, I'd drop everything to see him.

She's working. No worries.

Then we'll be right over.

As soon as I closed the front door behind them, Anusha pulled me into an embrace, and while she held me Ethan placed his hands on my back. When she released me, Ethan asked, "How are you doing? Noah said you're still having some trouble sleeping."

I swallowed. "When did you talk with him?"

"At the luncheon. We all wished you'd been there."

"I know." I studied the carpet, knowing I didn't have to explain further.

"Oh, Emma." Anusha sighed my name. "I'm so sorry about your grandfather. And about everything."

"I'm going to be fine." I gave her the We Can Do It arm pump, my healthiest smile, and changed the subject. "These past couple of days I've been organizing Grandpa Joe's things. It's pretty interesting."

"And how's your mother?" Anusha asked.

"She's hanging in there too. I mean, we knew it was coming."

"And you're *really* going to be okay?" Ethan still wasn't convinced.

"Please. I'm awesome at coping effectively with loss. Ask anyone."

Ethan chuckled.

I sat on my mom's floral couch and patted the cushion next to me. "So . . . to what do I owe this honor?"

Anusha glided toward the sofa and took a seat next to me. Never in my life had I met a woman so fluid. Her skin was a copper color, and her black hair cascaded over her shoulders in a curtain of ebony. Unlike me, she had no fluffy patches where she'd obsessively pulled at her split ends, and her eyes weren't circled with sleep bruise. Anusha's English carried the melodic accent of native Hindi speakers, a question mark at the end of most sentences, making me want to continue conversation beyond the point of topic exhaustion. I could see why Ethan was in love with her.

"We delayed our flight because we wanted a chance to see you," Anusha said, touching my knee as she spoke.

"Really? Well, that's nice."

Anusha smiled but didn't respond.

Visits with my brother and his girlfriend were typically so animated that we talked over one another in our exuberance, months of separation crammed into a couple of antic-filled days. But today the pauses between sentences were painful.

Ethan took a spot next to Anusha and cleared his throat.

After several beats, I stood. "Hey, I found something I want you guys to see." I ran to the bedroom to retrieve the wedding photo.

When I returned, the two of them were whispering. Ethan jumped from his seat like a fully extended bullfrog. "What did you find?" He was flushed.

"Am I missing something? You guys are acting weird."

"There's something we want to talk to you about, Emma." Anusha was standing now, too. "But what is in the envelope?"

"You first." I tucked the photo behind my back.

My brother stared at Anusha, though she'd spoken to me. In response she pulled at the charm on her gold necklace, spooling it back and forth, the movement creating a rattling zipper sound. This wasn't a regular visit.

"Ethan, come on. What's wrong?"

He took a deep breath and he finally spoke. "We've been thinking for a while now of starting a family, but with Joey's illness, it was too uncertain and—"

"We don't want to make this time any more painful for you, Emma," Anusha spoke for my brother. "But we wanted to tell you our plans, and we have a few questions, if they're not too hard to answer."

Ethan's shoulders sagged. He smiled weakly at Anusha, relieved she'd done the heavy lifting.

The photo I'd been clutching dropped to the floor. Ethan ducked to pick it up and placed it back in my hand. "A baby?" I meant to sound celebratory and light, but the question came out wrapped in a cry. They were going to have a baby?

But there was more to consider. Of course the genetic component of Joey's disease could affect my brother's children as well. I hadn't considered it until this moment.

"If it's too much—" Anusha touched my arm hesitantly, as if assessing an open wound.

"No. It's important. I'll be okay."

Ethan pulled the envelope from my hand, and I realized I'd been clenching it. The corner was damp from the press of my fingers. "Have you been tested?" I asked. "You should start there, because if I'm a carrier, you could be too, and if Anusha is—"

I twisted my hands as I spoke, digits crossing and grasping. This was a new habit of mine, born with the diagnosis of my son, a fruitless effort to take hold of something I couldn't control. Glad that Ethan held the photo, I pressed my palms against my thighs to stop them from clawing at each other.

"The test is critical," I continued. "If I'd been tested before we conceived, Joey wouldn't have been born with Canavan disease." I stopped and swallowed. "Actually . . . I guess Joey wouldn't have been born. At all."

What would we have done differently? Not conceived? But we didn't know about the disease. Aborted? Joey and his condition were inseparable. The disease was inextricably part of my child. Did I wish I'd never known Joey? No. If I couldn't have one without the other, I would never wish my son away. But Ethan and Anusha had an option, before they fell in love with their child.

"I already took the Ashkenazi Jewish Genetic Panel," Ethan said. "That's the one, right?"

I nodded.

"Okay, first question. Why Jewish?" Ethan blushed slightly. "The doctor at the clinic was named Silverstein, and I worried I'd offend him with my question."

"Well, Canavan and a bunch of other diseases, like Tay–Sachs, are more prevalent in the Ashkenazi Jewish population, hence the name."

"I'm quite certain I have no Jewish ancestors," Anusha said, pointing at her bindi, the decorative red dot between her Indian brows.

"Noah's grandmother was Jewish, but until we had Joey I was certain I didn't have any Jewish ancestors either. Or it would matter if I did. I'd never even heard of the disease."

"The poor Jews, first the Holocaust and now

a panel of genetic diseases they can call their very own." He bumped my shoulder with his, a reassuring movement all Ethan's. "Sorry, but sometimes dark humor minimizes the tragedy."

I returned the nudge, understanding.

"So you already took the test?" I asked. "What did you discover?"

"It's good news. I'm not a carrier."

I exhaled, my breath puffing through my nose. My chest constricted, and I wasn't sure if it was relief or envy. "That's so great, Ethan," I said with as much cheer as I could muster. "Full steam ahead?"

"I guess," he replied. "How do the genetics work on this thing anyhow? How is it possible you're a carrier and I'm not? I found some information online, but I still don't understand."

In the early days of Joey's diagnosis I believed if Noah and I could unravel the scientific details, we could beat it. This, as it turned out, wasn't true. We'd failed our child at the molecular level. But I could try to educate my brother. I visualized the Punnett square from high school biology as I spoke.

"So, either Mom or Dad is a carrier of the disease." I held two hands out, one palm up, the other in a fist, an unbalanced scale of justice. "See, if *one* parent is a carrier, then each of their children has a twenty-five percent chance of also being a carrier but no chance of having the disease. I'm the carrier, the one in four. If *both* parents are carriers, like me and Noah, it means each of us has one of the faulty chromosomes." I clenched both fists and held them side by side.

"If we had four children, statistically speaking, one would have the disease because the child received two faulty chromosomes. Which is what Joey got, two faulty chromosomes—" Two chromosomes that ended his life.

"I'm with you," Ethan said when I stopped mid explanation.

"Right," I said, swallowing. "However, statistics say two of our children would be carriers with only one messed-up chromosome and no sign of the disease. And one would *not* be a carrier, or have the disease, at all. It's a little confusing, but I have this chart to help explain it. It's at my house, but I could take a picture of it and text it to you."

Ethan leaned back into the couch and pressed his thumbs to his eyelids. "So, it's possible I could *not* be a carrier. I would be the three out of four."

"Yes. That's why it's so rare. And it was my bad luck to fall in love with another carrier, and Joey's bad luck to inherit two faulty chromosomes."

"Don't you ever wonder where it came from?" Ethan asked. "Was it Mom or Dad?"

"Yes, I wonder," I said. "But Noah says it doesn't matter. We both carry the disease. End of story."

"Probably the wisest approach."

"Of course, we know where it came from on his side. Or at least we know Noah had a grandma who was Jewish. . . ."

On our first official date, Noah asked me to meet him at a bar. Hidden in his invite was a subtle challenge I'd experienced often when dating in Utah. Actually, this veiled test was not just for dates, it was often performed between coworkers and budding friends, because in Utah this question was the litmus test of religion, aka, lifestyle. If you said yes to the drink, it meant one thing: You weren't a Mormon. At that point, if your religious sentimentalities aligned, and with everything out in the open, the relationship could proceed (or not).

I agreed to the date and he took me to Bar X, where on the second round he punctuated the relationship/religion test by asking, no punches held, if I was a Mormon (nonpracticing). I raised my glass, happy he wasn't religious either, and said, "Four times a Mormon, twice removed." I was already a little tipsy.

He returned my smile and clicked his mug against mine. "Sounds promising, but what does it mean?"

"I've got family going back generations in Utah. So of course I have Mormon ancestors. It's the only reason people stopped here on their way to California, back in the day. But, no, I have no living relatives who are members. Scratch that, I have a cousin who I think married a Mormon guy, and I guess they go to church. What about you?"

I was having a hard time not staring at Noah as we talked. I was typically attracted to guys who looked like they'd dragged in from a hard night—dripping with overt sexuality—but not someone you could count on to run to the grocery store for eggs and bananas. But Noah was earnest *and* sexual. Earnestly sexual. He had a fair complexion with the residue of childhood freckles and dark hair, which was likely auburn when he was young. And his eyes. Incongruous to his coloring, they were chocolate brown, so deep I couldn't see his pupils, surrounded by a sweep of thick lashes.

He looked as if he'd played a college sport, because he was big, with enormous hands and double-jointed thumbs. His palms were so wide . . . and those thumbs. I didn't know why they were making me crazy, but they were. I licked my lips, then chided myself to keep a little control. But this guy could circle my waist with his hands and put me over his shoulder. And I kind of wanted him to.

"I'm going to disprove your theory," he said, grabbing my scattered thoughts.

"What theory?"

"About the reason people settled in Salt Lake City."

"Oh, right." I caught the thread of the conversation and tried to concentrate.

"My family has also been in this city for well over a hundred years. But my great-great-grandfather came to Utah not because he was Mormon but because there was a business opportunity in Zion."

"Let me guess. Mining?"

"Nope. He was one of the Auerbach brothers. They opened the first department store in the city called—"

"Auerbach's! My grandpa told me about the store."

"Yep, two Jews on their way to the California Gold Rush saw a lucrative opportunity selling goods to the Mormons. Bartering for goods wasn't Godlike, so enter the merchant."

"Clever men. So you're Jewish?" I'd never met a Jewish guy before. It was rather exotic.

He shook his head. "Let's see, using your vernacular I'd be two times Jewish, thrice removed, or something like that. I've never been to a synagogue . . . and we had a Christmas tree." He whistled a familiar tune. "I can sing the dreidel song, though. We learned it in elementary school."

I could sing it too. After our third round of drinks, we sang it together.

• • •

"Emma, I think you're crying," Anusha said, touching my cheek with her fingertip. "We can talk about this later."

I rubbed my face, surprised at the moisture, knowing this time my tears weren't for Joey. They were for Noah, and the role genetics played in our demise. "Actually, it feels good to talk. I've been a little in my head lately."

Ethan sat forward and picked up a family photo in a dated brass frame that had long sat on my mom's sofa table. It was of my mom and dad and me, before Ethan was born. He placed it in my lap and I stared at it, confused. In it, I was the only child, one leg of a triangle made by my parents, their arms surrounding me as I sat between them. We were a perfect triumvirate of blond heads.

"I want to get everything straight about the genetics of this thing, because"—he took a deep breath before blurting out—"I've always wondered if I might be adopted."

Anusha froze. Her hand, which had been patting my leg comfortingly, twitched. "Ethan, this isn't the time."

"What? Adopted? I must have zoned out for a minute. I'm not sure what you're talking about."

"Ethan!" Anusha hissed.

"It's relevant, Anush. And it's a distraction."

I blinked. "You might as well spill." I set the photo on the coffee table in front of us. "I have no idea what you're talking about, but you can't clam up now."

"Okay," he said, and Anusha sighed, leaning back into the couch cushions; clearly she'd heard this conversation before. "So, when I was a senior in high school I had this biology class, and we were talking about recessive traits. One thing the teacher mentioned was attached earlobes."

"Hold on, weren't we talking about Canavan disease? And adoption?"

"I'll get there. So attached earlobes like yours, and Mom's and Dad's, they are a recessive trait."

"Like Canavan."

"Right. Meaning if there was any hint of gigantic earlobes, like mine, one of my parents should have them too. They're the *dominant* trait, the trump card. They'd win every time. But Mom and Dad *both* have attached lobes. Mine came from out of nowhere."

I touched my earlobe while he spoke. I'd always thought my ears were one of my best features, tiny and trim against my head. I preferred dainty earrings, like a woman with a small waist would accentuate it with a fitted belt, showing off a favorable feature. "Canavan is unbelievably rare, Ethan."

"Exactly my point."

"Are you really telling me you think you're adopted because you have chubby earlobes? It's the craziest thing I've ever heard of."

"Well, like you want to know where the Canavan came from, I'm curious about the earlobes." He laughed, realizing how ridiculous he sounded. "Granted, earlobes are nothing compared to the disease, but do you see my connection?"

"I see it. But I think you're nuts."

"There's more. Think about eye color. Yours are blue."

"Yes?"

"And Mom's eyes are blue."

"Fascinating, Ethan. And Grandpa Joe's eyes were blue. Mom got them from him. I got them from her."

I loved that I'd inherited my grandpa's blues, because when he listened to my rambling childhood tales it was like seeing the vastness of the heavens beyond his shoulder, a universe of understanding I could glimpse through the windows of his sky.

"And Dad's eyes are blue," Ethan continued. "Recessive again. Blue-eyed parents tend to have a blue-eyed child. But what color are my eyes?"

The first time Joey opened his dark eyes, I thought, whose eyes does he have? Noah's or Ethan's? But the shape of them, the long lashes, they were without a doubt Noah's, and I didn't think of it again. "Your eyes are brown," I whispered.

"I've researched this one. It is possible two

blue-eyed parents could have a brown-eyed child, because more than one gene controls eye color. It's *unlikely* but not impossible, but taken along with the earlobes—"

"I still think you're getting ahead of yourself."

"And this test," he continued without acknowledging my opposition. "You're a carrier and I'm *not*."

"No, see? It would be more likely you *wouldn't* be a carrier. Because there's only a twenty-five percent chance that any child Mom and Dad had would carry the gene."

"I still think there's something there."

"And I think you're taking this too seriously," Anusha chimed in. "This is all just speculation."

"Plus, Ethan," I added, "I remember Mom when she was pregnant with you. I held my hand over her belly while you bounced against it. You aren't adopted."

Memories of my mom swollen wide with my little brother were some of my first true memories. I had snippets from earlier in my life, but they were the ones prescribed to me through story and sometimes photos. Like the time I ran headlong into the corner of a table at one of those kids sports arenas, and the subsequent five stitches. Or my favorite animal on the carousel at the zoo, the zebra with the broken stump of a tail, because I wanted him to know he was loved. Or the day I learned to pump on a swing, age two, the tiniest one at the park. But Ethan, his earliest presence, the rolling kicks under my mom's shirt, these I remembered on my own. There was no possible way he was adopted.

"Then why were we separated after the divorce?" Ethan broke through my memories.

"I don't know. To punish Mom? I don't think custody has anything to do with paternity."

The divorce and the fights leading to it were also etched into my album of childhood recollections. My dad booming like thunder. My mom cowering on the couch, her hands clasped together in her lap like two hard stones as she bore the cutting hail of his words.

"Have you ever talked to Dad about it? Your adoption theory? Or the custody arrangement?" I asked, returning my attention to the present, to the odd conversation I was having with my now adult brother.

A heavy silence filled the room. "Over the years, I've asked," Ethan replied. "Back then I just wanted to spend more time with you and Mom in Salt Lake. But about a month ago, after I took the Ashkenazi test, I mentioned the adoption thing, and the earlobes, to see what he'd say."

"And?"

"And he overreacted."

"But that's Dad. Overreact or ignore." In my case it had been ignore. My dad left me alone to spend most of my weeklong summer visits

101

to California in Ethan's room, searching his abandoned school notebooks and under his bed for clues to who my brother was becoming. My hours with him were precious few, so these were the threads that wove the cloth of our sibling relationship: the collection of dried praying mantises, the carved sticks, a signed baseball hat. As we both became teenagers I found photos of girls, a dog-eared *Playboy*, a couple of beers he'd taken from my dad's stash.

"So what did Dad say after he finished over-reacting?" I asked.

"Well, after stomping around and pouring himself a shot of whiskey, he said"—Ethan shifted in his seat so he could look directly at me—"well, he asked, 'What *exactly* did your mother tell you?' "

"What?" I gasped. "Was he implying there was more to the story? Other than an ugly divorce and an asinine custody arrangement?"

"Yes, it seemed so."

"So what did you say?"

"Nothing convincing enough. Mom didn't *actually* tell me anything, so I said something vague like, 'Oh, she's told me things.' "

"You were never a good liar."

"Seconds later, as I was thinking of something compelling to say, he turned on the shower and locked the bathroom door. I waited around for him to get out. I was an hour late for dinner with Anusha, but I couldn't get him to engage. I couldn't even get him out of the bathroom."

I glanced at Anusha as he spoke. "It's true," she said, shrugging. "He was late and it was an unusual reaction."

"I've tried asking Mom about the custody arrangement too," I said. "Though more often when I was young."

"So how did she respond?"

"She never stopped me from questioning. I mean, I wasn't shut out." I thought about some of the conversations I had with my mother, skimming through the facts I knew as solid truth about the divorce and the split custody. There weren't many.

"I think she may have used some of her special social worker mind tricks on me. I know we talked about it, but I can't remember how our fights ended. Despite all of my repeated and circular questioning, I never got any closer to the molten core of the truth."

"Well, I think my adoption theory has something to do with the custody," Ethan said.

"How do you propose we figure it out, considering we're both well into our adult years and so far we've failed to reveal anything amiss, despite our decades of effort?"

"I have a plan." He took a breath, employing the dramatic pause. "I'm going to get a full DNA test and you should get one too. I've been researching and it's like a hundred bucks." He quickened the pace of his conversation, excited about his plan and eager to get me to conspire.

"But you've already had the Canavan test."

"This is totally different. If we both test our DNA it will tell us if we're siblings. And if we are, there's no problem, aside from a shitty custody arrangement and my dangling earlobes, but if we aren't . . ."

"If we aren't, what do you propose we do with the information?" This was crazy.

"Then we ask again. You talk to Mom and I'll talk to Dad. We'll use the DNA test to punctuate the question. There's no denying science."

"I don't know, Ethan. This is sneaky, like we're trapping our parents. I'm a grown woman. I'll ask. No test required." I didn't want to corner my mom and force her into revealing the truth like a villain at the end of a syndicated crime show.

"You'll ask *again?* That didn't get you anywhere for all these years."

"I'll give it another shot, and if it doesn't work—"

"Ethan, don't pressure her." Anusha pressed her lips together, but Ethan plunged forward.

"This? From my sister who's notoriously conflict averse? I'll send you the link for the DNA test when I get home. Don't delete it, because I think there's something there and it's haunting me. Anusha, obviously, thinks it's not important."

Anusha rolled her eyes.

"But I need to know the truth."

"Fine, send me the link. But I'll talk to Mom face-to-face. I'll engage in conflict if you insist, then I'll call you."

Anusha tapped her watch. "I think we've tortured your poor sister for long enough. Besides, we need to get to the airport."

Ethan's face went bright, excited by the conversation. He stood and pulled me to him for an embrace. "Say good-bye to Noah for me. And let me know what you decide."

As I closed the door behind them, I realized I hadn't sunk into sadness while talking about Joey. While I considered my brother's scattered questions, I'd set aside the grief I'd been carrying like a heavy pack. It was a bittersweet epiphany. And when Ethan told me to say good-bye to Noah, I realized I hadn't been dwelling on my failing relationship either. Maybe *this* diversion, even more so than organizing Grandpa Joe's room of memories, would be just what the doctor ordered.

CHAPTER 10

I stood silently in the doorway watching my mother flit about the kitchen preparing dinner for the two of us. She was like a bee buzzing about, touching briefly on one surface and then another. The smell of bubbling cheese filled the brightly lit room as she chopped romaine for a Caesar salad. Like usual, she was talking to herself, and I hesitated to disturb her, caught for a moment in the quiet patter of her words. In many ways it was nice living back in my childhood home. My mom and I slipped into our roles very easily, and over the days I allowed the smells and sounds of childhood to release the tension in my shoulders, melting sadness like candle wax.

My mom, Diane Barlow Gontrum. She had always been beautiful, in a double-take way, and even as a child I was happy when strangers commented on our similarities. White blond at birth, she grew up during a time when no one worried about sunscreen and the contrast between a tan face and pale hair was a sign of beauty. I knew from photos, she was that girl. These days, sun-spotted and lined with age-appropriate wrinkles, she was still bright blond. Although she was typically dressed in a uniform of jeans and sweaters, her physique whispered of the days she could rock a bikini.

Grandpa Joe always said she was a born talker, and as a family therapist, using only her voice, she could create connection between clients, discover secrets, and urge reconciliation. The irony of her successful career juxtaposed with her own failed marriage and the estrangement of my brother never ceased to amaze me. But when I questioned her about it, she said her job satisfaction came from fixing in others what she couldn't fix in herself. And when claimed such, in her self-assured, gravel-filled voice (the lounge singer intonation I inherited from her) I totally understood.

As I used my own voice to fill the silence with my son, or lead a yoga class, I knew among the many things I inherited from my mom I'd also obtained her skill of a soothing one-sided conversation.

She finally noticed me in the doorway and gestured to a lemon and the zester with a nod. "Could you help me with this? The mac's about to come out of the oven."

On the surface, it was like every other night over the last two weeks, but tonight our easy conversation would be different. I'd promised Ethan a quick turnaround on a candid question-and-answer session with our mom, but I'd delayed. My mom was my comfort. I wasn't sure

I cared enough about Ethan's earlobe mystery to confront her. But Ethan did. And I cared about Ethan.

"So this morning you told me you wanted to talk?" she asked, setting the bubbling casserole dish on a trivet. She took a wineglass from the cupboard and poured me a glass from the bottle of cabernet she'd opened. After retrieving her own glass from the counter, she took a sip, and resumed chopping, her back facing me. "Are you ready to talk about Noah?"

I'd been so intent on planning my conversation about Ethan and the custody arrangement, her question caught me off guard. "No, Mom. I don't need your marriage counseling right now."

She stopped chopping, surprised at my tone. "It's been weeks."

I swallowed. I knew exactly how long it had been. I was painfully aware of each night I spent without my husband next to me in bed. "I'm not ready yet. I'm a little up and down these days." I took up zesting the lemon, the sound scratchy in the quiet room. "Sorry I was so curt."

She nodded. "Okay, then. How are things progressing at Grandpa's? Any new discoveries?"

The truth was, I hadn't been back to Grandpa Joe's either. Between finishing my résumé, sending copies out, and considering Ethan's questions, I hadn't wanted to step back into that place of memories where everything once solid now sat on shifting ground.

"No. Nothing notable." I took a long sip of wine. "I had something else I wanted to ask you about."

I resisted the urge to be lulled into a quiet comfort by a combination of my mom's husky conversation and the alcohol. Talking with her was like taking a warm bath. I didn't want to step out of the tub into the frigid air, not yet.

But there were questions I promised Ethan I would ask, only how to go about it? *Mom, Ethan thinks he's adopted because he has large earlobes and brown eyes.* She would think I was insane. And then it came to me: I would bluff.

"So have you heard Ethan and Anusha are thinking of having a baby?" I knew the question would get her attention, but I'd been holding on to this fragment of sorrow for so long, I blurted the words, simply to get the statement out of my mouth. "They visited before heading back to California to ask details about the disease. Or to ask my permission to conceive, I'm not sure which."

My mom's features fell at the news, and I knew Ethan hadn't included her in his decision. "So, no wedding?" she asked without looking up from the knife.

"I guess since Anusha's not marrying an Indian man, her parents don't care one way or the other.

In fact, I think no ceremony means her parents don't have to announce a poor marriage to family and friends in Bombay. Apparently Ethan is not a catch on that continent."

"A parent's lie of omission or otherwise known as, No news is good news." She set the knife carefully on the cutting board. "Well, I really like Anusha, and I hope once Ethan has a child of his own, he might understand that the decisions we make as parents aren't always as simple as a child might believe."

Was my mom actually directing this conversation toward her relationship with Ethan without my excessive prompting?

"What not-so-simple decisions did you make as a parent?"

"What?" She hesitated before resuming her chopping with studied strokes.

"Did you make any difficult decisions?"

"Oh, constantly," she said, sliding out from under the question. "Would you take the salad to the table? I'll bring the mac and cheese."

After we tucked in, my mom talked about a client, a young man who harbored anger at his mother for working long hours, never making it to any of his high school basketball games. She believed she was doing him a favor, taking overtime to pay for his college. The son didn't see it the same way. Listening, I knew my mom was diverting me by telling a story about difficult parental decisions having nothing to do with her.

I changed the subject back. "So the day Ethan came to see me, before they went back to California, he wanted to ask a few questions about Joey's disease. Like how the genetics of the thing worked."

She touched my arm, a reassuring caress. "Baby, I didn't think how Ethan's decision would make you feel. Are you going to be okay?"

I nodded, soldiering on. "I encouraged him to request a Jewish genetic panel, to see if he was a carrier for Canavan disease."

"Has he taken it yet? I hope he's not positive."

I nodded. "He took it. He's not a carrier. So that's good."

Relief swept her face.

"He took a different type of test, though. Different from the Ashkenazi panel," I continued. This time I was lying. As far as I knew, Ethan hadn't taken the second test. Yet. "It tested for Canavan, but it was also a full DNA test. It showed lots of cool things like the countries where his ancestors came from and how much Neanderthal DNA he possesses. It sounds pretty interesting." I learned about these bonus features from the DNA link Ethan sent me.

"Really? How much Neanderthal DNA does Ethan have?"

"He doesn't have his results yet, but most

humans are almost 3% caveman, and Ethan is hoping for average."

"Average? I guess he'll have to stop hunting with that wooden club and dragging his knuckles." My mom giggled, and I almost joined her. I took a deep breath. *Stay the course.*

I faced her as I made my next statement, forcing myself to watch her reaction. "The test also reveals maternal and paternal lineage, and shows the genetic similarities between siblings. So if I *also* took a DNA test, we could see how much of our genome we share."

My mom shuddered, a forkful of lettuce falling back onto her plate.

"So I'm thinking of taking it. The DNA test." I flushed as I spoke, fixating on the fallen lettuce. Was I getting at something, like a lawyer with a squirming witness on the stand? It felt wrong. I was trapping my lioness mother. And in her presence, I was wavering.

But at the same time, as Ethan claimed, there appeared to be more to the story than we'd been told. "I think it would be interesting," I continued, attempting to justify the test to my mother. "And it might show the origin of Canavan disease. On my side."

Strictly speaking, this was not entirely true, but it made me feel better to say it.

"Emma." She faced me. "Knowing the origins of the disease won't change anything. You and

Noah understand the situation already. Maybe it would be better to let bygones be bygones." She rested her palm over my hand, which I'd clenched into a hard ball.

I flicked her away like scalding water, both fists tight, like I was bracing for impact. She'd said exactly the wrong thing. "Bygones? Is that what we're calling Joey now? A bygone?"

"It's not what I meant, and you know it. But he *is* gone, and you're still here."

I turned away from her and took a sip of my wine, trying to settle my emotions. Joey was not a bygone, he was my baby. My baby, who despite my most careful care was gone. If I had betrayed my son with my genetics, had my mother betrayed me?

Now I understood where Ethan was coming from. If something was amiss, he wanted the truth. And I did too. He wanted the truth about paternity, and I wanted the truth about Canavan disease. Somehow the two mysteries were twisted in my mind. Together they were two secrets that must be revealed. The DNA test was a start. Without further questioning, I decided I would take the test for Ethan. And I would take the test for me. If there was something real to his claims, I deserved to know as well.

The next morning Ethan and I co-conspired, registering our kits at the same time, giggling like sneaky schoolchildren, but after I disconnected from my brother, a sinking dread pressed like a pair of heavy palms on my shoulders. After hitting the buy icon to submit my order, I took a moment to read the proffered several pages of Terms and Conditions, which I had accepted (without reading) minutes earlier.

The terms specified that I allowed my results to be used anywhere, by anyone, as long as they weren't identifiable as mine. A little dystopian scary but not unreasonable. However, the line that stood out, almost as if it had been highlighted, was this:

You may learn information about yourself you do not anticipate.

The Ashkenazi panel I'd taken in the course of diagnosing my son with a fatal disease contained information I didn't anticipate, and it was *not* welcome. This new test would use science to tug at the other corner of the veil. It would be my next step to knowing the truth. But did I really want to know?

What if the results pulled my brother further from me because he was right, because we weren't actually bound by blood? I was already precariously balanced on a tightrope. Without Joey or Noah or my grandpa, I needed all of my remaining family ties tightly knotted.

CHAPTER 11

Every day after our ill-fated breakfast, Noah texted me first thing in the morning: *Will you come home today?*

After several days of negative replies, his question was shortened to: *Today?*

Though I always replied *No,* or sometimes *I'm sorry,* I anticipated our daily ritual almost as much as my morning coffee when we lived in the same home. I wondered when he would stop. I wondered when he would move on. The truth was, I ached for him. I hoped each day without him would strengthen my resolve to let him go, but after the conversations with Ethan and my mom, the only person I wanted to hash over the details with was my husband. And today I had a legitimate reason. I planned to go home, for at least a few minutes, because I finally had a job, which meant I must retrieve more clothing from my closet.

After sending a first round of résumés into the world to no response, I halfheartedly contacted my old boss, Darcy, at the yoga studio where I worked before Joey: Downtown Dog. Darcy had continued to reach out to me, almost monthly, after Joey was born. I'd been consumed with his disease and his care, so I hadn't returned her calls. I hoped the bridge hadn't been burned.

I knew employment was a step in the right direction, but I was still having a hard time embracing the idea of returning to the studio. Stepping back through the knotty pine door and into the incense-filled room was a five-year rewind. Same job before I got married, before I became a mother, before I met Noah. In some ways I would be erasing Joey, a prospect that brought a pang of guilt mixed with relief. I wanted to remember everything about those years, to the tiniest detail. And at the same time I wanted to forget.

Darcy answered on the second ring, and as soon as I said her name, she said, "You called back."

"How did you know it was me?"

"Caller ID," she said. "And your voice. Remember the regulars at your seven o'clock class all those years ago? The other day one of them asked about the girl who could wrap her words in velvet."

Again, evidence of my inherited skill. I could create instant shavasana in yoga class with my husky recitation. My mom used it to soothe her clients (and me). I used it to put a class into a yoga coma. It was also a trick that caught me my husband.

Darcy kept me on the phone while she arranged

the class schedule to give me two sessions a day. My timing was perfect, she said. One of the teachers was headed for maternity leave. As Darcy spoke, I worked to release the tight bands circling my lungs. Maternity leave. For someone else. It was fine.

As we worked through the details, I remembered the first time I met Noah. Although our orbits apparently crossed several times through the years of our young lives, we met for the first time, face-to-face, in yoga class. Maybe this was another reason I didn't want to go back. I didn't want to enter the place where our relationship sparked and simmered with potential.

That first night had been like any other in the studio, the lights low and the music a barely audible mantra. Women dressed in Lululemon had shushed into the studio carrying their mats and unfurled them on the hardwood floor. The class had settled into relaxation breathing when Noah opened the door, and backlit from the foyer light he resembled a cowboy at a saloon, the wind following him through the swinging doors. Everyone had turned to watch, but *I* could scarcely look away.

I left my mat and directed the newcomer to the registry, hovering next to him as he signed in. Even as he wrote his name, I wanted to move closer, to tuck myself against him. It was an odd sensation, an actual magnetism, and I'd forced myself to take a step back just to see if I could. Mesmerized by his hands as he scribbled a few details, when he finished I'd read his name: *Noah Hazelton*. I imagined writing it over and over in different fonts on the cover of my middle school notebook, combining my first name with his last.

After acknowledging my red-faced welcome with a shy, knowing smile, he'd glanced around the studio, observing the room as if he were in a foreign land, taking note of the people who surrounded him: well-kept middle-aged mothers who once fit differently into their yoga wear; single professional women who ranked him on the date-ability scale, noting his strong legs and turning up their noses at his track shorts from college; and a variety of hot gay men who were also assessing him, but for different (or similar) reasons.

But unlike the rest of the class, Noah's whole physique screamed heterosexual, the masculinity rolling off him like the opening scene of a Clint Eastwood film.

I pulled myself together and started the session. It was clear Noah was strong, if not especially practiced in yoga, but during Warrior One, as he'd attempted the pose he'd winced and rubbed at the back of his hip before assuming the position again. Sciatic. And that's why he had come.

I circled the room, leading the poses until I reached him, and placed two flat palms on his hip bones, angling his pelvis toward the front leg. My hands had warmed as I touched him. "Talk to me after class, I may have some additional stretches you could use to help with the sciatic pain." I'd wanted him to stay after class. I'd wanted him to stay forever.

He'd startled at my touch, his face going ruddy in the dim light, but he didn't pull away.

As the class ended and everyone rolled their mats, Noah hurried from the room and was tying his shoes when I caught up to him. Without a parting word, he slipped out. Apparently he hadn't been interested in further instruction, and I'd been surprised at my sharp disappointment as this man fled, his whirlwind escape from the studio a missed sliding-door moment. I was sure if he'd stayed, everything would have changed.

But the next night he'd called me at the studio and asked if I would join him at Bar X. The moment he reminded me of his name, I knew he also felt our connection. As we shared a plate of fries and several drinks, tipsy together while we sang the dreidel song, I knew nothing would ever be the same.

He told me months after we were together that on that first night he'd fallen asleep during the "relaxation part," as he called it, to the rhythmic sounds of yoga chant and had awoken to the chiming of the tingsha bells visibly hard. He was mortified someone had seen. I touched him when he haltingly confessed and found him in the same condition.

"It was your voice," he explained, moving against my hand. "My God, listening to you I was laid bare, like you'd joined me in my bed." By then I'd joined him in bed, many times, and I still loved his reaction.

With the memory of the first time we met fresh in my mind, making my limbs weak, smothering my resolve, I was in a hurry to return to our home for my yoga wear. Thoughts of seeing Noah again pulled at me, more strongly than any particular article I would collect from the house. I planned my visit on a Saturday when I knew he'd be home. And curse me, I couldn't help showering and fixing myself up. All morning my stomach lurched with butterflies, and I tried to remind myself I wasn't going back for good. As strong as our connection was, our lives must diverge.

Noah wore his brown canvas camping hat as he pulled the rake back and forth across our yard, attempting to breathe life back into our lawn. It was working. Spikey tufts of green shot through the leaf rot from the prior fall. A day of yard work, just like any other Saturday, only today I wasn't by his side doing my part. I pressed my palm against the car window, imagining myself there, a gauzy reflection next to Noah, our son resting in his chair while we worked. There would be music piped into a portable speaker from his iPod, and if Noah and I weren't talking to each other, I would be talking to Joey.

While our son was alive, I loved mowing, weeding, and planting. Watching living things thrive under my care, even as my son withered, gave me hope. But after Joey died, I gave up. The manicured yard we were both proud of suffered as a result. Conflicted, I loved that Noah was taking care of our home and things were moving on as they should. The yard was cared for, the sun was rising and setting, and yet what was the purpose?

I stayed in the car for a few moments, watching him work, his biceps pressed against the short sleeves of his T-shirt. Eventually he turned and pulled out his earbuds, a smile lighting his face. "I didn't hear you. But somehow I knew you were here. Welcome home, Emma."

He dropped his rake and in several strides stood in front of me. I fell into him, absorbing his presence, and just as quickly pulled away. "I came for a few things. That's all."

His face fell. "Stay for a while. It's been almost a month. I've tried to give you some space, but we should talk about this new arrangement, face-to-face. You owe me that much."

"You're right, I do."

"Let me clean up and we'll grab some lunch."

"How about I make something here?" I could collect my clothing, and my ability to resist, if I had a few moments alone in the house. "Finish what you were doing and meet me inside in a bit."

"Just like old times."

I shook my head *no,* even as I said, "Like old times."

Upon entry, I realized the rooms of my own home were strikingly foreign, and I, the guest. I almost didn't want to open a cupboard. It felt like prying. The state of the kitchen indicated that Noah was eating out most meals. Kitchen duty had been my realm, and though I let other things fail, I usually managed to make a meal. But today the glass shelves in the refrigerator held several half-empty bottles of a variety of sauces and not much more.

Touching each in an effort to divine something from combining them, I settled on pasta with fridge pesto topped with canned olives. I discovered a block of parmesan, and if I sliced off the mold, it could be used. Plus, there was a full bottle of wine. It was a little early for a drink, but it was wine or water, and I opted for the wine.

Half an hour later, Noah grinned at my efforts and took a sip of the glass I poured for him before he made his way into the bathroom for a quick shower. He raised his arm like he was making a toast. "It feels so good to have you here."

After setting his glass on the counter, he stripped from his sweaty shirt and shorts. I admired the length of his muscular thighs and the strawberry hair on his broad chest as he entered the room, whistling lightly under his breath. In full view, he turned on the shower and got in. My God, he was beautiful.

I turned the pasta on low and fitted the pot with a lid, considering for several minutes the consequences of what I ached to do. Then I slipped out of my skirt and blouse and tiptoed into the bedroom. I lowered myself across the rumpled comforter.

Making the bed was another task he'd likely neglected for weeks. The pillows smelled like him, and I breathed in the essence of my husband as I waited. Why was I doing this? This wasn't creating separation. I willed myself to pull my clothing off the floor, dress, and get back into the kitchen. But I *wanted* him. I needed his solid presence so badly, it pinned me to the mattress.

At the familiar tug between my legs, an incongruous tear slipped along the curve of my cheek. Loving my husband, and he was *still* my husband, was normal. I hadn't touched him for months before I left, except the night of my grandpa's funeral. If Joey couldn't be in my arms, I wanted no one, but now I wanted this.

He opened the door, steam from the bathroom following him as he entered the bedroom and saw me waiting. He stopped midstride and dropped his towel to the floor. As we joined and held each other, he pressed his mouth into my hair, murmuring his love. Fully aware of the pressure of skin on skin, the living essence shared between our bodies, as he emptied himself into me, joining the two of us through heart and limbs, tears slid down my cheeks. All of this beautiful, natural expression of love, and for us it was an exercise in futility. Noah and I were a biological mismatch, the combination of the two of us toxic.

I pushed him off me with both hands, mumbling something about swallowing a hair, and I fake-coughed into the bathroom, masking my sadness with the guise of a rough patch in my throat. Palms filled with water, I touched the cool wetness to my cheeks and glared at my image in the mirror, convincing my reflection. "Be strong."

"Want me to pour you a glass?" Noah called through the closed door. "This bottle's decent. It might help the throat."

I coughed one more time for good measure and slipped on a robe. "Sure."

In the few minutes I spent lecturing myself in the bathroom, scolding myself back to calm, he'd set the table, lit a candle, poured my wine, and turned on some music. Song wove like a vibrant thread through our relationship, an iridescent shimmer, an infusion of hope within difficult days and broken colorless strands. Together we saw as many live music performances as would fit into our schedule and budget. And we always took Joey with us.

Noah was high, his good mood filling the kitchen. He tied my Carmen Miranda fruit-print apron around his waist, his chest bare and broad above the ruffles. "Hey, good lookin', whatcha got cookin'?" I forced levity into the room. Serious talk could come later.

Could we actually be together? This was so easy, the banter, the heat between us. If I pretended enough times to make a day like this real, rather than a polished veneer over a broken scene, it would be. Wouldn't it?

Three-quarters into the bottle and it was working. He was the man I'd fallen head over heels for, and there wasn't a bottomless divide between us. Noah leaned back in his chair, a sleepy grin on his face. "Does this afternoon mean you'll be moving home?"

Yes! I wanted to scream. "Soon . . . maybe."

"So, how long will it take to finish organizing your grandpa's things, do you imagine?" He was nonconfrontational, but I knew there was more to his question. To him, the end of the project meant the end of our separation.

"I've been working on my résumé, and things,

so I haven't been there very much." I wouldn't tell Noah how unsettled I was about my grandpa, about his country of birth, about the smoking, about the inconsistencies that made it so difficult to dive into his memories that I hadn't returned.

"There's actually something else I wanted to talk to you about." I held my wine suspended. For some reason, I was a little nervous to tell him about the DNA test Ethan had proposed. Noah and I both knew there were more important topics at hand, like our uncertain living arrangement, but my mom's unusual reaction was weighing on me.

"Ethan and Anusha are thinking of having a baby." I meant for the topic of their impending pregnancy to lead me into an easy discussion of the DNA test, minus a discussion about Joey and Canavan, but my statement was wrapped in sorrow.

Noah groaned, knowing already what this news would do to me. "Wow . . . well, I don't love the timing, especially since you're right in the middle of dealing with your grandpa's death. And with everything else. But I hope for them the very best."

"I do too." I took a sip of wine, and before I could stop myself I asked, "But Noah, why us?" The question stung my tongue, as if I'd touched a nine-volt battery with the tip. "Ethan will probably get a perfectly healthy baby. Why did Joey end up with this thing?"

"The doctors say—"

"I know what the experts say, but we didn't do anything wrong. It's not fair."

"You're right." He poured another finger of wine into his glass. "It's not fair."

"Don't you want to know where it came from? Not some vague reference to Jewish ancestry, but something solid. Somewhere to place blame?"

"It won't change anything. You know that."

"I know. Sorry. Okay, this test thing with Ethan doesn't have anything to do with the disease. Or not much. It has to do with my mom."

Noah listened silently as I explained the DNA test. Interested at first, he leaned in while I described Ethan's earlobes and his brown eyes. I detailed my brother's belief he might be adopted, telling him about my mom's shaky objections, but when I tried to justify my *own* DNA test by pulling Canavan disease into it, his grin faded and his eyes narrowed millimeter by millimeter.

I couldn't help myself from drifting toward the disease that claimed my son, try as I might, because any discussion of genetics always circled back to this. After I stopped talking, Noah pushed back from his chair, stacked the plates, and left the dining room. Our romantic meal was over.

On his return trip from the kitchen he took off the playful apron and slipped into shorts and a fresh shirt. He sat next to me and held my hands in his, not because he wanted to touch me but because he wanted my attention. He smelled clean, and his fingers were warm. I ached to lean into him, but I couldn't let myself.

"I'm going to agree with your mom on this one," Noah said. I kept my focus on the crumbs scattered on the surface of the table, remnants of something that once was whole and nourishing.

At his words, I pressed against the back of the chair until my spine ached. "But why aren't you interested in where you came from?" My questions were harsher than I intended, but I couldn't stop. "Wouldn't you like to know more about, say, your grandparents? And don't you feel a little deceived? I thought you, more than anyone, would understand. You're as much to blame for the disease as I am." I pulled from his grasp and touched an errant crumb with my thumb, pressing it into the whorls of skin, grinding it to dust between my fingers.

He didn't try to touch me again. "It doesn't help me to know that my grandmother on my mom's side was Jewish. She'll always be my grandma. I can't change who she was, or who I am. I can't be someone different just because I don't want the genetic disease she probably gave me. The reason I'm here is because of her, and, of course, a few other relatives. You and Ethan should realize the situation is the same for you. Move forward. Stop looking back."

I was silent, not able to trust what I would say next.

"This topic is a little broken-record, Emma. Do you, in all honesty, think one of your ancestors concealed a terrible secret, this disease, so it could leap from obscurity to attack you?"

"Of course not." I responded too quickly. "Yes. Maybe? I don't know. But I was wronged. Joey was wronged. Shouldn't there be a good reason for something so awful?"

"Bad things happen to good people."

"I hated it when people said that at his funeral. I still hate it because it sounds so condescending and trite."

"But the information you're seeking is a nonevent, Emma. It doesn't change anything." He walked away from me, heading for the bedroom. "Of course, any child of ours should know his genetics before he had a child of his own—" He spoke from a distance, then stopped abruptly.

"Any child of ours? *Our* child is dead." The statement resonated through the rooms. Dead . . . dead . . . dead. Truly the final word.

"If we were to have a biological child in the future." His response was weak, drowned by the only syllable that mattered.

I put my hand in front of my face as I replied. "You'd curse another child like we cursed Joey?"

"There are ways to ensure . . . did you even read the information I gave you?"

Now I stood, but instead of following him into the bedroom, I entered the bathroom and closed the door, locking Noah out, and stared at my image in the mirror. Who was I? A wife? Certainly not a mother. What did I want to be?

Every time I undressed since learning of Joey's diagnosis, I'd stand bare in front of the mirror and analyze myself without my shield of clothing. Exposed, I would search for some indication of the monster living within me. It waited to kill my children, hunched like a silent predator under my skin.

I pressed my forehead to my reflection so my eyes melded into one. I had failed Joey. Every cell of his unresponsive body was affected because of who I was. The beast hadn't disappeared. It flowed through my veins. It lived in every organ, but it scarred my heart.

"Let's get back to your original argument for the DNA test. For a minute, let's leave Canavan disease out of it. . . ." Noah called to me through the closed door, his attempt at peace making. "If you're considering this test to twist a rusty knife in your mother because of your childhood years spent without Ethan, I don't think it accomplishes much. The relationship between your mom and brother doesn't have to do with genetics and should be approached on a surface level. Meaning he, and you, should ask her some questions."

"I did ask. I told you she acted weird."

"Then why focus on a mystery that doesn't matter? Why concentrate on something that happened years ago? And I'm giving you and Ethan the benefit of the doubt that anything *actually* happened." He was getting louder and louder as he tried to make his point, as though we were separated by something even more impenetrable than a wall.

I opened the door abruptly, and Noah jumped back. His eyes no longer shimmered with love. He was ready for a fight. "How can we go forward if *you* won't stop looking back?" He yelled as if I wasn't right in front of him, making his point, forcing me to understand.

"I can't go forward, Noah," I whispered. "Until I know where I am. I need to know *who* I am."

"What do you mean?"

"I mean . . ." I took a deep breath so he'd believe the words I said, so *I'd* believe them, even as it broke me to do so. "It means I free you. I free you to move forward. Without me."

CHAPTER 12

The first thing I did when I returned to my mom's house was take a shower. Not so I could remove the touch of my husband but to disguise the cascade of tears in the rush of falling water.

Noah was no longer mine. Now he could move past me, and fill my place with someone a more perfect match. I pressed my cheek to the slick tile, letting the water fall over my face, but the image of my husband's arms around another woman hovered in front of me, eyes closed or not. *Stop.* It was the right thing. I was doing the right thing.

Steps. I needed a next step before I sunk back into the malaise of the prior year. The DNA test was the first. I'd received the brightly colored test kit several days earlier and had hesitated to open it, not sure I wanted the truth, but today before I could change my mind I would fill the test tube with saliva and send it to a faceless lab in an attempt to reveal who I was, and what I was made of.

I found the kit in a pile of paperwork I'd stashed in the corner of my makeshift bedroom and followed the instructions. Test tube filled and stashed in my bag for delivery to the post office the next time I got in the car, I moved on to the next item in the intentionally forgotten pile: the stack of reproductive options.

In all fairness, I had studied them, as I told Noah I would, and I was dismayed at the options. But it didn't matter now. Noah was free to find a wife who could give him children. I wouldn't need them anymore. I picked up the papers, walked them to the recycle bin under the sink, let my hand go limp, and dropped them in.

The final item was the manila envelope containing the photograph of my great-grandparents. I took it out and wandered to the mirror in the bathroom. I could hear Noah's words at breakfast telling me to find my doppelgänger, and start wearing my hair in a bun.

Twisting my hair in a topknot with one hand, I put the photo against my cheek. Noah was right, there was some resemblance there. The photo slipped from my fingers and landed on the counter facedown. Once again, I noted the script on the back: *Barlow Wedding 1916*. It was the beginning of a lifetime of happy memories and a houseful of children for my great-grandparents. My own wedding photos were on a dusty shelf in a home I could no longer call my own.

1916 . . . They were married almost one hundred years before I wed my husband. It was so long ago . . . 1916. Hold on. Clutching the photo, I ran into the kitchen, where my grandpa's obituary was suspended by a magnet next to the grocery list. I trained my focus on the small print, forcing it into absolute clarity:

Joseph Lewis Barlow (Dutch)
Born September 15, 1913, in
Manchester, England.

My memory *was* right. I had overlooked his year of birth as I fretted about the country. Grandpa Joe was born in England. In 1913. But according to the photo in my hand, his parents were married in 1916. How in the world had he been born three years *before* his parents were even married?

A few minutes later I heard the garage door close, and seconds after that my mom staggered through the door holding a paper grocery bag in each arm. "A hand here, Emma?" She panted, setting them on the kitchen counter. "If you're going to live here, can you help me unload the car?"

"What?" She pulled me from my pondering. "Oh, yeah, of course." I followed her into the garage and returned carrying another installment of food.

"What are you concentrating on in there?" she asked absently. Then with some suspicion, she added, "Hey, didn't you go home this morning? Did you see Noah?"

"I just discovered the craziest thing," I said, ignoring her question.

"Tell me about it while we put away the groceries."

"After. You need to be sitting. And you need to see the documentation."

My mom and I were quiet, weaving around one another in the small space as we shelved food for another week. I hoped she wouldn't ask me about Noah, and she must have understood my silent plea.

As we stacked the final cans of black beans into the cupboard she said, "All right. What did you find?"

I handed her Grandpa Joe's obituary.

"I've seen this."

"Read the date of birth."

"He was born in England. Which we've already established is probably no big deal, right?"

"The date."

"Okay. September 15, 1913."

"And now this." I put the photo in front of her. "Have I shown you this yet?"

"Oh my Lord, is this my grandma and grandpa Barlow? They're so young. Did you find this at Grandpa's?"

"Yes, that first day. I meant to show you and then I got distracted. Anyhow, look at the writing on the back. It says *Barlow Wedding 1916*, and I presume it's the wedding between the two of them because see how she's holding flowers in her hand, along with her hat? And he's dressed nicely."

"Yes, it must be. Oh, this photo is so fantastic! I should frame it." She walked away from me and held the image against a wall of other family photos on display. "What a perfect addition. I'll put it right next to this one of my parents."

"Mom. You're missing the point. The year Grandpa Joe's parents were married was 1916. Three years *after* Grandpa was born! The obituary says he was born in 1913!"

She stopped arranging and turned the photo to the back side again. "Odd . . . a typo in the obituary? Or, you know, the writing on the back of the photo is faded. The six could easily be a two or three."

"You think so? It looked pretty clear to me." I put my chin in my hand and stared at the obituary while my mom fussed around in the living room. "Do you think Great-Grandma and Great-Grandpa Barlow had Grandpa Joe before they were married?"

My mom laughed. "Naughty, naughty for those days. But maybe they'd been messing around and finally married when the dust settled, so to speak. Childbirth out of wedlock wasn't impossible in those days."

Suddenly realizing the connection, I jumped up and joined my mom, taking the photo from her.

"If that's the case, maybe . . . maybe this little blond child is Grandpa Joe." I squinted at the profile of the boy. "But then, who is this second woman. The one holding his hand? The nanny?"

I left the house before my mom woke the next day, determination marking my every action. I told Noah I couldn't move forward without knowing who I was, and it was the truth. There were too many unsettling surprises filling my mind, making it hard to concentrate on anything except the things just out of my grasp.

My first stop: the cemetery. A vase of poppies clipped fresh from my mom's front yard, bound for Joey's grave, was wedged between the passenger seat and the center console. Flowers for my baby. It had been a couple of days since my last visit, and I was antsy to get to him, a lingering remnant of my year of waiting. I was hopeful a quick conversation with my son would soothe the beast, the aching worry I would somehow forget him.

After the cemetery I would drop the DNA test kit into the mailbox. I prayed my nerve wouldn't fail me as I took this step toward untangling the strands of my DNA. And the final stop: Grandpa Joe's. My plan was to find my doppelgänger in the photo albums and determine who she was.

My first two errands finally complete, I used the key I was given as an adult to enter my grandparents' house, and leaning into the emptiness I hollered as I always would upon my arrival, "Grandpa?" For several seconds I waited for his approach.

After my dad left, cleaving our family of four into halves, equal but incomplete, most mornings my mom would wake me before sunrise, strap me into the car, and drive me shivering in my nightgown to my grandparents' house. Every school day and some weekends I was shuffled, shipped off, and left behind.

But if Grandpa Joe wasn't already waiting on the porch, golden light spilling from the kitchen window, the smell of coffee escaping through the screen, he'd quickly join me in the foyer at my call. Until I was too tall, I'd rush to him in greeting and he'd lift me under my scrawny armpits for a kiss, but instead of touching my lips with his, he'd rub his bristly chin against my smooth cheek. Safe in his embrace, I wasn't so alone.

How badly I wanted him to sweep me into the comfort of his arms today. I strained to hear his footsteps. Of course, there were none. Alone, I hurried through the empty rooms of my childhood and into the room filled with the past. Everything was how I'd left it: the Madame Alexander dolls, the stacks of correspondence, the open desk.

This visit was purposeful, and I was determined I wouldn't linger, so I quickly relocated the previously examined items into one of the plastic storage bins for safekeeping and continued to comb through the cluttered roll-top.

About ten drawers of various sizes created the backsplash for the leather writing surface, each fronted with a brass fingertip handle. Quivering slightly with anticipation, and despite my attempt to remain productive, I was excited to explore. I started with the flat drawers typically used to hold paper, and I wasn't disappointed. On top of a stack of yellowed parchment-like sheets lay a small booklet the size of a passport labeled *Your Ration Book, 1944 to 1945*.

On the cover my grandma had written her name in blocky print letters as specified: *Virginia Barlow*. The pages were a faded pink, corners rounded and wrinkled with use. Each page had a column for individual necessities: flour, coffee, sugar, bacon, eggs, bread. Some of the quadrants below each food item were darkened with pen and some had official stamps marking their consumption. I imagined my grandma at the grocery, book in hand, scanning the shelves for provisions.

"Two eggs sunny-side up, Ginny," I could almost hear Grandpa Joe say.

"With a side of whole wheat toast," my grandma would reply each morning. I parroted her not long after I began joining them for breakfast, taking her exact tone as she responded to his polite request, a chorus of two women in my grandpa's life who knew exactly what he wanted.

The first time I echoed my grandma, Grandpa Joe chortled a mouthful of coffee, drops of liquid showering the table. But it hadn't stopped him from asking in the same manner the next day, and the day after. The habits of a lifetime are hard to break and become more precious over the years.

After Grandma Ginny died, and Grandpa Joe and I resumed our morning schedule, her place by the stove yawned like a black hole threatening to pull us both in. Without him asking, I took the eggs from the refrigerator and made breakfast for both of us. Learning to turn on the gas and crack an egg into the pan was less discomforting than the disappearance of his request.

The first time I made breakfast, when he said, "Two eggs sunny-side up," he stuttered as he switched the name from Ginny to Emma.

"With a side of whole wheat toast," I replied, a gentle reassurance that when nothing was the same, at least this one thing remained.

Setting the ration book inside the plastic bin, I hoped my grandparents were already employing their breakfast call-and-answer when she used it to purchase the eggs and bread crossed out in this little pink booklet. Then I resumed my task.

The other drawers contained exactly what they

should: pencils, correction fluid, correspondence envelopes, and wide elastic bands that shattered into tiny pieces at the first stretch. But inside the last drawer, the largest, I discovered half a dozen packs of playing cards. How many times had Grandpa Joe touched each of these?

My grandpa was still working as an OB/GYN for several years after I joined my grandparents before school. I knew he left the house to help women have babies in the gloom of night or the glow of dawn, and he'd developed a solitaire habit when he was on call. Back then "on call" meant sitting by the telephone. There were no pagers or cell phones, and my grandparents didn't have call waiting. He didn't do home repair projects. He didn't run an errand. He played solitaire.

I tapped a pack into my hand. The cards were smooth and cool to the touch. I ran the ten of clubs over my cheek and brought it to my nose, then I cleared the surface of the desk with my forearm and shuffled the cards, my fingers caressing them like my grandpa's had at one time, and I laid them on the flat surface, pretending, for a moment, he was with me.

As a child I loved the snap of the thick cards as they grazed his thumbs, the ticking rhythm as one slotted on top of its opposite, sounding like the click of spokes on a bicycle. Three times shuffled, then laid out in front of him: first card face up, remainder down, stacks graduating into a wedge.

His movement was so assured, so routine, he didn't have to concentrate while he played. Sometimes as I sat beside him, I'd make a suggestion, but I had to be fast, because he dealt at lightning speed. Regardless of the worth of my contribution, he'd always take it, even if it cost him the game, his quiet trust filling me with self-assurance morning after morning.

As I moved the cards like he would have, creating a graduating sequence and shifting it to another pile, I listened for him. And for an instant, he returned.

"Emma," he whispered. "How old are you now?"

"Eight," I told him in my mind, wanting to exist for a moment in memory.

"So you're old enough to add to twenty-one?"

"Grandpa," I huffed. He knew I was working on times tables. He'd helped me with a math page the day before.

He dealt a card in front of me and one in front of himself. This was the first time he included me as a player in a game. "This game is called Twenty-One."

With extreme patience, he taught me the rules, the value of the cards, when to hit, and when to stand. But he soundly beat me fifteen hands in a row. Turned out, over the years I became a crack blackjack player, winning a thousand dollars on our honeymoon as Noah and I passed through Las Vegas bound for San Diego. But that was another time. This day, in this memory, I sought my way out of the game. I didn't want to lose. I put my cards down and slid them toward him.

He glanced at his own cards and flicked them against his chin, catching them on his whiskers. "Finish this last hand, Emma, and we can be done," Grandpa said, gesturing to my abandoned cards.

I shook my head and stuck out my lip. Daring him to make me.

My grandpa smiled, but his eyes were firm. "Number one rule in cards, kiddo, you have to play the hand you're dealt." He slid the cards toward my closed fist. I glared and picked up the stack. I lost again.

"Grandpa." I spoke to him as I restacked the deck, tapped them into a tidy pile, and slipped them back into the cardboard container. "I played the hand I was dealt, like you told me to, but I'm not sure if what I really want is in the cards."

Like a beanbag toss, one by one, I threw the packs into the garbage can, where they rattled against the empty bottom. *Don't give up, my girl.* The final pack rested in my hand. I opened it and counted the cards. A full deck. At his prompting, I placed it carefully into the box of items to save.

Next I took the photograph of my great-grandparents posing with a mysterious woman, who happened to look like a sepia version of me, from my purse and propped it against the surface of the newly cleared desk so I could refer to it as I made my way through the photo albums. As I searched, I figured I could throw away anything else random, broken, or inconsequential. It was progress. My mom would be pleased.

Five leather-bound albums were stacked on top of a metal filing cabinet next to the desk. After opening the one appearing to be the oldest, I examined the photos documenting the marriage between my grandparents: Joe and Ginny. In several photos Grandpa Joe, in a dapper three-piece suit, posed with an older couple. They embraced him, arms around his back.

I set the open album on the desk next to the wedding photo of my great-grandparents and determined, without a doubt, they were the same people: Grandpa Joe's parents—Emmeline and Nathaniel—thirty years beyond their own wedding photo but clearly the same couple. Emmeline had the same haircut, though in the later shot her hair had aged to a mixture of gray and brown, and my great-grandpa Nathaniel held his hat in his hand, revealing the defined triangle of a widow's peak.

Two albums later, my mom and Aunt Marsha were children posed in various positions around the same house where I'd spent so much of my youth. The decor was instantly familiar and remained constant as the two girls aged. Often they were surrounded by Christmas gifts, or Easter baskets, dressed in matching flared skirts and white patent-leather shoes.

The final album ended with a formal shot of Grandma Ginny and Grandpa Joe taken at a medical convention a month or two before she died. The remaining photos, school shots of the grandchildren, basically anything after Grandma Ginny's death, were tucked into the back of the book in a thick, disorganized stack.

My stomach growled. Hours had passed. Using the desk to pull myself to standing I tapped the corner of the sepia photo. It tipped into my hand. I hadn't found a trace of the blond woman. Had I missed something because I was trapped in other memories? But no. Not a single image of a pioneer-girl me.

After consuming an energy bar and a glass of water, I abandoned my fledgling piles of loose photos and decided to inspect the older things, the yellowed envelopes, the documents tied with ribbon, the contents contained in a rusted traveling trunk. I would find the girl.

Resting precariously on the antique trunk I wished to explore lay a white wicker bassinet, the delicate lace bumpers aged to various shades of pale yellow, like a cloudy, jaundiced sky.

It was filled with a stack of expired medical journals, a brittle construction paper Christmas chain (mostly flattened) made by my cousins, and several crafty caterpillars created with pompoms and egg cartons. Tucked into a corner was a gallon-sized ziplock bag filled with crocheted baby booties, two pair a pale pink and two pair light blue. Whose were they?

I set them aside and continued to dig, placing pieces of a broken ceramic bowl and a pack of dry felt-tip markers into the trash, along with the crafted egg cartons. The remaining items I stacked on the floor.

Two unmarked yellowed envelopes lay pressed flat against the lumpy bassinet mattress. They were sealed. But who was to stop me from snooping? I slid my finger under the flap on the first and unfolded an official, but aged, document.

Certificate of Stillbirth for
Robert Joseph Barlow in 1944

Two tiny footprints were ink-blotted at the bottom of the faded paper. I'd learned of my mom's infant brothers at my grandma Ginny's funeral, but at that time I didn't know how my fate would mirror my grandma's. Back then, the existence of the two children and their early demise were just words. Taking a deep breath I opened the second envelope.

Certificate of Live Birth for
Ronald Nathaniel Barlow in 1946

But this envelope contained a second paper.

State of Utah Certificate of Death for
Ronald Nathaniel Barlow in 1948

Like the woman at the cemetery who buried five of her children, and like me, my grandma had suffered the loss of a child, of children. I unraveled every day, when upon waking I would realize Joey wasn't in the next room, waiting for my arms to surround him, my kiss ready to press into a chubby cheek. How did my grandma go on? I placed the booties, which had likely been crocheted for each of my grandparents' four children—two living and two dead—and the certificates into the partially filled Rubbermaid. This was too hard. I wasn't up to the task. This mystery wasn't worth the pain.

I stood, then paced around the room, the movement soothing to my cramped legs. How was I supposed to clear out the memories of a lifetime? And yet, how could I not? I would keep working.

In the far corner was a bookcase stacked with encyclopedias from 1975 and a collection of *Reader's Digest* magazines, their covers dull and pages yellowed. I stepped closer; the case smelled like the used bookstore in my neighborhood. On one of the shelves, supporting a stack of books like a bookend, was an item I instantly recognized. I plucked it from the shelf, and the books it had been propping thudded like an avalanche to the floor.

"Dammit." I scooted them into a pile with my foot, unwilling to set down the old-fashioned cookie tin Grandma Ginny had always filled with cookies for me. Seeing it again brought a visceral response of pleasure, of love expressed through sugar and chocolate. It was during a different life I checked the contents daily for treats.

Grandma Ginny, once upon a time, told me the container belonged to Grandpa Joe's mother, and by the looks of it, it could easily be a century old. Rectangular with rounded corners, it was flatter than a shoe box and twice as wide. The hinges were more rusted than I remembered, but the image painted on the top, though faded, was like reuniting with a childhood best friend. Two girls sat on a stone wall, hair tied in matching kerchiefs, blond braids emerging to hang over their shoulders. They were obviously telling secrets. Their feet, which were dangling in red wooden clogs, were entwined. I had always imagined I could be one of their friends.

My grandpa had removed this biscuit container from the kitchen counter when Grandma Ginny was no longer available to fill it with sweets and replaced her daily baked goods with Velveeta. But based on the shifting, rattling weight of it, he'd filled the tin with something else and tucked it away for safekeeping. The hinges groaned as I lifted the lid to reveal the contents.

"Oh my God," I whispered as I pulled out the first item. "Who are you?" It was a fuzzy image of a soldier in a bowl-like hard hat with a short, circular brim. His nose was angular and his chin was sharp, pushed up firmly by the strap underneath it.

He was handsome, hauntingly so, and he also wasn't my great-grandfather Nathaniel. But who could he have been? Did Emmeline have a lover, a soldier who died in the war? I was told she trained as a nurse during World War I, but had she also served overseas? I turned the photo over. *Josef.* My grandpa's name.

After staring at the image for several minutes, I set it aside. The next item was a drawing made by a child—dark, smeary pencil on thin newsprint. It was a youthful representation of a girl or a woman, perfectly oval face, a crooked-line smile, button nose, and exaggerated lashes. Below the drawing was one name in ragged script. It was blotchy, like much concentration, and many attempts were required to complete the letters. It said *Mutter.* Or *Mother*, I imagined.

The final item was a small book about the size

of the ration book, although twice as thick. The cover was tooled brown leather, the binding fraying. I carefully opened it, and two pages pulled loose from the stitched center with a cracking sound. The book was written in what appeared to be a Germanic language of some sort, though I didn't know for sure. I searched the front of the book for a publication date, or an author, and from within the pages fell a lock of blond hair, the strands bound by embroidery floss.

"Grandpa," I called to the ceiling, a surge of frustration chugging through my veins. "Why didn't you show me these things before you died? Whose hair is this? And whose book?"

I typed a few lines from the foreign text into the translate function on my cell phone, but the phrases didn't make sense. I could call my mom and talk to her about my discoveries, but she acted more in the dark about my grandpa than I was. The library? Or wait, I had it. It was time to get out of this room for a while anyhow.

I looked up the number for Vosen's Bakery. Luckily the only German baker in the city also happened to run a booth, directly across from mine at the farmers market when I was selling my scarves. I had a friendly relationship with the apprentice. I knew he spoke German, and if I could track him down, maybe he'd inspect the book and tell me what it said.

. . .

"Lorenzo," I said as the burly, ruddy-faced man pulled me into an embrace as comfortable and welcoming as the scent of baking bread and sugared almonds steaming the windows of the bakery. Couples sat at wooden tables sipping dark roast, reading novels, and digging into German pastries. I took a deep breath, savoring it, wrapping myself in the safety of this friend from long ago. "How's my big, old German with the Italian name doing? How are your wife and your kids?"

"Same . . . same. Mornings at the bakery. Saturdays in the summer at the market. We've missed you there, Emma. What's it been? Five years?"

"Five, yep," I said, and clawed in my purse before he could ask what I'd been up to for the last half decade.

"Heard you were married with children? Helene wondered when you'd bring the baby by."

I kept my eyes buried in the depths of the bag so he wouldn't see them fill, ignoring his comment.

"Ah, here it is!" I emerged with the book and a thin smile on my lips. "You have to see this. This is the book I was telling you about on the phone."

I handed it to him quickly, turning the conversation to the tangible. He held it between two fingers still trapped in the plastic bag I'd used for

151

transportation. He was sufficiently distracted by the item. "Wow. This is really old."

"I think it belonged to my great-grandma. I found it stored in an old biscuit tin that belonged to her. Is it written in German?"

"If you don't mind?" He slid the zip open. Seconds later he said, "Yes, it's German. I think these are"—he gently turned several pages—"love poems. A compilation of sorts, Lessing and other poets. This could be worth some money. Who did you say it belonged to?"

"I guess it belongs to me now, but I'm trying to figure out who it belonged to before me, if you know what I mean."

"Is there an inscription or a name written anywhere?"

"There are some handwritten words I don't understand on the front flap, and I found a lock of hair tucked inside."

Lorenzo turned several more pages, reading a random line or two in German. "If you want, I could have my ancient auntie Greta take a look. Her German is flawless, mostly because she doesn't speak a lick of English."

"Would you?"

"Sure. You know, opening day at the farmers market isn't this Saturday but next. You should come by."

"Well . . ."

"It's bound to be crazy busy, but the old

gang would love to see you. And I'll have your translation from Auntie Greta by then. I promise."

"It's just . . ."

"You can say hello to Helene too. She'd love to see you. In the meantime, cherry strudel for the road?"

I left with arms loaded with strudel in three varieties and a promise to visit him at the market.

CHAPTER 13

The following days were filled with a hovering silence like the interior of a jetliner, loud and muffled at the same time. I sent out a résumé or two (Downtown Dog filled only three hours of each workday), I made dinner for my mom and me, I visited Joey, and I organized at my grandpa's house. My mom joined me several times to sort through boxes of memories, and I yearned to talk with her about the tangle of unanswered questions filling my thoughts, but there was the DNA test looming between us. She still acted cagey when we were together, our conversations newly forced and surface.

Plus, Noah hadn't called. I didn't want him to, but I expected he might, and when he didn't it was all I could think of. His absence was a cacophony of silence. Only a couple of days after I determined to get to the bottom of things, to figure out who I was, the mysteries surrounding my grandpa seemed trivial and Ethan's questions regarding his paternity insignificant. Had I left my husband to search for a truth that didn't matter?

There had been no other discoveries at Grandpa Joe's, almost as if my mom's presence had taken the magic out of the room. She didn't want to find anything unusual and so we didn't. Currently, my only hope was the translation from Lorenzo's aunt.

Two Saturdays later, the day I promised to meet Lorenzo at the market, I was excited for a diversion. Mornings were always festive when I worked my booth selling my rainbow display scarves. It would be a sweet respite to wander the market, stepping back into a time when I was a different person. Back then, we were a band of ragtag artisans pitching our wares to all who walked the paths between the temporary stalls, our customers ranging from urban housewives to hungover college students.

Maybe I'd go, retrieve the German poetry book and translation from Lorenzo (along with a German pastry or two), have some traditional African food, and listen to some music. It was the perfect way to kill an afternoon.

I chose a wrap-around tie-dye skirt and a tiny, black tank top. As the final accessory, I twisted my hair into one of the narrow hemp scarves my mom still had kicking around her house, letting the fringed ends emerge near the nape of my neck. Even if I was no longer the same person, I could dress the part.

My mom was in the kitchen when I emerged. "Going somewhere special?"

"The farmers market."

She touched my chin, raising it so she could

see my face. "You look like you did all those summers ago."

"Do I?"

"It's like the last five years never happened," she whispered against my forehead as she pressed it with a kiss. I leaned into her hand but didn't respond. Sometimes I wished they hadn't.

The weekly farmers market was held in Pioneer Park, the oldest park in Salt Lake City. However, because of its location in relation to the shelters, it was a green space unintentionally, but realistically, reserved for the homeless. Every Saturday morning, spring to fall, the usual inhabitants were pushed to the periphery, their rolled blankets and empty bottles removed from benches and under the slides, and the whole place was transformed.

Temporary stalls, tarp-shaded and full of items ranging from handmade soap to personalized stamped leather belts to fresh peppers so hot their purpose was medicinal, circled a wide gravel path at the perimeter of lawn. In the grassy center was a corridor of ethnic food trucks, coffee and kombucha vendors, portable tables, and a stage for live folk music.

Young couples with babies in strollers, couples with dogs on leashes, and those who visited the market once a summer for the handcrafted jewelry jostled for space with the regulars, their cloth bags bulging with seasonal vegetables.

Swimming upstream in the current of the jolly crowd, I headed directly to Vosen's Bakery.

Lorenzo spotted me right away and gestured for me to come to the front of the line. He handed me the book enclosed in the ziplock bag, apology written on his face. "I don't have much to tell you, Emma. The book was published in 1901. It's an antique, but my auntie said it was a book common to many German homes at the time. A trendy item, if you will. They are love poems, all right, and she helped me translate a couple, which I put in the bag.

"And the writing at the front"—he opened to the inscription melted into the grainy paper—"says, 'To my love—J'. That's about it. Sorry I couldn't be of more help, but it's really a neat book." He handed it to me.

"Well, at least I know it's written in German. And I have an initial to go on."

He nodded. "And here's more bad news. Helene is sick today. She's not here to say hello, or to help with the crowd."

As he spoke, he gestured to the line forming behind me. "Okay, then I'll buy a loaf of rye and one of those sweet loaves with the raisins, the stollen." I pointed at the shelves behind him. "Then I'll get out of your hair. But, Lorenzo . . . thank you."

"My pleasure. Come back and see us again and bring your baby." He handed me my bread and turned quickly to help the next customer. I was glad he didn't see my face.

I broke off a piece of the loaf and chewed as I wandered, afraid to swallow before the knot in my throat cleared. I missed this place, the smell of simmering ethnic food mingling with sweat and humanity. It was intimate and festive, but at the same time anonymous. I was another shopper, and the people-watching was divine. Alone on this outing, I could choose to engage, or not. I could watch, unnoticed, the parade of children strapped into Bugaboo carriages, or I could ignore them. Some of the vendors were familiar, and I made a wide circle around those I knew but whom I hadn't spoken with since my marriage. I didn't want a what-have-you-been-up-to conversation with a casual acquaintance and be forced to choose between a breezy lie and an awkward spilling of the truth. So I drifted aimlessly through the river of people flowing alongside me, until I saw him.

I could tell it was Barry from the triangle shape of his back. I'd touched his lean waist in another life, the warmth of his summer skin firm under my hands. His hair was no longer grazing his wing bones, the curls wrapping into dreadlock ringlets. It was cut short, the wave still apparent, but if he put on a suit and tie, he might be permitted into an office building.

The booth he operated had a line coiled in

front, and it appeared he no longer sold incense holders and other rustic carved items. The canvas sign above his head was painted with a logo I recognized from the Buy Local section of my grocery store. Did my stoner, Barry Runyan, own Barry's Blend? We typically had several versions of his fruit salsa in our refrigerator at home. Based on this crowd, and the array of items available at my regular grocery store, Barry's foray into farmers market commerce had fared much better than my own.

Standing in the line, I figured I'd buy a packet of seasoning for a curry dish I liked but hadn't made since I'd married Noah. He wasn't fond of it, and as I waited my turn I tried to revel in the fact that I could now cook whatever pleased me. It was meager consolation.

Once I reached the front of the line, Barry faced me, a grin of recognition playing on his lips. He still had a beard, but like his hair it was trimmed tight to his face, making him look like Colin Farrell during his wilder days. Barry had won over many a girl with his earlier unbathed hipster look, but this was much better.

"So I guess you're not selling handcrafted bamboo bongs anymore?"

"Emma, is that really you?" He put his hand on mine as it rested against the countertop.

"It is," I said as my hand tingled.

"You're one of the only souls who may bear

witness to the secrets of Barry from bygone years." He put his finger to his lips, shushing me. "Yes, I still carve pipes and I'd be pleased to sell you one, weed included, at a friends and family discount, but don't tell anyone."

I moved my hand out from under his touch and glanced at the banner blowing in the summer breeze. "I didn't know you were *the* Barry, from Barry's Blend. Congratulations! You've come a long way, baby."

"Are you getting anything?" A heavy man with two large bags stood behind me, his face red from too much time spent in the morning sun.

"Yes, sorry. I want—"

"Stick around for an hour, then come back, Emma. I want to talk with you. Things will slow after the lunch rush. Return and whatever you want, you can have for free." He winked and I blushed.

"An offer I can't refuse."

"Can I have something for free? Since I had to stand in this line for so damn long?"

"Sorry, buddy," Barry said, his demeanor taking all animosity out of the situation, and I slipped from the line. "The deal is only for the best of friends and family. Now, what can I get you?"

With an hour to kill, I continued to wander the crowded walkway, stopping for several minutes to watch a preteen pick at a banjo, earning money for a service trip to Panama. I left him five dollars for his resourcefulness more than his skill, and he grinned and bowed when he saw the bill. Further ahead, a crowd gathered around a woman holding an Australian shepherd puppy that drooped over her forearm. Joining the group of adorers, comprised mostly of teen girls, I reached in for a tentative touch of the loose skin and downy fur, and sighed. If I couldn't have a baby, maybe a puppy was the answer?

Barry was right, at two o'clock the line in front of his booth was almost nothing and the teenage boy he had helping him, at a gesture from Barry, took over the shop. "My nephew Pete. Good kid," Barry said, touching me on the small of the back and leading me deeper into the market. "Let's get one of my favorite treats before we talk. You have to know someone who knows someone to get the secret special."

At the Cache Valley Ice Cream stand he asked for two Irish coffee milkshakes. "And make them strong." To me he said, "You're going to love this." I poked my straw through the whipped cream into the thick, coffee-colored liquid and took a huge swallow. My throat burned with the sharp taste of whiskey, then cooled quickly from the ice-cream chaser.

"They serve alcohol at the market now?"

"Of course not," he said as I took another long swallow. "Now, let's find a place to sit."

He led me to a group of tables arranged on

lumpy grass near a low stage. A man played the harmonica and tapped out a rhythm with wooden clogs on the raised surface. It was mesmerizing.

Barry's gaze traveled along my body as I watched the show, the intense observation burning a line on my skin. "You look great, Emma. A little sad around here." He touched my cheek near my lips. "But you haven't lost the tight little yoga ass."

I snorted, the Irish coffee loosening the muscles in my neck. "And here I thought you'd become a professional with a solid product line and a respectable beard. But thank you, I guess. I've started teaching at Downtown Dog again. Just part-time."

"Compliment entirely deserved. Now about my beard, it *is* perfectly respectable, I agree, but don't let appearances fool you." He winked. "So tell me what you've been up to 'lo these many years."

My throat seized at his sudden question, and I coughed as camouflage. "This milkshake is deceptively strong. You tell *me* how you became the hot sauce king of the world while I catch my breath." I swallowed several times.

"It's quite the swashbuckling adventure."

"I'm sure it is, so start at the beginning." If he talked long enough we could both get lost in his story and I wouldn't have to tell mine.

"Well, about the time you closed your shop, I

162

decided to go on a pilgrimage to the holy land of Morocco."

"You mean Mecca, right?"

"Now that would be technically correct, but I met this dude who had family in Morocco, and he said I could stay with them for a month and bash around for almost nothing, so I saved my money and bought a ticket."

"Okay, pilgrimage to Morocco."

"But on the flight there, we encountered wicked turbulence. I thought I was dead, in all seriousness. It was one of those life-changing moments full of bargaining amid the foolishness of life. But we made it. I spent the next month in quiet contemplation, wandering the spice aisles of Morocco." He finished his shake with a slurp, leaned back in the flimsy lawn chair, his movements languid.

"You've never seen anything like it. It's like a full-time farmers market, except stall after stall is lined with wooden buckets packed with ground spices so tall they stand peaked like birthday hats. The colors and the smells . . . my God. So I bought bags of my favorites and mixed them, tasting each concoction one sprinkle at a time. When I decided to leave, I knew I couldn't fly across the ocean with so many bulging bags of spices, so I took a freighter back to the States, where on board I met this Jamaican guy—"

"Hold on, are you telling me the actual truth

here? A Jamaican guy on a freighter? When was this, 1910?"

His lids were heavy, and I was reminded of the evenings when we would hook up. He was never one for commitment, and I couldn't imagine a lifetime of his free spirit, but his mischievous gaze flashing under half-mast lids reminded me of lazy mornings on twisted sheets.

"You said to tell you the whole story, so I am. Antwan taught me to mix the spices, the elements of sweet, spicy, and smoky. By the time the boat landed in the United States I had the makings of my new career, and Barry's Blend was born."

I laughed. "How very immigrant of you. A boat ride across the Atlantic, a dream in your pocket."

"Plus a hundred pounds of exotic spices."

I relaxed as the purr of the harmonica resonated between my ears, the dappled sun warm on my face.

"So are you still with that guy you left us all for? The guy I met who offered you the stability of marriage and couldn't keep his hands off you? Because I see a ring on your left finger, if I'm not mistaken."

Had Barry met Noah? I'd brought him with me once to the market on a Saturday I wasn't working, not long after we were officially a couple. Noah didn't fit the scene, but every time we touched the charge between us was electric.

Standing in line for tomatoes or eggplant, I'd lean into his chest and he'd wrap his hands around my waist. Those hands. They were powerful enough to lift me, large enough to support me completely. The heat between us was undeniable, and when he pulled me close he would press his hips against my spine, hard. We played like this amid the fresh produce and flowers, me bending over to retrieve an item I wanted and him pressing into me as if the crowd had given him a nudge. Oh, but I knew right where he was, the energy between us painting my cheeks and chest pink. Two hours later neither of us could take it anymore. We had sex in the car, parked in the stall of a do-it-yourself car wash. I didn't remember introducing Noah to Barry that day, I was so engrossed.

I tucked my hand in my lap, the gold band hot against my skin. "We're not so much together," I said, hardly believing it myself. "At this time."

"Interesting." Barry was close to me now, and I met his stare. "So you're free?"

Taking a deep breath I said, "I'm not exactly sure. It's a long story that doesn't need to be told."

He nodded like he understood. "Well, if you're free, I want you to meet me next weekend at the drum circle in Liberty Park. I have to work this place for the rest of this weekend, but it will be like old times. You'll recognize some people.

We can dance barefoot and forget all about long stories that don't need to be told."

It was like he was speaking another language. I'd been several times to the Sunday drum circle at Liberty, but the woman who nursed a sick baby for three years would never dance amid a bunch of hippies to an uncertain beat. However, maybe I didn't have to be that responsible woman anymore. "I might meet you. I'll have to see."

He stood and stretched, his T-shirt rising above the band of his shorts. Before I could ignore the line of tanned skin filled with potential, he said, "I've got to help Pete disassemble the stand, but listen, Emma, I'd like to see you again." He put his hand on my shoulder and let his fingers trail down my arm as he walked away.

Almost immediately I determined I wouldn't go to the drum circle. It would be crowded with stoned twenty-somethings dressed in clothing hanging off shoulders and sitting low, like bath towels on their hips—feet bare and dusty, forearms and bellies decorated with a preponderance of tattoos. It hadn't been my scene, even years ago when I attended with Barry or other friends from the market.

On the other hand, why not have a whole night where I could pretend to be anyone I wanted, a night to forget about who I'd become. I slurped the last drops of my shake, the whiskey fuzzing the corners of my periphery with a satisfying numb.

I decided to finish my shopping and grab some beets and fresh blue cheese for a salad. I meant to make a pie using berries from one of the fruit stands, but the hours of the morning had slipped away, so the remaining half of the sweet stollen would have to do. I would go to my mom's house, make dinner for the two of us, and forget all about Barry's offer and the glimpse of something more.

CHAPTER 14

Back in my car, fresh vegetables arranged in the passenger seat, I realized I had two texts and two missed calls. From Ethan. Had something bad happened?

Before turning the key, I returned his call. Anusha answered on the second ring. "Ethan took the garbage to the curb, but he's been waiting for your call so I grabbed it," she said without a formal hello. "This DNA thing has him going crazy. He's subscribing his lactose intolerance to it, his skinny legs, his love of Thai food, you name it."

"Oh, this is about the DNA test? I thought there was an emergency."

"He's treating it like one, probably because—" I could tell she was still on the phone, but she stopped speaking.

"Because of what?"

"Hold on, he's at the door. Just a minute, he'll want to tell you." There was a full minute of silence before I heard her say to my brother, "It's Emma."

"Finally," he said from a distance. Muffled movement and then Ethan picked up the line. "Hey Em, do you have your DNA results?"

"Not yet. I was a little slow sending in my

sample, but Anusha said you're going nuts. What did you learn?"

"The big news is, I'm about twenty percent Asian. Here's what it says." Ethan was measured as he read aloud. "Half your genome comes from your mother and half from your father, a quarter from each of your grandparents, and so on." He continued speaking, becoming more excited as he ad-libbed. "Which would mean one of our great-grandparents was Asian, or specifically from East Asia. Or a combination of several other East Asian great-grandparents. Crazy. It shows the breakdown of the percentage of ancestry in my blood from different regions around the world. I'm mostly British and Scandinavian, with this huge chunk of Asian. And get this, Emma. I'm about ten percent Ashkenazi Jew. It could be where Canavan came from, right? You're a carrier because of something in that ten percent?"

I swallowed. Ten percent, the tiny piece of myself I wanted to slice away from the rest of my DNA, like using a paring knife to cut a moldy patch out of a slice of cheddar. But I wouldn't make this about Joey while Ethan was so hyped. This was his quest. So what I said was, "You said you were adopted. Now you're admitting we *both* have Ashkenazi ancestors? And by the way, I don't think you look Asian at all."

True my brother wasn't blond like the rest of the family, and his eyes were chocolate, but after

Ethan's hair lost the spikiness of a newborn, it had grown in as soft as my own, curling over his head in chestnut waves. We had the same straight nose and the same split between our front teeth requiring two years of braces to correct. In Ethan, I could see our mother's stride, the way she turned her feet when she took a step, like a dancer. While walking, Ethan and I were her clones, moving with the same heel-to-toe motion.

As a child, although our paths crossed infrequently, Ethan was always my brother. Despite the physical distance and the gaps in our time spent together, we shared an obvious bond. It was the tenacity of family.

"Fine. Be a doubter," he said. "But call me the minute you get your results. It's important to me that I know."

"Know what?"

"If I'm adopted."

"Oh, please, Ethan. Take a look at our school photos side by side. Or one of the more current photos, like the one we took when Noah and I brought Joey to California a couple of years ago. We're related. And Mom was pregnant with you. I remember."

"Switched at birth. Maybe there was a mistake at the hospital."

"I think you're being ridiculous. But I'll still call you the minute I get my results," I said, preparing to hang up.

"Emma?" He sounded hesitant. I wasn't sure he'd even spoken.

"Did you just say my name?"

"There's a little more I wanted to tell you."

"Oh no. You're mostly Neanderthal? I knew it." His tone was scaring me.

"Very funny, but that's not it."

"What then?"

He took a breath, then exhaled his next sentence. "Anusha is pregnant. It happened fast. We wanted you to know."

"Oh, Ethan. My God. So fantastic!"

"We think so, but—"

"Don't say another word. I'm fine. Thrilled. Please don't worry about me. Enjoy this time worry-free, because you already know you're not a carrier. And tell Anusha congratulations." I hung up before I heard his good-bye, pressed my head against the steering wheel, and wept.

After I pulled myself together enough to drive, I meandered, picking up a twelve-pack of Noah's favorite beer on the way home. I missed him desperately and hoped the smell of the open bottle in my hand would remind me of the summer evenings after he would come home from work, when he, Joey, and I would sit under the large oak tree in our backyard.

Noah and I would share a bottle, share our day (best and worst), and delight in our son. It was an active time for Joey, and when his hearing hadn't failed and he could still see, he would turn his head from side to side as the birds would call to one another among the verdant branches canopying us. A smile—a precious, fleeting smile—on his face. After we noticed Joey's interest in the birds, Noah hung several feeders from low limbs to entice avian activity, and from dawn to dusk our yard was a cacophony of song.

When Noah and I bought our home, just after our honeymoon, I imagined tree forts and platforms built in the branches. Rope swings, and whispered secrets shared between my children while they climbed among the shaded boughs. But for us, and our children, it wasn't meant to be.

So tonight with this familiar beer, I planned to get drunk. Because I could. Because I had no baby in my womb who needed me to nourish it, no child who would cry for my attention in the night, no husband who would take the beer out of my hand when I nodded off and direct me to bed with a gentle hand.

It worked out well. My mom was gone, a note on the table quick-scribbled saying she was going to dinner and a show with a couple of girlfriends. She wasn't waiting for me to make a meal using fresh ingredients from the farmers market after all.

I was two beers into my evening of wallowing

when my phone rang. I didn't recognize the number, so I ignored it and opened another beer. I was determined to forget. I found a half-empty bag of BBQ chips my mom had probably served at a yard party the summer prior. The phone rang again. And then again. On the fifth call I picked up.

"Is this a solicitor?"

"Emma?"

I bolted at the unfamiliar voice. "Yes?"

"So this *is* the right number. I'll try not to be offended if you don't recognize my voice. It's been a long time. It's Barry."

"I didn't recognize the number. Sorry," I apologized, popping a stale chip in my mouth. I was feeling tipsy, and the saltiness righted the spinning room. "Hey, wait, how did you get my number?"

"I called your home phone. Good, old online white pages."

"And?"

"And a man answered. When I asked for you, he said you weren't home, but he gave me this number."

"He did?" I shook my head, denying it. Barry had talked with Noah? And Noah gave him my number?

"I've been thinking of you since this afternoon. Nonstop. You have to come to the drum circle. Or maybe we could get together sooner? There was something hot between us before, but there's something even more enticing about you now."

I took a slug of beer without answering. On one hand I was flattered. I may not be the girl I was five years earlier on the inside, but on the outside I seemed the same. But I also knew what would happen if I saw Barry. He'd expect sex, because that's where our relationship had ended. We'd progressed from friends to the after-the-party go-to for each other, neither of us ready to commit but with no better options.

And then I met Noah. The relationship between us was nothing but potential and joy. Barry was immediately forgotten. Is this what I wanted now? Another season of bleary evenings with a man who was interested in me for one thing: a good time.

We talked for several minutes, and I hung up without agreeing to meet him, despite his urging. I angled the chip bag to dump the crumbs into my mouth and opened another beer, attempting to clear my mind of Barry, and the fact that Noah had offered up my cell number to another man, and distracted myself by searching for youthful memories of my brother, Ethan, something beyond the rolling pop of him cocooned within the confines of our mom. He was obviously wrong about the adoption thing, but he was just so insistent.

• • •

Ethan was tiny—not yet able to sit—lying prone on a blanket made of denim squares. My mom kept the quilt in the trunk of her car for the whole of my childhood and gave it to me as part of my wedding gift. It was the blanket on which Noah and I lay when we made Joey. It now rode in my trunk, under the jumper cables and reusable grocery bags, but needless to say it hadn't been used in some time.

In this memory, the summer sun was warm, and Ethan and I were surrounded by my mom and dad. There was no residue of battle between my parents. Things were peaceful. My dad reclined, his arms tenting to support him, his hands powerful and hairy but gentle and beloved. As an adult, these earliest memories of my father were hard to reconcile with the pinched man I knew the rest of my childhood, the man who raged at my mom before he left us, barraging her with a cutting waterfall of anger.

That day, my dad had his shoes off and his legs were long in front of him. The sun shining through the trees made a patchwork of shade and light, creating a shifting giraffe pattern on Ethan's yellow romper. My mom lay on the blanket, her body a comma curving around my little brother, talking to him in high-pitched tones. I also leaned over him, pulling his toes from his hands and giggling when, like a coiled spring, he'd tuck one big toe back into his mouth with a satisfied pop, rounding his spine like a potato bug.

My father, who was in a perfect position to join our gibberish conversation, was quiet. I wanted him to see Ethan's performance, but he was focused on my mom rather than my brother. There was concentration in his brow, like when he worked at the table with papers in front of him, like he was trying to figure something out.

"Can you see what he's doing, Daddy? He's sucking his toes." I forced a giggle, a bit unsettled at his intensity.

"What, honey?" My dad lifted me and put me on his lap, my straight legs mirroring the angle of his, reaching his knees.

"His toes. Don't you think it's yucky?"

He tugged at one of my toes, pretzeling my leg like Ethan's. "You did the same thing as a baby. I bet you can still do it, if you try."

I laughed and rolled off his lap. "No way!"

"Emmy, your toes are like mine. See?" He pulled his leg into a bend and placed his foot next to mine.

Wincing, I shook my head. "No, they aren't." His toes were huge and awful in a grown-up sort of way.

"Okay, mine are bigger, but see the shape? See how the little toe curves into the rest, and the shape of the nail on the big toe? You're definitely my kid." He said this staring at my mom, who glanced at my dad while he spoke, then quickly returned her attention to Ethan. "But your face, it's all your mom's. Based on pictures from when she was young, you're going to be her mirror image."

Now, that was more like it. As a child I knew my mom was beautiful, not in the unconditional way a child loves her mother but in a smooth-skin, wide-smile way. She sparkled when she laughed and soothed when she spoke. Cashiers at Albertson's rushed to help us to the car with our groceries, and neighbors lingered on our porch to listen to her long after I'd wandered back inside.

"So I'll look like Mommy. And Ethan will look just like you."

Again my mom's glance found my dad, for the briefest flicker. With a distant gaze he considered the future. When he finally spoke he appeared to be talking to my mother. "That my girl . . . is a mystery."

CHAPTER 15

My daily morning routine after my mom would leave for work: check for missed messages on my cell, check e-mail, and shower. I'd sent another round of hopeful résumés into the world, and I convinced myself I was waiting for an interview request, or my DNA results, but what I really wanted was a message from Noah. A virtual caress indicating he was still thinking of me. He'd messaged once, right after I told him we should separate, letting me know he would give me some space, and then no more. He wasn't chasing me this time. God, this was so hard.

The screen scrolled long with new messages (none from Noah) and I skimmed them, urging, "Come on. Give me something to chew on today."

And a miracle, there *was* something, second to last in the queue:

Good News—Your DNA results are ready.

After Ethan's revelation, I'd been nervous about what I might discover, but now I was antsy. I wanted to get to the bottom of all these secrets and be done with them. I wanted Ethan's suspicions to be a nonevent, as Noah put it.

"Here goes," I said to the empty room as I

signed into my account. After verifying I was the intended recipient of the results, I clicked on the tab reading *Your Ancestry Composition.*

A map of the world appeared, many countries highlighted in various shades of blue. To the right of the map was the breakdown of the origin of my DNA, region by region. At the top of the list, it tabulated that I was 100% European, and right below that, it catalogued details of my European heritage: British/Irish, Scandinavian, French/German in decreasing amounts. Like Ethan, I had almost 10% Ashkenazi Jewish ancestry, but unlike Ethan, who sported almost 20% East Asian/Native American, I had less than 1%.

Was it possible for siblings to have such a large discrepancy? Could the Bingo shaker cage of genetics create this type of variation between a brother and a sister? After clicking out of the screen, I scanned the home page for something that might answer this question. Another option available was a tab reading *Your DNA Relatives.* This was a listing of relatives who had also taken the test and the percentage of DNA we shared. Of those who had taken the test worldwide, I had more than two thousand relatives, detailed as such:

Close Family—1
2nd & 3rd Cousins—102
4th Cousins—786

The remaining relatives were categorized as *Distant*. Close family might be Ethan? But if he was adopted we would share no common ancestors at all. I clicked on the nameless/faceless icon of a supposed ancestor (which was the only method to contact *Close Family*) and scanned the prewritten suggested introduction:

Through our shared DNA, we have been identified as relatives. Our predicted relationship is Half Sibling. Would you like to compare our genomes? By sharing genomes we can compare our DNA using ancestry features and discover clues about how we are related.

Half sibling? If this message I was about to send was received by Ethan, what did it mean? And if it was directed to someone else? Oh God. But I must. Twitchy with anticipation, I pressed send and imagined it zipping to an unknown in-box.

After pacing around the kitchen for several minutes I picked up my phone and before I realized what I'd done, I'd dialed Noah's cell. Just a word or two. I'd tell him about the DNA results, or my résumés, or the book of German poems. I just needed to hear his voice. I was forwarded immediately to his recorded message. His phone was off.

With shaky determination, I decided to try him

at home. Typically, when I called the home phone I keyed in the number, digit by digit. It was much faster than searching for it in my contacts. This time, though, I was forced to retype the number twice. Finally, I asked Siri to call Noah at home. Again, no answer.

With frustrated steps, I stomped around my mom's kitchen waiting for a response from my half sibling. Ethan took the same test, so his results would be part of the data bank. The fact I didn't have a *full* sibling on my list of relatives meant we were half siblings, or not blood relatives at all. Ethan was right. Something was amiss.

If my mom was hiding something, and she wasn't willing to tell us, maybe while I waited (instead of fruitlessly pacing) I could find some indication of paternity in the divorce documentation. Granted, it had been over twenty years since the arrangements were made, but surely she would have kept something. The stairs leading to her office creaked as I made my way up them, protesting my progress. This was all wrong.

Although my mom converted Ethan's rarely used childhood bedroom into a guest room for his longed-for visits, the week after I left for college she changed my tiny loft bedroom into her home office. She said she knew I'd keep coming around even without a space to call my own. She was obviously right.

These days, a modular desk from Ikea filled the space formally occupied by my bed, and on each side stood a filing cabinet, where she kept bills and patient records on clients she'd counsel from home. Legally she'd be required to keep the medical records confidential, so those drawers would likely be locked, but maybe other, less sensitive files would be accessible.

The top drawer of each cabinet held typical office items: pencils, stapler, scissors, and paper for the laser printer. If the documentation was here it would be in one of the four remaining drawers. Three were locked, but one slid open easily. I crouched, but unable to support myself with knocking knees I plopped to the floor to rummage through the contents. What was I doing, breaking into my mother's private papers? But then again, if I found nothing incriminating, she'd never know I snooped.

Bills and insurance documents at my own house were thrown together by year, but my mom organized by category, so if anything was here, it would be easy to find. I shuffled quickly past a folder labeled Mortgage, one Medical, and one called Joey Medical. My mom kept a file on Joey's disease? Toward the back I spotted a file labeled Divorce Documents.

My palms were sweaty as I pulled it onto my lap, and I imagined leaving greasy prints on the paper, a clear indication of my guilt, but the file was light, flat with lack of documentation. I opened it. It contained a single page reading *State of Utah—Certificate of Divorce*. The form was complete with all vital information. However, it contained no line placing blame, or the reason for the split, but there was this:

Number of Children Under Age 18 Whose
  Physical Custody Was Awarded To:
Husband: 1 child
Wife: 1 child
Joint: 0

And there was the black-and-white truth of my childhood without Ethan. No joint custody.

The day, more than two decades earlier, when my dad and Ethan left town, my mom and I stood in the driveway watching the moving van pull away from the house. My mom reassured me after the taillights were no longer visible, "We'll see them lots, I promise."

But I knew from the way she'd gripped Ethan's tiny body to her chest before she set him into my dad's arms, the way she'd kissed his forehead and the tiny bridge of his nose, her hands caressing his chubby legs, dimpled knees, and the ladder of his spine over and over again, memorizing him, it might be a long time. And it was. I didn't see my brother for a year.

Each summer from then on I was forced to

spend one miserable week in California with my dad, and Ethan would stay with my mom, but the swap was lined with silver. The following week I'd fly home and spend the week with both my mom and Ethan. One measly week out of every year when I could finally be a big sister to a brother I barely recognized.

I rolled back onto the floor of my old bedroom clutching the divorce decree to my chest. Things should have been different, and now all those years of my childhood, of *our* childhood, were gone. It couldn't be fixed. But it didn't mean I hadn't tried.

When I was eight and Ethan was four, and we'd spent the second of our weeklong annual visits together, the vague promise of *you'll see him soon* rang especially untrue. So on the morning we were supposed to take Ethan to the airport so he could disappear for another three hundred sixty-five days, I hid him.

Our little house had a steeply pitched roof, and on one side of my loft bedroom (the room where I now lay curled on the carpet) ran a long closet the shape of a wedge. The door to the closet was about three feet high, and my mom avoided the space because to enter she had to crawl. But for my purposes it was perfect. I stretched out to read in that space, cocooning myself in thick blankets on the floor. I hid the homework I didn't want to do. And as a teenager I took boys to kiss in there, crawling and grumbling until I closed the door and pulled the string to turn off the light.

But that day of my childhood, it was the place to bury my treasure, my place to keep my little brother safe from marauders who wished to drag him away. I supplied him with his favorite trucks and pushed him deep into the darkest corner. I gave him a box of Cheese Nips, two cans of apple juice, and a large mixing bowl for him to use as a bathroom (if need be). I was prepared for a long standoff. I hung blankets around his hiding spot, securing them in the exposed rafters with heavy books and diaper pins. As I pushed my Barbie Dreamhouse against the door, (obscuring it with plastic dolls who were living the dream), I believed the entrance to the closet would disappear.

And it worked. Well, it worked for a little while. Like usual, my mom called from the kitchen telling us to come for lunch. She added that she wanted to get Ethan to eat a sandwich before he left, because it would be dinnertime before our dad had a chance to feed him. I pasted on a smile and trotted down the stairs, figuring if I kept in plain sight it would add credibility that Ethan was missing and his disappearance would have nothing to do with me.

"Where's your brother?"

I shrugged and took a bite of peanut butter and jam.

"Wasn't he upstairs with you?"

I finished chewing, swallowed in a great gulp. "I've been reading this whole time. Weren't *you* helping him pack?"

"I was packing *for* him. He was with you."

"Nope."

"Ethan!" my mom called again. "Come eat. Then it's time to leave!"

When my mom called, would Ethan remember my strict instructions indicating that he should not emerge or speak? After a minute of silence I shrugged again and smiled. In retrospect, my grin may have been a little wolfish, but ignoring me, my mom dashed up the stairs two at a time. I heard her in my room, calling out to Ethan. I figured she'd check under my bed and in the tiny bathroom near my room, but probably not in the closet. Several minutes later she came back, her face puzzled.

"Emma, will you help me?"

"Sure," I said, checking the numbers on the microwave. They were supposed to leave for the airport by one o'clock, so if I could slow his departure by forty minutes, he'd miss his flight and we'd get to keep him for another year.

"Let me get my shoes and I'll check outside." I was incredulous at how I could smooth my face when involved in an abject lie. My mom always told me I would feel guilty, deep in my gut, if I was lying. Instantly my palms liquefied, and my stomach churned with the sandwich I'd eaten moments earlier. Maybe this was what she was talking about.

Back in my bedroom, I chose the shoes requiring the most complicated tying, allowing a minute or two to communicate with my brother. I shifted the Barbie house and hissed through the crack for Ethan to keep quiet and that he was doing great. He called back, telling me he needed to go potty, so I reminded him of the bowl, trying not to think about his already shaky aim when standing at the toilet and what steps I'd have to take to flush the yellow mess when he was done.

There was a knock at the front door. Knowing it was my grandparents arriving to go with us to the airport to see Ethan onto the plane, I skittered down the stairs and out the sliding door leading to the backyard. I couldn't face my grandpa's piercing blue gaze. I bit my lip until it made my eyes water. Me, the girl he always said he was so proud of, I was a liar.

"I'll check in the yard," I said, rushing away from the scene.

The space behind our house was small and surrounded with a tall wood fence. It illustrated my mom's struggle to be a single parent. I remembered lying on the fresh-mowed green lawn with Ethan, before he and our father moved to California, but now the yard was filled with knee-high weeds, their barbed leaves scratching me as I walked into the parched-earth jungle. No one had come out here in months. Not a single weed was crushed by the fall of a foot, but I still took my time on my fruitless search.

When I stepped back into the kitchen, bracing myself to see my grandparents, my mom was hunched over the table with Ethan's uneaten sandwich between her elbows. Her face was in her hands and she was sobbing. My grandma sat next to her rubbing her back.

At the sight of my mother, the rock in my life, reduced to sand, I cracked. I met her sob for sob before I could make my way ten feet across the kitchen and into her arms. "He's not gone, Mommy. He's not. He's in my closet. I wanted to keep him." She pulled me onto her lap, pressing her face into my hair.

"I want to keep him too," she whispered, her response tickling my scalp. "More than anything. But we can't." She took a shuddering breath. "We just can't."

"Why? Please!"

Grandpa Joe entered the kitchen carrying Ethan, who was giggling and not wearing any pants. My mom shifted me to one knee and received Ethan from my grandpa's arms on the other side of her lap. She pulled us together between her arms, pressing us into one another, firm against her heart. I thought she'd be angry I'd hidden him. I thought she'd be mad that Ethan wasn't wearing all of his travel clothing, but she wasn't. She held us there for several minutes, her breath hitching as she tried to control her breathing.

Eventually, my grandpa said, "We should probably get going."

And we did. I didn't clean Ethan's hideaway for two weeks, imagining him there with me. He'd finished one apple juice and he hadn't peed in the bowl, but he'd been there, tucked into my closet. And then he wasn't.

I slipped the divorce decree back into the folder and returned it to the cabinet. After using the edge of the desk to pull myself to standing, I grabbed a tissue to wipe the moisture from my palms. Tucked under the cardboard Kleenex box lay an envelope from the University of Utah Medical Center. On the front stamped in red, it said *Test Results—Do Not Forward*. It was addressed to my mother.

Fear tripped an uneven rhythm in my chest. Was my mom sick? I didn't expect to find *this* information in my clandestine search. So much had recently been taken from me, it couldn't be bad news. Not so close to losing Joey. Not so soon after Grandpa Joe.

But I also knew sometimes the worst news came dressed in a white envelope with a bland message. It seemed there should be fanfare accompanying devastation, like a movie sound track indicating the approach of tragedy, but that's not what happens in real life.

I glanced about the room, almost wishing to see my mom standing at the door so we could open it together, and even if she was angry she could reassure me everything would be okay. But she wasn't, and I couldn't stand another minute of uncertainty. Not now, not with so many edges of my life fraying. I pried the lip of the envelope and unfolded a page of familiar letterhead. Typed in the middle of the empty sheet was

Ashkenazi Jewish Genetic Panel (AJGP)—
Carrier Screening Results
Canavan Disease—Positive

She'd taken a blood test to answer my question about Canavan disease. Relief filled my eyes with quick tears that she wasn't sick. However, now I knew she was a carrier. Like me, she was the harbinger of illness. It didn't change the end of Joey's story, but somehow knowing my mom and I were connected, bound by blood in this way, was a small comfort. I was also touched she'd take this test for me, because she knew I was questioning. Or . . .

I dropped the results to the floor. Or, she'd had her blood drawn so I wouldn't continue to research my own ancestry using the DNA test. She'd sought a genetic panel of her own so I wouldn't be compelled to join Ethan in discovering who we were, and how we were related to each other as siblings. The fresh fuel of injustice fed the fire in my gut.

Seconds later my phone rang, accusation echoing in the empty room. I wasn't sure who I wanted to speak with: my husband who was avoiding me, or my brother who may not be my brother, or my mom.

It was Ethan.

"I just received an introduction notice from my half sibling, your contact information attached. Emma, what does it mean?" Before I could respond he continued, "Find your detailed results and go to the Ancestry Composition section. Let's compare."

"Hold on just a second." I tucked my mom's Ashkenazi screening results into the envelope and, clutching it to me, walked downstairs. After starting the coffee (I needed something to clear my head while speaking with Ethan) I reopened the e-mail and peered at my results.

I was 100% European, more than 50% Northern European, as Caucasian as Caucasian could be. Knowing what Ethan was going to ask, I wished for something different than I'd seen before, but taking a deep breath I put the phone back to my ear. "Okay, I'm here, and I've pulled up the site. What do you want to know?"

"What's your overall genetic makeup?"

"Pretty white bread, Ethan."

"What do you mean?"

"I'm one hundred percent European," I said.

"No Asian?"

"Less than one percent."

"And I'm 18.7% East Asian/Native American. The note you sent indicates we share enough DNA to be *half* siblings, which would explain why you remember Mom being pregnant with me. It would mean I'm not adopted. And it would also explain where I got my brown eyes and unattached earlobes. Which would mean—" In the middle of his rapid-fire analysis, I heard a hitch, the edge of a whimper I knew well from when he was a baby and I was a big sister hovering over him in his playpen.

"Ethan?"

He gulped back a sob. He was a full-grown man and no longer willing to allow himself the luxury of crying, the inevitable childhood response to pain or injustice. "Which means we have different fathers."

"But Dad is the only dad I remember. He's the guy in the photos at my first birthday and he's the *same* dad who held you in the hospital as a newborn." I spoke to convince myself. "Maybe Mom was married before. And she had me with another man? But why wouldn't she say so?"

"Or maybe she was raped after you were born? Maybe I'm the son of a rapist."

"I can't go there," I said softly. "But it would make sense she'd hide the truth. However, if that's the case, why the split custody? It makes more sense if our dad isn't *my* dad. He left me with Mom because *you* are his true son and I belong to someone else."

Although my dad and I hadn't shared a solid relationship since he moved out and stole my brother, saying this aloud tugged at my already ragged heart. If he wasn't my father, who was?

After listening to light breathing on the line, the near silence growing earsplitting as we pondered our results, Ethan said, "Well, you and I both know who has the answers."

"Mom." We echoed against one another.

"You should ask her," Ethan said. "You're there. You can see her face when you talk with her. I'll talk to Dad."

"Okay. I will," I said after a long pause. "But give me a day or two, please. I need to wrap my head around this before I confront her."

Hurt and deceived, I knew if she'd hidden a secret for this long, it would take some maneuvering on my part to get it out, and I would need to be calm. We rarely fought, and I was currently dependent on her for my mental well-being, as well as a place to sleep.

"You have no idea how much it means to me,

Emma. Please hurry, because I need to figure out who I am." Again the familiar wobble in his voice.

"I think you'd be surprised how much I understand. But things are bad with Noah, and Mom's the only constant in my life right now. I need her."

And I did need her, but I also knew if I saw her today, armed with this fresh knowledge, I wouldn't be able to avoid a confrontation. After finishing my conversation with Ethan I glanced at the clock: eleven-thirty. My mom would be home in less than a half hour from her Saturday morning couples therapy. If I encountered her now, I'd likely blurt out something I'd later regret. But where could I go until then?

Grandpa Joe's? No. I was a spinning miasma of unanswered questions. The frayed end of a rope. Being alone in his house without anyone to answer my questions would be too much. Home? If Noah wasn't around I could hide out there, and if he was home . . .

I scribbled on the envelope containing the Ashkenazi Panel: *This is interesting. Talk later?* The note might distract my mom from my sudden departure and allow me some time before we encountered one another.

Even from a distance, my house appeared unwelcoming. The blinds on the front windows were closed, and a paper lay abandoned in orange plastic on the drive. How long had Noah been gone?

In the seconds it took for me to reach the back door, keys in hand, I imagined a dozen scenarios, each more horrific than the last: He didn't answer because he'd moved out. He was asleep in the arms of another woman. He'd killed himself, his hunting rifle at rest near his side.

Holding my exhale until I entered, I called his name in a breathy whisper, then inhaling I yelled louder, attempting to summon him with the vigor of my call. No response. The house was eerie in silence and he'd left the lights on vacation setting.

Walking into the kitchen, I saw a piece of the graph paper he often used for work, filled with his familiar script. It was addressed to me. He anticipated I'd come home, eventually. He knew me. I imagined him stepping behind me as I leaned close to read his words. Sometimes I'd flip through the mail in this position, standing at the kitchen bar, and he'd wrap his arms around me from behind, resting his chin on the top of my head. I ached for the reassurance of his touch.

Emma,

I've gone to St. Louis for work. There was a last-minute issue at our Missouri branch and they asked if I could fill in. I took it because I needed to get away. I'll be gone a few days. I didn't call because I'm trying to give you some space and actually, I didn't want to talk.

I understood you when you isolated yourself in our home. You were aching for Joey. You were sad. I was too. But now I feel like I don't know you at all.

What we had was good and I want you in my life. What do you want, really? Before I am really free, as you put it, we need a long conversation. And I want a solid answer.

I do love you. More than you know,
Noah

My throat constricted. He hadn't moved on. Yet. Oh, how I wanted him. I wanted this. But surveying the house, the rooms once filled with Joey, the bittersweet memories of our child left me empty. Considering we might never again be parents together, the years of just the two of us loomed long, rattling disjointed in these same rooms, both of us aching for a different life.

Through the bolted windows, the sounds of summer filled the air. The finches and doves that frequented our yard called to one another in a spontaneous opera. Maybe I would find peace outdoors. I unlocked the back door and walked into the yard.

One lonely feeder hung exhausted in the branches of the oak, swaying lightly in the breeze. The high-backed chairs we once used daily were dusty and pocked with droppings, and the seat cushions were nowhere to be seen. A few persistent sparrows hovered about the hollow plastic cylinder and perched on the lip, encouraging me with their vigorous voices to refill it with seed, while several fat doves pecked at the ground between the exposed roots. Noah's abandoned rake leaned against the trunk. As I reached for the tool, my feathered friends exploded into the heavens, a torrent of pinwheeling, whistling wings startling me.

"That's right! Leave," I yelled at the sky, suddenly furious at the direction my life had gone. "I'm taking it all down, so tell your friends there's nothing here for them!"

I hoisted the rake and with all my strength swung it at the feeder, smacking at it as if it were a tiny, empty piñata. Again and again, I aimed the tines of the gardening tool and batted, my hair sticking to the moisture on my cheeks. "You all get out of here! No matter how long you hover around, things will *never* be the same."

I was breathless by the time the chain caught between the metal teeth, solidly this time, flinging the container across the yard, where it hit the fence and fell to the ground, the red plastic perch separating and rolling across the lawn. On cue, the doves swooped back into the yard, unafraid, ready to examine the carnage. I chucked the rake at them, and again they scattered, their wings whirring in protest.

If Joey were alive, he would be four years old and our yard would be filled with sand toys and rubber balls. I could imagine Noah doting on his children, throwing a football with his boy, playing tea party with his girl, sitting amid beloved dolls and stuffed animals in these unused chairs. But there were no children here.

If Noah married another woman, he could choose one who would give him healthy babies. For that matter, if I chose a different husband, so could I. And I was back to the solution that made me ache: Set him free.

Or . . . I sat on the dusty Adirondack, glaring at a magpie inching close to my shoe. Or what if I conceived a child with another man, one who wasn't a carrier for Canavan disease, one who, in our meeting at the genetic level, wouldn't create a toxic slurry of DNA? What if, like my mom, I had a child with a man who wasn't my husband? She hid a similar secret for my whole life. Was there a purpose?

I knew *I* had a reason. A good one. After I became pregnant, Noah and I could test the fetus. I would be carrying a healthy child, a welcome accident. Noah would never have to know. I could keep Noah, I could be his wife, and we'd have our longed-for child, the completion of our family.

Scrolling through my call log, I found the *unknown* number in my list of received calls. Barry. I could call him. I could sleep with him. I could solve this. If I could get pregnant while Noah was gone . . . and if Barry was the father, the baby wouldn't have Canavan. Noah and Barry were both tall. They had slightly different coloring, which could be explained away. And they both had dark eyes. Together, Noah and I could move forward like a regular family. Could I make it work?

"Stop it. This is stupid!" I yelled at the ground, trying to scare the damn bird that hopped near my feet. A hot, thumping shower is what I needed, and I'd move forward with my day. I would do something to stop my circular thoughts from pulling me into the deep.

While I was in the shower, the text indicator chirped. I peeked at the phone before grabbing my towel.

Hey girl. Drum circle tomorrow? I'll bring some Barry's Blend salsa and a devil's lettuce salad. You game?

There was a woman I didn't recognize in the bathroom mirror. She held a phone and an opportunity in her hand. Drips fell from my wet hair onto the screen like tears. Knowing I was going to go, to meet a man who wasn't my husband, who I intended to sleep with, made my blood run hot. But it wasn't a pleasant heat. It resonated like poison through my limbs, making me sluggish, angry, weak with guilt, and consumed by the ache of fever.

I'll meet you there.

CHAPTER 16

The drum circle gathered at Liberty Park after lunch on Sundays, and the crowd stayed late when the weather was good. Outside it appeared to be another bluebell day in my high desert city, sapphire sky and not a cloud to be seen. Many would linger from midmorning to midnight on a day like this one.

I'd attended the circle a handful of times in my former life, always with Barry, where with his encouragement I would be convinced to lead the group in twenty-minute sessions of yoga, often ending with timed headstands or tree-pose competitions for the less coordinated (or more inebriated). But the late-evening activities were overwhelming to me, and today I hoped to accomplish my mission before the night lit up with fire batons, neon hula hoop dancers, and stilt walkers.

After replying to Barry, confirming my plans, I stayed the night alone in my own home, weighing my options, calculating the risks, avoiding my mom. By noon on Sunday, I found a mustard-yellow knit skirt I bought before I met Noah. A knot on one side of the fabric created a slit midthigh and made the whole outfit appropriate for the crowd I'd encounter. After parting my hair in the middle, I created two loose braids and tucked a silk daisy from my craft cupboard behind my ear.

Repeatedly I checked for missed texts, pleading under my breath to Noah, "If this is a bad idea, stop me." The phone was silent. I spun in front of the mirror. It would do.

Liberty Park was as integral a place to my childhood as my elementary school playground. It was a block from my mom's practice, so during long summer days when I didn't visit Grandpa Joe, after I'd exhausted the arts and crafts projects in her little office using the copy machine and highlighters, I'd wander the meandering pathways. I was forbidden from using the restrooms (it was where the perverts hid, waiting for preteen girls, my mom told me), but the rest was mine. It was the only place I knew of in the Salt Lake Valley where a person could find constant shade from morning to long-shadowed dusk. The towering trees had been planted long before the wide streets of the city were paved, and the rolling hills and stone pergolas were created for picnics a century earlier.

Even as an adult, during my years before Noah, I spent hours reading on the lawn, the sun warm on my body. Easy afternoons would drift into night, when the stars would reach their spires toward one another and speak to me of my future.

I saw a husband there, and children, dreamy, peaceful and just ahead. I determined I would bring my babies to the park, their hands sticky from cotton candy, wrapped in my equally sticky ones. We'd feed the ducks and roll down the hill. We'd nap in the shade.

And I did bring Joey to this park. It was our weekly adventure. The smooth sidewalk circling the rolling lawn was plenty big enough for his elevated wheelchair, leaving room for the multitude of joggers and the girls in black spandex shorts to Rollerblade past. We were all going the same direction, so most of the time no one would alter their course, but if they did, their smiles would be a thin line of sympathy, and I would look away. I didn't want their sympathy. I just wanted my baby to be happy.

Because Joey enjoyed it. I know he did. Though he didn't smile, his eyes would crease at the corners like Noah's when he grinned. Maybe it was his reaction to the sunlight as it shone between branches to caress his upturned face, fading into shadow, and reemerging brightly as we strolled, but I hoped not. I wanted him to sense the other children as they dashed about the playground, jostling for a turn on the slide or pumping the swings, backs arched horizontal to the sky. Scraped knee, sweaty-headed, Popsicle-stained childhood would forever be out of Joey's reach.

Though my child sat strapped next to me in his chair, his limbs flaccid, and a feeding tube in his delicate nostril, I was filled, bursting with love for him. I'd touch his head, the downy waves tickling my fingers, and mourn the childhood he'd never know.

In my gnawing indecision about meeting Barry, I wandered our familiar walking path until I could practically feel the spongy black handles of Joey's chair pressed against my palms. The last time I'd trod this ground, I was still a mother. Now what was I? The title had been stripped and might never return. I was a woman I didn't recognize. I was an uncertain wife. I was the daughter of a woman who lied to me. I was the granddaughter of a grandpa I didn't know. I was the carrier of a rare disease. Shapeless as a specter, I could be anyone now. Anyone at all.

I smelled the pot before I saw the crowd. More than twenty people were tucked at the base of a hill in the deepest shade of the park. The gathering was younger than I remembered (or maybe I was older), and they appeared sadder somehow. Some pierced and tattooed, some shirtless and dirty, and some looked as if they'd stopped here on their way from Trader Joe's, but all were bound together in various states of intoxication.

A woman in a glittery full-length gown with an iridescent cape attached to the arms, like the wings of a bat, wove through the crowd, dipping and swaying, her music in her head. Girls spun in enormous hula hoops or twirled weighted poi balls in elaborate patterns. Dogs outnumbered the humans. One man held a raven, and another walked an iguana on a leash.

Who of this odd menagerie sought a carefree day, the rest of their life humming along in perfect harmony? And who intended to numb a pain so significant nothing else worked? I knew to which category I belonged today, and the realization made my desire to forget more intense.

Hesitant at first, I felt my strides grow longer as I picked my way through the crowd. The swish of my skirt against my thigh, the choppy rhythm of the novice drummers, the earthy smell of damp lawn and bare feet, and I could almost feel the glass bong in my hand, my lips against the rim, the smoke hot in my mouth.

Barry noticed my approach and waited at the bottom of the hill under the deep shadow of a cottonwood tree. He held a familiar pipe, his thumb stopped over the hole at the top, trapping the smoke he'd pulled for me. He held it in my direction, and I put it to my mouth. He released the smoke, and I inhaled.

Moments later, loose limbed, I followed Barry back to the blanket he'd set near the edge of the circle. About half of the bongo drums were unattended, as were half a dozen guitars; the others were being tapped and strummed with various amounts of enthusiasm. I recognized Barry's blanket. More than once we'd kissed lying on the Navajo wool, the familiar chevrons of black, red, and gold leaving an imprint on bare skin.

It was like no time had passed at all. Joey and Noah were a dream I had the night before, vivid, haunting, but not real. True to his promise, Barry brought a buffet of food, and my mouth watered. I finished a jar of roasted corn salsa and half a bag of chips before I spoke.

"My God, this is the best salsa I've ever eaten." I tapped on the label. "Barry's Blend, of course."

"Thanks, girl, it's probably been a while since you smoked."

I agreed as I hungrily scanned the other items he brought for the daylong picnic.

"So, Emma." Barry leaned back on the blanket, supporting his head with his hands. "Tell me your story. I told you my adventure, but the same five years passed for you. You married that same guy, right?"

No. I didn't want Noah in this space with me. I knew what I wanted to accomplish, but I didn't want to think about it. Dream-like or not, he didn't belong. After crawling several feet off the blanket, I snagged a double bongo from the circle, brought it onto my lap, and tapped on it several times. "Less talking, more music."

Barry grinned. He wasn't intent on serious conversation, after all. He filled the pipe while he watched me pick out a tune, a few others in the crowd joined in, a galloping rhythm played by one or two decent musicians and many more who, like me, held the music in their bloodstream.

Barry stood and held the pipe to me under the cover of his palm. I let the smoke fill my mouth before gulping it into my lungs, never losing contact with the drum. The ends of my braids touched my shoulders like heavy feathers, and through closed lids I appreciated the sense of well-being settling over me, top to bottom, individual hair follicles, cheek muscles, crooks of my elbows.

But when I looked again, I thought I saw him. Noah, standing in the shadow of one of the spruce trees, his fists tight with accusation. He turned away as I jumped from my seated position, the drums falling off my lap and rolling across the cushion of pine needles. Barry caught my hand before I ran to my husband and pulled me back to the blanket. I fell to my knees at his tug.

"Easy there, girl. Take a minute."

I blinked long and concentrated on the tree. The shadow was empty. "Do you see someone there? Over by the pine tree?"

"The park is full. There are loads of people over there. Don't worry, Emma, lay back and relax. No troubles today."

Resting on the blanket, I peered into the layers of green canopy over my head. No troubles. If this was the right thing, why did it feel so wrong? And if Noah saw me! I didn't want to hurt him, and more important, he wouldn't believe my lie.

I bolted upright and Barry pushed his hands against my shoulders, returning me to the blanket, where the spinning in my head receded somewhat. He lay next to me on the ground. "No one is there, it's just the weed. Twenty minutes and you'll be dancing, relax." He pulled at one of my braids and tickled my arm from shoulder to wrist and back again. It felt like a waterfall of warm sand covering me grain by grain. I tried to settle the jerking behind my eyelids by exploring the sensation on my limbs.

"You still haven't taken that wedding ring off, my girl," Barry whispered in my ear, his lips caressing the lobe.

I turned my head away, both from his comment and from his mouth on my skin. I was too tired to move very far. Barry's hovering presence receded, and I knew I was alone on the blanket. He joined the circle and was pounding on a bongo. I watched through cracked lids until I fell asleep. When I woke, my cheek was wet against the damp wool under my face. I could smell the fiber of the woven fabric, musky and dank. Had I cried?

I sat and blinked to clear the haze. Barry pulled me to standing.

"Better now?" he asked, pulling me close. "You should dance." He pushed me into a crowd bouncing to the beat. Some shuffle-stepped and some swung their arms like anime fighters, but it didn't matter, the crowd pulsed in unison.

Finally exhausted, my face covered with a sheen of sweat, the afternoon gone, and the sun a curl of tangerine on the horizon, I returned to the blanket and pulled my knees to my chest. I watched as the woman with the translucent wings flitted through the crowd.

From behind, strong arms surrounded me, and without thinking I leaned into the solid chest at my back. I tilted my head to expose my neck. I knew it wasn't Noah, didn't I? This is what I planned, wasn't it? As his lips traced the flutter of my pulse, I leaned into his mouth. "I miss you," I whispered. "I miss this."

The kissing intensified, delicate nails skimming the insides of my arms, tracing my hands to the tips, moving with hesitation to my thighs.

"Should we go home?" I pressed his hands against my legs, wanting more.

"Your place? Or mine?" And suddenly I knew the man behind me wasn't my husband. And no matter what I hoped to gain, it was wrong.

Crouching like a feral cat, I crushed a platter of cut fruit and felt it, warm as blood, slip under my bare feet. Empty bags of chips popped like cap fire under my weight. Cornered and hackles raised, I made my retreat.

Barry was standing now. "What the hell?"

"This is wrong. I'm not supposed to be here." I scanned the ground for my sandals, not turning my back to him, not allowing myself to be deceived. He approached me holding the pipe.

"If you're coming down?" he asked, holding it toward me.

"No. Oh God." I was crying now. Noah's anguished face filled my mind. Without another word I ran up the hill, out of the party. My feet, which were once used to walking barefoot, now throbbed without shoes.

Barry found me sitting on the wooden pier where the paddleboats were launched. He held my purse and sandals. "Emma, you might want to unload your five years of baggage before we party again." He put my bag in my lap. "I tried to call someone to come get you, but your phone is dead." He reached in his pocket and handed me his. "Is there anyone you can get ahold of?"

Like the time I was sixteen and had thrown up after too much peach schnapps, I dialed my mom, my movement jerky over the illuminated screen.

She answered, sounding far away. "Mommy?" I whispered, and started to cry.

● ● ●

Ribbons of heat fell across my body like the canvas restraints in a mental hospital. My head throbbed as I attempted to twist free from the sensation. Where was I? Opening my eyes to thin slits, a shard of white summer light hit my retinas, and I remembered. Once again, I was sleeping in the guest room at my mom's house. Harsh morning light lay across me in zebra-stripes created by the slats in the plantation shutters.

Rolling onto my stomach to block the sun, a braid caught under my cheek and the loose ends tickled my forehead. The drum circle, and my hangover, and . . . I stiffened, my skull thumping. And Barry.

"Mom?" I croaked, patting the bedside table for the digital clock. Numbers illuminated in red blinked: 10:15.

"Mom?" No answer.

It was Monday, which would mean she had already left for work. I needed to get out of bed and find some noise to soothe the silence amplified in my head. And right after I found my equilibrium, I would call Noah. Had he been at the park? I could have been paranoid from the pot. But what if he'd lingered in the shadows witnessing my behavior? Please, no. I pressed my palms against my cheekbones, attempting to push the thoughts from my head, and found my hands streaked with prison stripes of mascara.

The yellow skirt lay in a puddle on the floor, grass stained and smeared with dirt. My bag was next to it. I groped the interior for the familiar rectangle of my phone, at last dumping the contents onto the bed. In the mirror over the dresser, I caught my reflection. My face was shiny with layers of sweat, my eyelids red-rimmed, and one cheek was smeared with brown dirt from swiping at a tear with a dusty hand.

And my phone was gone. I'd used Barry's phone to call my mom, but I could swear I had mine when I got home. At my panicked thought, a text indicator chimed from the nightstand on the far side of the bed, and I was filled with a Pavlovian sense of relief. My phone wasn't lost. And my mom had charged it.

In my haste to grab it, I rammed my toe into the base of the stand. My head thumped again, pain coursing along my leg, the additional sensation causing my already fragile body to shudder. Collapsing onto the bed, I rolled onto my back, moaning. My feet were filthy and my nail was now cracked deep into the nail bed. The reminder ping on the phone sounded again, and I held it to my face.

My mom. *Are you awake?*

Sorry for last night. I typed. *I'm a train wreck. Let's talk when I come home for lunch.*

Like a lazy teen, I'd slept until almost 10:30. I pushed my knuckles into my eye sockets and then I remembered . . . I was scheduled to teach at 10:30! I dialed the number for Downtown Dog and spoke with Darcy, claiming stomach flu and apologizing profusely. She told me she could take my classes, but it was clear she wasn't pleased. After hanging up I pulled the covers over my head to block the light. What was I doing with my life? If I wasn't careful, I would lose the only job I'd managed to get.

Ensconced in my cave of shame, I scanned the text log to see if Noah had tried to contact me during the night. Nothing. Oh God, maybe he had been at the park. He was supposed to be out of town. However, I didn't know when he wrote the note. Maybe he came home after I left for the drum circle.

Not knowing for sure, I texted my husband, clicking out the letters *I'm sorry,* but before pressing send, I deleted it. I hadn't cheated on him, not exactly. I typed again, this time only his name: *Noah?*

Holding my phone to my chest, I pleaded for it to buzz, to give me a lifeline. Twenty minutes later, after no response from him, the throbbing in my foot had finally steadied to a low hum and I pulled myself from the covers to standing. I'd have to wash the sheets. They held evidence of a night spent with bare feet pounded into clay-like mud. I touched my nose to the creased pillow. And there was also clear evidence of marijuana smoke. After stripping the bed, I deposited the linens and all of last night's clothing into the machine and set it to the sanitize setting. I would attempt to erase my missteps with baptism through hot water.

In the shower I decided I would leave before my mom came home. It was a chicken move, and I knew it. She'd saved me, yet again. Didn't I owe it to her to stay? One part of me ached to talk to her, to discuss the DNA test, but the conversation would involve a discussion about my childhood, about my brother, about lies.

There were answers I'd have to provide about my activities at the park and a lengthy discussion regarding my shattered relationship with Noah. In this hungover state, I wasn't strong enough to hold a mirror toward my mother, to make her face her truth. And I was terrified to have it aimed at me. Who would be staring back?

I dressed as quickly as possible and rushed out the door. Invisible chains held me in front of the house, the late-morning sun searing the part in the middle of my hair, as I realized I wouldn't be rushing anywhere. My car was still at the park. Hell. First order of business, retrieve my car from Liberty Park, the final piece of evidence from a night filled with shame.

I could call a cab and spare myself the walk,

but after my sordid night at the drum circle, some retribution (or suffering) was deserved. I would walk the sun-parched sidewalks between my mom's house and Liberty, and I hoped the thump of my steps would provide a rhythm to smooth my jagged emotions.

As I limped along the street, literally in the gutter where there was no sidewalk, my hair stringy and wet on my back and my toenail bleeding, I realized I had never been more alone. I couldn't get ahold of Noah, and if I did I didn't deserve to be rescued. I wouldn't call my mom, because I needed my head straight before I saw her; Ethan was in California; Grandpa Joe was gone; and after spending all of my emotion and time on Joey, I didn't have a single real friend.

Not to mention, I didn't know who I was. And, in all honesty, I had no idea who I was becoming.

The streets between my mom's house and the park, the roads I'd only witnessed as blurry smears of color whizzing past the window of my car, were surreal on foot. The commuter concourse rarely experienced pedestrian traffic, and the squares of disjointed sidewalk lay like crooked teeth, the enamel eroded by scrappy weeds.

An hour into my trek, thirsty from my marijuana hangover, I knelt on the ground near a leaky sprinkler to pull water into my cotton-filled mouth. Somebody yelled from a passing car as

I crouched on the ground, "Get a life!" I stayed low until they passed. I deserved everything I got.

After another hour of hobbling through a familiar landscape turned into a foreign country, sweaty, blood from my toenail dried in the rubber foot bed of my shoe, and sunburned across my forehead and shoulders, I received a fellow-comrade nod from the woman who was a regular panhandler on the freeway off-ramp near the park. How many times had I driven by her, wincing at her weathered skin and grungy backpack?

Now I waved back, thankful for a familiar face, realizing there weren't very many steps between where we both stood at this moment. With my own safety net full of gaping holes, it would only take a few more fragile lines to break before she and I would be swimming in the same choppy, unforgiving waters.

My phone rang and I checked the caller. My mom. The voice mail indicator was followed by a text.

Are you okay? I'm home now. Call me.

Several more blocks and another call. My trudge in the afternoon heat, interrupted by the ringing of my phone, was quite the opposite of soothing. I wouldn't answer, because my mind wasn't clear. My stomach growled like a denied lion. I should have eaten something before I left. I groped the edges of my purse for a dusty granola bar as my phone pinged with another text. I pulled it from my purse in lieu of a snack.

What happened last night? Honey, we should talk.

And now I knew what my mom wanted: to slip into therapist mode, to counsel her wayward daughter, when *she* was the one who was the liar. She'd raised me in a world of lies.

As I neared the park the phone rang again. Another voice mail. "All right already. Jesus." I held the phone to my ear and listened to the messages.

"Emma, we should talk about the test. I just received the results and I was going to tell you. It was a surprise to me. I'm sorry."

She was talking about the Canavan test? "I've got more unusual test results you'll need to explain," I said into the silent phone, jabbing at the delete prompt.

The next queued. "Baby, you're probably confused about my test results and troubled about your evening. Things will get better if you can talk through what happened, candidly, honestly. Call me."

"That's rich," I whispered. "How can she preach?" The words were poison on my tongue. I continued the conversation with myself as I walked, sweaty and hungry. "How could I possibly hold my marriage together? I was raised in a dysfunctional home, missing a father, kept from my brother. And all the things I believed were true—" I wiped a hot tear from my cheek. "Shut up, Emma."

I was in public having a lengthy conversation with myself. What the hell?

My phone rang again. And again, my mom. She'd worn me down. This time I answered.

"There you are," she said. "Where are you right now? We need to talk." Instead of being soothing, her plea covered me with a thick merengue of anger. The heat, my hunger, and my humiliation churned below the surface, mixing into a sickening sludge. "Emma?"

"It's rich," I whispered. "You calling me, saying we need to talk. Like *you* can counsel me through my problems."

"I want to talk to you as your mom." She was surprised. "I'm worried."

"But nothing you say is the truth," I hissed. "You lie as easily as you breathe."

"Emma?" Her voice shook.

"Don't call again." I pulled the phone from my ear and disconnected. Holding it in front of me like a bloody weapon, I stumbled back and sat on the curb, rocking myself, cradling the instrument to my chest.

Realizing where I was, deep in Liberty Park and only a couple of yards from my car, I staggered there and dropped into the front seat. After turning the key in the ignition, I directed the vents to my pulsing face and pulled my sweaty shirt away from my chest. As the air conditioner dried the moisture from around my brow and under my hair, I could think.

From where I sat, I could see the ground worn by the stomp of bare feet from the drum circle crowd, disbursed now, since it was Monday. Still holding the phone I prayed for it to ring. Would I apologize to my mom? Would I answer?

And when it did, I startled. But the number wasn't one I recognized, so I set the phone on the passenger seat. Minutes passed, and when the voice mail indicator sounded, I was surprised. When a solicitor called my cell, they rarely left a message. Suddenly desperate to talk to someone, anyone, in my solitude, I listened to the message. It was Noah's boss.

I was halfway to the hospital, his words filling the empty interior of the car, before the message ended.

CHAPTER 17

Two elevators, two flights of stairs, and I finally made it to the third level. And there I hit a dead end. Access to entry could be gained only through a locked door equipped with a doorbell and an intercom. I rang it, and not even a second later rang again. Then again. "Hello. Who are you here to see?"

"My husband." I leaned against the wall feeling like my legs would collapse. "Can I come in?"

"What's his name?"

"Noah." I gulped so I could tell her our last name. "Hazelton." As I said it, I hoped she would tell me I'd made a mistake, because there was no one named Noah Hazelton in this hospital.

But a buzz and a click indicated I said the magic words. As I walked through the door I read the sign above the intercom: NEUROTRAUMA CRITICAL CARE. *No.*

The nurses' station was only a few feet from the door, but I couldn't catch my breath, and I stumbled forward on the last step, catching myself on the countertop just before landing on the tile. A tiny woman with a short black ponytail rushed toward me. Her caramel eyes quickly assessed my condition.

For a moment I worried about my appearance,

wanting to appear respectable, knowing I'd just walked hours in the heat to retrieve my car from the park. My hair was likely stringy, my face sunburned. Would she know I'd done something awful and my visit to the hospital was penance for my misdeed? Or maybe she knew I didn't have claim to the husband I called my own.

Almost instantly, her features softened and she smiled warmly. "You must be Mrs. Hazelton."

She knew my name. Someone was expecting me. I nodded. With a guiding touch to the middle of my back, she escorted me to the entrance of a room several doors down. I could see activity inside, but before I could barge in, she said, "Let's stop here for a minute or two. I want you to know what to expect." I kept walking, trancelike, not heeding her warning. I had to see him. I had to see him for myself.

She touched my arm, pulling my attention to her. "I'm Talli."

I stepped away from the entrance. Manners somehow trumped more pressing things in this situation and I responded appropriately, which gave her a chance to redirect me. "I'm Emma Hazelton. But you can call me Emma." As I allowed her the familiarity of my first name, part of me wanted the nurse to continue to refer to me as Mrs. Hazelton because it was a solid reminder I was still Noah's wife.

"Nice to meet you, Emma." She stayed my

forward progress by continuing to hold fast to my elbow. "Okay, as you know, your husband has been in an accident. When you see him, he won't be able to respond to you. He's in a medically induced coma so we can reduce the swelling on his brain. What this means is, we want very little stimulation from his surroundings. Loud voices, bright lights, even continued manipulation of his hand, causes brain activity, and we want his brain to rest."

"I can't talk to him?" I leaned against the wall. How could I let him know I was with him and he wasn't alone?

"You can say hello and touch his hand gently. While we're in his room, I'll talk to you a little about what we're doing to help him, about the machines. Over several days, as the pressure in his brain subsides, then, yes, you can talk to him."

Uniformed people moved quietly around a shadowy table. In a crowd, Noah always directed traffic, his physical presence and personality large in the room. Not sensing him, I retreated. Even injured, I should be able to feel him here. The nurse had clearly directed me to the wrong place. "I don't think this is right—"

I stepped back from the wide door to double-check the room number, embarrassed that I'd nearly invaded the most intimate of scenes for this ailing stranger, and found myself pressed against the resistance of a small, warm hand steady against my spine.

At my protest, Noah's boss, a friendly man named Doug Winters, turned around. I blinked several times, thinking it was odd he was here. Such a small world.

"Emma," he whispered. "Come in, they've just got him settled."

I took another step backward, but with a tender touch Talli blocked my departure. "It can be a little unsettling at first, but come in and I'll explain what's happening."

I shook my head, even as I walked forward. It couldn't possibly be him. The man who lay like a felled statue, surrounded by whirring machines and covered with tubes, couldn't be Noah. But two more furtive steps into the room and I recognized the strong line of his nose. A tiny sob escaped as I moved nearer. The rest of his face was mutated, made alien from attachments and swelling. This figure wore a frightening, yet familiar, mask.

Someone had shaved a swath of hair at his crown, and the flash of naked scalp surrounded by his thick, coppery strands reminded me of a patchy fox. The baldness was punctured by a tube sewn into his skin with dark, jagged stitches accentuating the ghostly white. The thin hose protruding from his head was hooked to a bag, and pale liquid seeped from his skull into a clear plastic container. As I studied it, a second nurse adjusted the angle of the line.

"Spinal fluid," Talli told me. "We're draining it so the swelling in his brain doesn't cause damage. And the bolt"—she pointed to a piece of thin metal rammed into his scalp next to the tube—"that's an intracranial pressure monitor, or you'll hear us refer to it as an ICP. It tests the pressure in the brain and sends the results to this machine, here."

I felt as if I was at a car lot with a salesperson leading me through the features of the latest model. This information couldn't be about my husband, a man so vibrant he couldn't be defined by the machines keeping him alive.

A different hose, a reticulated one the size of my pinky, protruded from his gaping mouth and was taped to his upper lip, pulling his features into a sneer, and a separate tiny line curled from his nose. He looked as if he'd been overtaken by aggressive plastic snakes.

And his hands. Those hands that held me, that once held our child, were still. Before this moment they were never at rest. Noah spoke with his hands, worked with his hands, loved with those hands. And now they lay curled, like wilted blossoms. I touched his thumb carefully, wanting him to respond and at the same time not wanting to disturb him.

"You can touch him for a minute. Just watch out for the IV lines on his forearm."

"When will he wake up?"

"Not until we let him. We're keeping him calm and asleep so he can heal."

My fingers quivered against Noah's thumb, and I couldn't help myself. I leaned toward his ear. "Come on, baby, wake up. Come on, Noah?" I touched his hip, pressing into the solid warmth beneath a thin sheet.

"Don't worry, we'll wake him when he's ready," Talli said gently, pulling me away and leading me to an empty chair in the corner of the room. Before I knew it, I was sitting. She pulled up a chair next to me.

Though Talli appeared calm and not out of breath, as she sat beside me a heavy inhale then a lengthy exhale filled the room.

"What's that noise?"

"Which one?" And then I realized the otherwise subdued room was full of sound: chirping monitors, whispering doctors, and a suctioning, groaning noise that increased at measured intervals, then subsided into a nearly subliminal sigh.

"It sounds like the room is breathing."

"The ventilator. The tube in his mouth. We're breathing for him while we have him sedated, otherwise his body would forget to do it on its own. Plus, we monitor his blood pressure. He's getting IV antibiotics and liquids. The NG tube in his nose is to drain stomach secretion."

"Why?" I didn't know what I was asking. Why Noah? Why the pressure? Why the coma? Why?

Nurse Talli understood. "Say you roll your ankle, it would swell, right?"

I nodded. I didn't know what she was talking about, but her explanation held me to the chair and stopped me from breaking into pieces.

"Well, the brain swells when it's injured, but the trouble is, the brain is encapsulated in bone. There's nowhere for the swelling to go. The body responds to this pain and injury by rushing even more blood to the site, which is typically the right thing for the body to do when damaged, but since the brain can't swell freely, the swelling *itself* will further damage the brain. So we sedate to take away the pain response. We take over vital functions so the brain can go on break. We also drain the spinal fluid, anything to give the brain room to expand. Sometimes we even cut the skull and remove a piece—"

I gasped.

"But we're not there yet. Don't worry. Our initial steps so far seem to be working."

I stood again, wanting to crawl onto the bed beside my husband and feel his arms wrap around me, making everything fine.

Noah's boss was talking to a man taking notes on a clipboard. They spoke in hushed tones, but sensing my inspection, Doug smiled and welcomed me into the circle. "If you want to step into the hall with us, I was just giving a report so the hospital can initiate the workers' comp benefits. I can start at the beginning for you."

The second man gave me a sympathetic nod and closed his notebook. "I think I have enough for now. I'll put this into the system and you can fact-check the documentation later."

Alone in the corridor with Doug, a man I always liked, I could get answers. He was a burly fellow with a round belly and balding head surrounded by thick fringe (when he donned a hard hat, he gave the impression of a full head of lustrous gray hair, so he rarely took it off). He wasn't wearing it this afternoon.

"Why is Noah here?" I blurted. "Wasn't he in St. Louis?" If I could relocate my husband back to Missouri, then he couldn't possibly be lying in a hospital room in Utah. "Why?"

"In the hospital or in town?"

I blinked. I couldn't wish him away from this. "The hospital."

Through the open door I could see Talli moving near my husband, noting the levels in the IV bags hanging on either side of the bed. She typed several things into a computer suspended on the wall and then she stepped out. "Emma, I'll be back in a few minutes. Collect your questions and we can talk more soon."

I nodded, and Doug started his explanation.

"Noah flew in from Missouri this morning. He was on his way from the airport when he stopped at the site. His travel bag is—" He pointed to the duffel Noah purchased for our honeymoon and now used for business travel. It lay unattended in the corner of the room. "Anyhow, he decided to check on the Civic Center project between the airport and home. I was in the construction trailer and I didn't see what happened, but the guys say he was on the roof when some of the tar paper must have come loose. It was windy, and it may have startled him. I don't know. The pitch wasn't steep, but he stepped back and lost his footing. He was close to the edge.

"The fall was only twenty feet or so, and he seemed to land fine. He started to stand, even after hitting the ground, but then he crumpled and we couldn't get him to wake up. I was out of the trailer by then because of the commotion. We immediately called an ambulance and they brought him here. He's only been at the hospital for an hour or two."

I stared at him unblinking, hoping for some reassurance.

He had none. "You know, Emma, it seems crazy. He was wearing a hard hat." He knocked on his skull. "I've seen men get up from a similar fall and continue to work, but he just must have hit wrong."

I willed a rewind of the scene: Noah falling but landing like a cat low on its haunches, then sauntering away like nothing had happened.

"I think he's gonna be fine. He got up. He started to walk—"

The room inhaled, and I matched the slow exhale before speaking. "He doesn't look fine to me."

Doug left and the medical staff moved in and out of the room, but no one asked me to leave, so I stood by Noah's side and, instead of holding his hand, I rested my palm on the mattress next to it. I imagined his fingers finding mine. I willed them to move. "I'm right here, Noah," I said quietly. "Please open your eyes. Stay with me and I'll never let you go."

Time must have passed, people swirling about me while I remained still, like a pylon at high tide. Before I knew it, my mom was next to me.

"Emma." She wrapped her arms around me from behind. "I'm here," she said, her lips next to my ear.

"How did you—"

"You texted me Noah's name. But when I questioned you, you didn't respond to any of my return texts or calls. I tracked your location on Find Friends."

"I texted you?"

She held her phone toward me. I had. But I

didn't remember. Asking for her support was so reflexive I'd called out to her without conscious thought.

"Oh, baby. Tell me what happened."

So I took her into the hall and told her as well as I could, standing at the doorway, pointing out tubes and what they were for, my explanation enhanced with technical terms by Talli, who joined us after hovering in the background. Her shift had ended an hour earlier, but she stayed with us to repeat the specifics with Noah's parents when they arrived only minutes after my mom.

It was clear Noah hadn't told his parents I'd moved from our home. There was no hesitation in their support of me. Of us. As we surrounded him, Noah's mother took a moment to caress her son's shoulder through the printed hospital gown. I imagined her cradling him when he was a child, when he could fit easily into her arms.

Tears fell as she touched him, and Noah's dad, unable to take the emotion of the room, left and paced outside the door. Eventually she said, "I'll take Ben home. He doesn't do so well in these situations."

And then it was just me and my mom.

There were so many things between us, so many questions I wanted to ask and none of them mattered. She was here and I needed her.

She pulled up a hospital regulation straight-backed metal chair next to mine, and I leaned into her shoulder. "You hanging in there?" she asked quietly.

"I can't believe he's really here." I rested my head against hers, whispering so if Noah could understand my words, he wouldn't hear me. "I was going to give him up. I was going to walk away from him. He was mine, and now I might lose him."

"You won't lose him, baby."

A night nurse came in and further dimmed the lights in the already dusky room. "We're changing shifts again. You're free to stay, but he should be fine through the night. Things are stable"—she paused while she checked his monitor—"right now."

"You should get some sleep, Emma."

I shook my head. "I'll stay."

"We can bring a cot, or the recliner can be adjusted so you're nearly horizontal. We can work around you."

Relief in the form of immense fatigue made my eyes burn, dragging me unwillingly toward slumber. The nurse adjusted the recliner so it lay next to his bed. "This is probably the most comfortable of the options."

"Thank you."

"I'll bring clothes tomorrow, or sit with him in the morning while you go home to shower." My mom stood and stretched. "My goodness, it's after midnight."

"It is?" I'd been in a time warp, another dimension where huge, crashing events could occur while no time passed at all.

After all the nurses left, I reached across the arm of the recliner, the stickiness of the artificial leather adhering my forearm in place, and I caressed the swell at the base of Noah's thumb twice. Then I removed my hand and let it rest next to his. "Noah. I'm still here. Just stay with me and I'll be here as long as you need me."

And I meant it. But when he woke and remembered everything that had passed between us, would he still want me around?

CHAPTER 18

"I think your phone is ringing." A man I didn't recognize, a nurse with an earnest face and round glasses, leaned over Noah to inspect the IV site on the arm closest to me. It was a little startling to see a stranger's face so near mine and to realize amid the continual muted cacophony of the room that I didn't even notice my phone, a sound that typically triggered a primal response.

I managed to get it out of my purse and into my hand before it stopped ringing. "Ethan?" I whispered.

"I woke you, didn't I? I'm sorry."

"It's okay. I was only able to nod on and off through the night anyway. The hospital's not like a room at the Hilton."

"Mom texted, and Anusha talked to her for an hour last night, so we know what happened. I can't believe it. How is he?"

I gazed at my husband, silent and still on the bed. His accident hadn't been a bad dream. He would appear almost peaceful if he wasn't taped and tied up like a poorly wrapped gift. In this medically induced tranquility, he could also be mistaken for . . . I turned away. I wouldn't think of it. "I haven't talked to a doctor this morning, so I don't know if he's any better, but there was no emergency during the night. Ethan, it's eerie. I keep staring at his face thinking he'll open his eyes and he won't. He can't."

"I want to see him. To see you."

"Please come!" I whispered. "Mom and I would love to see you—" I stopped, realizing there were still many questions between the three of us that hadn't been answered. Of course they mattered, but looking at my husband, the import was insignificant.

"I want to see Noah," Ethan said quietly. "But I don't want to see Mom."

"Could you put this aside for a while?" I tried to stand, to maneuver the recliner so I could leave the quiet room and convince my brother.

There was silence on the line. "Let me talk to Anusha and check my schedule at work."

"Ethan, please."

Before I could stand, a neurotrauma surgeon I'd seen the day before walked through the door, and two nurses followed him like a tailwind. One was Talli. She smiled at me. The other was the man who'd checked on Noah minutes earlier. "I've got to go, Ethan," I said before he could respond. "The doctor is here." I disconnected before I heard his answer. These doctors didn't dillydally, and I wanted to hear everything he had to say.

The surgeon had a military haircut and ice-blue eyes. I could imagine him healing the infirm using his laser-like vision alone. But when he smiled at me, he revealed a wide gap between his two front teeth, and he was immediately human. I watched silently as he ran his fingers up and down Noah's arm, checking his pulse, lifting his hand about an inch and dropping it to the mattress. He pulled back Noah's eyelids, checked the readouts on all the monitors, talking as he worked. The nurses took notes as fast as he could speak. ". . . EVD drain looks good. How were his pressures over the night?"

Talli responded, "Between the fifties and sixties. Well controlled."

The doctor nodded. "Let's keep sedation where it is for today."

Finally he turned to me and extended a hand. "Good morning, Mrs. Hazelton." I took it, feeling his confident strength embrace my fingers and race up my arm. Nothing bad could happen on this doctor's watch.

"Noah is doing fine this morning. We're going to keep him sedated today, so you won't notice any change in his behavior, but things seem to be progressing appropriately. The swelling in his brain is slightly lower, which is good news. After the pressure is closer to normal, we'll take him off the sedation and see what we have."

"What do you mean?"

"The best way to gauge brain function is through observation. I believe he was unconscious upon arrival?" He looked to Talli to verify this fact, and after she nodded he continued. "If he'd been conscious in the trauma bay we wouldn't have sedated so we could judge the brain functionality, but at the point we worked on him he was unresponsive. We took further measures to sedate, to reduce the pressure in his brain."

"Wait. Will he be the same when he wakes?"

"We were lucky. We controlled the swelling early in his injury. I have high hopes, but we'll know better once we reduce his medication."

"His parents," I whispered. "They'll be here in an hour. Could you tell them? His dad will want all the details, and I don't think I can . . ." Pressure filled the space behind my cheekbones until tears from lack of sleep, and lack of certainty, pooled in my eyes.

"I can talk with them," Talli said. "No worries. I'll watch for their arrival."

I nodded and fussed with the footrest on the recliner, trying to get my toes to touch the floor. To give the appearance of control, I needed my feet firmly planted.

Talli rushed to my side and pushed a flat button near the armrest. "This thing is tricky."

The doctor extended a hand to help me upright, and finally I was standing.

"I feel good about his progress," the surgeon said, meeting my eyes directly. "There will be no change today. You can go home, get some real rest, and be ready for more news tomorrow."

I nodded again, emotion too close to the surface to speak. Every ounce of kindness was magnified when the uncertainty and horror of the situation were so close at hand.

The flock of medical personnel flew out the door as abruptly as they arrived. Alone again with my husband, I touched his jaw, marveling at how his whiskers continued to grow overnight, unaware everything had changed.

I put my cheek next to his, letting the bristle scratch my skin, employing the morning greeting I used to receive from Grandpa Joe. Grandpa called it the "whisker kiss." Once I described it to Noah, he incorporated a variation of it into our mornings as newlyweds, waking me with a scruffy cheek, then chasing me around the room. Once caught, he would flip me onto the bed and tickle my stomach with his chin.

"Good morning, baby," I whispered against his neck. "It's been too long since we've awoken in the same room, but this"—I looked around the tiny space, boxes of lifesaving equipment surrounding my husband—"this isn't ideal either. You need to get better so we can go home. Together." My volume increased as I spoke, the last word nearly a shout. I wanted to shake him awake, to reach him in his slumber with my cry. *Open your eyes! Be okay!*

The ventilator inhaled and exhaled. Noah's chest rose then fell with artificial breath.

"Good morning, sweetie." I pulled away from Noah with a jerk, caught. My mom stood at the door, two Starbucks coffees in a cardboard tray in one hand and a bag of clothing in the other. "How was your night?"

"Never a dull moment in a hospital room," I whispered, scolding myself for speaking desperately to my husband, for doing exactly what they told me not to do.

"How is Noah?"

I pulled her into the hall. "Less swelling on his brain, but they're going to keep him sedated today." I wouldn't tell her how they would not be able to fully assess the damage to his brain until they allowed him to wake.

She set my bag on the floor and the tray of coffee and scones next to it, then she took me in her arms. After she released me, she pulled a paper cup from the carrier and handed it to me. "Caramel macchiato?"

"Yes. Oh God, nothing sounds better." I cradled the cardboard mug in my hands, allowing the warmth to travel from my fingers into my palms before taking a sip. The sweetness on my tongue and the warmth in my belly, and I was thawing. "Noah's parents will be here in a few minutes."

My mom glanced to the corners of the tiny room. "I'll wander the halls while they're here so you can all fit, but until then, let's have a quiet coffee together. Even when nothing else is good, coffee is."

A few minutes later, Noah's parents arrived. His mom, Delia, who was typically well out-fitted, her hair a short, impenetrable bob of dyed auburn, had it pulled back into a sloppy ponytail. She appeared more youthful than I'd seen, the vulnerability in her face making her childlike. His father, on the other hand, looked years older. His face was puffy and like his son, he was unshaven. Today he appeared more a vagrant than a businessman. His mom hugged me and his dad nodded, as if words were more than he could muster through his sorrow. As promised, Talli breezed toward them and began explaining their son's condition.

As she spoke, Noah's dad turned toward an empty corner and inch by inch made his way to the edge of the room, where his face was invisible to the crowd, but I could tell from the shaking in his shoulders that he was crying. And he was embarrassed that we were there to see it. I stared at his quivering back not knowing if I should approach him, or touch him, or ignore him.

Of course my mom knew what to do. From the open doorway she said, "I was going to take Emma home for a warm meal and a shower. The doctor's already told her that Noah's condition will remain constant for the day, so I may insist on a nap. Besides, there's only supposed to be two visitors at a time in these little ICU rooms." She patted at my arm, pulling me from a trance. "What do you think, Emma? Should we leave now and give the Hazeltons some time with their son?"

"Um . . . yes, we should." I took a step backward, away from my husband's side.

Noah's mom looked at me, then at her husband, who hadn't removed his attention from the wall, and mouthed, "Thank you."

CHAPTER 19

I fell asleep in the car, like a sentry guard finally off duty. My mom led me to the spare bedroom, turned back the sheets, and closed my door.

I must not have moved for hours, because when the text indicator on my phone chimed, the east-facing bedroom was lit with early evening dusk.

"Noah!" I dove for the phone resting on the nightstand. He was awake and texting me to pick him up! I believed it, and as the message hovered on the screen for several seconds before fading to black, I was disoriented to the point that I inspected the case on the phone, wondering if I held the wrong device in my hand.

Hey girl. How you faring?

The number wasn't familiar. And then it hit me. It had been only two days since I met Barry in the park. Only two days and he wouldn't know everything had changed, that my world and my plans had been forever altered. I scrolled to the bottom of the screen and blocked his number. If I saw him at the farmers market, I could apologize and say I lost my phone. No need to be rude, but I didn't want him in my life. Not now, not ever again.

I was summoned to the kitchen by the gentle click of my mom's shoes on the tile floor.

241

Tonight, along with chopping and stirring, it was clear she was preparing for a conversation about her Ashkenazi test panel. And about Noah. And about the future. But did she suspect the reason for my angriest words? Surely she wondered, but obviously other, more serious issues demanded our attention.

The food smelled delicious and my stomach growled, but I was anxious to get back to the hospital. Did I have time for this conversation with my mother? With quick fingers, I checked for other messages as I listened to my mom's circular conversation, out of sight but not out of earshot. There were no calls from the hospital. No indication of a change in condition. Noah's parents texted an hour before I woke, letting me know things were fine and they were going to leave for the evening but would be back the next morning and hoped to see me then. Delia thanked me for giving them some time to be alone with their son.

Since Noah's condition hadn't changed, and he'd had company all day, I realized this might be the perfect time to talk to my mom about the DNA test. I would take the evening to dig to the bottom of this pit of uncertainty, then I would join my husband for the night. I hoped the truth would give Ethan purchase to scale the invisible barricade separating him and our mom. And hopefully once he made it to the other side, he would feel strong enough to visit Noah. To visit me.

My mom smiled when she saw me standing at the archway leading into the room. "Hey, sleepy. I wondered if you were out for the night."

"Can I help with anything?"

"You slept like a log." She reached toward me and touched the pillow marks on my cheek.

"I know." I put my own hand to my face. "I saw them in the mirror. I don't think I moved an inch."

"Sure you can help. Or you can relax and I can finish up."

"I want to be useful."

"Okay, then, you can stir the garlic and onions while I finish chopping the tomatoes." She pulled me next to her at the stove. "I'm making spaghetti sauce the old-fashioned simmer way. I figured a warm dinner might be nice."

"It should give us plenty of time to talk."

She looked at me but didn't respond.

"And we might need some time, because I have some questions I didn't want to ask you at the hospital, when Noah was right there."

"Okay. I imagine this is about the test?" Her tone was cautious and at the same time gentle. She wouldn't fight me with her sharpest weapons when she knew my softest spots were exposed.

I cleared my throat, wondering where to begin. Worry about Noah coated all the surfaces in my mind, and yet the truth of the DNA test pulled my attention to a darker, more suspicious space. If I wanted an unfettered path into my mom's arms while he was sick, it must be now.

"So . . . before the accident, when we spoke on the phone you sounded really angry. What was going on?" My mom broke our sizzling silence, glancing at me sideways, her pause inviting me to respond.

"I'm sorry I was a little crazy on the phone. It was a rough day." As it turned out, even when I hit rock bottom, the day still managed to become worse. So much worse. "I need a little truth now. Can you do that?"

"I'll try." My mom's face was wary, covered with a controlled calm.

"Mom, have you ever kept a secret?" I wanted her to guess my intention. I wanted her to tell me the truth without forcing her hand using the test results. I wanted her to blurt it out like it had been burning her up all these years. And I wanted her to apologize.

"We all have secrets. What kind of secret?"

"Like one that might hurt someone if they found out?"

She stopped chopping for a second. "Do you want to talk about what happened at the park the other night? Is there something you want to tell me?"

I shook my head. Not yet. This wasn't about

me. I gestured to the pan I was guarding. "I think the onions are soft. Should I turn off the heat?"

My mom responded by bringing over a bowl of chopped tomatoes and dumping them into the pot. She added some salt, turned the burner to low, and poured two glasses of red wine. "What if we go outside while this simmers?"

The backyard of my youth was different now. These days my mom had more time to garden, so the space was no longer filled with weeds. She had a bountiful, if tiny, garden and the trees were bigger. It was pleasant, but like most things from my childhood much smaller than the jungle I roamed when I was young.

I changed my approach. "Mom, do you know any women who've been raped?" I asked her as we sat, not really thinking about the harshness of the question. My mom choked on her wine, coughing into her hand. In pondering the genetically confirmed differences in my paternity from Ethan's, I'd attached myself to this explanation. My mom was raped and she didn't want us to know about it.

"Oh my God, Emma!" She dropped her therapist facade. "Did something happen?" Her face was pale.

"Not to me. I mean, in general." I tried to speak calmly. I meant to shock her into admitting to an incident in *her* past, something to explain the difference in the DNA results, not to turn this on myself.

"Sure, many of my patients have been raped." She resumed control.

"Have any become pregnant?" I studied her face, which remained placid.

"Honey, you're bouncing all over the place. Where are you going with this?"

"Nowhere." I swallowed. "That was a stupid question. I just read an article."

My mom wrinkled her brow. "How about we talk about you and Noah? And Noah's accident."

I shook my head. I couldn't talk about Noah, not yet. But my mom and I had all night. What *did* I want to talk about? We had so much to discuss, I didn't know where to begin.

"How about we talk about lies?" I lapsed back to my original accusation. Lies were a vital strand in the DNA that bound me to my brother, as well as separated me from him. The threads, the chromosomes, were a tangled, confused knot.

"First secrets, then rape, now lies. Maybe you're redirecting your uncertainty over Noah into this conversation." She spoke with a forced monotone.

I started to protest. She held up her hand.

"But, baby, I want to know what's on your mind, so let's talk about lies."

I took a deep breath. "How could a person tell a lie lasting a lifetime?" My thoughts, like an indefatigable fly, flitted about Ethan. Why would our mother lie to me and my brother for so many years? We had mismatched DNA. It was a secret she harbored for my whole life.

"A vague question." She paused to see if I'd fill in the gap. When I didn't, she continued. "There are many reasons a person would lie. Most of the time the person wants to spare someone from pain, either their own pain or the pain they might cause the person they are lying to." She swirled her wine, studying it. "Maybe the lie is easier than the truth. For everyone."

"But when the lie is discovered, doesn't it cause more pain?"

"Often," she said. "Is there a particular lie you'd like to talk about?"

"Yes. It's about the test."

Like she'd been stung, my mom jumped from her deck chair and ran into the kitchen. "The sauce!" she yelled from inside the house.

By the time I joined her in the kitchen, she was draining the noodles as if nothing was amiss. She busied herself with the meal, employing the distraction technique she'd used through the years of my childhood, allowing her to leave the discussions about Ethan and the custody arrangement incomplete. I wouldn't fall for it this time.

I followed her and retrieved the block of parmesan from the refrigerator and the box grater. She poured us both another glass of wine. I forced myself to hold to the topic at hand until we could return to the conversation.

In step, we walked toward the sliding glass door, full plates and drinks in hand. The reflection of the two of us side by side emphasized how similar we were. Same height, same curves. My mom had her hair in a ponytail, and mine was in a knot at the base of my neck. Our cheekbones were illuminated by the overhead light. We had the same heart-shaped face.

I smiled at my reflection to define myself as one of the two specters in the glass. My mom smiled in return, translucent mother and daughter connecting through a wavy image.

How much would I hurt her by forcing her to tell me the truth? Yes, I needed to know why Ethan and I weren't full siblings, but I also knew it wouldn't change anything. My mom would always be my mom. The same woman she'd been two days ago, the same one who cradled me as a child. And my brother would always be my brother.

Resting my plate on the small side table between our chairs, I sat and cleared my throat and resumed the conversation. "Mom, we were talking about lies. There's this test—"

Before I could finish my sentence she blurted, "Canavan disease. You saw my results on the genetic panel. I'm a carrier too. I'm so sorry,

Emma. If I'd known . . . if I thought to take the test earlier . . . I would have."

She believed I was talking about *that* test. Again, I'd almost forgotten she'd taken the Ashkenazi Jewish Genetic Panel. It was inconsequential now, compared to what I was about to tell her.

"You couldn't have suspected," I dismissed. "You're not Jewish, and neither is Dad, I don't think. But it doesn't matter. I'm talking about a different test. I'm talking about a complete DNA panel, like the one Ethan took."

Silence fell between us as I plotted my next move, but before I could tell her about my results, she spoke. "So, you had a wild night out? You were a little out of it when I picked you up from the park the other night, and you smelled like a Grateful Dead concert."

Derailed from my intended conversation and tongue-loose from the wine, I giggled. This conversation was so absurd. My husband was in a coma, my son was gone, my grandpa was dead, and we were talking about the park. "You noticed?"

Like a fine crack in a dam, the laughter released a flood and I choked between guffaws, my ribs aching. I set my plate on the patio and gulped at some water to control the hiccups that followed. Before I knew it, I was weeping.

"Baby girl." My mom stood behind me and

stroked my hair. She didn't speak until I finished, supporting me with her presence.

"Okay," I sniffed after several minutes. I didn't even know where to begin.

"Okay," she replied, leaving the conversation to me. "Tell me about the park."

"The park . . ." I paused. Fine, I would start there.

I recounted pieces of the night, the desire to be someone else, to forget who I was, if only for a few hours. She nodded, understanding. And it *was* understandable, until I examined my true reasons for the excursion.

"There's more."

My mom rested her hands on the crown of my head, a gentle reassuring pressure. "Do you want to tell me?"

"It's more than what I did. It's what I *wanted* to do."

"What did you want to do?"

"I didn't cheat on Noah, if you're asking." I took a deep breath.

Silence was her response to my defensiveness.

"I could have. But I didn't," I said, lashing out, angry at myself. "And yes, I was stoned."

Now she returned to her chair so she could communicate without words. Her therapist goal: to allow me to move through the emotion before worrying over a solution. God, I was a volatile mess.

"I went to the drum circle to meet this guy Barry I used to know from the farmers market."

She nodded. She'd likely met him once.

"I planned to sleep with him that night."

She shook her head, telling me it was a bad idea.

"I planned to sleep with him . . . so I could get pregnant! I want to have a healthy baby, and I can accomplish that much easier if Noah isn't the father. And I considered it. I considered conceiving a child with a man who isn't my husband. And not telling Noah."

"Why?"

"I want a rewind. I want a baby. I want Joey back." I gulped as I said my son's name, and continued speaking in a rasp. "I want a family and I want Noah. But those two things are mutually exclusive."

My mom drew in her breath, her scrutiny leaving my face and resting on her own hands, and I knew I'd hit home. Without meaning to, somehow I'd turned this conversation the direction I intended to take it in the first place.

How similar were we? What independent decisions, separated by decades, might my mom and I make, leading us to the same point? Somehow she'd had a child with a man who wasn't my father, and I was considering the same.

"I think you might want to seek some marriage

251

counseling, you and Noah, with a therapist who isn't your mother." She spoke while picking at a crumb on her pants. "I'm finding it hard to separate my own emotions from yours."

She placed her plate back on her lap and slowly spun her fork in the cold noodles. She chewed and swallowed with forced concentration, but I didn't turn from her. Finally, she faced me, the lines in her face deep with anguish. "You understand, don't you, Emma?"

"I don't understand anything, Mom. But I'd like to."

"I can refer you to someone. You and Noah need to work this out together. When he's out of the hospital, of course."

I would say it. I would just throw everything I knew sky-high, like shards of glass, and I would attempt to bandage the deepest cuts.

"Mom, Ethan and I *both* took a DNA test," I said. "We know we are only *half* siblings. Is that the reason you're having a hard time talking about this? Because it has something to do with you? Because you had a child with a man who wasn't your husband?"

Her hands shook, and her fork rattled against the ceramic plate. I took her dish from her lap and set it on the small table between our chairs.

"Please help me understand why we got these results," I begged.

"It was my fault," my mom said. "I was to

blame. And I can't tell you, because I promised your father."

"You weren't raped?" I'd centered myself over this explanation. My mom had been raped, and I was the product. After I was born, I figured she met Greg Gontrum and they had Ethan together, but in time fell out of love. Greg took his biological son and left me with my mom.

"Raped? No. I was a willing participant, and though it happened only twice, it unraveled everything we'd created together."

"Who? You and Dad?"

She nodded. "It was so long ago, but the consequences continue to resonate."

I thought of Ethan, his infrequent visits, his tense relationship with our mother, and I knew what she was talking about.

"You asked why a person would lie?" she asked. "I'll tell you. It's because you can't bear the weight of the enormous mess you've made, because you pray things will work out for the best, or they'll change given enough time. At first, it's avoidance of pain, but the truth drifts away, the distance between reality and the original lie are so far removed from one another, the situation can't be bridged with words. Soon, the lie is the truth. The lie dictates how things are, in reality."

"Where did your lie start? Tell me, so I can understand."

"It started with protecting your dad, with protecting Ethan. It ended by harming Ethan and harming your dad. All these years later, I don't think the truth can change anything. Our truth is where we are now. It's where we've lived for over twenty-five years. The moment to change things passed a long time ago."

"But maybe if we knew what happened, it would help? Please, Mom."

She turned inward. "What does Ethan think? I can talk to you about this, but will he ever talk to *me?*"

"He's the one who suspected things weren't as they seemed. I think he also wants to know what's real. It's what's driving him now, *knowing* is what matters."

"And after he knows? What then?" She paced the length of the wooden deck.

"He talks to you? We pick up the pieces?"

"It's not what happened to you years ago, it's what you do from this point forward." She spoke to herself, soothingly, as she might consult a patient. "The *next* step is more important than dwelling on past mistakes."

"But if we don't ever know the past, Ethan and I will be in this limbo forever," I pleaded. "Maybe what's important *is* the next step, but before we take it we have to see where our feet are."

She shook her head. "I promised your dad."

I followed her lead. "You tried to protect Dad. What were you protecting him from?"

"From my mistake. From my betrayal."

"Okay." I used her banal acknowledgment, and it worked.

"I was at the end of my clinical training, and Ethan's father was a patient. He was damaged and vulnerable. He was beautiful and broken. I believed I could fix him with my love. All graduate students were warned how easy it was to develop a connection with a patient, and how easily the connection can become sexual. It happened twice, the thing between us, and after the second time we were together, I changed clinics. I severed contact with this man, but it was too late. I was pregnant. I convinced myself Ethan could have belonged to your dad. We were happily married and sexually active. My betrayal was short lived, so I didn't tell him. And right after Ethan was born, your dad had a vasectomy. You know Greg, the environmental idealist: two children, only enough to replace yourself. . . ."

"Recycle, wind power, organic. Passionately self-righteous, bordering on insane."

Her laugh was wistful. "Always uncompromising in his passion. It's what brought us together, and in the end it was what tore us apart. He always stuck to what he thought was right. And what could I say? 'Don't get a vasectomy. This baby might not be your child'?" She sighed.

"But it was fine. It was good. We had our girl and our boy, our complete family. Until your dad began to suspect."

"Why did he suspect?"

"Ethan's eyes never turned from baby gray to blue. They were, and are, the darkest brown. I don't know. . . . His coworkers teased him, asking what the mailman looked like, and Dad started to compare you to your brother. Your baby pictures, the shape of your hands compared to his, and to mine, even Ethan's lactose intolerance. Your dad wouldn't stop questioning me. I didn't know for sure, so I laughed it off. I didn't offer an explanation and we continued to live, tense but together. Until Ethan was two."

"What happened when Ethan was two?" I would have been six, right before my parents divorced and my dad took Ethan away.

"Ethan's father found me," she whispered. "It wasn't like I was hiding. After I left the clinic I didn't hear from him, so when I quit working to have Ethan, I didn't think to conceal my personal contact information. Turns out he'd been institutionalized not long after I was transferred. The next thing I knew, this man was on our doorstep."

"Ethan's father?"

"Yes. Greg told him to leave, and I tried to talk to him, to tell him I wasn't practicing anymore, to refer him to another counselor. We finally got a restraining order because he wouldn't leave us alone. I was scared your dad would figure out this man was Ethan's father, because seeing him again, the resemblance to Ethan was striking, same almond-eye shape, same olive complexion. But I was more scared of the man himself. He was unstable and drawn to me."

"So what happened? Why did Dad leave and take Ethan away from us?" Déjà vu overwhelmed me as I asked the question. I was certain throughout my life I'd asked the same thing many times, but my mom had never given me the answer she was giving me tonight.

My mom averted her gaze to the velvet night, collecting herself. I went to the kitchen and got her a glass of ice water, placing it between her limp hands. After drinking to the bottom, she set it on the table and continued without prompting.

"Greg told me he knew who the man was. My ex-patient had returned while I was out, and from his restraining-order-required fifty feet, he yelled to the whole neighborhood that Ethan was his son."

"And Dad believed it?"

"It confirmed his suspicions."

"So you told Dad the truth?"

"Yes. I shattered him with the truth."

"So if Dad isn't Ethan's biological father, why did he want custody?"

"Ethan's biological father was unstable—

dangerous, in fact. I won't go into details now, but we were afraid. The police were involved on several occasions. It was terrifying."

"Oh God."

"Greg and I both loved Ethan. We were both worried this man would make a justifiable parental claim. And if he did, Ethan would be paternally bound to someone who could cause him harm. It scared both of us. That was when your dad talked about moving. I thought he meant all of us, that we'd get out of town until things settled. But a week later he served me divorce papers. He packed his bags that night. When I saw the terms—he would get full custody of Ethan and I would get full custody of you—I was shocked. I got on the phone with a lawyer right away. I was ready to fight.

"But he convinced me it would be wise to move Ethan out of the state, away from this unstable man. At first I believed it would be a short-term move. I insisted we should all go, even if we were legally separated. I told him we could continue to be a family, and didn't he want a family? I wouldn't sign the papers."

"But then?"

"He wouldn't change his mind. As a last-ditch effort, I asked him why he wanted Ethan if Ethan wasn't his biological son. At my question, your dad sobbed, a man who never cried." My mom's voice wavered at the memory. "He reminded me about the vasectomy, that ours was the only family he'd ever have. He said I had robbed him of it."

"So why did he leave? He could have stayed and continued with our family."

"He said he didn't want me to be his wife. I wasn't who he thought I was and he didn't want to pretend that everything was as perfect as it had been. He didn't want to live in the place where all his hopeful memories lay. He told me I caused everything to come crashing down. And I had.

"But he didn't want part-time children either. He wanted a child who wouldn't remind him of what could have been. You were my tiny twin. You reminded him of our life together. He said Ethan was a blank slate. He could have a new home with a new family."

"I think I understand," I murmured to myself. "Maybe just a little bit." My dad believed everything once precious and beloved, everything imbued with possibility and hope, would be forever tarnished by what happened. He wanted to run from his dreams, from what could have been, and I understood. Sometimes I wanted to run from mine.

"So I signed the divorce papers because it was my fault. Because I was guilty. Because I believed given some time to heal, your father would soften his position. You are, after all, his biological daughter."

"But he never did." I remembered my father's stoic features, sometimes lingering too long on my face when I was a child, enduring my annual weeklong visit. I remembered him clearing his throat over and over, like something was stuck there, when I caught him staring.

She shook her head. "He never did. He had the legal right to keep Ethan. I filed an appeal when it seemed your dad wouldn't come around. But I withdrew it when I learned that Ethan's true paternity would be addressed in court. I didn't want to pull his biological father back into his life. Not after all we'd sacrificed to keep him out."

"I understand," I said.

"I also worried that if I dragged Ethan from his home, I might strain Ethan's relationship with Greg. If I upset Greg by taking partial custody, things could have turned out much worse. Not to mention, all those years away from your brother stretched and snapped the fine bands of affection Ethan had for me when he was a baby. I was the mother who abandoned him, who sent him away. He loved you, his sister, but he was wary of me."

"Would it have hurt to tell Ethan the truth? Sometimes believing you were lied to is worse than facing it. Don't you think Ethan could have handled it? At least when he became an adult?"

My mom nodded her agreement. "On several occasions, once we believed Ethan was safe, once this man had disappeared for several years, I urged Greg to tell Ethan the truth. Ethan was still young, and it wouldn't have mattered any more than telling a child they were adopted. There's no stigma there, maybe a little curiosity, but it's not the end of the world."

"True."

"At first Greg said he would. But he delayed. As Ethan got older, Greg was scared to present him with evidence he'd already been lied to for years. And when Ethan questioned him directly and Greg denied everything, he said he could never go back. You see, your father didn't want his uncertain bond with Ethan damaged in any way. He was worried that with any information Ethan would search for his biological father, find him, and leave forever."

"The snowball lie. You told the snowball lie."

Her lips were pale, pressed against one another. "Sometimes a knife wielded with the best intention cuts the deepest." My mom took a breath and leaned back in her chair. Her story had been told.

In the silence, thoughts bounced in my head like caroming pinballs: But what about me? What about Ethan? What were we owed? When I learned the results from my DNA test, I wanted a tearful apology from my mother. I wanted her begging for my forgiveness. I wanted to go back to the fateful moment when my dad stepped away from our family and deprived me of my brother. Ethan and I were the innocents. We deserved to see our parents' remorse. After all, my mom was guilty and my dad was proud. Like the tails on two wayward kites, Ethan and I were forced to follow them as the wind blew our family apart.

My mom's face reflected the pain, which had been bottled up all these years, now uncorked. How could I ask her to comfort me when she lost her son? She was overwhelmed with guilt *and* loss. Though Ethan and I were raised apart, we always knew we were apart, *together*. We were distant allies, fighting against a common enemy, and as such, when we became adults, it was easy to resume a friendship.

No longer did I want to punish her. Her pound of flesh had been paid. I stood, and this time I was the one who reached for my mother, to comfort rather than be comforted.

CHAPTER 20

It took twenty-four hours to organize my emotions before I felt I could contact Ethan. I spent all of them at the hospital. When I arrived that evening, at peace with the explanation from my mom and well rested, the night nurse informed me that Noah's mercury levels, meaning the swelling in his brain, had receded enough that I was allowed to hold his hand. For as long as I wanted. I could also freely talk with him, and after my unsettling conversation with my mom, lifting this restriction was like removing ankle weights. I could talk with my husband! Although Noah couldn't answer, I could touch him with my voice. I could explain everything that had happened over the past several days and together we could swim to the surface.

So I did. I talked for hours about Ethan's suspicions, Anusha's pregnancy, my mom's mistake, and how that mistake—and all the decisions made afterward—affected my childhood. When I ran out of words I pulled out my phone and set it on the mattress. I turned on the Joey playlist, as we called it, and together we listened to music from all of the outdoor concerts we took our son to, moments of summer perfection as our baby sat between us, surrounded in song.

Eventually, I laid my cheek on Noah's chest. The filling and emptying of his lungs may have been accomplished by a machine, but his heart thrummed strong.

"I forgive her," I murmured against him. "We can't know what would have happened if she didn't hide the truth. Ethan may have been raised by this other man, who may have harmed him."

Noah's chest rose and fell. "She was trying to do the right thing, but we never know exactly what's right, do we?"

At some point in the night I fell asleep with my head on the mattress next to my husband and my arm draped across his torso, his warm body a familiar presence even in this foreign place. By the time the cafeteria brought a breakfast of watery cream of wheat and flaccid bacon, I had decided what I would tell my brother.

More than anything, I wanted to give him my sense of peace, of forgiveness. I wanted the truth to heal rather than sever. Ethan didn't see our mom on a regular basis. He didn't have a good relationship with her, and he didn't hear her speak her story. He was also the one raised by a man who wasn't his biological father. Indeed, his wounds were deeper. They'd leave a larger scar. I hoped I could convince him to visit, not only to see Noah but also to talk with our mom.

After considering carefully crafted phrases designed to convince and inspire my brother, I gave him the facts, as well as I could, without too much personal bias. In the end he'd be the one who would forgive. I did, however, remind him that the first cut in our relationship was made when my dad decided to move away. Ethan could now choose to bring the edges of the wound together and see if it would heal. He could have a relationship with our mother and a grandmother for his children. He only had to open the door and let her in. I knew from the rose-colored weeks we spent as a threesome—Ethan, our mom, and me—that she'd been knocking his whole life.

"Will you reconnect with Dad?" Ethan asked, after I had my say.

"You know, I'm not sure," I replied. I hadn't considered the possibility. "Mom always reached out to you, but I never got that from Dad. He built the wall surrounding the two of you so solid and secure, I don't know if there's a way for me to enter."

Ethan acknowledged the truth with his silence.

"Now that you know what happened, will you try to contact your biological father?" I asked. "You worked so hard to discover the truth, aren't you compelled to see who he is?"

"You know what scares me?" Ethan paused long before continuing. "My father is a man with a mental illness. He gave me enough of himself, genetically, that I knew I didn't belong to our dad and our mom. But what else did he pass my way?"

"What do you mean?"

"I mean, is there a genetic component to mental illness? I've got his earlobes. Does it mean in a few years I'll be headed to the loony ward?"

"You and your leaps. God, Ethan, not everything has to do with genetics. He could have suffered some trauma as a child. Or maybe he had an addiction."

"I'm *not* going to find him," Ethan said all at once. "I don't want to know."

"Dad will probably be relieved to hear your decision."

We were both silent for several seconds. I smoothed the condensation off the glass of ice water I'd nursed while we talked. There was one question I wanted to ask my brother. A question only he could answer. We were the two people equally affected by these events.

"Ethan, now that we know the truth, who do you blame? Was it Mom's fault for the affair or Dad's for being too proud to forgive?"

"Mom's," he said without hesitation. "If she hadn't slept with that man, none of this would have happened."

"Right, but if she hadn't slept with him, you wouldn't be who you are. You wouldn't be you. You wouldn't exist . . . at all." As I said it, I understood what Noah had been telling me all along. About being Jewish. About the disease. About placing blame.

Noah was who he was because of all his ancestors who came before him. And I was the same. We couldn't help who we were or what diseases we carried, but we could control who we were to each other. We had to choose. We could build from where we stood, but we couldn't change where we were standing. In that instant, I wanted my husband to open his eyes. I had something to tell him. I knew what I wanted.

"You're right," Ethan said. "I didn't consider it that way. I am who I am because of Mom's mistake. I'm not sure what to make of it."

"So? Will you visit? Noah and I could use your company."

There was a pause, so long that I pulled the phone away from my ear. But he hadn't hung up; our connection was solid.

"Anusha and I will leave in the morning."

I loved that Ethan was my brother. And I loved that we were in this together. Whether we were half siblings or whole, we weren't alone.

CHAPTER 21

A week had passed since I'd lobbed my last round of résumés into the world. So much had happened since I sent them, I nearly dismissed the e-mail from Nordstrom as an online advertisement until I noticed the header: *Open Position.* I opened it.

Nordstrom, the largest department store in the city, was interested in interviewing me for a retail position in the activewear department. It was a sales job and didn't exactly match my prior experience, but perhaps my combined years of yoga instructor and organic scarf curator would be adequate preparation for the job.

I held the phone toward my mom so she could read the e-mail. "So fantastic, honey! Call them now and set something up."

Glancing at Noah, I expected his mouth to curve into a smile at the news. He'd been so patient for a full year after Joey's death, I knew he would be excited to see I was taking steps. But I couldn't leave him. "I can't go to an interview," I told my mom. "It's hard enough to go home to shower. Shouldn't I stay here?"

"He's not going anywhere soon." My mom smiled gently. "If you want, I'll stay while you go and I'll call if there's any change. But you know, honey, you might want to pursue this. Who knows what will happen when Noah wakes. Even if workers' comp helps, there will be expenses, you'll need insurance if he can't go back to work, and there are other things to consider. Nordstrom is a good company."

I nodded. She was right.

Ethan and Anusha arrived that evening, and the next morning Anusha helped me fix my hair, hovering as I dressed. I was thankful for her cheerful company as I slipped into a form-fitting athletic dress I purchased from Nordstrom the summer before Joey died (figuring the dress would show solidarity). I was nervous, but not about the interview. With Anusha by my side, I knew Ethan was at the hospital with our mom. Alone.

As I applied my makeup and pulled my hair back into a loose bun, I wondered if anything my mom would say to Ethan would soften my brother's resolve.

"I think he already forgives her, you know?" Anusha realized my preoccupation wasn't about possible interview questions. "He came here to see you and Noah, didn't he? Despite everything, he feels better simply knowing the truth."

I placed the final bobby pin as she spoke, and upon seeing the end result, Anusha applauded. I felt it too. I was at the bottom of a well, darkness surrounding me, but there was light above. The interview was the first foothold toward reaching it.

After I got ready, I called the hospital one more time. Talli must have memorized my number, because she answered, "Hi, Emma. Things are stable, but tomorrow could be a big day. His pressures are nearly normal, and in the morning the doctor plans to wake him. Don't worry about him today, and good luck with your interview."

"Thank you. Wait, how did you know about the interview?"

"We nurses keep tabs on our favorite patients."

I smiled. I was surrounded with care.

The artificial hush of the high-end department store was soothing—the music not blaring, just loud enough to lull shoppers to stay and spend. Spend and stay. Perhaps working at Nordstrom would offer the perfect amount of superficiality to fool me into believing everything was as perfect on the outside of the air-conditioned walls as on the inside.

I checked my phone to see if I had a few minutes before the interview to indulge in a tiny browse. I had three. Not enough time to buy anything, which was fortunate. The danger of working here? Obvious, I thought, as I passed through the shoe department, unable to resist touching several pairs of heels to graze the leather, turning each over to scan the price, and placing each back on the display table as if they were made of glass. Expensive glass.

Quickly I made my way to the human resources department to ward off further temptation. After registering with the receptionist I wandered the large waiting room. The ceiling-to-baseboard windows on this floor provided a bird's-eye view of the Salt Lake City Temple, the headquarters for the Church of Jesus Christ of Latter-day Saints.

The immaculate grounds surrounding the temple were maintained as if they'd been touched by the hand of God himself. Rows of color-coordinated blossoms marched alongside the sidewalks and were mounded in terraced beds. From my vantage, I couldn't spot a single wilted petal or brown leaf. Tourists mingled below me in the square, staring at the cut granite walls of the castlelike temple, mouths agape as they arched their necks to spot the glistening gold statue of the Angel Moroni perched atop one of the six spires.

As a child, when my family and I would walk the grounds to celebrate a tulip display rivaling the Netherlands, or Christmas lights better than anything in Rockefeller Plaza, I imagined the hidden contents of the great temple would be spectacular. For if the grounds of Temple Square, which were shared with members *and* nonmembers, were this beautiful, imagine what kind of heaven would be held within the walls of the temple building itself.

Though I'd never been a member of the Mormon Church, after Joey's diagnosis I'd allowed the missionaries into my house, seeking some kind of answer to the situation I was facing. If polite conversations with two young men in tidy white shirts and matching name tags could provide some solace or perhaps a miracle, I would partake. I would have gone to a chapel, a synagogue, or a pagan altar if there were some hope of reversing Joey's condition. It just so happened in Salt Lake City, the most readily available contact with the divine was through the Mormons.

And the members were so kind, offering to help around the yard, bringing casseroles and open invitations to neighborhood gatherings. Turned out I didn't have a problem with the Mormon Church, just with God in general, because when faced with a crisis, wasn't everyone praying for the same thing? A miracle?

Of course, miracles weren't guaranteed, regardless how hard people prayed. Or to which church they belonged. Or to which God they appealed. In response to my questioning, the answer was always placating: God gives you what you can handle, or God wanted your child back in his sacred arms, or bad things happen to good people. All of which I thought was crap. I wanted my son to live.

Although I eventually rejected the doctrine, a person could appreciate the physical beauty of Temple Square. So, maybe after the interview, if things were fine at the hospital, I'd cross the street and wander the grounds for a few minutes, taking peace where I could find it, hidden in the interplay of shadow through the quaking leaves of a redbud or reflected in splashes of pastel light in a bed of lavender hydrangea.

The receptionist gestured me to her desk. "Your interviewer was just pulled into a quick human resources conference call. I don't think it will be long, but if you're in a rush, we can reschedule."

"Oh." I glanced at my cell. It was still early. Ethan had probably just arrived at the hospital. If anything, I should give him and my mom some time. "I guess I can stay."

"Great! I can get you water, and there are magazines on the table."

"Water would be nice."

As she left to retrieve a bottle of water, I fished in my purse for my lipstick and emerged with the ziplock bag containing the book of German poetry. I hadn't used this handbag since the day I went to the farmers market. It seemed like decades ago, but in fact it was not even two weeks earlier. How could it be?

The binding crackled as I opened the volume and touched the German script.

To my love—J.

This book, a lock of blond hair, and a child's crayon drawing were all tucked into the cookie tin belonging to my great-grandma, Emmeline. Why? An unknown woman in a wedding photo. Who was she? My grandpa's foreign birth. And he never told me? These were the simmering questions before Noah's accident, before everything boiled over, scalding me.

"Emma Hazelton?"

The woman standing in front of me wore a tailored navy suit. Her hair was pulled into a chignon so tight that it stretched her wrinkles into smooth creases. But her smile was bright, and despite the rigid updo, her lipstick was fuchsia. The moment I shook her hand the burning questions about my grandpa fell away and I was thrilled to speak with a contemporary who didn't have the slightest idea about the rest of my life.

I didn't want to talk about Noah or Joey or Grandpa Joe. I didn't want sympathetic eyes searching my face, almost wishing I'd shed a tear to illustrate my justified sadness. I didn't want a consoling hand on my forearm, the gentle squeeze accompanying the sentiment *How are you doing?*

"Quite a view, isn't it?" She nodded toward the window. "I wish they'd come to my house and work a little magic in my front yard. Why don't you come with me and I'll tell you about the open position."

The conversation went well. After we talked, I got a quick tour of the building and met the woman who would be my manager. After the interview, instead of celebrating with a purchase I couldn't afford, I made my way out of the store.

I called the hospital. Again Talli answered. "All is well. Take an hour or two. Doctor Zhang will check his levels on his evening rounds, and if all is well, we'll start reducing sedation. You'll want to be here for that. So enjoy this beautiful day. This may be your last chance to take a few minutes for yourself."

"Okay," I said, turning my back to the sun, letting the heat soak into my spine, melting department store goose bumps from my chilly arms.

Talli was right, the weather was perfect, and a few minutes out of the artificial light and climate of the hospital was liberating. After grabbing an iced coffee, I decided to wander. I always told my yoga clients to steal a second or two to breathe, no matter where they were, so for a moment I'd follow my own advice.

As I entered Temple Square, enormous trees cast cool shadows on the wide, flower-lined sidewalks under my feet. I inhaled. Of course, there were multiple pairs of Mormon missionaries milling about (in case the beauty of the place inspired religious conversion), but they were unassuming and smiling and they kept their distance.

Several minutes of relaxation breathing created a gentle hum between my ears. I enjoyed the pace of my steps until I crunched my way through the ice at the bottom of my cup. It had been a good day. A productive day. Noah appeared to be on the mend. Who knew what the next weeks would bring? But in this moment of no projection, no looking back, things were good.

Peaceful and satisfied with my tour, I headed to the nearest exit to navigate my way back to the parking garage.

Typical to most large urban areas, in downtown Salt Lake City beggars were quick to set up in the path of tourists leaving a popular site, and the sidewalks surrounding the temple were no exception. Just outside the gates, a weathered man sat on a yoga mat, his legs crossed and splayed. He was absorbed in his own relaxation breathing, apparent from the even fall and rise of his chest. Watching him, I was reminded of the slow metronome of Noah's ventilator, his breath of life.

The yogi's hands were at rest on his bent knees in the position of Gyan Mudra, the Mudra of Knowledge. His presence calmed me, and without meaning to, I matched my breath with the deep rhythm of his. Aware of me now, he bowed his head and chanted the word I would say at the end of each of my classes. It was a greeting or a closing. *"Namaste."*

"Namaste," I whispered.

Tucked between the thumb and pointer on his right hand, as he maintained the Mudra position, he held a small sign with script that read:

For One Dollar Discover What You Seek

Resting near his knee was an old, black bowler hat partially filled with dollar bills. Clever. Most people, and especially the religious, the ones who might visit the temple, were seeking answers: Where did I come from? What is my purpose? Where do I go after I die? This man promised sought-after knowledge, for just one buck. This beggar, Zen in his promise of discovery, touched me. And wasn't I also questioning? I recalled my conversation with Noah before I set him free. *I need to know who I am.* Could this man answer my questions for one dollar?

Not one to give in to panhandling (I'd been schooled in giving to homeless organizations rather than individuals), today I opened my purse, took out a dollar, and tucked it among the others.

Sensing my payment, he spoke like a coin-operated fortune-teller. "Thank you, young lady.

The answers to the questions lingering in your soul are much closer than you imagine."

He didn't continue, so I nodded at his horoscope-like statement, closed my bag, and turned to resume my course to the underground parking garage. His advice wasn't overwhelmingly helpful, and definitely not worth a buck. Before I could take a step another beggar, a woman in clothing that had likely been on her body for several weeks extended a hand. Her mouth was barren of teeth.

"Since your purse is open?" The stench of her rotting gums hit me like a wave. I pawed the depths of my bag for another dollar, shoved it in her direction, and made for the crosswalk to separate us by the width of a road. Once across I was farther from my car, but I figured I could angle back at the corner and circumnavigate the long way, avoiding the remaining panhandlers stalking the popular tourist sight.

Glancing to the street corner to gather coordinates, I spotted a sign on a three-story brick building. In permanent metal letters it read:

FAMILY HISTORY LIBRARY

And below the sign hung a temporary banner, which read:

Find Your Ancestors—Find Yourself

I took a step back and put a hand to my chest; my pulse beat rapidly against my palm. Would it be possible to find myself in this library? Was this information what the gnarled man had promised? The answers to the questions I'd been asking?

Pulling my bag to my chest like a life vest, I wandered close to the reflective-glass front doors to peek in. I couldn't see movement inside, so it was probably closed. But before I could raise a hand to tug on the handle, the door was swung open by a round-faced, bald man who was likely over eighty years old. He ushered me inside. The building engulfed me in the embrace of air conditioning similar to Nordstrom, like a hug claiming, *Things are better in here.*

But this newish building didn't carry the perfumed fragrance of a department store. It held the lingering smell of an old library full of leather-bound books, ancient volumes of pressed paper, and gold-embossed spines.

Another eager gentleman in a two-piece suit led me from the door to a welcome desk. These men were dressed like the young Mormon missionaries who visited my home, with an additional sixty years under their belts: same uniform white shirt, same name tags. However, they had rounder bellies and less hair. There were women in here too, each clad in a conservative floral skirt and boxy linen jacket spanning the colors of the rainbow. They were all smiling at my approach. There was no turning back now.

Within seconds I wore my own name tag, reading *First Time at the Family History Library* and my first name, which I'd written with excited, loopy script. I thought briefly about returning to the hospital, whether or not I was needed, but this much attention from people who reminded me of Grandpa Joe was intoxicating.

A short informational video for newcomers told me the library contained genealogical information from 245 countries, more than a billion individuals were listed on their search site, and I would have access to millions of rolls of microfilm records. There were thousands of books and periodicals from around the world on a variety of floors: floor B-1 for International and Scandinavian countries, B-2 for British Isles, and so on. Plus, there was an experienced staff of volunteers who could help me to discover the identity of my ancestors. Right this minute. For free.

The entire building was purposed for ancestral discovery, aiding in my own effort to prove my significance as one tiny drop in an ocean of humanity. Perhaps not everyone searched for truth among the branches of their family tree because they carried a genetic condition that killed their baby. Or had a grandfather who hid the truth about his country of birth. But they had their reasons. I wasn't an outlaw for questioning, and I wasn't alone.

I was ushered with brisk steps from the introductory movie room into a gigantic, open space full of flat-screen computer monitors, occupied by people like me. Each searcher was attended individually by a church-dressed octogenarian. A woman named Sister Callahan swooped over and directed me to my own monitor. There would be no waiting to ask a question at this library. With expert guidance, she walked me through the search sites available.

I touched the book of poetry in my purse as she set up my account. Could I find my grandpa in the records of this enormous library? Could I really find myself?

Pulling out my phone, I checked the time. Hours must have slowed. It wasn't even noon. And no more news from the hospital. With a sense of purpose, I slipped the phone back into my purse.

"Is there a particular person you're interested in researching?" Sister Callahan asked after finishing my registration. The cursor blinked with anonymous patience on a field reading:

Deceased Ancestor's Name

"Deceased?" I questioned.

"They have to be deceased, due to privacy laws and all," she explained as I studied the screen. "The living folks tend to be a little touchy about being researched by strangers. But the deceased? I'm sure they're happy to have a little recognition."

I pulled out the worn leather book. "I want to learn a little more about my grandfather. I guess."

"And he's deceased?"

I nodded, eyes glued to the keyboard so she couldn't see my face. "Recently."

"You could find the online obituary for sure. After you have a date of birth, you can start filling in the blanks."

"Oh, I already know his date of birth."

"Then you're ready," Sister Callahan whispered. "I'll be back to check on you in a few minutes. Have fun."

I studied the empty blinking field, considering, then I typed *Joseph Barlow*. Below his name, it read *Search with a Life Event* and gave me the option of *Birth, Marriage, Residence, Death*.

I chose the event *Birth* and was presented with two fields requesting *Birth Place* and *Birth Year*.

I'd memorized the obituary hanging on my mom's refrigerator and I ticked in the information *Manchester, England* and *1913*, then I pushed the Search button.

Three pages of Joseph Barlows scrolled on the screen in front of me, but nothing matched the other details I knew about my grandpa, like date of death, or spouse. Not one Joseph Barlow listed here was *my* grandpa Joe.

I backed up and retyped *Joseph Barlow*, but this time I searched with the life event of *Death* and added the date. Immediately displayed on the screen was a carbon copy of my grandpa's obituary. Below the obituary, on the same screen, was a census report from 1950, containing other verifiable details. And just that easy, I found him!

Head of Household—Joseph Barlow—aged 37
Wife—Virginia Barlow—aged 30
Daughter—Diane Barlow—aged 0

Oh my God, reading the names, my breathing stalled. My own mother a newborn and my grandma the same age I was now. They didn't know about my aunt Marsha, and at this particular moment, decades stretched long before I entered the scene. Several other digitized documents verified his existence; another census from 1960. This time, Diane (daughter) was aged 10 and Marsha (daughter) was aged 7. Growing up.

Still nothing about Grandpa Joe's birth, however.

So I reset the search again, this time considering the *Deceased Ancestor's Name* field for several moments before typing the name of my great-grandfather, Nathaniel Barlow. At the *Search with a Life Event* prompt I chose *Marriage*. I typed in Salt Lake City for the place and 1916 for the date.

A full page of Nathaniel Barlows appeared on the screen. I scrolled through the information for another snippet of information to triangulate against, anxious to determine if any of these men named Nathaniel was my great-grandfather. There were several men named Nathaniel with pensions on record, some as far back as the Civil War. Several resided in Salt Lake City, but without a corresponding listing of a wife or children, I couldn't know for sure.

At this point I wasn't sure of my great-grandpa Nathaniel Barlow's birth date or his death date. After several failed attempts, I cleared the search bar and typed in *Emmeline Barlow*, then I chose *Search with a Relationship*, tagged *Spouse*, and entered *Nathaniel*. Again random references to several women named Emmeline Barlow, some married to men named Nathan, but nothing definitive.

This search was a little less rewarding than I anticipated. I shifted in my chair, tapping my feet on the caster, until the man next to me looked up. I smiled apologetically. I should just leave. I wanted to see Noah, but first . . .

I raised my hand, and this time a Sister Lambson responded. She was wearing an outfit I recognized—long floral skirt, nylons with orthopedic sandals, and a black tag with her name etched in white. "Can I help you find something?"

"I'm searching for someone, and I don't know enough about him to find the other information I'm looking for. Is there another way to search for the missing details?"

Sister Lambson rolled a chair next to me. "I see you've already searched for an online obituary?" She clicked a tab behind the search box. "If this is your person, then click on this icon, which looks like a headstone. There may be more information available using a gravesite search engine."

I did as she said.

"Now, from here you should be able to search for the person's actual headstone, using the approximate year of death. It will report more accurate results if you have a city, or at least a state, of interment, but this engine is a powerful tool. Many times you can find an actual photo of the grave marker."

"So, someone takes a photo of all the head-stones in *all* of the cemeteries?" I asked as we waited for the search results to generate.

"Well, not *all* the headstones, but you can find most gravestones from most cemeteries, all across Europe, and in many other parts of the world."

Three Joseph Barlows emerged on the screen as we watched. And one was my grandpa. There was a photo of the double marker placed when my grandma Ginny died, and someone had already established the relationship between my grandparents. "Wow! This is crazy."

"If the deceased don't have many other records, you may learn a little more this way. It's all about zeroing in on your target." Sister Lambson turned to walk away. "Check it out and call me if you have other questions."

I stared at the screen. There was another headstone at the same cemetery I could search. But I wouldn't. I pressed my lids together to clear my head. This computer wouldn't help me find my son.

So what did I want to know? I wanted to verify where my grandpa was born, right? And I could do that by expanding my search to his parents, my great-grandparents. But I had no idea when my great-grandfather Nathaniel had died. Scanning Grandpa Joe's obituary again, it stated his mother, Emmeline Barlow, practiced medicine with him until her death in 1955. 1955! I had her death year.

Not even a minute later, I had her, an image of a side-by-side headstone for Nathaniel and Emmeline Barlow, birth dates and death dates for both of them. I leaned forward, my face only inches from the monitor. This was like solving a puzzle, following clues, each piece of information leading to another.

After targeting Nathaniel Barlow using his date of birth, the first result that seemed to correlate

with the other information I knew was a cer[
from 1930:

Name	Role	Age	Birthplace
Nathaniel Barlow	Head	38	Utah
Emmeline Barlow	Wife	36	Utah
Joseph Barlow	Son	17	England
Blake Barlow	Son	13	Utah
Deacon Barlow	Son	11	Utah
Hyrum Barlow	Son	9	Utah
James Barlow	Son	7	Utah
Aaron Barlow	Son	4	Utah

Grandpa Joe was a teenager! I couldn't picture it. He was seventeen years old and living with an overabundance of brothers. I touched the screen. What I would give to emerge in their house in 1930, a silent spectator, viewing my deceased ancestors as children. They existed like this, in this snapshot of a moment, my grandpa in a houseful of siblings. But more practical than interesting, this report confirmed his birthplace and date.

I clicked back to the search results. There was one more possible match. I clicked on the record, a census from 1920:

Name	Role	Age	Birthplace
Nathaniel Barlow	Head	28	Utah
Rosa Barlow	Wife	25	Germany

Emmeline Lansing	Boarder	26	Utah
Joseph Barlow	Son	7	England
Blake Barlow	Son	3	Utah
Deacon Barlow	Son	1	Utah

Rosa Barlow—*Wife?* It would appear this was the wrong record, except everything else matched. I raised my hand, and within seconds Sister Lambson appeared near my elbow. "Have you seen this before?" I touched the screen where it read *Boarder*.

"Sure, a census is a listing of everyone in the household at the particular moment the census was taken. I've actually seen a census taken at a prison, and the role of every individual was listed as *Inmate*." She peered closer at my screen. "It was pretty common to let a room to a friend of the family, or rent a room for money, or have a widowed auntie live in as a boarder to help with the children. Perhaps it's what happened here."

"Yeah, but look at this." I clicked the back arrow to the census from 1930, ten years after the one listing Rosa Barlow as the wife. "See, here, Emmeline isn't a *Boarder*, she's the *Wife* and there's no sign of Rosa. Emmeline was my great-grandma, and I've never heard of anyone named Rosa. Could there be a mistake?"

"Sure, it's possible. The people who key in these records are just that, people. But sometimes there's a digitized copy of the actual census and—" She leaned forward and touched the screen. "Click right there, where it says *View Image.*"

The screen shifted and a document written in uniform, old-fashioned cursive verified the information I'd seen on the screen. Sure enough, Rosa was listed as *Wife* and Emmeline below her as *Boarder.*

"You're lucky, not many of these actual documents are digitized." She printed the documents for me.

"Would this be the head of household doing the writing? Because these other names on either side of the family"—I touched the screen again—"are written in a similar hand."

"No. An official census taker would write these documents, walking from house to house, asking questions of the inhabitants. These listed names were their neighbors. See here, you can read the address. It's easy to see where mistakes could be made, but often you can find other documents matching your search and piece things together. Often, though, it does take some time."

"What time is it now?" I asked her as I reached in my purse for my phone and clicked it to see the illuminated time. Two hours had passed. Butterflies flew to my throat, knowing I'd been gone from my husband for so long. It was too easy to follow one clue to the next, sometimes not remembering what I was searching for, backtracking, and losing myself in the digitized documents. I didn't even notice I missed lunch.

"I've got to go. My husband . . . I can't believe I've been here so long."

"It's easy to do. Just tell him you've spent the afternoon tucked into the branches of your family tree. I'm sure he'll understand."

I dashed out the door, an empty feeling in my gut. If I told him, would he hear me? But if he could, I knew he'd understand.

CHAPTER 22

I rushed from the Family History Library directly to the hospital, where I talked to Noah late into the evening. Contrary to what I saw in the movies, there was no such thing as visiting hours at this hospital. I even asked the night nurse about the policy, wondering why no one scolded me to get out.

"It's been clinically proven that patients heal faster when surrounded by family. So stay as late as you want. Tell him about your day. Help him remember there's life outside the walls of this hospital."

And so I did. I talked as the room glowed with sunset and blackened with night. I told him about the job interview and my hope to work in the city. I described my homeless yogi meditating outside the temple grounds and his prophetic sign, and I detailed my visit to the Family History Library. I asked him what he thought about the strange woman named Rosa who was listed as my great-grandfather Nathaniel's wife on the 1920 census.

The hospital settled into a muffled silence, the halls dimmed, the footsteps of the night nurses became panther-like as they prowled from room to room.

As I drifted, I promised, "Tomorrow you'll

wake up and I'll be here by your side. Just like old times." I pulled the somewhat comfortable recliner closer to his bed, linked my pinky through his, and together we slept.

Talli woke me while it was still dark. "Big day today. They started to wean Noah off the sedation in the middle of the night, so we hope he will show some signs of awareness by early rounds. You might want to get up and grab some coffee. Once the doctors get here, you'll want to be available."

I stood and gently uncurled my fingers from Noah's hand. His digits were still eerily unresponsive, but I imagined them flexing, grasping my hand and never letting go. Today. And it couldn't be soon enough.

I removed the tie holding my hair back in a ponytail and wiped the sleep from the corners of my eyes. "I finally remembered to bring a toothbrush, and coffee does sound nice." The wall clock said it wasn't even six. "What time should I expect the party to start?"

"Probably by seven."

"I should call his parents."

"Call them if you'd like, but I detailed our plans with them yesterday. Mr. Hazelton was hesitant to be here when I told them what to expect. Don't be surprised if they want to visit later, after things settle. It can be intense these first few hours."

The room squeezed around me, blocking my air. Noah's ventilator wheezed and reminded me to inhale. Talli's foreboding tone worried me, but at the same time I would get Noah all to myself. I wouldn't have to temper what I said to him, or move aside for his mom to take her spot next to her son as he woke. "How bad will it be? Maybe you should tell *me* what to expect."

"He's not going to peacefully open his eyes and say your name, like in the movies. It would be nice, but that's not the way it works. We hope for early eye contact or recognition, but often, even in our patients who make a full recovery, this takes time."

I took a step toward my artificially calm husband and touched his cheek. "How will I know if he's going to be okay?"

"One good sign is purposeful movement."

"Purposeful movement? Will he be able to hold my hand?"

"At first he won't want to hold your hand. There will be coughing, gagging, pulling at his lines. Which is good. It means he's fighting. The ventilator is very uncomfortable when conscious, and pulling at his lines is purposeful movement. He won't be able to talk until it's out, which could be hours. When his coughing is vigorous and he's able to breathe on his own, we'll pull it. Even then, when he speaks, he may not know who you are or what happened. It will take a while before we can assess where he is cognitively. He'll likely be fearful and in pain. It's a hard time for most loved ones."

It was unsettling to imagine my husband being anything but in control and unafraid, but because of Joey's condition, my child's inability to purposefully move his hands or head as he withered, it was also strangely familiar. "I can handle it. I told him I would be here."

In the hour before the tiny room filled with medical professionals, I brushed my teeth and tried to fix my hair in the attached bathroom, bending at a ninety-degree angle to see myself in the mirror, which was tilted to accommodate those who might primp from a wheelchair. Talli offered me coffee from the nurses' lounge (which was leaps better than the lukewarm brew delivered by the cafeteria), and I called my mom.

She told me that she, Ethan, and Anusha were standing by ready to visit whenever I needed them. She sounded giddy when she told me she was making breakfast for the three of them and apologized for moving my things to her office for the night because Ethan and Anusha spent the night in the guest room.

Ethan was at our mom's house. On past visits he would stay with Noah and me, or get a room at a nearby hotel, but last night he stayed with my mom. Which meant the conversation must have gone well. Was she forgiven, or was Ethan trying to keep things easy and drama-free for my sake?

I imagined my brother once again sleeping in his childhood bedroom after all these years, the one decorated for his infrequent visits, the room he'd not slept in since turning eighteen. The bright morning sun would find entry through the shades, filling his room like it had when he was a child. Would he roll closer to Anusha and touch her belly, cradling the tiny being growing within, and be happy he had reconnected to his youth? I hoped so.

At five to seven the neurotrauma surgeon who spoke with me the first morning after the accident arrived with a team. He introduced me to a second surgeon, Doctor Zhang, and a medical student. Talli followed close behind with a nurse I vaguely recognized. They surged into the room and surrounded Noah's silent form, like dancers around a maypole.

The doctor described what he would be doing to Noah (though without giving as much detail regarding Noah's possible negative reactions), and the team made room for me near his face. I leaned in and spoke to him while they further adjusted his medication. I tried to visualize him, the way he was before he'd been pricked with needles and constricted by life-giving tubes. I imagined him smiling and saying my name. Once again, he'd be strong and able to hold my hand

and we'd walk away from this place. But I'd been warned not to expect so much.

He was unresponsive as I described the first night we met, the atmosphere in the yoga studio, my impulse to write my married name next to his on the registry, his escape from the room after shavasana, and his explanation for his speedy departure. "It was my voice, remember, Noah? Listen to me now and follow me here."

Nearly a half hour later, he opened his eyes. He didn't find me in the crowded room, his gaze softening with recognition. Two orbs rolled under heavy lids before filling with fear. Like lightning, he raised his taped and tubed arm to clumsily claw at the hose filling his mouth, scraping my cheek with nails that hadn't been trimmed in several days. I jumped back, holding my face, as the medical student stepped into my spot and restrained my husband's hands. Noah writhed.

"Is this normal?" I asked Talli, gaping at the man who pinned Noah in an attempt to keep him on the bed. The surgeon's face was bland, completely unconcerned at the commotion.

Talli nodded and made her way to Noah. She touched his shoulder. "You're in the hospital, Noah, and you're waking up. You're doing fine, and we're all here for you." He didn't seem to hear her. She gestured to me with her chin, to resume my spot near his face. "Go ahead and talk with him. You won't know exactly when your words will start to sink in, but he'll want a familiar voice in the dark."

For two hours Noah drifted and groaned. He opened his mouth like a fish gasping for breath. He didn't turn toward me, though I continued to speak. All the while the medical team monitored his breathing and pressure in his brain.

By noon he was coughing almost nonstop, filling his lungs and gagging, grabbing at his neck, his eyes rolling and wild. The veins in his arms were ropey and pulsing with effort. It was awful to watch, but Talli reassured me this was a good sign, and as if to punctuate her claim, the doctor decided to pull the breathing tube.

Finally free from the garden hose in his throat, he appeared to drop into unconsciousness, and Talli cleaned the tape residue from his slack mouth. Eventually he started to move again, and I leaned close enough to touch his ear with my lips. "I'm here. Noah? Baby? Look at me. You're in the hospital, but you're going to be all right. Can you hear me?"

His jerking movements settled for several seconds. I pulled back to see his face. His lashes parted, the whites were nearly scarlet with broken vessels, but he found me. His mouth moved, gasping. I leaned closer. "What?"

His breath was ragged, hitching, warm on my face, smelling of antiseptic. Not human breath, but medical. "I heard . . . you." He pushed the words out and sagged against the mattress, exhausted by the effort.

His mouth went slack again and I panicked, calling to Talli. "What's happening, where did he go?"

She touched my back. "That's all he has energy for right now. He's medicated and weak. But he saw you. He knew you. It's a very good sign."

Two days later, Noah could sit at a steeper incline for several hours at a time. They removed the tube from his nose, which had provided nutrition, and he was able to eat clear food: a variety of broths, gelatin, tea, and coffee. They'd also removed the spinal fluid drain from his skull. However, he still had an IV line in each hand and could speak only a few seconds at a time because his throat was so raw. But the conversation was comprehensible, and each word he pushed through his lips brought the whole room scurrying to his side to respond, to listen, to fetch, eager to gather the dropped jewels, the syllables that indicated he was coming back to us.

Ethan, Anusha, and my mom spent much of those days with me, all of us perched on uncomfortable chairs. We surrounded Noah's bed, talking across him as if he was part of the dialogue, staying on light subjects, including him like he was participating. Sometimes he appeared to follow our conversation. Most of the time he slept.

The day came when Ethan and Anusha were scheduled to return to California. My brother stood, making a last round of good-byes, but instead of staying with me and Noah, my mom gathered her purse and packed up the knitting she carried with her to busy her hands, ready to accompany him. "Let's pick up your suitcases from my house and grab some lunch on the way to the airport," she said to Ethan and Anusha. "We have time."

As Ethan bent to give Noah the typical man hug they reserved for one another, I reminded my brother that Noah had three broken ribs. He resumed the hug, gentler this time, but from behind the embrace, over Ethan's shoulder, Noah found me, wrinkled his brow, and then darted his gaze quickly between my mom and my brother. I understood him immediately.

"I'll tell you when they leave," I mouthed.

Of course, the biggest elephant in the room hadn't been discussed in front of Noah. He was sharp enough to know something happened between my mom and brother, because the suitcases were at my mom's place. Of course, every day they'd visited at the same time, but Noah was in and out, groggy from the medicine. Until this moment he hadn't noticed they'd arrived and departed together.

The room was empty and silent after everyone left. I pulled a chair next to Noah's bed. "DNA test?" he croaked. "I guess nothing amiss?"

I stroked his shoulder to the middle of his forearm, where he was pocked with craters from IV lines recently removed and relocated to the back of his hand. His arm was thin, and the freckles were especially bright on his translucent skin. This diet of liquid, no matter how much he ate, wasn't enough. "Hush. I'll tell you everything." I held the large plastic mug with the bendable straw toward him and he drank gratefully, his dark eyes not leaving mine.

"The results weren't what we expected," I said after setting the mug on the nearby tray.

So I told him about the test, the fact Ethan and I weren't full siblings, about my mom's indiscretion and the custody arrangement, about the Ashkenazi part of myself and of my mom. I speculated about the direction of her conversation with Ethan.

Typically on visits, when my mom and brother were forced into proximity, Ethan's jaw would twitch, his exits were abrupt, and my mom's conversation jangled as she cast energetic lines that Ethan wouldn't nibble. But over these past days in the hospital, they were at peace in the same room. Anusha and I watched the two of them, warily at first, but as the hours progressed we allowed their conversation to take the spotlight, relieved we didn't have to hold the ends of the thin rope binding the two of them together.

"But how are *you?*" Noah's lids drooped. He was fading.

"I was angry at first, but Ethan and I have always had each other, and we can't revise the past. Plus, I understand that my mom thought she was making the right decisions. At the time."

"Aside from the decision to sleep with Ethan's biological father?" Noah's sleepy smile softened his statement.

I swallowed. "That was a mistake. But who would Ethan be if she hadn't done it?"

Noah nodded and closed his eyes.

"Ethan is the one who must decide to forgive our mother, but I think he has. And no matter what, my mom is still my mom, and Ethan will always be my brother."

Noah's hand dropped from his lap to the firm mattress and his chin hit his chest. I lowered the incline on his bed so he could sleep.

I was awakened hours later by Talli checking Noah's charts. "Don't you ever go home?" I whispered, checking the corners of my mouth for drool. Sleeping while sitting was not glamorous.

"Don't you?" She smiled as she typed his vitals into the wall-mounted computer. She was the constant comfort to our days, and it seemed she was always available. "But, in actuality," she said, "I just got here. Swing shift today. How are things? I've been off for two days, but you've been so busy you didn't notice. I can see from his chart that things are going well."

"I think he's coming along."

"I'm alive," Noah croaked from the bed. He struggled to find the button to elevate the headrest. Talli found it and pushed it for him. When he was vertical, he grinned and I melted. This was his first smile that wasn't unfocused or untimely.

"Good nap?" I asked. "I slept too."

He was quiet for several seconds, as if internally monitoring his systems. "You know, I feel pretty good, considering."

"Uh-oh," Talli said. "You know what that means? You'll be leaving me soon. Another room . . . a new set of nurses."

"No one will ever replace you."

"Oh, you probably say that to all your critical care nurses."

I'd be happy to get out of this room, but Talli had been the calm in our particular storm. I *would* miss her.

My phone rang. The room was quieter now without the numerous machines keeping Noah alive. It was particularly jarring. Noah raised his brows.

"It's Nordstrom," I mumbled, then louder as it sunk in. "It's Nordstrom! I have to take this." I slipped out the door so Talli could continue to examine Noah without disruption.

After the conversation I stepped back into the room. "Doing some shopping?" Noah asked.

"Second interview!"

"What?" He shook his head. "How long was I out?"

"Well, some of these balls were rolling before you . . . you know? Before your fall. I was applying for jobs, trying to take a few steps toward—"

Noah focused on his hands.

"Toward being more independent," I said weakly.

"Where are we now, Emma? Are you still working on your independence?" Noah asked softly. His words weren't filled with pain from forcing them through a swollen throat, but his face told me they were agonizing all the same.

"No matter what happens, I'll need a job. I needed a job a year ago, after Joey—" I swallowed. "This is a good opportunity. There will be benefits, and it will help pay the bills."

"When I leave this place, do you plan to come home with me?" This was the first sentence Noah had spoken that lacked the swimmy tones of painkiller. His words were crisp, and he wanted a real answer.

"You'll need someone to take care of you." I avoided his stare.

"Do you plan to come *home* with *me?*" He raised his head, sitting straight, even without the support of the mattress.

"Do you want me to? Considering . . ." I bit the inside of my cheek to keep my voice from shaking.

This time he looked away. He sank back into the bed. "You and I hadn't spoken for weeks before my accident, you know? I wasn't sure where we were headed . . . things between us have been so crazy."

This was not a welcome mat, and I didn't deserve one. I was so concerned with Noah waking up and healing that I hadn't considered he may have already changed his mind. His note wasn't a continuing declaration of love but a closure. His intent, before the accident, was to do the right thing and end it decisively.

"I could just come home for a little while, to help you get settled." I rushed to fill the silence, to ease the awkwardness between us. "I could help out where you need it. I could drive you to doctor appointments, or whatever. It doesn't have to mean anything if you don't want it to. . . ." I took several shuffling steps backward toward the door as I spoke.

"That's not what I . . . never mind. I need to . . ." Noah pressed his palms to his forehead, his hands shook with the effort, but his features shifted after several moments, losing the hard lines. "When is the interview?"

"Tomorrow morning."

"Sleep at home so you're fresh. I'll be fine here tonight. Alone."

"If that's what you want." I stayed by the door, newly unsure of my place.

"But eat dinner with me," he soothed, taking his hands from his face and reaching one toward me, beckoning me to his side. "Nurse Talli said I get creamy liquids: mushroom soup, mashed potatoes, and pudding for dessert." He smiled more widely than this bland menu should warrant. "It's a celebration dinner. But then I want you to get a good night's sleep . . . at home."

"At home," I agreed, our words mingling in the air between us. But I still didn't know, did he mean *our* home?

CHAPTER 23

Our house, like my grandpa's, after only a few days of abandonment seemed to settle in upon itself. Empty of the people who inhabited the rooms on a daily basis, it had become smaller, the ceilings sagging without the buoyancy of human energy. I planned to clean the place after the interview. Even if it no longer belonged to me, the least I could do was fix things up, to make it ready for Noah's return.

The next morning, after dressing as professionally as I could on short notice, I pulled up Nordstrom's online catalogue and compared the items for sale to those available at Athleta and Kohl's. In an hour of quick prep, I was firm in my knowledge of bandeau versus removable cup bras and was ready to go. Dressed in leggings with a subtle print, a drapey cashmere shawl, and a silk tank top, I hoped I looked like a casual professional, the perfect example of a woman who knew her gym-to-office clothing. I needed this job.

And then the phone rang.

It was Lydia from Nordstrom asking to delay the interview until the afternoon. I assured her it was no problem, sighed into the mirror, and called Noah. I'd visit him until the interview, if he'd have me. The hospital was close to the store anyhow, so it would be easy.

Noah answered his cell, but he sounded out of breath.

"Are you okay?"

"The room is full of people. Can I call you back?"

"I'll come up now. My interview was delayed."

"One second," I heard him whisper. The commotion on his end of the line faded. "They're getting me ready to change rooms."

"Hold on, I'll be there in minutes."

He was quiet for several seconds. "Wait for a little while. Then come." He sounded sheepish.

"Why?"

"They're removing the Foley."

"And you don't want me there?"

"And giving me a laxative. All this bathroom stuff is embarrassing."

"Gotcha." I laughed. "But important. Everybody goes."

"I hope that's true." He chuckled.

"My interview is this afternoon, so I won't be able to visit until after that. It could be quite a while."

"Then come later and tell me how it goes. By the time you get here I'll be showered, shaved, and able to piss like a man."

"Okay. But if you change your mind, I have the morning free."

"I guess you could come if you want. . . ." He hesitated before speaking again. This time his voice was timid. "I have a few other things I need to take care of. Some paperwork and stuff."

"The workers' comp? I saw a stack next to your bed."

"Yes. That's it. The workers' comp." It was clear he didn't want me to visit.

"I know what I'll do." I paused, hoping he'd change his mind. He didn't speak. "I'll go to my grandpa's. I still have a bunch left to organize, and maybe I'll discover something new about this Rosa woman I told you about."

A variety of muffled sounds and several sharp clangs rose through the phone on his end. "I've got to go," he said. "They're back and waiting to torture me. See you this evening?"

"Yes," I said as he disconnected.

On this visit to Grandpa Joe's, tucked into the hush of the cluttered room, I decided to explore the closet. I hadn't ventured there yet, and I optimistically set the nearly empty trash can next to me, determined to be productive, to ignore the twinge of uncertainty about Noah that seemed to color all of my actions.

The wooden closet door slid easily in the metal track, and as it opened a familiar scent engulfed me. Butterscotch. My grandpa's coats, along with everything else from the front of the house, had been relocated. I reached into the pocket of the puffy green jacket, the one I associated most closely with Grandpa Joe, and pulled out a stubby pack of Life Savers. The foil had lost its glimmer, and the candy was covered with lint. I popped one corroded piece off the top and put the second, mostly clean one, into my mouth. Grandpa. Then I reached in his other pocket and emerged with a different partially used item. A pack of Camels.

"Everyone has a few secrets, huh, Gramps?" I whispered as I threw the cigarettes into the trash and pocketed the candy.

On the floor directly beneath the coats was my grandpa's leather medical bag. I recognized it from the mornings I spent with him before he retired. I was never allowed to explore the contents when he was working, and now, even though he was gone and obviously hadn't practiced medicine for a couple of decades, I expected I'd get a scolding for opening it. But taking a deep breath, I did it anyway. Folded on the top was a white lab smock embroidered with his name. He probably packed it up, along with his stethoscope and the framed print of his degree, on his last day at the hospital. Aside from those items, it was empty.

Tucked behind his bag was another leather briefcase, a similar style, also a medical bag, but much older. I twisted the clasp and pried it open, the metal hinges groaning with the sudden activity. It smelled like the shoe repair shop near my house, tanned hides and time. First up was an item that looked like an overly starched napkin. Attempting to unfold it, I poked my palm with a hairpin and realized it was a nurse's cap. Stretching the stiff oval headband, I placed it on my head, where it instantly snapped back into the flatness of fifty years, slid over my forehead, and fell onto my lap.

"Hello, Emmeline. So this bag must be yours," I whispered as I drew out the next item: a framed certificate from the Westminster School of Nursing. A diploma awarded to Emmeline Lansing in 1917. The edges of the document were dotted with rust from the frame, but the script was still legible. The remaining items consisted of a photo of Emmeline and Nathaniel standing arm in arm, likely forty years old, and six framed black-and-white headshots of young boys. Her sons. Which one was my grandpa?

Each child had an identical haircut, likely administered by Emmeline herself, but I placed the images in a line and studied them closely. After several passes, I recognized him, the lighter hair, the shape of the brow. So many brothers, and I'd never met a great-uncle. What were their names? I glanced over my shoulder to check which purse I carried today. The one hanging on the doorknob was the same one I took to my first interview and my first visit to the Family History Library, which meant I had the printed census reports. They would tell me. I pulled the pages out and smoothed the creases, examining the names from decades ago.

Wait. Here was something I'd originally overlooked on the census: the address of my grandpa's childhood home. What if a relative or a cousin still lived there? Or I could find a neighbor who remembered the family? I could ask them about Emmeline. And about Rosa.

I pulled out my phone and keyed in the address listed on the census. Seconds later it reported the location was unavailable. I tried again, and it gave me coordinates of a house in Texas. Clearly that wasn't the one. The listed city on the census was Murray, a bedroom community south of Salt Lake City, maybe five miles south of my grandpa's house. And it was just past noon.

If I grabbed lunch at a drive-thru, I could make it to Murray, try to find the incomplete address, and race back downtown before my three o'clock interview. But I'd have to be fast.

As I left the room of memories, I realized I'd accomplished very little. But this thing with Rosa, this loose end, beaconed like a neon billboard, demanding to be seen. After the DNA test, I knew who I was at my core, at the genetic level, but it didn't answer a single question about Grandpa Joe, a man I thought

I knew through and through, a man I hadn't thought to question while he was still alive.

Murray was a city settled in fits and starts. There was no clear grid system defining a downtown, or planned neighborhoods stretching from one intersection to another in orderly rows. Rolling hills of horse acreage butted up to the Walmart, an abandoned dairy fronted a new subdivision of homes arranged in a bouquet of curving streets, and the car dealership was plopped next to the historic city hall. At some point, Murray had committed to development on demand, and it showed.

After forty minutes of misdirection, the navigation system on my phone put me smack in the middle of a neighborhood of split-level homes, each adorned with a double carport. Clearly built using 1960s cookie-cutter design, none of these places were standing when Grandpa Joe was a child. After driving back and forth along the winding streets, among houses with burnt orange or avocado shutters, all bearing a distinct resemblance to the *Brady Bunch* home, I eventually emerged next to a freeway on-ramp. I flipped illegally at the light and reentered the neighborhood, this time on a different street. And at the new entrance, I saw it. Displayed on a low cinder brick wall, in cursive font and wooden lettering, it said,

BARLOW MEADOWS. Barlow. So I *was* on the right path.

This street was slightly different in appearance. Scattered like unpopped kernels among a well-buttered bowl were several small, old houses. And by old, I meant historic, bricks made of cut sandstone or adobe, a few with porches, a couple with gravel driveways, and none with a carport.

After directing me to a third location on this new street, the increasingly inept-sounding navi-voice insisted that my destination was on my right, so I stopped the car. I could see the house number and knew I was on Mill Brook Lane, which put me at a distinctly different address from what the census said, but it was almost time to give up. The clock on my dash blinked 1:45, and I didn't want to be late.

After staring at the house for several minutes, I turned the key to leave. As I put on my blinker, a man in a Honda hatchback pulled into the carport directly in front of me. He was my dad's age, dressed nondescriptly in tan pants and a jacket. He hurried toward my car. Startled at his approach, I locked my doors. But his smile was wide and he didn't appear dangerous, so I relaxed in my seat and waited to see what he wanted.

"You're early. Or I'm late." He was muffled through the glass, but understandable.

I put down my window, confusion creasing my brow. "What?"

"Aren't you the home health nurse? I thought you said three, but—" He looked at his watch. "I zipped to the pharmacy, but he's waiting just inside. Don't worry, early is no problem. Come in."

"I'm not a nurse. See, I was searching for an address and my phone told me to stop here. But this isn't the spot, I'm quite certain."

He gestured toward the house where I could see the curtains sway with the movement of someone watching. He held up a hand and yelled, "Just a minute, Pop." He turned back to me. "What's the address you're looking for?"

I read him the cross streets and he studied the sky, pondering. Finally he said, "Yep, those coordinates would put you right about here, but all of these streets have names, like Mill Brook and Oak Hills, not numbers. Who do you want to find?"

"Well, someone, I guess *anyone,* with the last name of Barlow. I saw the sign back there saying the subdivision was called Barlow Meadows and—"

"Okay, I see now. Well, Barlow owned this farmland, way back, before all of these houses were built, as I understand it. But I've lived here for over twenty years and I can't say I know of a Barlow in the area these days."

A sharp rapping sound came from the large, curtained window. "Coming." The man grinned at me. "Good luck." He turned to retrieve something from his car, but before I could roll up my window and pull away, he hollered, "You know, you should talk to my dad. He grew up around here, and if you can deal with a grumpy old man, he may be able to tell you more."

Another knock on the plate glass. "Yes, Pop, I said grumpy."

The clock said 1:52. I hoped that it wouldn't take long. But I should grab this opportunity. There was an old man who lived in the area willing to talk to me. How often would I get this chance?

"If your dad doesn't mind?"

"Mind? Gosh, he'd be thrilled to talk. I'll get him in his chair and wheel him out. The air would do him some good."

At the old man's wheeled approach, I was reminded of a hovering eagle on a nest, his white hair circling his crown like sinuous vapor. His brows were nearly as long as the wispy strands on his head and just as vivid. Like most old people, his nose had become his most prominent feature, as the rest of his face melted.

"I'm Dick Stevenson," he called across the yard. "Who are you?" He was a wise, old bird.

After I explained my search he stretched his legs, pushing a pale foot out from under his brown fleece blanket.

"You can't get up, Dad."

"I'm just adjusting, don't bust a stitch," he grumbled, and turned to me. "Ezra Barlow, the original Barlow of this area, owned this land. But he died well over a hundred years ago. If you're a Barlow you're likely related to every other Barlow in the valley, because old Ezra kept himself nearly a dozen wives. Had siblings who were polygamists, too. Hell, you're probably a cousin of mine. I've got Barlow blood somewhere in my veins . . . which means, you and I, we shouldn't date." He winked one watery eye.

"Dad!"

"I'm teasing. When I was young, this area was still undeveloped and these houses"—he pointed down the street to one of the adobe shotgun places—"held the wives or the children who were married and starting their own families. The Barlow Meadows development was built around them, leaving the old houses intact, grandfathered property and such. No Barlow wives here anymore, though. That time has come and gone."

He continued to talk, reminiscing about his childhood, the dirt roads, the irrigation ditches. I didn't know what else to ask. His stories didn't fit into any of my memories, so I just listened. Several minutes later another car pulled up next to mine and a woman in pink scrubs patterned with cartoon kittens emerged from the vehicle.

"The home health nurse, I imagine," Mr. Stevenson's son said to me.

"I should go anyway," I stuttered. "But thank you, both of you."

It was nearly three o'clock. The nurse was early, thank goodness, or I would have missed my interview. I left the neighborhood, head reeling. Grandpa Joe grew up on a polygamist commune? It didn't jive. He'd never mentioned it, not at all. He had a loving mother and father and several brothers. But then again, who was Rosa? Why was she a part of the picture? Questions swirled as I drove into the city.

While I'd spoken with Mr. Stevenson, Noah had called and left a message, wishing me good luck on the interview. I ached to return his call, but I didn't have time. All spare minutes were occupied by my frenzied freeway drive, navigation of the parking garage, and jog to human resources. I'd be with him soon and I hoped I'd have a job. Perhaps he would want me to stay the night and we'd celebrate with a meal of soft foods, together.

CHAPTER 24

I checked my hair in the reflective chrome of the hospital elevator. A little disheveled, but my lip gloss was still fresh from the interview. It would do. At the appropriate floor, I dashed through the barricaded door, tucked closely behind a doctor I didn't recognize so I wouldn't have to be beeped in, and I rushed to Noah's room. The door, was closed, and I knocked gently, wondering if he was sleeping. Before anyone answered, a nurse called out. "Mrs. Hazelton? He's been discharged from the ICU. Remember?"

"Oh, right. He said that was happening today. Sorry." I glanced apologetically at the closed door, then scanned the hall, suddenly melancholy at leaving my home away from home for the past week. It was odd that the corridor of a hospital could become familiar and, in a strange way, beloved.

At my pause, the nurse on duty said, "Talli's not on tonight, but she said to tell you she wishes the very best for you and Mr. Hazelton."

I smiled. The interview went well. Noah was healing. I was hopeful, too.

"Mr. Hazelton is on this floor, but to find him you'll have to go back out past the elevators and into the opposite wing."

I retraced my steps and directly across from the elevator spotted a women's bathroom. The second I glimpsed the familiar cutout of the faceless woman, my bladder clenched. In my rush from my grandpa's, to Murray City, to the interview, and to the hospital, I hadn't gone in hours. The iced tea from my drive-thru lunch at McDonald's sat heavy on my pelvis.

As I took care of business, relief filling me as I emptied my bladder, the swinging door from the hallway opened and a woman rushed through, speaking loudly. I listened for the response of her companion and hearing none, I figured she must be on a cell phone. It was hard to ignore her.

"Of course he looks good. How could he not? He's got a couple of shaved patches in that hair of his, but even in a hospital gown, he's not bad."

I stopped mid-flow. Shaved patches? Was she talking about Noah?

"This was my first chance. He's been in the ICU . . . only family admitted."

Silence for several seconds, and I tried to relax enough to stop my heart from thudding in my ears, muting her voice. Shuffling around in my bag, I tried to make normal bathroom sounds. Maybe she would think I was searching for a tampon rather than listening.

"Oh, I'm sure she's been there. They're still legally married, but from what I understand they're separated. I don't know what the situation is, exactly. We didn't discuss it, because the nurse was in the room most of the time."

She *must* be talking about Noah. And me. I tried to see who was speaking, but where she stood in relation to the crack between the stalls didn't allow me a direct line to her face. Did I know this woman? She sounded somewhat familiar. Was her visit the reason Noah wanted me to delay my own?

"I think he's okay. He's a little thin, but he could carry a decent conversation. He said he hopes for a full recovery. It's hard not to be charmed. . . ." And a pause. "Of course I did. Flowers. Not red . . . too presumptuous. Some Gerbera daisies."

Ears straining to understand every word, I heard her snap the lid on a lipstick, her next comment marred by the attention she paid to her mouth. Did she kiss my husband?

"He'll probably be home in a few days and then we'll see." Pause. "Talk to you later."

She clicked off and entered the stall next to mine. As she disrobed, I yanked my leggings over my hips and ran from the bathroom without bothering to wash. Any hospital-borne disease I carried on my hands didn't matter. I had to get out of there. I jabbed at the down button. After several seconds without response, I ran toward the emergency stairs at the end of the hall. I didn't want her to emerge behind me as I waited.

I didn't know who she was, but if she recognized *me* . . .

I passed a room on the right-hand side of the corridor advertising the name *Hazelton*, written on a tiny white board next to the metal surround. The door was ajar, and the sound of the evening news drifted toward me. I slowed. I could see the foot of the bed. Two lumps encased in a blanket told me Noah was watching television while reclined. I almost entered. I could have misheard the conversation. It was probably nothing. But then I saw it. On a moveable cafeteria table, tucked into the corner, under the wall clock, sat a vase. The wilted flowers I'd brought earlier in the week were gone and in their place stood a bright orange bouquet of Gerbera daisies.

CHAPTER 25

I reached the parking garage without considering what I would tell Noah. I could go back in and fight for my spot in his life. But did I deserve it? I could angrily question him and demand to know about the woman. But it wasn't like I hadn't deliberately distanced myself from my husband. I told him to move on. And my past few weeks certainly weren't spotless.

When I finally slammed the metal door of my personal sanctuary, I hunched low in the leather seat. I was parked next to the stairs in the visitors' garage, a busy thoroughfare leading guests from the main entrance of the hospital deep into the lot, and though alone, I was not without inspection. Pedestrians eyed me curiously as I sat, hands gripping the steering wheel, trying to catch my breath.

More than once I'd pulled myself together in this very parking lot, so this experience was not unfamiliar. Noah and I had visited this medical complex not so long ago. But on those numerous occasions, sitting in the car after heart-stopping news, Noah and I cried together.

Suddenly I ached for Joey with a wrenching that burned beneath my ribs. I turned in my seat, willing him alive, willing him to be buckled behind me. "Momma's coming," I whispered, and finally I could start the car. I turned toward the cemetery, knowing the comfort to be found among the headstones was for the living rather than the dead.

After moving aside the vase of wilted tulips I'd brought a couple of days earlier, I took my usual spot with my bottom positioned on the corner of Joey's flat headstone.

"No fresh flowers today, baby. I came to talk."

Noah offered to get me one of those stone benches that marked a grave here and there, but I preferred this position. Joey and I could sit side by side. It was as close to having him on my lap as I could manage.

"Daddy's been hurt. He's been in the hospital, which is why I haven't been by so often. I think he's going to be okay, but I wanted to tell you we're having some trouble without you here, buddy. It's not your fault, but it's been really hard."

I imagined him understanding me as we spoke. He would have been wise. One of those old souls, I knew it. Our child's eyes, coffee brown, sparkled with life, with wisdom, only days after he was born. We watched as he slowly lost the ability to focus on our faces, as the windows into his mind grew muddied and confused by the disease that ravaged his brain.

Even still, he was beautiful, a dimple in his

chin like Grandpa Joe's, a wide forehead like mine. His fingers were shaped like Noah's, and I imagined those hands growing strong like his father's. Strong enough to catch a ball, to climb a tree, to hold his own child. And at first Joey *could* clutch things, a toy or a lock of my hair as I held him over my shoulder. But eventually he lost that too.

If I stayed with Noah, we could never have a child like Joey, a child who reflected back at us, like a mirrored ball, tiny parts of ourselves. Noah was beautiful, strong, and smart. How could I rob him of that experience? Of a chance to see himself in a child?

I freed my husband once. And he moved on. This woman, whomever she was, was interested in him. It was likely early enough in their relationship, and soon enough after Noah's accident when I sat with him, summoning him with my voice, that I could fight for my place next to him. I could continue to be his wife.

But we'd buried one child together. I'd forgotten about this, lost in the relief of his recovery. We were exactly where we were before the accident. The cost of the procedure to create a healthy child, given the medical bills flying toward our mailbox (coupled with those we were already responsible for from Joey's care), made any in vitro procedure out of the question. Together we'd never have a child who would allow us to say to each other, "He has your chin, but I think he has my smile."

There were too many tangled roots in our family tree, a gnarled crisscross of faulty chromosomes that created Joey. After some time, after pondering all the options, I stood. There were no answers here.

"I'm going to visit Grandpa for a few minutes, but I'll be back soon," I said to Joey, and I reversed the steps taken after Grandpa Joe's funeral, tracing my path from Joey's grave to his. My grandpa's date of death still wasn't inscribed into the granite marker, and the sod was a lumpy blanket from his recent burial, artificially greener than the established lawn surrounding it. Grandma Ginny lay to his side, her blanket of grass smooth from her lengthy slumber.

"So, Grandpa, I have a few questions." I touched the headstone tentatively, like I might have tapped his shoulder to get his attention when I was a child. "I've been organizing the spare room in your house, you know, the one full of memories. I feel like I shouldn't be in there, I mean, you never let me open the rolltop desk when you were alive. Was there a reason? Because I'm finding things I don't understand. I can't free myself from these questions, these loose ends. I'm trying to move forward, but they keep pulling me under." I sat on the edge of his elevated headstone.

"And I have some decisions to make about Noah. I wish you were here so you could tell me what I should do."

As I spoke, I glanced about me, once again noticing my grandparents' eternal neighbors. Barlow . . . Barlow . . . Barlow. Most of these Barlows died in the early nineteen hundreds, so maybe I could find Nathaniel and Emmeline. I knew what their gravestone looked like via the image at the Family History Library, I just didn't know where it was.

Like my grandparents, they rested under a side-by-side marker, light granite, almost white. I circled Grandpa Joe's grave in larger and larger loops, reading the headstones. No Emmeline, no Nathaniel, but enough Barlows to fill a school bus or two. The old guy at Barlow Meadows wasn't lying—this family got around in the day.

I crossed one of the narrow paths used by the hearses to access the burial sites and continued into the next plat. Quickly I ran out of Barlows and found myself in a field of Hansens. I shivered. It was quiet here in the older part of the cemetery, and though it was midsummer, the breeze carried a chill of the deceased. I pulled my shawl around my neck and continued to search.

Maybe fifteen minutes later, I found it: the gravestone of my great-grandparents, of my namesake Emmeline Barlow and her husband, Nathaniel. Across the distance I could see my grandpa's fresh plot. It really wasn't so far away, and from this higher point in the cemetery, his parents could watch over him.

"I've got some questions for you guys too," I said as I stood near their grave, letting the last of the evening sun warm my shoulders. In no time, where there had been long shadows now there were none, and the charcoal of night was fast approaching. How late was it? I pulled out my phone to check the time and saw three missed calls from Noah and a text. I'd turned my phone to silent for the interview.

Emma? He'd sent it an hour earlier.

Hey. I responded as I walked back to Joey.

He responded immediately. *You're done with your interview, right? It's nearly dark.*

At the cemetery, right now.

Say hello to him for me.

I already did.

So are you coming to the hospital? I have a snazzy new pad and a bigger TV. I've been waiting for you.

I paused, fingers hovering over the tiny screen before responding.

I'm beat. But the interview went well and I got a bunch done at Grandpa's.

The phone rang in response. I was standing at the foot of Joey's grave watching a bright orange strip of sunset fade to black. "I miss you," he said. "But if you want to get some sleep, I understand.

Come up first thing tomorrow. Or will it be your first day on the job?"

"I don't know if I got the position yet." The night sky rested heavy on my shoulders. "But in the morning I might take a few more hours at my grandpa's. Now that you're in your new room, you can have other visitors. I'm sure plenty of people from your office have been dying to visit . . . people who couldn't visit you while you were in the ICU." He didn't respond, so I continued talking. "My mom wants to get my grandpa's house on the market soon. There's still so much to do, and it might give you a little space—"

"Don't do this again."

"Noah . . ."

"Can't your grandpa's house wait?"

My grandpa. I would hold fast to my grandpa, and the task at hand, and the mysteries surrounding him, so I wouldn't blurt out that I'd seen the flowers. So I told Noah about the drive to Murray City and Barlow Meadows. He listened silently. "I keep discovering things about my grandpa I don't understand. Who was he, really?"

"Who was *he?* Your *grandpa?*" After minutes of forced silence, Noah's anger scalded my ear. "You were here every day while I was sick and now you're avoiding me again, chasing around the valley in search of your dead relatives. The questions you should be asking yourself, Emma, are: Who am I? And who do I *want to be?*"

"I saw the flowers." The words filled my throat as I tried to pull them back into my mouth, but it was too late. "And I saw the girl. And there are things we need to talk about, because there was this guy I dated before I knew you. And I saw him again. And I've been a mess. I've done some stupid things."

"Ah . . ." He exhaled long into the phone. "I was going to tell you about her when you visited. I want you to know that nothing happened between us. She's the sister of a guy I work with, you know, Travis? We were set up. I mean, I thought you and I were done, so I agreed. I saw her twice, and never alone. She joined me at a work barbeque and at a concert."

I swallowed to clear the hard lump from my throat. Until he admitted there was someone else, the wish-making part of my brain denied it. "She seemed interested in more."

"I think she is, but Emma, it's *not* what I want. I tried to tell her when she visited that you and I were back together again, but there was always a nurse in the room. And then I expected you to arrive at any minute, and I—"

"Didn't want me to see her?"

"Yes. I figured I could work things out without upsetting our balance. Sorry."

"It's okay."

If we were confessing our sins, should I tell him about Barry? And how much? He went to a barbeque. I got stoned with the intent of sleeping with another man. I planned to lie about my indiscretion to my husband. Why did I think my actions would ever be forgivable? But before I could confess, Noah spoke again.

"I'm going to ask you one question." Noah's voice shook with his words. "I don't want any details, other than *yes* or *no,* because I don't want that movie in my head."

"Okay."

"Did you sleep with him? That guy you mentioned."

"No. But—"

"Stop." I could picture him holding the phone away from his ear, his hand indicating I should not proceed. "As long as I know you weren't with him and you're not planning to see him again, I don't want to know more. It will be easier if I can't imagine."

"Okay."

"So, are you still at the cemetery? Are you planning to visit?"

I was standing at the foot of our son's grave. As we spoke, the loss that hovered between us was as real as the grass under my feet. "I'm standing here with Joey. And I realize that even after your accident, and your recovery, that you and I . . . we're in the same spot. We're still the same people, genetically. We haven't changed. But you're alive and maybe there's a reason."

"I don't understand where you're going with this."

"We can't have a child together. Don't you see? There will never be a little Noah. All the great things about you, they'll go to waste. . . ."

"And there won't be a little Emma either." His voice was crisp over the telephone, lacking the softness from moments earlier.

"I guess that's true."

"Maybe that's what this is all about, Emma. I want a family, one way or the other. And I want you. But maybe you can't love a child who is not genetically yours."

"That's not true." But as I said it, I remembered the joy of carrying Joey, a living, growing child. He was a tiny part of me, and not part of me at all. He was a beautiful secret I could hold next to my heart. Until I realized that by creating him, I also killed him.

"This is too confusing, Emma. You're confusing me."

"I'm trying to figure things out. There's so much I don't understand. So many things I can't change."

"You know what has changed?" The words burned my ear, because I knew.

"I have."

His long silence confirmed that I answered his

rhetorical question correctly. "Emma, I love you, but I don't want to see you again until you figure out what *you* want. I can't keep doing this." He was silent for several seconds, and I intended to speak, but I couldn't get the words past my throat.

"The doctor said I likely have two days before I can go home. You take some time to research your ancestors, or talk to Joey, or read books, or meditate, or reconnect with that guy, or whatever you need to do to feel solid in your decision. My dad has my truck right now anyway. I'll have my parents bring me home from the hospital."

"Wait, what decision are you—"

"Emma, listen, this back and forth is breaking me." He swallowed several times. I couldn't tell if it was from emotion or fatigue; either way, his fragility pricked my tears. I was doing this to the man I loved. I was causing him pain.

"If you decide to stay with me, you'll need to commit to counseling," he continued. "You need to commit to me. To us. To the family we'll be, even if it's just the two of us. I'll know your decision when I come home. Because either you'll be there, or you won't." He sounded out of breath, his conversation progressively weaker.

He disconnected before I could respond, and the distance between us increased exponentially, like turning a telescope to the wrong end, and the thing you expected to see closely was no longer distinguishable across the miles.

Sometime in the pre-dawn I had the nightmare again. The repetitive dream was frequent in the first year of Joey's life, but the uncontrolled fear of those first months became more tolerable, and in time I stopped dreaming all together. While Joey was alive, I was forced to deal with nightmarish emotions in numerous daytime, real-life situations, hour after hour. A living nightmare, so dreaming wasn't necessary. But it was back. I woke gasping and sweaty, my comforter smothering me under a nighttime blanket of dread.

I was at the pool, the one in the rec center a mile from our home, the one where I envisioned taking my children during warm summer afternoons. Joey sat in my lap in the zero-depth entry, our bottoms resting in a couple of inches of water. The surrounding light had an eerie quality, bright but brittle. Other children, clad in water wings, played around us and pool toys bobbed nearby. Joey kicked his chubby legs, a sprinkling of water glistening like snow crystals on his skin. But the splash of water made no sound, nor did the calls and laughing of the other children. Absolute silence.

For some reason, in this dream I would glance away, maybe to answer a question asked offstage or to watch a robin flick, drop onto its back at the edge of the pool, and when I would reach for my son, the tile floor where he'd been sitting would be gone, leaving a bottomless, water-filled tunnel. Before I could respond, Joey would swirl away from me, pulled from my lap like soap suds down a drain, spiraling into the void.

I would stretch my arms into the sudden depths. I would shatter the silence. "Hold on to me!" But his hands floated like limp tendrils of seaweed above him, and I couldn't catch his wrists.

In each dream, I would try to dive into the narrow pipe, knowing if I caught him in his descent I'd never be able to right myself and swim us both to the surface. But it didn't matter. With every fiber I tried to throw myself into the watery grave. But I couldn't.

After waking, I would chide myself for not being strong enough to save him. I would promise the next time I had the dream I would sacrifice myself and maybe it would make a difference in the real world. Night after night, restrained from following my instincts, I watched him, horrified as he drifted away.

But this night, the dream shifted. One second I was reaching for my son and the next the hand I stretched toward was Noah's. I was relieved. He was stronger than Joey; he could catch my fingers and I could pull him to the surface. Together we'd be saved. But he didn't. He shook his head, tucked his hands to his sides, eyes locked on mine, and allowed the current to pull him farther and farther from my reach.

CHAPTER 26

Midmorning sun streamed through the window, rousing me later than usual. My arms and legs felt fatigued as I woke, as though I'd fought a swift current through all the hours of darkness. I rolled toward Noah's side of the bed and embraced his pillow, imagining him dozing beside me like he had until I moved away: his arms tucked under the pillow, the rise and fall of his breathing visible in his shoulders, his dark lashes touching his cheek, the rough stubble on his jaw. But he wasn't next to me. He was in the hospital alone. And I'd abandoned him again.

I was dressed with keys in hand before I realized what I was doing. In flight mode, my body viscerally urged me to run to him. *Stop it, Emma.* I set the keys on the counter. *You can't do this to him.* Two days. He was right, I had to decide. My indecision burdened him. If I was jangled, imagine how he felt.

As I made a cup of coffee in my familiar yet out-of-sorts kitchen, I thought about Noah. I didn't want to admit it, but over the past year there were times I was furious at my husband: for moving on, for failing our son, for everything and nothing at all. Together, we were to blame for the tragedy that befell Joey, but when I could no longer maintain fury or sadness at myself, I focused my excess emotion on my husband.

And at the same time, I was afraid of the hurtful things I might say or do. So, for the last several months while we lived together, we were increasingly further apart. Though we spoke often, I kept the conversations between us as surface and placating as the polite discourse you'd have with a long-winded and often ill neighbor, someone you couldn't avoid but who you didn't want to engage in a lengthy driveway discussion.

I didn't understand what was happening to me. Noah and I had stuck together through the toughest times. Through all three years of Joey's illness, we were a team. When I could hold my son in my arms, my job was clear. I was his mother. I would parent him in any way I could. But once he was gone, I was helpless.

Noah tried to be patient, but a year after Joey's death he was still treating me as if I were a filigree of spun glass, too fragile to hold. In some regards this was true, because if my emotions broke through the thin barrier and released the seething beast, I'd most certainly lose my husband too. And maybe that's what I deserved. Or desired.

Without Noah's presence in the house, the silence rang in my ears. I held my phone in my hand urging him to call. I dialed his cell number, but before pressing the green call icon, I turned it off. *No*. Two days.

I could go see my mom, once again retreating into the familiar. I could ask her professional advice about Noah. And if her counseling was unhelpful (or unwanted), I could tell her my discoveries about Grandpa Joe, my interview, the woman who visited Noah in the hospital. Did he already call her and ask her to come back to visit him again?

Stop.

I longed for a best friend to confide in, someone who wasn't connected by blood to my mess of a family. But through one year of pregnancy, three years of disability, and one year on the couch, I'd lost every single friend I'd ever had.

I could attend a session of yoga. I'd taken some extra time off while Noah was in the hospital and I wasn't scheduled to teach again until the following Monday. But I could participate. I looked at the clock. I'd already missed the morning classes. The next session wouldn't start until five. Almost out of options, I dialed Ethan, but the call went unanswered. Often during a workday he'd silence his cell. He would call me back at some point, but when?

Like a stranger in my own home, I shuffled into Joey's room. The nursery furniture was disassembled and stacked against the far wall, leaving the rocking chair the single functional piece. I'd done the initial disassembly myself the week after he died, moving his tiny clothing into plastic bags and returning his medical equipment to the hospital. I hoped it would be cathartic, a letting go, but as I peeked into his room hoping to find him lying in his crib and finding it not only empty but disassembled, it crushed me. I wasn't ready to be done with him, yet in my frenzy I'd exaggerated his absence.

Several months after slamming the door to the nursery and shutting out the image of the disassembled furniture, I dared to list all the pieces on Craigslist. That day I wanted no reminders a baby lived in the room, ever. But after the first inquiry, I told the pregnant woman who stopped by it was already sold and removed the online ad. I was foolish to think I could let him go.

A month or two later, I decided to reassemble the crib, forced to quit when I could no longer see through my tears. The day of the half-cocked half-reassembly, after I pulled myself together, I closed the door again. I left the Allen wrenches spread on the carpet and the crib slats strewn on the floor. Noah tidied the room several weeks later.

These were the types of knee-jerk, crazy-girl activities that filled the blurry months after Joey's death. For the past year I swung this weighty pendulum directly at Noah. No wonder things were in shambles.

Who lives in this house now? I tiptoed to all corners of the nursery, caressing the walls with my fingertips. Not a baby. Not a blissfully married husband and wife. I ached to talk to Noah. There was no one who would understand the loss of our son more than my husband. When I was a child, I could always talk to my grandpa Joe, the man who had always been my island as the waves battered the shore. But he wasn't here, and thinking about him left me unsettled. After all of my discoveries, I was no longer sure who he was.

Emma . . . my grandpa's presence filled the empty room. I sat carefully in the rocking chair to silence my footsteps so I could hear him if he spoke again. Several minutes passed.

"Grandpa?"

Silence.

"What should I do?"

Silence.

"Where are you? I want to talk to you. I'm lost."

Count the steps, Emma. You'll see I'm not so far. I pressed my finger into my ear, and the words muted. It was almost as if he'd actually spoken. I shook my head. I was contriving this conversation because I wanted so badly to hear from him. My grandpa wasn't at the cemetery. He wasn't at his childhood home. He wasn't in a cluttered room full of memories. It was silly and indulgent to chase after him.

But on the other hand, I couldn't visit my husband at the hospital. I had two days to figure out who I was. Maybe I would follow this whim, because it was the only path that wasn't blocked. I would go back to the Family History Library. And maybe if I found my grandpa there, I would also find myself.

An hour later, perched in front of a computer, my fingers hovered over the keyboard. Here's what I had: I knew Emmeline and Nathaniel Barlow were listed as husband and wife in 1930. I knew the 1920 census listed Rosa as the *Wife*. And Emmeline was listed on the same document as a *Boarder*, the whole family living in Utah. I knew my grandpa Joe had been born in England in 1913. This meant at some point between 1913 and 1920 he made his way to the United States. But with who?

I sat with my right hand hovering over the mouse and my attention fixed on the home screen trying to channel inspiration with my glare. Unwanted thoughts drifted to Noah and the other woman. He'd done exactly what I told him to do. I'd freed him, but why did it hurt so badly? I caught a tear sliding down my cheek with my tongue before the drop hit the keyboard.

Noah and I were destined to fail. We were both reeling from loss, bouncing against circumstance. I made the decision to stay with him in the hospital, but it was made in the haze of relief that he was still alive. I wasn't being fair, I was being greedy. And what about Barry and the mess I'd nearly made? After my close call, all of my decisions were suspect.

Barry . . . something niggled as I considered him, trying to worm its way to the surface. He was a little too wild for my comfort, but I admired his pilgrimage to Morocco. He came home on a ship carrying enough spices to build his little empire. Talk about taking a risk and landing on your feet.

Wait. Barry took a *ship* from Europe. My fingers froze in midair, and Barry was wiped from my mind like raindrops from a windshield, replaced with the image of a young boy on a ship: Grandpa Joe.

The only way my grandpa could get from England to the United States in the early 1900s was by *ship*. What if there was a record of all passengers arriving in the United States, a roster of some sort? This would be the place to find out.

I raised my hand, and a woman came to my side. "Is there any way I could find a person who came to the United States from England via passenger ship?"

She took a seat in the chair next to me. "Do you know the exact year? Point of debarkation or arrival, by any chance?" She adjusted her glasses on her nose. More than my other volunteer guides, based on her questions this woman projected an abundance of confidence on the subject. I glanced at her name tag: Sister Mills.

"I know a range, from 1913 to 1920. And that's about it."

"So, the years encompassing World War One."

"I guess so. Is that a problem?" I hadn't considered the war.

Several seconds later she continued. "It makes things a little harder due to the soldier traffic and the uncertainty of passage across the Atlantic. Not many passenger ships sailed from about 1915 to 1918. In fact, after the *Lusitania* was torpedoed in 1915, there was minimal travel that wasn't military. The waters weren't safe."

"Oh, I didn't realize. Maybe he traveled before 1915? Where would I look then?"

"You said you didn't know where this person landed, right?"

I shook my head. She was going to tell me this was a dead end.

"Okay, let's see," Sister Mills mused. "Was

your individual already an American citizen, or were they immigrating to the United States?"

"I'm not sure. He was born in England and was in the United States by 1920. He was a child."

"Hmm." She regarded the screen, contemplating. "With very little information, you could still try the Ellis Island site. It's like shooting into the dark, but if your person came through Ellis, there would be a record of the year, the age of the traveler, and the ship, which would get you going."

"And if he didn't come through Ellis?"

"There's a library full of books downstairs on B-1 detailing all persons immigrating into the United States; however, some volumes are organized by name, some by year, some by port, and most by ship. Without corroborating information, you could search for years and still not be sure you had the right individual. Plus, if your person was already a citizen, sometimes their records weren't taken, since they weren't immigrating but simply traveling, you see? Who would he have been traveling with, if he was a young child?"

"I'm not sure. His parents, I guess?" But who were they, if he was born *before* they were married?

This line of research wasn't answering any questions. It was only posing new ones. Fighting an urge to flee, I stood from my chair under the guise of stretching my legs. The first time I visited the Family History Library, the information appeared abundant, but then I wasn't looking for anything specific, so any tidbit was a new and revealing detail.

Sister Mills stood next to me and put her hand on my arm. "Don't get discouraged. Try the Ellis Island site, and if that fails I'll help you search downstairs." She clicked on an icon of a ship from the home screen, which redirected me to the Ellis Island site. "I'll be back to check on you in a few minutes." She tucked in her empty chair. "Good luck."

With two fingers I typed my grandpa's name: Joseph Barlow, with no filters, and was rewarded with over a thousand immigrants. Next to each *Barlow, Joseph*, was the year of arrival, the last place of residence (which was often blank), and the ship name. Sister Mills was right, there weren't many ships arriving after 1915. The boom time for immigration was the late 1800s to the beginning of World War I.

After scrolling for several minutes and clicking on anything hopeful, I decided to try a middle initial. Remembering Grandpa Joe's obituary, I included *L* for Lewis and tried again. Much better: fifty-seven matches, and four occurred during my window. "Come on," I whispered, examining the screen.

The first three were grown men at their year of arrival, but the fourth proclaimed

Joseph L. Barlow
Year of Arrival: 1915
Age at Arrival: 2
Debarkation: Liverpool
Arrival: New York City

I stood and my chair rolled backward, smacking into the man sitting behind me. "Sorry," I whispered, and he grunted. I ignored the rest of his muttering and raised my hand for assistance as if I were hailing a cab at rush hour.

"Oh my God! Sister Mills!" Several heads swiveled in my direction, and I turned pink as I realized my mistake (Mormons don't sprinkle their language with the sacred word *God*). Since I'd essentially yelled a curse in one of their buildings, Sister Mills was at my elbow in an instant.

"What did you find?" she asked, allowing my verbal misstep without reprimand.

"This could be him! How can I find out who he sailed over with?"

"Interesting." She leaned close, talking to herself. "Says here the ship was the *Mauretania*. You've probably heard of her. But I thought she was repositioned during World War One to a battleship. If you don't mind?" She slid the keyboard closer to her and typed in *Mauretania WWI*. An image of a great steamer, much like the *Titanic*, appeared on the screen, but the entire boat was painted white and the hull was decorated with a multitude of red crosses.

"So that's why it says *hospital* next to the ship's name. It looks like your person"—she clicked back to the listing of names—"Joseph Barlow, sailed on a hospital ship. He may have crossed with Canadian troops, since the United States wasn't in the war at this time. So why didn't it sail directly to Canada?" she asked herself. "Wartime research . . . anything can happen."

"All is fair in love and war," I added, and she smiled, still captivated by her own imaginings. I thought of Noah, knowing that in fact nothing was fair in love, or in war.

"This unusual circumstance might make it easier, or harder, to discover who he traveled with. It was my understanding that Ellis Island practically shut down during the war, but this information, here, disagrees."

"Do you think there's a roster available? I'd be interested in seeing who he crossed with." I was falling into this quest as if it was the only certain thing in my life, and in some regards it was.

"Well, we do have the ship name. We could go downstairs and see what we can find. If you have a bit of time to kill, that is. Research slows significantly if you have to reference a source document."

I needed a distraction. I'd stay here all night if I could.

With a ping, the elevator doors opened and we were deposited onto floor B-1. Several people sat hunched at enormous wood tables, staring at encyclopedia-sized volumes. Beyond the tables stretched rows of leather-bound compilations. The stacks appeared to extend for miles, the far wall disappearing into a dot in the distance, like an exercise in drawing perspective. Yes, this is what I imagined the History Library would be like, but barraged by this massive amount of written information, I glanced at Sister Mills and wrinkled my forehead. Was she up to the task? Was I?

"This floor contains volumes on immigration, information about early life in the United States, and sources for ancestral ties to various European countries," Sister Mills said as I gaped at the vertical shelves of rainbow-hued leather-backed books. "Other floors have information about the British Isles and other countries of origin. Plus, the church has over four thousand other history libraries around the world. However, this library is our largest. Go ahead and wander around while I try to locate a few possible options to begin our research. I'll call you over when I think I might have something. By the way, I don't have your name."

"It's Emma." I didn't mention my last name. It hurt to consider that Hazelton, a beloved half of myself, may no longer belong to me. "Thank you, Sister Mills," I said as I made my way into the labyrinth.

Scanning the titles, I could see that many of these books contained the original documents that had been digitized for easier access on the main floor: There were bound volumes of cemetery records from every county in every state, *Who's Who* books from the 1800s in the colonial states, books listing typical Americanization of foreign surnames (a separate volume for each European country of descent).

Farther in, there were compilations of census reports from every state, each spine-width bigger than my palm, going back to . . . I gasped seeing the date: 1790. How in the world could I find my grandpa in this mass of information? Did the history of one little person matter?

Twenty minutes later, Sister Mills found me in the Utah section, holding a volume of records from the Salt Lake City Cemetery. As far as I could tell, the Barlow family arrived in Utah about the same time as the Mormon prophet Brigham Young. That would explain the numerous antiquated headstones surrounding Grandpa Joe's, all bearing the name Barlow.

The arrival of Brigham Young and his wagon train of persecuted believers was essentially the first chapter in Caucasian occupation of this Native American territory. Turns out the prolific Barlows had decades, centuries actually, to populate the city.

"Emma, I've collected several books that might prove fruitful in your search. I'd love to stay and help you, but my shift ends in five minutes and I'm expected at home. If you don't find what you're looking for, you can ask for assistance from someone else, or I'll be back on Saturday and I'd be happy to help."

"Thank you so much," I said, pulling out my phone. One text from my mom saying *Good morning*. Nothing from Noah. "I'll take a quick peek at the information you've found and if I'm lucky . . ." I slipped the phone back into my bag.

Sister Mills stopped at one of the tables, gesturing for me to inspect a haphazard stack of books standing almost three feet high. "Here they are. Take care, and I hope I'll see you soon." She made her way to the elevator.

Three volumes were similar to one another, gigantic taupe-brown indexes with titles reading *Passenger and Immigration Lists*, two more pertained to passenger arrival records for the

Port of New York, one was from the Immigration and Naturalization Service, and one was a compilation of passenger lists leaving the United Kingdom on the *Mauretania.*

I opened one of the books containing passenger lists. Passengers were listed alphabetically (kind of), each volume starting at *A.* Hundreds of pages later the list *restarted* at *A*, with a different port of arrival. Turns out there were dozens of ports running the length of the Atlantic coast. After an hour (and several hundred Barlows later), it was clear this source was too broad. Next I tried the *Mauretania* book, which ended in 1914. At the end of the book it said, *For listings beyond 1914 consult* and it listed several additional titles.

I scanned the room, trying to find a helpful volunteer. This section of the library was sparsely staffed, as most searchers ended their journey of ancestral discovery at the main floor computer lab. Maybe I would look for it myself.

I stepped into the aisle labeled U.S. IMMIGRATION. A whole floor-to-ceiling case was dedicated to immigration after World War II: German, Japanese, Jewish, Wartime Brides. I would keep searching. Farther along the aisle, books on World War I appeared, several detailing the Immigrant Act of 1917. I was closer . . . and there! One of the titles pertaining to World War I Wartime Immigration looked familiar. I scanned the *Mauretania* book to verify the title. It appeared to be the right one.

I trotted back to my desk. Perched in front of my impressive collection of materials, the newest volume on the top, I swirled the air over them like a sorcerer, willing the information to be in there, willing it to float to the surface so I could find it.

"Immigrant traffic through Ellis Island dwindled during the war years," I whispered, skimming the text aloud. "After war erupted in Europe in 1914 passenger traffic across the Atlantic was erratic. For example, less than 200,000 immigrants came through in all of 1915, which was a significant reduction from the years 1900 to 1914, when up to ten thousand immigrants were processed *daily*."

I turned the page to the alphabetical passenger list, silently pleading for him to be there. And minutes later, in the year 1915, I found him.

I gripped the edge of the desk to steady myself. Directly across from me sat a man about seventy years old, wearing a set of magnifying glasses perched on his nose and another pair on the top of his head. He winked a gigantic eye. "Guessing you struck gold?"

I nodded. Yes, I'd found Grandpa Joe, and though I knew he'd been hiding something, he still wasn't who I expected him to be.

1915
Barlow, Nathaniel; 23; New York
Wife: Rosa 22
Son: Joseph 2

If Rosa was the wife, Nathaniel the husband, and my grandpa the son, then who was my *true* great-grandma? Rosa? Rosa from Germany? But what about *Emmeline*, the great-grandmother whom Grandpa Joe always talked about? The woman who'd given me my name?

CHAPTER 27

By the time I arrived at my mom's house, her windows were dark, which is exactly what I hoped for. I hadn't called ahead, not sure I'd even end up at her place. I figured no matter what, I'd let myself in clandestinely to avoid a discussion about my repeated abandoned-puppy appearances on her doorstep. At the last minute I'd stopped by Grandpa Joe's and picked up a few things. In the morning, I planned to discuss the mysteries about my grandpa with my mom.

After brushing my teeth in the kitchen so I wouldn't wake her, I stripped to my tank top and underwear and hoisted the plastic container of Grandpa Joe's memorabilia onto the guest room bed. I crawled beside it and took the contents out, one piece at a time, pondering each. Who was Grandpa Joe, if his beloved mother wasn't Emmeline? Maybe Emmeline was his stepmother? Not a big deal, but why no mention of Rosa, ever, if she was his *true* mother?

And what about the sepia photo of the soldier and the book of German poetry? The mystery man in military attire seemed to be a piece from a different puzzle, fitting nowhere. The poetry was written in German, and Rosa was born in Germany. But the serious young man? No idea.

After looking them over, and having no answers, I set both articles back into the bin.

One last item to study: the black-and-white wedding photo. I held it near my cheek and balanced myself between the edge of the mattress and the dresser to catch my image in the mirror. Yes, there was a similarity between me and the blond woman, who may be Rosa, in the roundness of the cheekbones and the angle of the chin. Noah was right. I couldn't tell from the monochromatic print if her eyes were blue, but it appeared they could be. And the child holding her hand, the tiny face in profile, was he my grandpa?

The photo said *Barlow Wedding 1916*, and the taller woman whom I recognized from other photos as my great-grandma, Emmeline, held flowers. But Rosa came to the United States with Nathaniel and baby Joseph in 1915 . . . and Rosa was listed as *Wife* on the ship roster. Plus Rosa was listed as *Wife* on the 1920 census. If Rosa, a German girl, was Nathaniel's wife and Grandpa Joe's mother, why did she disappear from one census to the next, never to be mentioned again by her son?

It was too weird. The whole thing. I checked my cell for messages from Noah. Nothing. After moving the empty box to the unoccupied side of the bed, I turned off the light and fell into a fitful sleep.

• • •

"Emma?" My mom's face loomed above me, and the decades slipped away. Once again I was a child. I sat upright, thinking I was late for school. Several seconds later, I remembered the truth. She continued speaking as she extended a hand to pull me from the bed. "I was on my way to the kitchen and I nearly called the police when I saw this door closed, but then I noticed your car in the drive. Why are you here this morning? I thought you were sleeping at home or at the hospital these days."

"Painting." The lie rose from me without conscious thought. "I painted a wall in the living room to get the place ready for Noah's return and the smell was a little noxious to me."

My mom wrinkled her brow in disbelief.

"Okay, Mom, you're right, that's not the truth." I sighed. "Noah and I are . . . I don't know. I'm trying to figure out what I want from our marriage. Again. He doesn't want to see me until he's out of the hospital. So here I am . . . a basket of crazy on your doorstep." I tried to smile to stop my lurking tears and turned my palms to the ceiling. "Surprise."

She touched my hair. "And you brought some of Grandpa's stuff?" She gestured at the haphazard stacks on the side of the bed opposite of where I slept.

"I did."

"Do you want breakfast?" With her response, I knew she'd let me talk about Noah, and everything else, when I was ready.

"I have an off-topic question," I said as we walked together to the kitchen. "Grandpa had a bunch of brothers, right? At least, it says so in his obituary." I pointed to the news clipping on the refrigerator as evidence. "Did you spend much time with cousins or know any of your uncles? You've never mentioned them, and from what I can tell there aren't any photos of Grandpa with men who were about his age."

She cocked her head to one side, thinking. "You know, I think I attended a reunion or two. But I was pretty little when Grandma Emmeline passed. After she died, we didn't spend much time with extended family." She shrugged her shoulders. "I didn't think too much about it. We spent plenty of time with my parents' friends and their kids, other doctors at the hospital, and so on. Why?"

"I've been doing a little ancestral research. It's no big deal, but if Grandpa was raised with a bunch of brothers, where are they now?"

She pursed her lips considering my request. Finally she said, "You know, I have my parents' old Rolodex in one of the kitchen cupboards. I haven't referenced it since well before Grandpa died, but if there's any contact information for his brothers, it would be in there."

"I'd love to grab anything you have. Did any of them come to the funeral?"

"I'm not sure. I was a little distracted that day."

"I was too." I tried to ignore the memory.

"I know you were, baby." My mom put her arm around me, and I melted into her side. "How about I make you some coffee and we'll see what we can find."

Within seconds we found five listings for Barlow men, organized one after the other in the ring of index cards, my grandpa's doctor scrawl detailing the addresses, spouses, and various other pieces of information in forced tidiness. I recognized the names of his brothers from the census report, when all these old men were young boys living in the household of Nathaniel and Emmeline.

I'd uncovered so many details during my hours at the Family History Library, a time or two I'd scribbled notes on a piece of scrap paper or printed a few screens, like the census reports, but I never knew what information would be significant. When I went back again, *if* I managed to go back again, I'd do a better job of documenting my search. With proper documentation, I could take my mom, or Noah, on this journey with me.

Written as a diagonal slash across four of the five names in the card file, like a sold sticker on a real estate sign, Grandpa Joe had scripted the word *deceased* and the year. Though he was the oldest child, he'd outlived most of his brothers. According to the obituary, the one living sibling was Aaron Barlow. Without further conversation I picked up the phone and held it to my ear, keeping my finger on the only viable card. "I guess I'll call."

"Hold on there," my mom said, handing me a cup of coffee. "Have you checked the time?" I glanced at the digital on the microwave and set the receiver in the cradle.

She sat next to me. "Before you herald the dawn with a telephone call, do you want to tell me what's actually going on?"

I wrapped my palms around the warm mug and took a sip without looking at my mom. What was going on? I had a compulsion to search for the answer to a hundred-year-old mystery about my grandpa, meanwhile losing all sense of myself. Or was it that Noah wanted another baby? And any other baby I had might be defective? Or was it that my baby was gone and it was my fault?

My baby was gone. Joey was dead. I bit my lip to stop it from quivering. The root of my search, the root of everything wrong, was right there. "Joey's gone, Mom. And I can't fix it." My voice was foreign to my ears, a croak rather than a whisper. "He's truly, truly gone."

"Oh, Emma." My mom slid close and grabbed my hands, which were grasping at the air, trying to catch hold of something that couldn't be found. Tears fell onto our bound fists, mine or hers, I didn't know.

"And what if I forget him? His morning smell tucked into the folds of his neck, the butterfly tickle of his hair across his forehead, the pink color of his cheeks while he slept." After several minutes, my sadness spent for the moment, I whispered, "And I'm messing up the rest of my life. And I'm not sure why."

"Grief is a process. Each person moves through the stages differently. Give yourself some time. You do seem like you're in a different phase these past weeks, but that doesn't mean you aren't grieving. You've been through so much: Joey, Grandpa Joe, Noah's accident. Hopefully, Noah will fully recover, but it doesn't mean you're not affected by the uncertainty."

She released my hands, reached behind her for a tissue, and handed it to me. "I tell my adult clients that grief is like the teenage years—you must take the time to get through them and try not to make any serious mistakes. At the end you will emerge a different person, functional, and able to experience joy. I hope you'll be able to forgive yourself for what you believe you've done wrong. Someday soon, your days will be good."

We finished the rest of our mugs in silence. After my mom took her last sip she put some bagels into the toaster. "Now, do you need to call Noah? Does he know you're here?"

"I'm not ready to talk to him." I set my empty mug on the table with a hollow thud. *Truth.* "Actually, he doesn't want to talk to me."

"So, something to eat?" she asked.

I nodded. There was comfort in being a child perched at the table with her mother, asking for breakfast.

"Okay, then, more questions." She took a bite of her poppy seed bagel as she brought me mine. "Why do you want to call Grandpa's brother?"

This mystery was clean, interesting, and not fraught with my personal mistakes and missteps. It was separate from me and yet still part of who I was. I would tell my mom what I knew.

"Hold on for a minute." I walked down the hall to retrieve the photo of my great-grandparents, detouring in the bathroom, where I secured my hair into a loose bun. I returned holding the photo. "This woman, right here." I touched the woman whom I believed was Rosa and held the photo near my face. "Who does she look like?"

My mom studied the photo, then she looked at me. "She looks like you, especially with your hair like that. I wonder if she's Grandma Emmeline's sister. Didn't I mention my grandma had a sister who died quite young in childbirth and Grandma Emmeline helped raise her little girl after the sister died?" She squinted at me again. "But you're right. There is an amazing family resemblance."

I released my hair, letting it brush against my shoulders so I'd no longer resemble the girl in the photo. "Oh. I didn't remember you talking about a sister." I tried to process this new piece of information with everything else I knew.

"But I do love this photo," my mom continued. "I'm so glad you found it. We'll have to hang it." She set the image next to my coffee cup. "So why are you searching for Grandpa's brothers?"

"Well there's a bit of a mystery I'm trying to work through. Would you help me sort it out? I can't get my head around all of the information I've found."

She nodded. "I'm ready."

"Grandpa was born in 1913." I held up the obituary. "And this photo says his parents' wedding was in *1916,* three years *after* he was born. Because of this inconsistency, and a few other things, I've spent some time at the Family History Library. The one run by the Mormon Church." I started at the beginning, detailing the inconsistencies between the documents and what I knew about Grandpa. I told her about my time spent researching, the skeleton sketch of my process and discoveries. It took a while, and I had to follow her into her bathroom, talking the whole time she dressed for a counseling session.

When I finished speaking, she touched her temples with her thumbs, then slowly ran her fingers across her hairline. Finally, she took the photo from my hands and she held it close to her face, as if she could discover the truth with her meticulous inspection.

"I'm not sure what I think about these claims," she said. "This is *my* dad you're talking about, and lies he may have told. And it's my uncle you want to get ahold of. Maybe I should be the one to call him?"

I shook my head. "Can I? This is the next step in my search, if that makes sense."

She handed me the phone. She got it. And she was more curious than hurt.

Slowly I keyed in the number for the youngest Barlow son, Aaron.

An old woman answered on the second ring, and at my question she called out, "Honey, there's a young lady on the line. Wants to speak with you."

After several minutes a scratchy voice reached my ear. I explained who I was and why I was searching for information about a woman named Rosa Barlow who may have lived in his home when he was a child. I didn't want to imply his mother might not have been who he thought she was, so I dangled Rosa's name without explanation.

"A relative of some sort?" he asked, unaffected.

"I think so. I'm not sure. She may be some relation to me. And to you, I guess."

"So you're Dutch's granddaughter? Good old Dutch . . . he was the oldest of all of us. The role model. The one we all looked up to. I was just a kid when he became a doctor and my mom went to work with him as his nurse. I'll admit I was a little jealous he got to see so much of her, but my dad was always around."

"Nathaniel?"

"That's right."

"Did you call my grandpa Dutch?" I asked, remembering the word listed in the obituary.

"That's what we all called him. I wish he'd stayed in closer touch after Mom died. Busy, I suppose. I saw his obituary after the service so I couldn't come. My brother James passed two years ago . . . and now Dutch. It's sure strange to be the last man standing."

"I'm sorry."

"No, no. I'm sorry for *your* loss, my dear," Aaron said. "I can tell from your voice he meant a lot to you."

"Yes. He did." I pressed a finger against my lips to stop them quivering and changed the subject. "I know it seems a little after the fact, but I'm kind of on a quest to learn more about my grandpa's life. I'm wondering if there might be someone who kept track of, I don't know, photo albums or any family journals, something that might mention this woman, Rosa?"

"Hmm." There was silence on the line for a touch too long.

"Aaron? Mr. Barlow?"

"Sorry, dear, just thinking. You know, we were a household of boys, not ones to go in for sentimentality. But I did have a girl cousin who lived with us when I was a kid. Bitsy was her name. She was a few years older than me. She died not long back, but maybe she held on to a few things."

"Bitsy? But you said she passed?"

"Bitsy!" My mom mouthed the name so she wouldn't interrupt the call. "I recognize that name! She's the sister's child. The one who lived with Grandma Emmeline."

"Let's see, what was her married name? Hold on." There was shuffling on the end of the line. "Hon, grab me the address book." After several minutes Aaron Barlow said, "Here it is. Bitsy Carlisle. Lived in California most of her adult life, but near the end moved back to Utah to live with her daughter . . . who I'm not sure I have a listing for. If you have a minute?"

"Sure, take your time."

He mumbled to himself as he turned the pages of his book, "Meg, Meg, Meg . . . what was her married name? Meg, Meg . . ." He spoke louder now, "Well, wouldn't you know, here she is, second to last page, Meg Yamada. What in blazes kind of name is Yamada?"

"Um, Japanese, I think," I answered, though I wasn't sure he was talking to me.

"Yeah, it's her all right. Do you have a pencil?"

"Pencil," I mouthed to my mom, who slipped one into my hand and put a piece of paper in front of me.

After I wrote everything and returned the phone to the cradle, my mom said, "I counsel an AA group at the Unitarian church at nine-thirty this morning, so I need to go. See what you can discover and let's talk this afternoon." She kissed me on the head and cupped my cheek with her hand, a gesture she often used when she would tuck me into bed as a child.

I filled my coffee mug again and sat, staring at the name: Meg Yamada. This woman was a little distant, the daughter of a cousin who lived in my grandpa's childhood home, but she was all I had. I would call her, but first I'd check on Noah.

He didn't want to talk with me, but I needed to know he was well. I longed to speak with Nurse Talli, but the pleasant-sounding nurse at the new station told me what I needed to know: Noah was currently with an occupational therapist, he was doing fine, and he'd likely be released from the hospital the following evening.

I hung up, relieved, and dialed Meg Yamada's number.

In the middle of the first ring, a chipper-sounding woman answered, and again I explained my quest, detailing her mother's relationship with my grandfather, asking about a woman who may have lived in their childhood home named Rosa Barlow. I mentioned that Aaron Barlow considered her mother, Bitsy, the keeper of memories, or at least photos.

"Mmm . . . hmmm," she muttered several times while I spoke, amid a variety of noises on the end of the line, including her labored breathing.

After several minutes, I stopped talking and waited for her response. "My mother died six months ago," she said. "But since she didn't live with me until the last two years of her life, most of her things are still in the boxes she packed for her move from Sacramento. Except . . ." More shuffling. "Except a few months back, there was a woman asking about my mom's childhood, and Ma had me dig through one of these boxes for a stack of letters, which I was trying to find as you were speaking . . . but I think I left the letters with the woman."

"The woman?"

"I know where she lives. I dropped my mom off there one afternoon. But I don't have her phone number, or her actual street address." She groaned. "How could I do that? I need to get those letters back. She's not even part of the family."

"So did the letters have anything to do with Rosa Barlow?"

"That I don't know. I haven't read them. I meant to, after I got them out. But Ma took a turn for the worse, and she wanted this woman to see the letters. Most of them were between her aunt Emmeline and her uncle Nathaniel. My mom lived much of her childhood with them, after her own mother died in childbirth." Fresh angst filled her words, maybe not for the little girl but for her own mother, who had once been the orphaned child.

"Oh, I'm so sorry," I said.

"No . . . no. I'm sorry about spilling." Meg blew her nose. "I miss my mom. It's so silly. I'm in my seventies and I still miss my mom."

My own mother's caress fresh on my cheek, I knew what she meant. There were issues in our past, but I loved my mom. I wanted to be a mom. A hot tear blurred my vision, finally landing on the paper where I'd written Meg's name and number.

"Where do you live? Are you local?" Meg asked. "Maybe I could take you to that gal's house, the one who has the letters. Or I could describe where she lives and you could go there by yourself, if you're in a hurry. My husband and I are heading to St. George this afternoon, so . . . ."

"I live in Salt Lake."

"Good, are you familiar with Sugar House?"

"I'm just south of there. I bet I could find my way through the streets."

She described the house, the location in relation to Westminster College, and a few other identifying features, along with a promise that if I got lost, she'd help me find the house in a week. She also asked me to tell the woman, whose name was Ivy, she'd be by to retrieve the letters and that Ivy could make copies if she wanted.

This was going to be so awkward. I'd arrive on the doorstep of this random house asking for a stack of letters that weren't mine, all in my search for a woman I didn't know existed until a few days ago, who may or may not be my actual great-grandmother.

CHAPTER 28

Following the directions given to me by Meg Yamada, just past Westminster College I turned east toward the Wasatch Mountains and wound my way through streets canopied with massive trees.

The whole neighborhood spoke to the passage of time. The houses weren't grand. They were bungalows similar to one another in original construction, smaller versions of those built in brand-new subdivisions, but these homes had been standing for a century, each progressive owner making enough changes that they were no longer uniform. Some were run-down, but many had been gentrified, the yards updated with trendy grasses rather than looming 1950s shrubbery. Roofs had been replaced, peeling wood patched. Many were painted brick, and several had felt a carpenter's hand, a remodeled addition resting on top of the original structure like a mismatched wooden block from a child's building set.

Meg said the house I should look for was red brick with a wide porch, a wooden porch swing, and a huge metal children's playset on the west side of the home. "Not one of the new kinds with a climbing wall and colorful slide," she said.

"This set is as tall as the house, metal triangular supports, and three swings with wood slat seats."

Four separate streets, all named something-or-something Avenue, ran east from Westminster College. This matched my directions, so I cruised each one, idling in front of every red brick home, scanning for the remainder of the clues. On the third street, one called Downington Avenue, two blocks from the college, I spotted it. Stopping the car on the opposite side of the street, I opened the file and reread Meg's notes. Porch, check. Red brick, check. Swing set, check.

I patted the passenger seat, where the physical manifestation of my story rested, the manila file full of printouts detailing the research I'd conducted, along with the notes taken when I spoke with Aaron Barlow and his grand-cousin, Meg.

I picked it up and held it in my hands, caressing the corners, attempting to muster my courage to leave the car, when a woman walked from the backyard dragging her enormous, green plastic trash bin to the curb. She glanced at me, and I put my silent phone to my ear. Maybe she'd think I'd pulled over to receive a call.

Her hair was thick and hung in a braid down her back. She appeared fifteen years older than me, about forty-five, and in decent shape. Her stride told me she got things done. This was garbage day and the bins were her job, no need to delay.

This meant in seconds she'd reappear with the blue recycle can. I set the phone on the passenger seat and shut off the car. If this was Ivy, she'd seen me now. I couldn't slink away and return in ten minutes. *Face this, Emma.* This was a step I had to take. Besides, it was the only decision I dared confront.

Sure enough, the woman brought the second can to the end of the driveway. When she saw me walking across the street in her direction, she waved, smiled with closed lips, and called out, "I already know who I'm voting for. I just talked to another guy." She pointed to her front lawn, where a campaign yard sign for the mayoral race had been pounded into the ground.

"That's not it. Um . . . this is going to sound a little weird. Are you Ivy? I'm sorry, I don't know your last name."

"Yes, I'm Ivy. Baygren." She grinned, and I wasn't so embarrassed. "Who are you?"

"My name is Emma Hazelton . . . and see . . . it's kind of a long story. I was directed to you by a woman named Meg"—I opened the folder to unnecessarily consult the name—"Yamada, who is related to me. Somehow. Maybe a second cousin to my grandfather. Anyhow, she told me you had some letters that may have belonged to my great-grandmother."

At this, Ivy loosened her grip on the recycle

bin, letting it bang onto the concrete driveway, and rushed toward me. "Meg . . . that's Bitsy's daughter. Oh my God. What was your great-grandmother's name?"

"Emmeline, I think. Or Rosa. I'm not sure. See, I've been doing some research on my ancestry and I've hit a dead end. I'm not sure who I belong to, and Meg mentioned some letters, so . . ."

"Come in. I didn't know how to return the letters to Meg. She didn't leave her address or number. I'm sorry to have kept a family heirloom, but please come in and I'll get them for you." I trailed behind her as we walked toward the house. She stopped suddenly and turned, poised on her toes as if she wanted to embrace me. "If your research and my research both led us to these letters, I do believe we may be kindred spirits, Emma."

She continued to lead me along the driveway past a rose garden, a riot of multicolored fists of fragrance perched on thorny stems. The heat from the midday summer sun was staggering, but it didn't seem to burn the roses. Their essence hovered about the garden, a mixture of lavender and vanilla. Or was it butterscotch? Yes, for a whisper of a second it smelled like Grandpa Joe, and then it was gone.

She opened the back door and trotted me through a kitchen, where a lanky preteen boy pulled a plate of nachos from the microwave. "This is

373

Porter," Ivy told me. "My daughter, Naomi, is at the pool. Ah, the lazy days of summer."

Porter waved with his free hand and made his coltish way to the dining room. We walked past him, and Ivy had me sit on her couch. "This is probably the best spot. We can spread out here with no danger of smearing melted cheese everywhere. I'll go get the letters and a couple other things. You can read them now, if you have time. I have a few details not found in the letters Bitsy told me, if you're interested."

"There are quite a few here," I said as she placed them in front of me. With deliberate movement, I sorted the fragile yellowed paper. "1914. Wow." These were so much better than the impersonal census lists on the computer at the Family History Library. These handwritten letters were textural evidence of lives lived.

"They're between Emmeline, your great-grandma, and your great-grandfather, Nathaniel. They were written before they were married." Ivy was giddy as she spoke. "Their love story was fascinating! Oh, but I shouldn't skip ahead. You should read them for yourself, and afterward we can talk."

I opened the envelope and read the first letter, written by Emmeline. In it, she was lamenting that Nathaniel must leave for a Mormon mission to England. It was written in 1913, maybe a month before Grandpa Joe was born. There was no mention of a child-to-be in this letter. The next letter was Nathaniel's response, equally as infatuated. These two people were young and in love, sad about the two years they would be apart and nothing more.

Trying to hide my frustration that these letters may not contain the answer to my search, I turned to the following installment. Ivy was wistful, gazing over my elbow at the old-fashioned cursive as I read. When I shifted so she could see where I was, she said, "Sorry. I feel like I've spent so much time with Emmeline, searching for her story, pondering her life, and here *you* are on the same journey. Their fledgling relationship is captured in this script. Young lovers caught in the crossfire of World War One."

I nodded, trying to catch her enthusiasm. "Why were you researching my great-grandma? You say you're not family, right?"

"I'm not family. But Emmeline lived in this house over one hundred years ago. I researched her after I found a few things she'd hidden, before she moved on." Ivy slid back on the couch cushions so I could read the next letter without her hovering. "I've been told she planted the oldest rose bush in my garden," she said after a few minutes. "It's named the Emmeline rose."

"Really? The Emmeline rose? Your garden is beautiful."

"Thank you. Inspired by your great-grandma."

She gestured at the page I was holding. "Keep reading. I don't want to disturb you."

I read the next letter. This one was a reply from Nathaniel to Emmeline, detailing his days as a Mormon missionary, his devotion to Emmeline apparent in his writing. Again, no child.

Dismayed, but still trying to hide it, I must have sighed loudly enough for Ivy to hear. She sat forward and put her hand on my arm. "Emma, are you okay?"

I set the stack of papers on the coffee table. "These letters are fantastic, and I want to read them all, but I'm looking for a specific piece of information. These are confirming my existing research, but they aren't filling in the blanks." I picked them up again and held them carefully so she wouldn't think I was ungrateful for this amazing history. "I feel like some of the stories told to me as a child about Emmeline were lies. I was named after her, and I've always loved this connection between the two of us, but some things I discovered don't make sense. I want to get to the truth because, somehow, I think everything wrong in my life hinges on it. . . ."

The events of the past months tumbled together into an avalanche as I spoke—Joey's disease, the arguments with Noah, the questions about Ethan, the letters—the combination threatened to crush me. This woman, whom I didn't know an hour ago, was now my only confidante.

Ivy was quiet for several beats. She was dreamy as she gazed out her front window to the canopied street, as if she expected Emmeline to wander up the steps and wait for us on the porch swing for a revealing conversation. I could picture Emmeline as she was in the photo of the wedding: a black-and-white two-dimensional woman, dark hair tucked behind her ears, wearing a light-colored dress. She held flowers in her hand and had a suggestive smile on her face.

Who was she when she was alive? A nurse who worked side by side with my grandpa, a man who claimed to be her son? A beloved wife? A mother of six boys? But was she *my* great-grandmother? If my grandpa was born *before* she married her Nathaniel, how could she be?

Studying my face, Ivy spoke. "If you don't mind telling me what you're looking for, maybe I can help. If you can't find your information in the letters, I had several related conversations with a woman named Bitsy."

"Aaron Barlow mentioned her."

Ivy nodded. "He probably told you she was Emmeline's niece, but she spent much of her childhood in her aunt Emmeline's home. She's the one who gave me these letters and told me the rest of the story."

So I explained to Ivy how I found the wedding photo of my great-grandparents dated 1916, but my grandpa Joe's obituary said he was born in

1913, in England. I continued through my list of original clues and what I discovered at the Family History Library. I likely spoke for an hour. Here and there, Ivy's teenage children peeked into the living room and were dismissed with a quick movement from their mother's hand.

As I spoke, Ivy shuffled and sorted the letters, contemplation etching her face. She was realizing they didn't contain a gentle love story in my mind but were an additional component of my angst. Two times, she moved through the stack. Finally landing on the right installment, she rested it on her knees, tracing the worn corners until I stopped speaking.

"You may want to read this one." She handed it to me. "I'm going to leave you so I'm not a distraction, but call me when you're ready to talk. You might be surprised at what you find. You will have questions. I want you to ask me anything. Please understand there's more to the story."

The letter was dated Christmas, 1915.

December 25, 1915

Dearest Emmeline,

Merry Christmas, my love. I am writing to you from New York. We have been here for nearly a week and this whole week I have been willing myself to write you. I have started this letter so many times, and even now as I write, my hand quivers.

If I tell you anything at all, I have to tell you everything. So please keep reading. Please try to understand why I have done this. I did what I had to do, to save her. Please remember I love you. I love you, Emmeline. I can hardly write these next words.

Emmeline, I am married. I have married Rosa Lewis and have brought her and Dutch back to the United States with me. When I told Rosa about the death of her husband Joseph at Ypres, she fell into my arms. Things had been hard for her after her husband Joseph left. She had been so worried about his safety. She had waited for a letter or some word telling her he was alive. I know from your letters you have the same fears. I know this part you will understand.

As I wrote in an earlier letter, I was the one who baptized Rosa. I hoped her baptism would provide her with protection given by her brothers and sisters in the church. And I also wanted her to be protected by the Lord. But things continued to get worse, Emmeline. As I was preparing to return to the United States, someone broke into her flat while she was sleeping! They broke her dishes and painted on her walls terrible, threatening things—in blood. She and Dutch hid under their bed, and they were unharmed, but Rosa was inconsolable.

As I attempted to comfort her, I couldn't shake the image of her husband as he lay gasping in his bed. As he was dying he asked me to save her. You see, Emmeline, he asked me to save her and I said I would. How could I save her if I was leaving? So I prayed, and very quickly I knew what I had to do. I had to bring her to the United States with me, where she could start fresh. So I tried.

I bought her and Dutch tickets for passage on my return ship, but when we tried to leave the country, they wouldn't let her travel. She didn't have the proper papers. They accused her of not being Dutch's true mother. They said they were going to send her back to Germany and keep Dutch in England. The officials at the port told me the only way she could leave England for the United States was if she was my wife, the wife of an American.

And so I married her. I believe the Lord called me to be her husband. How could I deny the signs that God had a hand in our union? Now she is saved. She is my wife and Dutch is my son and my responsibility. I am trying to do what is right. I am trying to keep the promise I made to Joseph, as he lay dying. His wish and my promise were his only comfort as he drifted into the arms of God.

But Emmeline, you are my first love and I need you. I don't know what to do now. All I know is I need to see you. I will come to you as soon as I return to Salt Lake City. Please don't turn me away.

I love you, Emmeline. I love you so much and I am so sorry.
Nathaniel

Dutch. Dutch was part of my grandpa's name in his obituary. Dutch was the name his brothers called him. The little boy in the photo *was* my grandpa. I retrieved a wrinkled scrap of newsprint from the file, his obituary, and read his name again: Joseph Lewis Barlow (Dutch). It was a nickname, not an indication of heritage. And Lewis wasn't a middle name, but his last name, the surname of his father, my biological great-grandfather, who died during World War I. Holding my breath, I studied the stack of letters for a postmark later than 1915, aching for the end of the story, but this was it. The last letter.

"Ivy." My call sounded strangled. She entered

the room like she'd been waiting for me, holding a mug between her hands.

"I know it's summer, but sometimes swallowing something warm helps me to soothe any lump that sticks in my throat." She set the ceramic mug on the coffee table in front of me and gestured to the letter still open on my lap. "Is that what you were looking for?"

I grasped the cup, warming the tips of my frozen fingers, pulling me to safety. "It answers some of the questions, but it creates more. Now I know the facts, but I don't know the why. . . ."

"The why?"

"If Rosa was his mother, why did my grandpa always claim his mother was Emmeline? What happened to Rosa, his true mother, my actual great-grandmother? I ache for her because she was forgotten, denied by her own son, married to a man who loved another woman."

Pushing the stack of letters toward Ivy, almost intending to deny the newly discovered facts, I continued, "Do you know what happened next? Did the woman you mentioned, Bitsy, tell you? According to this letter Nathaniel was married to my great-grandmother, Rosa, in 1915. But he wasn't the father of my grandpa. I know from the wedding photo that he married Emmeline in 1916. How does that work?"

Ivy sat next to me. The letter fell off my lap, fluttering to the ground. She retrieved it, holding it like a fragile gift, and returned it to the envelope. "Nathaniel Barlow was married to two women. Rosa *and* Emmeline. By official definition, he was a polygamist, but I think theirs wasn't a polygamist marriage in the religious sense, meaning he didn't marry two women because of doctrine. According to Bitsy, Nathaniel and Emmeline had a true love, not one prescribed by religious dogma."

"Nathaniel and *Emmeline?* But what about *my* great-grandma? What about Rosa? How sad if she was a sidebar to a tremendous love story, forced into a marriage she didn't want. My grandpa, up to his dying day, claimed *Emmeline* was his true mother." My nails cut my palms, and I was happy I wasn't holding the fragile letter.

Ivy sat quietly for several minutes. "I'll admit I did think of Rosa that way, as an aside to the love story between Nathaniel and Emmeline. I've always contemplated Emmeline's story because she was the young woman who lived in my home. Hers was the life I imagined. But let's think this through together. Wait here." She stepped out of the living room and returned with a spiral binder. "If you don't mind, I think better if I'm writing. I make a lot of lists."

"You remind me of my husband." Noah always used paper and pencil to work his way through a confusing set of issues. We had a stack of spiral notebooks he'd filled with calculations

383

and musings as he'd tried to figure out Canavan disease, as he'd tried to work his way to the root of the problem, both of us searching for a cure.

I ached for him. We'd been through so much together. I wanted him next to me now, learning the details of this mystery, making notes we could sift through later.

Ivy lifted her pen, writing as she spoke. "Rosa was widowed. She was a young German woman in England during World War One. From what I've heard, anti-German sentiment was severe as the war dragged on. So she's there, alone and frightened with a small child, Dutch, your grandpa. And Nathaniel, well, he's her safety net, likely the only one she has. Does she love him?" Ivy asked me.

"Probably not, but she needs him to survive," I conceded.

"They are connected through their religion, now that she's been baptized into the Mormon Church. It was written in the letter you just read."

I nodded and she continued. "And they were both connected to her husband, Joseph Lewis, as Nathaniel was with him when he died." Ivy drew an arrow connecting Rosa's name with Nathaniel and Joseph and then continued her list, handwritten facts and speculations filling the page. She was right, it helped to watch her write these things in black and white. It stopped them from swimming around in my head.

"So they were polygamists? Like the first Mormon pioneers?" I asked myself. Suddenly Barlow Meadows made sense. I continued speaking to Ivy. "You know, my grandpa wasn't a Mormon. No one in my family was ever a member of the church, as far as I knew," I said, and paused. "But what do I know?"

"Well, these letters confirm that Nathaniel went on a Mormon mission," she said. "But if he was actually married to two women in 1916 . . . I've done some research on the church and I know it was illegal to be a polygamist in 1916. In fact, plural marriage was against the law *and* church doctrine by about 1890. They would have been breaking the law to marry, plus they would have been excommunicated from the church."

I nodded, realizing what she was saying. "So, they left the church. And that's why my grandpa wasn't raised Mormon."

She put a star by the words *Left the Church*. I liked this woman so much, the way she worked through these issues, considering them but not ruminating. "The question"—she put the pen to her lips—"is what happened to Rosa after she came to the United States? And why did her little boy, Dutch, your grandpa . . . sorry, I've thought of him as Dutch for so long, it's hard for me to imagine him being a grandpa, or an old man."

"It's okay. It's like we're talking about strangers."

"So why did Dutch claim that his mother and father were Emmeline and Nathaniel Barlow? Why didn't he tell you about his true mother, Rosa?"

"I think I know what happened to Rosa," I said, suddenly remembering a story my grandpa told me about a woman named Rosa. I was so young then that this newly revealed memory was more a fuzzy dream than fact.

I bounced on Grandpa Joe's knees because my mom's lap was taken by the lump that would become my brother. We were at my grandpa's kitchen table, the same table where I would spend countless hours learning to play solitaire. My grandpa was in his scrubs. I was clinging like a barnacle.

"Why do you have to leave?" I whined.

"There are ladies like your mama who need help having their babies. I have to go. They need me."

"Why do you do it, Grandpa? Is it fun?"

"I wouldn't call it fun. It's rewarding, I guess. See, I decided to become a doctor when someone very special to me died giving birth. She is also one of the reasons your great-grandma Emmeline decided to specialize in childbirth. Her death hurt both of us."

"Was it Grandma Emmeline's sister? You've told me about her before, I think," my mom asked, lifting me from his lap so he could stand.

Grandpa was quiet for several minutes, long enough that I noticed. "No. She wasn't your grandma's sister, so to speak. Grandma Emmeline was already a midwife when her sister, Cora, died."

"Who then?" my mom asked, holding me tightly on her lap, her round belly bending my spine at an awkward angle. "You've never told me about someone you knew who died in childbirth."

"Rosa," he said quietly. "Her name was Rosa."

He left, or I was distracted, or both, but the conversation with Grandpa Joe ended.

"Rosa is a pretty name, don't you think?" My mom touched her stomach as she continued to squeeze me. "Maybe if this little thing is a girl, we'll name her Rosa."

I remembered this story because until Ethan was born, and he was without a doubt a boy, my mom called the baby in her stomach Rosa. In fact, for a month after he'd been officially named Ethan, I still called him Baby Rosa.

"She disappeared because my grandpa's mother, Rosa, died in childbirth." I returned to the conversation with Ivy. "That's why she's gone from one census to the next. Her death was the reason my grandpa became a women's doctor." That had to be it.

"Wow." Ivy was staring at me as if she'd discovered a lost treasure.

"Grandpa Joe practiced as an OB/GYN with my great-grandmother, or his stepmother, Emmeline. She served as his nurse until her death."

Ivy scanned her page of notes, her face turning wistful. "So they were close? Emmeline and Dutch? He considered her his mother after his own mother died."

"I guess so."

"I think it's touching."

"But what about Rosa? Why was she forgotten?" I stood, still angry at the injustice. "Hold on. If Rosa died in childbirth, but my grandpa Joe was already born, it would mean she was pregnant here in the United States. Nathaniel didn't just bring her to the United States to save her. They had sex. She was pregnant!"

"If they were polygamists, then Nathaniel had two wives. It's likely they were living the lifestyle."

"Oh God," I gasped. "How awful. He was sleeping with both women? Do you think that's why my grandpa never mentioned his mother after she died? He was embarrassed they were polygamists and once Rosa was gone, their family appeared more . . . normal."

"Maybe. There have been many polygamists in Utah throughout history, so having multiple wives wasn't so uncommon. But it was illegal."

"That's why Emmeline was listed as a boarder on the census. . . ." I mused to myself.

Ivy stood next to me and put her hand on my arm. "You might never be certain of all the facts. If there's no one to ask, you have to consider the clues. And you guess. Was your grandpa a kind man?"

"Oh, yes."

"Did he love his family?"

"Yes."

"He honored his mother, Rosa, by becoming a doctor, serving other women so they wouldn't suffer her fate. And it seems he loved Emmeline, his adoptive mother."

"All these things are true," I said. "But why lie?"

Ivy shook her head. "I don't know. Sometimes people make decisions thinking they are following the best possible course of action at the time. Maybe once his mother died, it was easier to say Emmeline was his true mother. Polygamy wasn't accepted in the community. Maybe it was easier to deny this one part of his heritage." She shrugged. "I don't know, I'm only speculating. You should talk to other people who loved your grandpa. Maybe without knowing it, they might have more clues as to what happened."

"I've been following a crisscrossed path for so long—"

"Don't get discouraged, it's fun," she said. "If you don't know the whole story, you can speculate, you can envision great untarnished love, bittersweet romance, and grand adventures. Think about the Ken Burns documentary about the Civil War, romanticizing battles never considered romantic by anyone who fought in them. But now reenactments are all the rage, people ponder sepia daguerreotypes, books are written—all through rose-colored lenses. I do it too. There's no harm, because the tragedy has already played out."

I shook my head, unable to get past the unforgiving facts. "But Rosa was cheated. She was the second favorite wife in a plural marriage. And my grandpa was cheated out of his own mother."

"Or maybe she was saved, and in turn, so was he. Think about where she was, who she was, a German girl in England during World War One. It's probable she would have been separated from her son during the war. Or, if not, she would have been forced to work long hours away from him. She was a single mother in a hostile country. Perhaps she made the best of a poor situation. And maybe, just maybe, she loved Nathaniel, and he loved her. Think of this, her death inspired Emmeline to specialize as a midwife. Although they were sister-wives, they must have been close."

"She came over here, took on an undesirable lifestyle, and she still died."

Ivy shook her head. "Her life created your

grandfather, which led to . . . you. Her death made him a doctor who, through his occupation, saved other women from a similar fate. And your grandfather's solid relationship with Emmeline and Nathaniel, his adoptive parents, made him a grandpa worthy of your love. His history doesn't change the man he became. He's the same grandfather who loved you."

"But I'm named after a lie."

"No, you were named after a woman your grandfather considered a mother, a woman who *earned* his love rather than assuming it because they were bound by blood. I think, Emma, you should consider your name an honor."

While visiting with Ivy, my phone rang once and I received one text message, both of which I ignored. Even as I hoped they were from Noah, the conversation with Ivy filled all of my reserves and I didn't want to disturb the flow of her musings.

The indulgent pondering I'd done about my ancestry, the messy facts I'd been rolling in like a pig in the mud making things muddier, were tidied by her analysis. Ivy gave me the scribblings she made during our conversation, mostly because I refused to let go of the paper, tracing our assumptions and connections, talking it through in my head.

Before I left, she took the letters to her little

office and made copies while I hovered at the door, drinking another cup of tea, which softened the edges of everything I'd been forced to digest. She caressed the stack, once again folded, enveloped, and organized by date, for several seconds before placing it in my hands.

The events in the letters were precious to her because they connected her to her home, but they were traces of my beginning. They belonged to me. They were part of who I was, and of who I would become. I would make copies of them and return the originals to Meg, but right now I wanted to hold the actual letters in my hands.

I hugged Ivy on the front porch before we parted, not wanting to let go.

"Emma, I want you to call me sometime soon." Ivy touched my arm, almost begging. "I've researched Emmeline and the other women who lived in my house for several years now. At first, I chased the mysteries to forget my own loss. My own pain. But in the end, Emmeline's story, and the other stories, they helped me heal."

"What happened? What did you lose?" I asked as my phone chirped again. I silenced it.

"I'll tell you my story later. I know you need to go now, so I'll save it for another day. But I get the feeling you're doing the same thing I was, running from real life by focusing on the past."

She was right.

"Inspecting the past, it's not a bad thing.

Sometimes understanding that everyone has a story means you're less alone. Emma, you're not alone. So call me and let's visit." She slipped into my hand her telephone number on a piece of paper. "And, of course, you know where I live."

CHAPTER 29

I kept the story about Grandpa Joe's lie, or lie of omission, as my mom would label it, to myself while I waited for Noah to return. Of course, I planned to tell my mom, but for the moment the secret was tidy and compartmentalized. It was distant enough that it didn't ache and burn. Quite the opposite. Learning that my grandpa had been raised by a woman who wasn't his biological mother was a beautiful discovery, like finding a pearl inside a craggy oyster.

There was treasure hidden in Ivy's words, when she told me my name was an honor. Emmeline wasn't Grandpa Joe's mother by blood, or *my* biological great-grandmother. But she was still my namesake. She was his adoptive mother, who raised him as a beloved son. He was who he was, because of her tender care. And her love. It didn't matter that the two of them weren't bound by their DNA. Her family consisted of the children she held next to her heart, no matter where they came from.

And then there was Ethan and the secret dividing us. Forgiving my mom for a childhood separated from my brother was the initial shimmer under dark waters. Ethan, who was my half brother in blood, was the full (and only) brother I carried in my heart.

These seemingly unrelated facts, braided together, created a gentle certainty. I knew I could move forward with Noah because I finally understood where I was standing. I chose Noah and he chose me. Together we were the foundation of the family we would cobble together, regardless of origin: biological, adopted, or otherwise. Because here's the thing: There are many things that connect one person to another. It could be shared history. Or biology. It could be blood. Or it could be love.

I knew these things and I was ready. I was home. However, as the minutes trickled by, hour by hour, as I waited for Noah's return, I was flooded with fresh doubt. What if the moment things became clear to me, he changed his mind?

I paced in front of the windows waiting for his return. This path was well worn, as I'd trod it incessantly, waiting for Joey. Realizing what I was doing, I stopped myself midstride. With determination, I left my post and found the carryall of cleaning products stashed at the back of the bathroom cupboard. The house reflected my disassociation with the place, from Noah and from my life. Debris from sorrow and inattention filled the corners, stacked deep on the table, and coated the countertops. With each swipe of the dust cloth and pass with the vacuum, I was more resolved.

By the end of the day our little house sparkled. I even mowed the lawn. It was midsummer, and thanks to Noah's care, the blades were uniformly green, showing no signs of a year of neglect. At the nursery, I bought geraniums for the flower boxes in the front and a replacement bird feeder for the one I'd unceremoniously knocked from the oak tree.

Like they'd been long anticipating its return, the doves hopped among the branches as I mended the chain, hung the container, and filled it with seed. The finches embraced me with their twisting, breathy whistle, then fluttered to the ground as I worked, finding the stray pieces of feed near my feet, surrounding me like friends from long ago.

Like most days, I made a trip to the cemetery with a flower for Joey's grave, but on this visit I selected several stems for Grandpa Joe and Grandma Ginny. I also brought a blossom for the woman, Marguerite Snow, who lost five of her children. Finally, on the way home from the cemetery, I went to the grocery store for a week's worth of meals.

It was near dark when I made my way to the front yard. If Noah was coming home today, it would be now. I knew we had many issues to work through and hard decisions to make, but once again the rest of my life lay just around the corner. There was a whisper of hope in the summer breeze. I just had to be in the right spot, looking the right direction, for it to lift my hair.

Not many minutes later, I heard the low rumble of Noah's truck, but instead of pulling into the driveway, his dad cut the engine tentatively at the curb, like a visitor. Seconds later his mom pulled up behind them in her car.

Noah sat for several moments in the cab staring at the house, and then he opened the door. He stood carefully on the sidewalk, as if not trusting his next step, either physically or emotionally. I rushed to help him from where I waited in the darkness of the porch. Suddenly shy, as I came close, I dipped my head, moving closer until he pulled me into his arms. He rested his hands on my shoulders, and I embraced his fragile body with careful hands.

Silently, after a nod from Noah, his father pulled the duffel from the passenger seat of the car and walked it to the steps. Together, his parents pulled away from our house.

"You came home," I whispered into Noah's chest, a knot forming in my throat, my words seeking access to his heart, the fragile organ tucked behind broken ribs, the one I hoped still had room for me.

Grasping me by the shoulders, he pushed me to arm's length, then fixing me with his gaze, and using both hands, he touched my forehead, my lashes. He slid the mound of his thumb along my jaw, tracing my lips, caressing my throat to my clavicle. Finally, cradling the back of my head, he wound his fingers through my hair and pulled me against him, this time desperately, clinging to me. "So did you."

EPILOGUE

Winter hovered close at hand, the whisper of it. A promise. Leaves swirled in the street, released from their branches by a nighttime frost. The day, however, was perfect autumn: blue sky, crisp sun, long shadows, and air like spotless glass.

Noah's hair had grown in, and with the exception of pain in his ribs when he sneezed, he was himself again. He'd been back at work for more than two months, but on this flawless day we'd both taken the day off. We decided to take a trip, together, into the city.

He drove my car, opening my door, formalizing the event, making me feel fragile and worshiped. I didn't mind. I was fragile. We both were. True, he was recovered, and on the surface we blended with the sunny-day revelers, our smiles wide, but our casual appearance was braided with invisible ropes of anxiety, hope, tension, and love. Our goal was to cut through the restraints with a multitude of distractions. And so a day out.

The sidewalks were jolly, crowded with people getting an early start on holiday shopping or office workers taking an extended lunch. As we walked, we held hands, never losing contact, reassuring each other with a small squeeze or a caress of the thumb. Noah reserved an alfresco table at a trendy new restaurant, where gorgeous, young people with scarves and rosy cheeks sat beside us. I hoped we wouldn't encounter any of my coworkers from Nordstrom, because I wasn't ready to talk. The intent of this busy location was to people-watch and eavesdrop when our own conversation stuttered, when we got lost in silence, unable to make passable small talk.

Light chitchat on this particular day would not be easy, because both of us were consumed with the topic of all the *big* talks of the past several weeks. Today, we sought something all-consuming to take our minds from the thing happening tomorrow: We would be conducting a chorionic villus sampling on our baby.

Yes, our baby.

After Noah came back to me, and I came back to him, we studied the family planning options for couples with increased risk. We went through comprehensive genetic counseling, and we were still in weekly marriage counseling. We were committed to having a family, and we wanted it together.

We knew the sacrifices we must make. In vitro fertilization would be close to fifteen thousand dollars. We analyzed our finances. We still had significant bills from Joey's care, but workers' comp had saved us from financial ruin after Noah's accident. All things considered, we had enough money, after taking small loans from our parents to try it once, and only once.

We also initiated the adoption paperwork. It was also very expensive and still carried some risk of birth/developmental defects, depending on the prenatal care of the mother or the age of the child at adoption, but we were ready for anything.

There was one final option: We could conceive naturally and test the baby at the tenth week with a chorionic villus sampling.

And if the baby had Canavan disease . . . I didn't want to consider the options. But they were real. We had three chances out of four to have a healthy baby. And if the child was affected, the awful one-in-four, we could abort or keep. We both understood what keeping the child would entail. And we both understood abortion. Together we decided we wouldn't go that direction. It was too uncertain.

Our decision: in vitro and debt *and* adoption and debt. We might get twins with IVF, and the idea thrilled me. A family of four . . . all at once. Five, if the adoption also went through.

We took the first steps. I had my IUD removed, started a daily prenatal vitamin, and per the detailed IVF instructions I waited for my first regular cycle before starting a course of birth control pills. After my hormones were consistent on the birth control, we would start Lupron injections, then stimulation injections, then egg retrieval, then fertilization, then testing of the embryos for Canavan disease, then implantation. Final result, a healthy baby!

However, my cycle didn't resume according to schedule. And there was the nausea. I knew from all of the medical literature I'd feel rough on the IVF drugs. But we hadn't started the IVF drugs. After several weeks, my doctor wanted to see if my cycle was regulating properly. At the visit, a blood draw confirmed what I already knew in my soul. In all of the juggling of birth control, I was pregnant. The decision of how to proceed was stripped from us. In that moment I was giddy and horrified. After all of our careful planning, we'd been careless when it meant the most. But . . . but . . . I could already sense the new life resting within me.

From that point, we had four weeks to consider the options—before we'd know. The results of the test tomorrow loomed larger than any test we'd ever taken. By the time we were originally tested for Canavan, we already had Joey. There was no decision, only dismay. But after this villus test, we would have to decide.

After lunch, step two in our day of distraction, Noah and I planned to walk three blocks to the Family History Library, where I would introduce him to the world of ancestral research. As I picked at my fries and Noah finished my sandwich, I tried to keep my mind firmly on our next destination. I reached into my bag, patting the corners for my stack of notes, the letters between Emmeline and Nathaniel, and Grandpa Joe's obituary. I didn't know which piece of information would be the clue leading us the right direction, and it was good to have everything, just in case.

When I told Noah about my original research, about the conclusion to the mystery surrounding Grandpa Joe, and about Ethan's biological father, he saw how the two situations became one in my mind, like twisted roots of the same family tree. With all of the unanswered questions swirling in my mind, I needed to discover the truth, about everything.

When I finished my recitation and reassured him I was at peace with my discovery, even the lie about Ethan's paternity, I witnessed the lines around Noah's mouth soften and the hard knot in his jawline relax.

However, it was Noah's idea to further the search, to investigate Rosa and Joseph Lewis, my biological great-grandparents. Maybe it was his attempt to divert my attention from the pregnancy, because I hadn't considered following the breadcrumbs to my next ancestral layer. But Noah said he wanted to see my process and he wanted to experience the library. Once he suggested it, I was willing to investigate, knowing I'd find my way out of the dark forest, because this time I'd conduct my research with my husband at my side.

Although I knew I couldn't change the outcome, I did wonder about my great-grandmother Rosa, my look-alike prairie girl, as Noah called her. We'd never know exactly why she was hidden, but I'd seen from my own life how a well-intended deception could expand from a single exhale, breath by breath filling the room, suffocating the truth.

Cutting through the temple grounds on our way to the library, we avoided much of the street noise, so when I whispered, "I wonder if he'll be there," Noah heard me.

"Who?"

I glanced at the sun-washed street. "My homeless yogi."

"The man with the profound signs?" Noah shaded his eyes with a hand, searching the street with me. "Have you ever paid the man for his sage guidance?"

"Not more than a couple of dollars, but if we see him today, no matter what his sign says, I'm dropping in a five."

Before I could fish around in my bag, Noah placed a folded bill in my hand.

"From both of us," I responded, keeping it light, but inside I was aching to see my guide, to observe the wisdom or direction given to me on tattered cardboard. I wanted an indicator of the future.

Unfortunately, the sidewalk between the Salt Lake Temple and the Family History Library was bleached by afternoon sun and void of beggars holding signs asking for money or providing advice. Scanning both sides of the street, hawklike, I was likely the only pedestrian eager to find a panhandler. "Maybe later," I said, dropping the money into my bag.

A pre-centenarian man opened the door for us at the Family History Library, bowing slightly. Like my original escort, he wore a dark suit and was capped with combed-over strands. He had a black-and-white name tag and an eager smile.

Noah received his *First Time* sticker and we were led with several others into the introductory movie room. We started at the beginning, because I wanted Noah to experience this place the way I had, the first time I visited. I wanted him to see that my compulsion to reach into the past wasn't a crazy thing. This whole library was created for people, like me, to search for ancestors, their connections stretching back hundreds of years, originating from countries I couldn't place on a map.

After the movie, we were led to our private terminal, and I sat with my hands hovering above the keyboard. "What do I want to know?" I whispered to Noah, who shrugged.

"You're the expert. Show me how it's done."

The cursor blinked on the home screen, asking me to type in my *Deceased Ancestor's Name.* I typed in *Rosa Barlow* and in the next field, where it asked which event parameter I'd like to coordinate my search, I chose *Marriage*, with a date of . . . I checked the letter from Nathaniel to Emmeline, the one stating he'd married Rosa and brought her to the United States. The year was 1915.

Results scrolled. Nothing matched.

"Try Rosa and Joseph *Lewis*, rather than the marriage with Nathaniel Barlow," Noah said. "Try to find her original marriage certificate in Europe."

"But I don't know the year. I don't even know the country where they were married." I inspected the screen. What did I know? I knew Rosa died in the United States, but I didn't know the year. Or did I? Flipping through the census reports, I found the printout of the 1920 census where she was listed as *Wife.* By the 1930 census report, she had disappeared. So somewhere between those dates, Rosa died.

I began a new search, starting with the grave-stone search site. I typed in *Rosa Lewis Barlow. Place of Interment: Utah*, and a death year of 1925, splitting the difference between the dates I knew.

Bingo. One Rosa Lewis Barlow buried in

the Salt Lake City Cemetery in 1922. The icon blinked over *View Image*, and I held my breath as a pixelated photo appeared, the image crystalizing as I watched. "Come on . . . birth date," I whispered as Noah slid his chair closer, inching toward the screen in anticipation. And there it was: a small, carved granite rectangle.

ROSA LEWIS BARLOW

BELOVED WIFE AND MOTHER

BORN OCTOBER 12, 1894

DIED JULY 17, 1922

"Oh my God, I think I recognize the location of her headstone. It's right by Grandpa Joe's grave." I touched the corner of the image. "See the granite obelisk right behind it? You can just make out the base, but I recognize it from my grandpa's funeral. I don't know why I didn't notice her grave before." I swallowed hard, understanding. "Rosa wasn't forgotten by her son at all," I continued. "My grandpa was buried near his mother."

"That's probably why he's in the older part of the cemetery," Noah suggested. "The plots would have been purchased when Rosa died almost one hundred years ago. I wonder if Nathaniel and

Emmeline chose a plot for Rosa with enough room for your grandpa Joe?"

"I wonder."

"Maybe today, while we're at the cemetery, we should find everyone," Noah said. "Rosa, Grandpa Joe and Grandma Ginny, Nathaniel and Emmeline. After we visit Joey."

"After we visit Joey," I confirmed, leaning forward and touching my forehead on Noah's shoulder. Now that Noah and I were reconnected in our grief, every time we were out together, we visited Joey's grave. Most of the time we brought him something: a flower, a pretty rock, a note. Sometimes we simply stopped by to let him know we were thinking of him. Like before, the frequent visits eased my anxiety about leaving my child alone, but visiting with Noah kept me from spiraling. Together, we were doing what we could.

"So you have Rosa's birth date. What do you do from here?" Noah drew me back into the search.

"Yes. I have the birth date," I said as I typed in Rosa's name, her date of birth, and I triangulated with the possible country of birth, Germany. I pushed enter, and together we waited for the results.

"You know, her last name wouldn't have been Lewis when she was born. I don't think you're going to find what you're looking for with this search," Noah said as a screen full of women with the name of Rosa Lewis appeared.

"Dammit, you're right," I said.

Noah shushed me, giving me a sidelong glance. "You're right," I corrected myself in a whisper. "I need that damn maiden name."

Noah grinned.

I raised my hand, and a woman I recognized hurried over. "Can I help?" she asked. I read her name tag: Sister Mills. I remembered her. This sister knew what she was doing.

"I'm searching for the maiden name of a woman born in Germany in October of 1894. I don't know the city, but I have her married name. Actually, she was married twice. I have both her married names, but I can't find anything else."

"Was she married in the United States or Germany?"

"I know her second marriage happened during World War One in England. My great-grandfather, or I mean, her second husband, got her out of Europe by marrying her and bringing her to the United States. See, she was in danger because she was German," I explained.

"So a wartime bride? Sometimes those marriage records are difficult to find, or information is found in unusual places. It's fascinating, really. They put brides from various countries all over Europe into what they called Bridal Camps, before they were allowed to immigrate to the

United States. The camps were often old army barracks on the French coast. In the camps they taught the women English and schooled them in American customs. Often the girls were issued emergency passports. If her new husband was an American soldier serving in Europe, often the wartime marriage certificate will be linked to his veteran service records. Do you know where he fought?"

"Here's the thing. He wasn't a soldier. He was serving a mission for the Mormon Church during World War One."

"During the war? And he got married on his mission? That usually doesn't happen."

"The war started while he was over there, and I have this letter he wrote to his fiancée"—I held out the copy of Nathaniel's letter—"letting her know he brought his new wife with him from England at the end of his mission."

"A fiancée *and* a bride. Oh my, this is a sordid love story." Sister Mills clapped her hands when she said *bride,* and I couldn't help but catch her enthusiasm. The story, when seen through a backward lens, was the stuff of a historical romance.

I tugged several pieces of information from the manila file. "I also have a ship manifest stating they traveled to the United States as husband and wife." I pointed to the names I highlighted on the copy of the manifest.

"Wow, you searched source documents? This is a photocopy from a book, if I'm not mistaken." She studied my face. "Wait. I remember you, I think."

"Yes." I blushed. "You helped me before."

"I can see why you aren't giving up. This *is* a good mystery. Tell me more details, maybe something else will tell us where to search. What was her name? The name you know."

"Rosa Lewis Barlow."

"And you want her maiden name?"

"Yes. I'm not entirely sure why, but she's my biological great-grandmother, and I feel like she's been forgotten," I explained. "I guess I want to gather anything I can about her."

"Okay, tell me what you know about Rosa."

Holding the ragged stack of papers I'd collected over the months, I tapped them against the laminate work surface. I didn't need to read from my notes, I had everything memorized. I'd been through it so many times, but all the same, it was nice to have the information at hand.

"She was born in 1894, likely in Germany. She was married to a man named Joseph Lewis, an Englishman. I don't know when they were married, but in 1913, they had a son they also named Joseph, and *that* son was my grandpa Joe. My great-grandfather, Joseph Lewis, fought in World War One and died after a battle in the

Belgian city of Ypres, from exposure to chlorine gas." I held the letters as proof.

"Tragic. I've read about the Battles at Ypres," Sister Mills said.

I nodded and continued. "So, on his death bed he asked this man, Nathaniel Barlow, who had been teaching them about the Mormon Church during his mission, to care for his wife after he died. Nathaniel met his promise. He baptized the wife, Rosa, into the Mormon Church and hoped the members in England would protect her. But times were tough for Germans in England."

Sister Mills nodded her acknowledgment.

"Finally, he decided that in order to keep Rosa safe, he would bring her to the United States. But they wouldn't let her on the boat unless she was his wife, the wife of an American."

"So he married her."

"Yes, in 1915. There's more to the story making it a little crazy, but the last thing I have on Rosa is that she died in 1922 and was buried in the Salt Lake City Cemetery."

Sister Mills had crossed her hands over her ample middle and stared into the distance as I finished speaking. "So the wartime marriage certificate may contain a maiden name, but it's not certain, since it was her second marriage. The original marriage certificate is a possibility, though searching by name without a location could be a long row to hoe in an overgrown garden." Noah winked at me as I smiled at her metaphor.

"Wait, you said she was baptized?" Sister Mills sounded giddy. "She became a member of the Mormon Church?"

"Yes, I believe so. The letters lead me to believe it was just before the second marriage."

Sister Mills rubbed her hands together like a sultan. "Baptism into the Church of Jesus Christ of Latter-day Saints? Now we're cooking with gas."

This time I giggled, her excitement was so infectious. "So, baptized in 1915 means her records would show up in the three-part form. They were in England, you say?" She sought confirmation. This woman's mind was like a steel trap. "We may have to search for it on microfilm, but the information will be in English and easy to read."

"Will it contain her maiden name?" I questioned. "She was married before she was baptized."

"Oh, yes, that's the beauty. The three-part form asks for the name of the individual being baptized at the time of baptism *and* the names of said individual's parents. Voilà, maiden name! Not to mention another layer of ancestry you may be interested in tracing," she added.

"Let's start with Rosa," I said. The idea of searching any further back was daunting.

She reached for the keyboard and typed for several minutes, made a cryptic list of numbers, and rolled her chair backward. "Yes, baptism forms are available on microfilm, and now I have the film and image number. Let me inform the desk I'm leaving this floor and we'll go a-hunting."

"Wait until you see the basement," I whispered to Noah as we waited. "There are several floors, and when I was here I never spotted a far wall. For all I know, the subterranean rooms might never end."

"Oh, I know what's at the end."

"What?"

"Heaven."

I snorted. "Or hell."

"Depends on which direction you walk, so be careful. If the floor burns your feet, turn around."

"Hush, you've got to admit this is cool," I said. "All this information at our disposal. No-strings-attached ancestry."

"It's because the Mormons baptize every name they locate, posthumously. Not the actual corpse, of course, but in proxy. It's called Baptism for the Dead. So there's your string."

I thought for a minute. "I guess I wouldn't mind being baptized when I was dead. Better to be safe than sorry."

Sister Mills led us to B-1, and as we exited,

the elevator doors closed with a space-lock pop. Noah's mouth was agape.

"See?" I whispered.

Trailing Sister Mills past the never-ending shelves of books, we made our way toward two dozen microfilm projectors. Ten were occupied by fellow searchers, tucked close to the whirring machines in rolling chairs, myopically glued to the screen as details whizzed past like ribbons of dusty sky out the window of a bullet train.

After threading the film using several large dials, she stood, allowing me to take her spot. "You can start here." I backed away from the machine as if it might attack, and she noticed my hesitation. "Or, it might not take me too long. Do you want me to see what I can find?"

"Would you?" The monster purred as she spun the dial, the film sliding by in fast motion.

She stopped it several times murmuring, "Closer . . . closer." Minutes later she rolled back and stood. "Here you are: Baptisms in England in 1915. You'll need to be deliberate with these screens because there's so much information. But the records kept for baptisms and new members are well documented. If it occurred, you should find it here." She turned to walk away. "I've got to return to my post, but if you'd stop by the desk, I'd love to see what you find."

Noah slid a chair from a nearby station to help me. "The names are cataloged with the first name first and not alphabetically, so turn the dial slowly and let's both look for an *R* for Rosa."

Floating amid an ocean of information, I might drown, but when given tiny parameters, like searching for the letter *R*, it was doable.

"Stop," Noah said, nearly an hour later. My vision was already blurring from the search. "Go back. You missed one."

I reversed the film and Noah touched the screen. "Right there. Rosa Lewis. She wouldn't have taken the Barlow name yet, since they weren't married before the baptism, right?"

"It seemed that way from the letters."

"Then there she is."

No.	575
Name	Rosa Lewis
Father's Name	Rubin Hammerstein
Mother's Name	Sarah Yudelson
Date	11-2-1915
Place	Manchester

Reading the names, I gasped, and then I reread each slowly, contemplating the identity of my ancestors. Noah spoke first. "Well, based on these names, it appears your German great-grandmother Rosa was also a Jewish girl." He put his hand on my arm, settling my reaction through his warm caress. "And there's *your* connection with Ashkenazi."

"A Jewish girl." Now it was my turn to touch the screen, to absorb the results with the tip of my finger. There was my Jewish ancestry, the root of Joey's disease and my broken dreams. I could sense Noah's worry, and I leaned into him for comfort.

"And now you know who you are," he said, moving his hand to rest on my cheek.

"And now I know who I am. And I'm okay with it." I blinked hard, trying to pull back the unexpected rush of tears.

"I've always known who you are, at your core. You consist of many parts making only one you. You're the girl I love."

"Thank you," I said, as he pressed his lips to my forehead.

"But you had to figure it out for yourself."

"I did. And I had to accept it."

The weight of possibility, a breath of new hope fluttered in my abdomen. I caressed it as I studied the screen listing the names of my ancestors.

"Are you okay?" Noah looked worried.

"I'm fine. Let's print this screen. I think we're done here."

As we made our way back through the leather and cloth volumes cataloging the loosely woven ancestral connections, the bonds shared between generations of people, twisting them like strands of DNA, I considered the results of my own DNA test. The explanatory video on the ancestry

417

website explained humans are identical in 99.5 percent of their complex genetic code, to *all* other humans. All of our intricate differences are located on one half of 1 percent of each genetic coil. In reality, we are not so different from one another. But one tiny mistake in the code could ruin everything. I knew. I'd seen it.

In the elevator I touched my stomach again, and Noah's glance was questioning. What were the odds that this time we would win? Because our cards were already dealt. Noah and I didn't mean to get lost in the hum of the casino. We didn't intend to sidle up to the table again. But now the two of us were tucked in, elbows on, and the dealer had placed the cards facedown.

I remembered Grandpa Joe sitting in his kitchen playing hours of solitaire, or teaching me patience through endless rounds of blackjack. What did he say when I wanted to quit? "Not until you play the cards you're dealt."

We showed Sister Mills the screen we printed, and she echoed Noah, "So now you know." She told us she'd return the film to the vault. As the glass doors closed behind us, separating us from the cool hush of the library, the departure was final. It was time to face the future.

"Is that him?" Noah hadn't let go of my hand since we saw the search results, even during the long minutes of contemplative silence, caressing my wrist with his thumb, holding me together.

He gestured to the right, using both of our hands to point, not letting go, leading me along the crowded sidewalk.

"Who?"

"Your homeless yogi."

Gripping each other, we walked toward him. I was apprehensive now. Superstitiously, I wanted his guidance, but what if his sign told me nothing? Or what if it hinted at the worst?

We stood in front of the man as leaves swirled about his still figure. His legs were folded, thin and knobby in dirty brown pants, a multicolored scarf wound around his head. His face was grizzled and heavily whiskered, but his eyes were piercing blue. He smiled and tilted his sign so we could see it. Tattered at the corners, stained from long days of showing it to passersby, the uneven script read

Joy Lies Within

I pulled my hand from Noah's. Staring at the sign, I pressed one palm against my flat stomach and one to my heart. A calm certainty filled me. Those three words told me all I needed to know. Noah quietly exhaled. Silently, he reached into his wallet, pulled out a hundred dollar bill, and placed it into the upturned hat.

DISCUSSION QUESTIONS

1. Emma wants to know who she is, genetically and ancestrally, because she's reeling from the loss of her son, Joey. Although her discoveries won't change her circumstance, or Joey's fate, do you think the search is worthwhile? Have you ever done any ancestral research on your own family? What was your purpose for searching, and what did you hope to discover?

2. Emma and Noah have a one-in-four chance of having another child with a rare and deadly genetic disease. Though they didn't mean to become pregnant the second time, how do you feel about this unintended pregnancy? Hopeful? Frustrated that they've been careless when things matter the most? What ending would you write for Emma, Noah, and their unborn baby?

3. Emma and Noah love each other, but they approach the loss of their child in very different ways. Whose reaction is the most understandable to you?

4. If you were a carrier of a rare but deadly condition like Emma and Noah, how would you approach parenthood? Which of the

options available to Emma would you have chosen, and why?

5. If you were suspicious about your parentage, like Ethan, would you dare to question it? And would you forgive? Do you think Diane was justified in keeping the secret? Finally, did you as the reader forgive her?

6. Betrayal is a big theme in *Where the Sweet Bird Sings*. Emma feels betrayed by her body, in some regards by Noah, by her grandfather, and by her mother. Who betrayed her the most? And should she forgive that betrayal?

7. Emma's memories of Grandpa Joe are a touchstone, or a comfort when things seem out of control. Most stories, even when they are very suspenseful, employ this literary tool. Did you feel a sense of calm when you read about him, that everything would be okay? Think of your favorite book or movie. Who (or what) was the touchstone?

8. It's likely that each of us is a carrier of an undesirable trait, be it bad teeth, a bad heart, an autoimmune condition, or something as rare and awful as Canavan disease. Have you or your family been affected by a genetic condition? How have you dealt with it?

9. If you were adopted, or didn't know the identity of one or both of your parents, would you be compelled to take a DNA test? What would you hope to find?

10. If you could determine that you carried a gene that would likely cause an unpleasant (but not terminal) condition, would you want to know about it? And if symptoms had already manifested, would it make you feel better to know where your condition, be it lactose intolerance or migraines (for instance), came from?

11. Many who search for ancestral ties try to trace their lineage back to a famous person—a king or a president, for example. Why are these connections to important historical figures significant, do you think? Who would you want to be related to?

12. People love to blame a certain behavioral predisposition on a family tendency—think bullheadedness or over-spending. Do you really think there is a genetic link to these behavioral traits? Speak to one that "runs" in your family.

Center Point Large Print
600 Brooks Road / PO Box 1
Thorndike, ME 04986-0001 USA

(207) 568-3717

US & Canada:
1 800 929-9108
www.centerpointlargeprint.com